Anotech Chronicles Book 3:

Reshner's Royal Guard

By Julie C. Gilbert

Aletheia Pyralis Publishers

For information about special discounts available for bulk purchases, sales promotions, fund-raising and educational needs, please email: devyaschildren@gmail.com

http://www.juliecgilbert.com/
https://sites.google.com/view/juliecgilbert-writer/

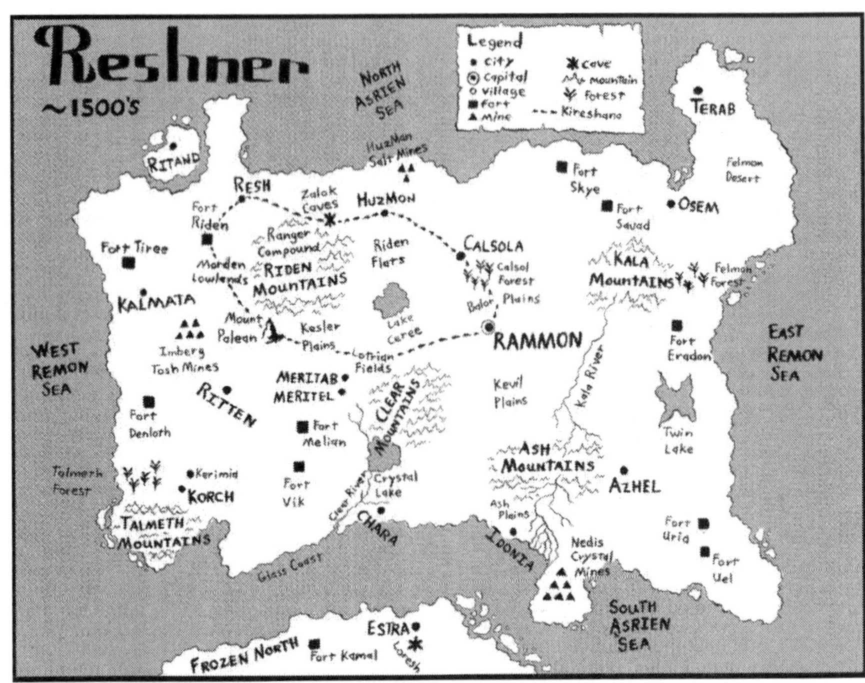

Visit: **http://www.juliecgilbert.com/**
to request a full-sized map.

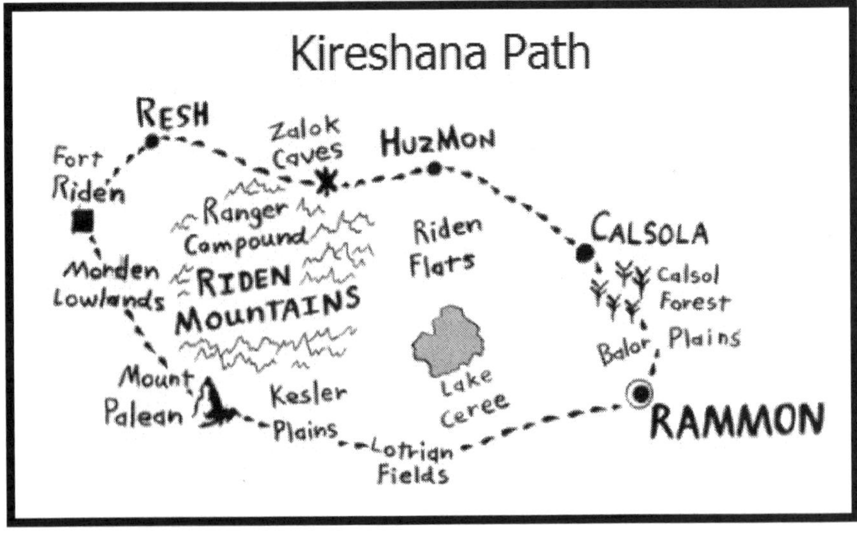

Acknowledgements:

Special thanks to:
Lucas Dalenberg, Jenny Shin, Chewie, J. LaRocco,
Timothy Sparvero, and Deb Monroe
for helpful suggestions

Note: This book may be read on its own,
but it might help to start with Reshner's Royal Ranger
and Reshner's Royal Threat.

Table of Contents:

Cast of Characters:

(Spoiler Alert)

Royals:
King Terosh Minstel – ruler of Reshner
Queen Reia Antellio Minstel – ruler of Reshner
Prince Teven McKnight – Crown Prince of Reshner
Princess Rela Minstel – Princess of Reshner
Prince Tavel Minstel – Second Prince of Reshner

Rangers:
Kiata Antellio Wellum – Nareth Talis Ranger, Reia's sister
Todd Wellum – Nareth Talis Ranger, Kiata's husband
Kayleen Wellum – Todd and Kiata's daughter

Other:
Sarie Verituse – Melian Maiden, caretaker of Princess Rela
Ectosh Laocer – Captain of the Royal Guard
Talyon Keldor – former RT Alliance operative
Jalna Seltan – daughter of the anotech creator

Villains:
Lord Kezem Altran – usurper; Terosh's cousin
Merek – Kezem's advisor

Prologue:

Ferrim (December) 29, 1546
Kezem's Private Retreat, City of Idonia

"Get up," Lord Kezem Altran's voice commanded from above.

King Terosh Minstel blinked up at his cousin. The stone floor dug into his back, but his head, which rested in the groove between two stones, felt oddly comfortable for the first time since he woke up a few hours ago. He lifted his head slowly, relieved to feel no new pain.

Terosh's poor vantage point made his cousin seem taller and more menacing than usual. Kezem's features hardened into a mask of hatred, disgust, and sadistic pleasure. The Gardanian enhancements had given him new height and breadth. His body trembled with energy as he kicked Terosh's left side, just below the battered ribs.

Terosh grunted and instinctively curled to protect his side, breathing slowly to minimize the pain. Anotechs rushed to the abused area and started repairing the damage.

With an annoyed grunt, Kezem stooped down and hauled Terosh off the floor as if he weighed no more than a small child.

Terosh whipped his arms up under Kezem's arms and slammed the flat of his hands into the crook of Kezem's elbows.

Kezem dropped him and laughed.

"Fight all you want. It won't save you or your family."

Terosh kept silent. He would not beg Kezem for mercy. The man had none. Terosh's heart ached to hold his wife and kiss his children, but he let nothing show on his face. Killing Kezem might be the only way to protect his family, so Terosh gathered the anotechs for a final attack.

"You can't win," said Kezem, pulling a small device off his belt.

"Even if you seized this, my men have a different set of controls to subdue you. Do not let the crude stones fool you. This room is fully equipped to deal with a royal prisoner. My mother designed it, thinking it might one day hold her siblings, but other plans prevailed first. Would you like to see what it does?"

Despite his determination not to play games with Kezem, Terosh shook his head.

"Experience can be so educational," Kezem commented. He pressed something on the small, gray device.

Terosh shouted as his arm and leg muscles suddenly clenched, dumping him to the floor in a mass of quivering muscles.

Kezem plucked Terosh off the floor again and pinned him to the wall with his left forearm across Terosh's throat.

Air rushed out of Terosh. Soon, his arms and legs were bound to the wall.

Kezem stood back to take in the scene.

"My mother also left me several interesting people," he said pleasantly. "I think I'll introduce you to Kellen and Lash. With your self-healing abilities, I'm sure you could entertain them for days. Should I arrange for your wife to join us? Look, she could even stand near you." He gestured to the wall to Terosh's left where a similar set of bindings awaited another prisoner.

Anger brought a flush to Terosh. He hated that Kezem could get a rise out of him so easily.

"Is that what they taught you on Gardan?" Terosh asked. He didn't have to work for the tone of contempt. "How to torture people chained to walls?"

"These walls have hosted many distinguished guests over the years," said Kezem. "Spice traders, informants, spies, ambassadors, minor nobles, but you might be the first king, Your Grace."

"Princesses," Terosh added.

"Indeed." Kezem looked mildly impressed. "Your brother's wife spent some time here, but alas, she did not last long."

"Deanna," said Terosh. "Her name was Deanna."

"Was it?" asked Kezem. "Good to know. I had forgotten. So much has happened these past nine years."

"Does Elia know?" Terosh asked. He tried to stop the question, not wishing to remind Kezem of the girl's royal blood.

"Who?" inquired Kezem. His feral smile contradicted the question.

Terosh waited out the moment.

Kezem's expression said he really wanted to gloat.

"You must be referring to Taytron's daughter. I am keeping her alive for now. Luckily for her, she has no idea the trouble built into her lineage." Kezem shrugged like he didn't care, but his expression darkened. "Should she ever discover her past, I will have to kill her. Do we understand each other?"

"We do," said Terosh.

Silence would keep Elia alive and safe, but no such solutions existed for Terosh's children while they stayed on Reshner. As his hopes for peace slowly crumbled, he abandoned his stance on not reasoning with Kezem. A crazy thought struck his heart with equal parts pain and hope.

"Let me annul my marriage." The words turned sour as they left his mouth. He forged on anyway. "Reia will have no claim to the throne, and you can seize control as you like once I'm dead."

"Her death will void the claim quite nicely," Kezem responded. "Besides, your plan has three tiny flaws."

The reference to his children hit Terosh harder than any blow.

"Reia could take them away," said Terosh. "Help me arrange transport. There must be a thousand of planets suitable for—"

"The trouble with exiles is that they tend to resurface at inconvenient times," said Kezem, cutting him off. "No, cousin, they must die."

Guilt tore at Terosh. If he had never entered Reia's life, she might have married some Ranger or merchant or farmer and lived in relative peace. He wished with every scrap of will left that he could protect his children.

We will watch over them, King of the Chosen, the anotechs promised.

With that assurance warming his spirit, Terosh snapped the bindings holding him and used anotechs to rip the controller from Kezem's hand. He would not wait to be slowly tortured to death. If Kezem wanted his throne, he would have to earn it.

***

Ferrim (December) 30, 1546
Kezem's Private Retreat, City of Idonia

No turning back.

Cold exhilaration filled Lord Kezem as he watched recordings of the queen's reaction to Terosh's homecoming. Laocer had delivered the body mere minutes ago, and the timing could not have been better. The three moons set, and the sun reached out cheerful beams to caress the palace as it claimed the planet for day. Kezem could not help seeing it as a metaphor for the events he had set into motion.

"You will not mourn for long, Your Majesty," Kezem murmured as he replayed his favorite short scene.

Queen Reia Minstel hurtled into the vidrecorder's range. Pain and irrational hope battled in her expression. Spotting the body, the pain proved victorious, and Reia froze in the hallway and swayed slightly. Her muscles tensed and her eyes clenched. She tilted her head and leaned forward like a woman bracing against strong wind. Then, she staggered forward and fell beside the hov sled holding Terosh.

Hope rekindled for a second as Reia reached out and touched Terosh's chest with her palms. Her eyes bore into the king's tranquil, pale face with a fierceness bordering on anger. Whatever magic she used to snatch him from death by poison all those years ago failed. In a second stretched over an eternity, her features changed as the reality tore through her and dashed her hopes in a flood of pain. Several long seconds passed, dominated by mute horror. Then, the queen gasped and surrendered to sobs.

A sympathetic pang stabbed Kezem in the chest. Startled, he crushed the feeling with anger. He could not afford such weak feelings. Determination flared in him. He needed to move quickly. If the queen's grief could shake him this much, he could only imagine what it would do to the ignorant masses.

Chapter 1: Dark Days Come

Idela (January) 2, 1547
Royal Palace, City of Rammon

An enormous crowd waited in the courtyard for her to speak. Reia's mind flew back to the time eight years before when she stood here with Terosh. Now only Sarie Verituse and Aster Captain Ectosh Laocer filled the balcony space that ought to hold her husband. Reia froze the emotions so she could think long enough to form words. When this was over, she would return to her grief, but for now, she needed to be much more than a heart-broken widow and terrified single mother.

She needed to be queen.

Drawing desperate breath and praying for strength, Reia turned her stinging eyes to the crowd.

"My people, I find myself hard-pressed to find words to comfort you." She tried to steady her voice. "My husband, my best friend, my children's father, your guide and king, is gone, and we mourn a mighty loss."

Hope lives, whispered the anotechs.

Reia swiped a hand across her eyes to catch some tears. The cool night breeze offered little respite from the hot despair clinging to her.

"I come before you today to ask your aid. Let Terosh live on in your hearts. Remember King Terosh of House Minstel as a man who stepped into his role with equal parts strength and compassion."

House Minstel is not yet broken, Queen of the Chosen.

The anotechs' reminder restored some peace to Reia. She

forced herself to look over the gathered people and meet as many gazes as possible. She briefly wrestled with the idea of sharing the insight with the people. It might ease their pain, but Terosh's murderer might take it as a challenge. She couldn't think about him or the depths of his betrayal.

"Some of you may be frightened by so many changes in such a short time," said Reia. "Some may also claim me unfit to rule because I came by the Minstel name by marriage rather than birth. I have not the strength to argue with you, but I assure you my life belongs to you. There are three strong reasons you should not despair. Their names are Prince Teven, Princess Rela, and Prince Tavel." The palest ghost of a smile brushed her lips. "Come what may, this Royal House will not bow to a tyrant."

Chapter 2:
Chaos in the Palace

Jira (March) 2, 1547
Throne Room, Royal Palace, City of Rammon

Death comes not-so-softly in the night.

Queen Reia Minstel felt this truth reverberate in her chest as she recalled Aster Captain Laocer's painful report. The East Quarter had fallen to Lord Kezem. Only five hours into the attack, Reia knew that Kezem's forces would breach the palace by daybreak. Then, she would be dead, he would be Reshner's ruler, and her people would be plunged into civil war.

War is anything but civil.

Sweeping aside some unruly strands of wavy light brown hair escaping the braid, Reia turned sharply and smashed the polished floor with her right boot.

"For what?" she demanded, wincing at the hoarse voice she barely recognized. Hours spent arguing with servants and soldiers bent on standing with her to the bitter end drained her. She had been thinking of years ruling with Terosh, searching her heart for something they had done wrong, something they could have done better, something that would justify Kezem's bold coup.

"For greed, hate, revenge; does it matter, Your Grace?" asked a grave voice, loud only because of the previous silence.

Reaching for her sword, Reia stiffened as adrenaline banished the weary shoulder droop. Then, she recognized the voice.

"Have you something to report, Captain?" Her hands released the weapon, and she drew herself up regally.

"The fortifications are complete," reported the Captain of the Royal Guard with a bow. He paused to consider his next words and lowered his voice. "But they will not hold." Concern etched deeply across his strong, square face, which carried a fair number of scars.

"I know, Captain Laocer," Reia assured him, eyeing the man with something akin to pity. She took in his sweat-matted, black hair, and tired eyes. Nothing in his posture or appearance betrayed fear, but she felt it rolling off him anyway.

What do you fear?

"Lord Kezem really wants my job," the queen added with a sad grin. A bit of humor sparkled to life behind her green eyes and vanished just as quickly. She sighed, like she was exhaling the weight of the universe. "I will not last this night."

"We will—"

"Are the arrangements made?" Reia asked, interrupting his predictable protestations of her fatalistic views. There are times to dream and times to be pragmatic. Since dreams would not save her, Reia figured she might as well accept it. After much thought, she concluded she had done everything possible for her people. The future would be played out by others. Her mind flashed a series of faces, family and friends she had finally convinced to flee. She sent a prayer after Kiata, Todd, Kayleen, the McKnights, the Etans, and Dr. Dentelich.

"They are, Your Grace," Laocer reported with a stiff nod.

"Good. Then, let them come." Reia spun on her heel, glad for the microgrips built into her boots. The highly polished throne room floors would be good for thwarting the enemy for a while. The battle's outcome was certain, but nothing said she had to forfeit her life peaceably.

"We will be ready," Laocer promised, saluting out of habit. He turned away then hesitated. "Your Majesty, may I speak as a friend?"

Reia nodded permission. Her thoughts turned to the last conversation with her sister. The memory of Kiata's desperation haunted her. It was strange how fate had reversed their roles. During their early years, Kiata had been the protector and Reia the one protected. Now, it fell to Reia to save both her sister and her people.

If only I could have preserved our parents as well. I'm sorry, Kiata.

Laocer's words interrupted her dark thoughts.

"Flee into the Riden Mountains! Accept exile. Gather the Rangers and the people will rise with you. Overthrow Lord Kezem when your forces are strong again."

"I cannot do that, Captain. Lord Kezem's wrath will cease once he claims the throne. Ruling is not as easy as he thinks it will be. If I escape he will feel threatened. I will not give him reason to pursue my children." Her tone left no mistake that the line of conversation was over. She knew the words consisted more of wishful thinking than facts, but she also needed Laocer as far from the palace as possible. "I have one last order for you."

"Anything," he said instantly.

She faced him again, and her expression said he wasn't going to like the order. Weariness, worry, and fear fled her face and stance. She studied Laocer carefully, then spoke with conviction.

"Aster Captain Ectosh Laocer, you are to quit this battlefield. You—"

"No!" Laocer dropped to his knees. "Please, let me serve! I can defend you. I—and every soldier here—swore by the three moons that my last breath would be spent in your service."

Like any good diplomat, Reia waited until Laocer finished. Then, she covered the five paces that separated them and knelt in front of him.

"You *are* serving me. My children matter most. Their survival is all that matters now. I know their fate is tied to yours. You must escape. The servant guardians are loyal, but they are no soldiers. Teach my children to defend and serve the people. If they cannot learn that, Reshner will surely suffer. Will you do this?"

Laocer nodded.

Reia could tell that it took much effort for him to meet her gaze. She was glad to see that he braced himself like a soldier.

"Thank you," she whispered, regaining her feet. "Come, there is much to be done before chaos enters the palace."

***

Jira (March) 2, 1547
Same Day
Princess Rela's Private Chambers, Royal Palace, City of Rammon

The haunting quiet in Princess Rela's nursery contrasted sharply with the muttered curses and loud commands filling the rest of the palace. Soldiers hurried to their stations. Servants who defied the evacuation orders rushed to quarters for weapons then reported to the throne room. Those who found no serlak or kerlak guns borrowed steel blades from the historic displays. Some even raided the kitchens for meat cleavers and mallets.

The princess's nursery remained calm only because Sarie Verituse refused to let anyone upset her charge. Her beady, dark eyes darted from one rushing servant to another. Her dark skin would have allowed her to blend in with the shadows had her cloak not already done so. She stood outside the nursery's heavy doors using a hard stare to threaten those who might disturb the princess. She refused to carry a weapon, clinging to the belief that even Kezem's brutes wouldn't cut down an unarmed woman.

"May I see her?" asked a soft voice from under a green cowl usually worn by the Melian Maidens. The female servants sworn to serve the queen for life were named in honor of their founder, Aster Captain Aria Melian.

Sarie flinched with surprise, yet she knew there was nothing unusual about Queen Reia wanting to see her daughter. Willing her heart not to break, Sarie immediately granted the queen access to the haven.

"Will you place the Ralose Charm upon her, Your Majesty?"

"I already have. It will preserve her life for a time," said Queen Reia, throwing off the hood and gently caressing her daughter's cheek. "Sarie, warn Lord Kezem about the charm and watch over my daughter. She will be safe in body but not in mind. Promise me you will guide her. Teach her to be loving, honest, and fair. When Kezem discovers her, he will try to twist her to his ways. That would be a fate worse than death."

"I promise, my Queen," Sarie whispered. Unable to say more, Sarie struggled to keep her sobs silent as she watched Queen Reia gently cup the slumbering toddler's chin. The expression on the young queen's face was hard to decipher. Sarie had not seen her this relaxed or vulnerable since before King Terosh's assassination two months before. She stared openly at the queen's profile, swiping at hot tears trying to blur her vision, determined not to miss one moment of the queen's farewell. Her efforts started to succeed until the queen spoke again.

"Sarie, see that Rela receives this when she is old enough to understand," said Queen Reia, pressing a small object into Sarie's right hand and embracing her tightly.

The gesture broke Sarie's resolve to not cry. Her hand clenched around the ring tight enough to make the emerald stone dig into her palm. She did not need to see the ring to imagine its elegant beauty.

"She and her brothers are Reshner's future," the queen reminded Sarie softly.

The queen continued whispering encouragements, but Sarie heard none of them. Instead, she concentrated on studying the queen. The hood was back on again, framing Reia's smooth, cream-colored skin. Her long, braided hair draped over her right shoulder. Her green eyes glistened with the emotions of the night. Her lips, though devoid of their usual smile, still appeared kind and gentle. Sarie memorized every graceful line of the queen's face then bowed and took her leave, knowing the queen needed time alone with the princess.

***

Reia gazed down at her daughter and thought about the Ralose Charm. Knowing that only she, her sister, and perhaps a high-ranking Ranger could break the charm tightened her throat with worry. She remembered whispering the ceremonial words and willing the anotechs to accept Rela as mistress.

What's done is done.

Reia concentrated on planting messages in her daughter's mind, messages that would not activate for years. Infopads could have been left with trusted servants, but these thoughts were meant for no one else.

"Always be sweet, my love. Never be bitter of the fate that befalls you," murmured Reia. A tear fell and the little one stirred. Reia resisted the urge to pick the child up, knowing she might crush her with the fierceness of goodbye. Instead, she drew two ragged breaths, leaned over, and kissed the tiny face. Her lips barely brushed the soft skin. More tears escaped and rained down upon the child, resulting in a scrunched up nose and a piercing whine.

Sleep, little one, thought Reia, soothing her daughter with anotechs.

Once certain the child again slept, Reia leaned back, laughed softly, and wiped the tears from her daughter's face. She wondered how much Rela would resemble her one day and how many features would come from Terosh. The toddler already had her father's piercing, deep blue eyes.

The servants would save Teven, the Rangers would save Tavel, and the Ralose Charm would save Rela, but no one could bring back Terosh or save the people from what would surely be long, dark years.

"Ensueltsom icretton, mef sela," she murmured.

In your heart, I will dwell, my daughter.

An alarm programmed into her infopad drove her from the room. She paused to encourage Sarie Verituse one last time. The servant's intense stare spoke of her strong loyalty. Reia lent her what strength of will and courage she could, before leaving to continue her heartbreaking farewells.

After seeing her eldest child into the secret tunnel below the old prison level in the care of the McKnights, Reia tucked her younger son into the life capsule that would protect him until he reached Osem. This third and final goodbye brought her so many mixed feelings that she feared she would burst open and spare Lord Kezem the trouble of killing her. The other farewells were said with some certainty that the children would end up where she intended. But as she clicked the life capsule locks into place, she felt a great distance between herself and her son. Doubt lingered.

The Rangers will care for him well.

She did not like the idea of shipping her son out of the palace like a crate of sweet nuts. If only Terosh could wrap warm arms around her, the pain might be more bearable. Having finished her task, Reia returned to the throne room to prepare for the last stand. At least she could join her husband knowing the children would be safe.

As she waited, Reia fingered the anotech-laden steel blade gently bouncing at her side. She could have simply drenched the blade with poison, but that would have been dishonorable and dangerous to her daughter. The tiny machines had been reluctant to obey her, but she had convinced them of the necessity of this long, strenuous mission where they would have to endure silently for years.

The few hundred servants, Melian Maidens, Palace Security, and Royal Guards arrayed before Reia held their shoulders back defiantly, serious gazes fixed upon her.

Rolling thunder crashed, causing everyone to flinch. It was as if the planet itself protested the political unrest. Reia smiled, putting every ounce of strength she possessed into maintaining the illusion of calm. They would feed off her emotions because she was their queen. She wished upon all the good left in the universe that she could order them to escape as she had Captain Laocer, but they would not listen. They had pledged their lives in defense of hers, and she could no more steal that honor than she could escape as an exile.

When she stood upon the dais and held up her hands, the surrounding murmur ceased.

"Lord Kezem will come soon to capture, conquer, kill, and

destroy. This is a dark day for Reshner, but hope remains. Let us make sure he never forgets this night!"

Chapter 3: Shipment to Osem

Jira (March) 2, 1547
Same Day
Spaceside Inn, City of Rammon

Reshner's not bad. If this moody Edge planet could kick its habit of forming acid storms every three months it would be downright pleasant.

As a former freight hauler captain, Trina Kiren liked the semi-metallic tinge left in the air around the spaceport.

Love's worth some sacrifices, and we could have fled somewhere horrible, like Moza.

The thought of that evil little ball of dirt where earthquakes were a daily occurrence and only the nobility ate regularly put a sour taste in Trina's mouth. She forced her thoughts back to the current situation.

On the other hand, Lord Kezem's violent bid for the throne makes Moza sound like a vacation hot spot right now.

Spending time with her man was one thing. Being trapped in an apartment half the size of her cockpit with her incessantly pacing husband was quite another. Queen Reia's version of martial law had been bearable. But now that Lord Kezem controlled Rammon's only spaceport, the situation had taken a turn for the worse. It seemed every two-bit, grouchy bounty hunter, mercenary, and other flavor of scumbag had chosen to join Kezem's rebel army.

Trina loved Kel, despite his unfortunate tendency to out think himself.

Safer closer to danger—humph.

Trina mentally cursed herself for letting Kel win the stay-or-go argument with idiotic logic.

Never again. My kerlak pistol—set for stun, of course—is doing the talking at the next family discussion.

She moved to stare listlessly out the grimy window and absently noted the click as Kel turned off the thought monitor.

"Hate to interrupt your mental bashing of me, dearest, but we're leaving," said Kel.

Trina's head snapped up and met her husband's cool blue eyes. His serlak pistol and kerlinblade were already donned. Although they'd been married four months, she still hadn't gotten used to him reading her moods, expressions, and thoughts.

"And where exactly are we going?" she asked, cocking an eyebrow.

"Away from here," Kel responded. "I doubt we'll have a chance to interview Queen Reia about me being a distant cousin of her late husband. So, anywhere away from that psychotic man who wants to be king will do." Kel handed her the weapon belt he had been adjusting.

With a slight frown, she took the belt, slung it around her slim waist, and clicked it snuggly into position. The move, made with grace earned through nineteen years of space lane travel, marked the shift from restless fugitive to self-confident captain.

"Do you think we could convince the queen to leave with us?" Trina inquired.

"We won't even get an audience with her now, but we should keep that meeting with Ranger Wellum," Kel said.

For someone in hiding, Kel did a lousy job of keeping a low profile. A mere two days after landing, they had received an encrypted infopad from Ranger Todd Wellum informing them of an urgent job. Today—day seven of their visit to Reshner—Trina checked the charge on her weapon and grunted at the thought of fleeing yet again.

We need to find a nice, out-of-the-way planet where the rest of the galaxy will ignore us.

"When, where, and how many do we have to take out to get there?" Trina asked, pushing the thought aside.

"That's why I love you," Kel said. His tender tone threw Trina off balance as much as the sudden kiss-embrace combo that followed. "Forty minutes, Rinten Tavern, and unknown but no more than four or five bounty hunters and the odd Kezem lackey too drunk to recognize humble fugitives like us." He flashed her that blasted smile that rarely failed to turn her heart into mush.

Trina agreed with his assessment of the opposition. This section of Rammon, the Southern Quarter, had fallen first, and the assault on the palace had most of Kezem's troops thoroughly occupied.

Precisely forty minutes later, Kel and Trina sat facing each other in a private booth and stared into miniature tankards of local ale that smelled strong enough to take off space-grade paint. After one whiff, Trina poured the offensive liquid onto the fuzzy, plant-like thing that was creeping too close to her arm for comfort. A high-pitched, ecstatic yelp startled her.

Kel's laughter at her expression morphed into a cough followed by muffled cry of pain when her steel-tipped boot brushed his shin.

"I forgot to warn you that bovas like Reshner ale. They'll tickle your arm until you either surrender your drink or smack them," he informed, swatting the bova that had been steadily approaching his drink.

Somehow, Trina doubted he'd simply forgotten, but she let it go because his eyes narrowed, telling her their contact had arrived.

Kel cautiously took a sip of ale, coughed, and gladly surrendered the remainder to the bova.

"The ale is an acquired taste," said a synthesized voice.

Trina watched Kel as he shifted to have easier access to his pistol. Engulfed in oversized robes that hid species, gender, age, and weapons, the being seemed harmless but Kel's wary expression made her cautious. The timeless, tense moment of first contact grated on her patience.

"Please, join us," Kel said cordially, gesturing to the empty chair next to their table.

The voice volume dropped, and Trina had to lean forward to hear.

"I am Nils Clavon. I give you my name as a sign of trust. My time is short. My master apologizes for his absence. He had urgent personal business to attend to, as do I."

"Lord Kezem moved much quicker than anyone anticipated, right?" Kel guessed.

"Your reputation precedes you, Master Kiren. My master heard of your inquiries and informed the queen. She conducted her own investigation and now asks that you prove your loyalty by accepting a dangerous mission. Here is the information. Please consider the job.

Many lives hinge upon your decision." The being dropped an infopad onto the table and left.

Trina watched Kel snatch up the infopad and rise to leave. She settled the ale account while Kel searched the infopad for tracers or malicious traps. She feared they would be accosted, but they exited the tavern without incident.

The only place private enough to view an important message was their Glaborn pleasure craft: *Zipper*. They met only one patrol on the way to the ship. The short confrontation went down like a great harvest celebration including lots of flashes, curses, and crashes. It ended with more than half the participants unconscious.

Three of the foes fell before Kel's flashing kerlinblade. One opponent, a particularly pungent Tedgmian, absorbed four energy blasts from Trina who then resorted to a more hands-on approach. She leapt onto the short man's back, rung his filthy neck, and held on for dear life.

When the Tedgmian finally lost consciousness, Trina tossed him aside with a disgusted grunt.

"I thought only Bozme could smell that bad," she commented, fondly recalling the elderly furball of a first mate.

"Well, I doubt this fellow's captain is quite as emphatic about personal hygiene as you were," Kel said, while relieving the unfortunate mercenaries of their various weapons.

Old pirate habit, Trina thought at her husband.

"You know those die the hardest, my love."

She shot him a read-this look and proceeded to mentally call him everything from an Asher tree toad to a Julip banker and worse.

"Such language is unbecoming of a lady," Kel said, smirking.

A kiss stamped a satisfactory end to the brush with death. They hastened on toward their ship. Although *Zipper* was greatly modified with illegal weapons and defense systems, Trina futilely wished for Kel's old Driden cruiser *Kel's Swift Hand.*

That beauty was a flying fortress.

Kel had been torn between his lucrative plundering business and her, but he had made the right choice. She would even have settled for her old cruiser, *Sassy One*, which had been rechristened as *Pride of Zopha.* The new name had come from the Driden god of fortune, a fitting name for the moderately armed cruiser that had survived several bounty hunter poundings. But wishes would get her nowhere so she pushed them aside.

Trina warmed the engines while Kel locked down the loading bay and swept for tracers. She was surprised and grateful that the engines worked. Kel found three tracers in the usual spots and two more in creative spots like the lavatory door handle. They worked swiftly and silently. Lord Kezem's nosy lackeys were no match for professionals.

Once secured in the cockpit, Kel activated the sound damper and flipped the infopad's active switch. The face that appeared on the screen was far younger than Trina had expected.

The man's fiery, rust-colored hair was balanced by his deep, concerned hazel eyes.

"Greetings, Master and Lady Kiren, I am Ranger Todd Wellum, and my faith in you rests upon your distant relation to the Royal House Minstel. By carrying out my mission you will greatly aid the queen. She is concerned. The informants in Osem report that Lord Kezem's forces have bombed the water reserve, set fire to the fields, and cut off aid to outlying villages. The death toll is rising. There is a special shipment at Ranger Corida's house in the West Quarter of Rammon. The shipment must reach Osem safely. I trust no one else. Fly safe."

Kel slapped the active switch again, and his brows furrowed in concentration.

"Well, I guess that solves the personal mission here," he mused. "What's so important about Osem?"

"He's hiding something," Trina said, not bothering to speculate on Osem's significance.

"But what? And why trust strangers, even related strangers?" asked Kel.

"Being the king's fourth cousin six times removed counts for something," Trina said deadpan. "Seriously, look at how his eyes shift when he speaks of the shipment," Trina urged.

Kel did so and his eyes softened ever so slightly.

"This is a dangerous time for the royal family," he said.

Trina's mind replayed clips from conversations overheard in the past few days. Her fingers lightly massaged her temple while she sifted through the rumors, double speak, and outright lies. Then, she stopped and muttered an imprecation.

"These people are crazy. How the flipping horn bats do they expect to smuggle anyone out of the palace?" The objective half of her recognized that the ranting meant she had committed herself to the task.

"That's not our problem," Kel reminded. "We only have to see the passenger or passengers and other supplies safely to Osem." He unlocked further instructions, flew to the site, and maneuvered the ship into the narrow alley without lights.

The Rangers had the supplies ready for transfer to *Zipper*'s cargo hold.

They're well organized; I'll give them that.

The moment the cargo was stowed, Kel shot the tiny ship straight into the air, hoping to surprise any anti-spacecraft guns Kezem might have on hand looking for a good target. As soon as he'd cleared the city limits, Kel made the ship dive until they were traveling mere meters above the ground. Twelve minutes later, Kel sat straighter in the pilot seat and relaxed a micron.

"We should be at Osem in fi—"

"It's gone." Silent tears crept down Trina's pale face as she pointed to the screen.

"Gone," he echoed. "The entire city? That's not possible!"

They set the security vidrecorder to look at Osem and zoomed in. Smoke rose from the city, spiraling upward and disappearing into the moonlit sky. Dark storm clouds followed closely behind *Zipper*. The pending rain would drown the fire and smoke, but the port city would be nothing more than a collection of craters for a long time.

"What will we do with the cargo?" Trina asked.

"We'll take it with us when I run the pathetic little blockade," Kel declared, throwing switches and pressing buttons. He gathered every scrap of energy he could temporarily borrow and added it to the engine reserves.

Trina worried about the dozen ships set up as a blockade around the planet. Lord Kezem didn't need to have a massive blockade to hinder travel around Reshner because its three tiny moons created unstable gravity wells which made many exit vectors unsafe. Trina nodded and sent some of the power Kel had gathered to the weapons systems. They had been hugging the planet's surface and powered down many systems to avoid sensors, but with the decision to run the blockade, subtlety could be ditched.

"Correction: you punch a hole in Kezem's blockade, and *I'll* run it," Trina said. As soon as Kel surrendered the pilot's chair, Trina slipped in, adjusted the safety restraints, and moved the chair forward to compensate for the height disparity between herself and her husband. She flew by instinct, veering sharply left to avoid the first shots. Belatedly, she hoped Kel had had time to strap in. A dull thud, yelp, and incoherent stream of angry words told her he hadn't.

Seconds later his voice came over the ship's communications system.

"Maybe I should fly."

"Since I want to live and I'm realistic about my shooting abilities, we stick to this plan," Trina said. She threw the ship into a thrilling series of spirals, partly to avoid the bullets and energy blasts trying to turn them into scrap and partially for fun.

"Dearest, unless you want to be scraping Reshner ale and the crackers we had for the midday meal off the walls, I suggest you stick to the less exciting evasive maneuvers!" Kel shouted.

Trina grunted but acquiesced to his request. Forgoing further fun, she skipped through the blockade in the most efficient manner possible. She tried to count the explosions but lost count around five. Then, they were out of range, and the ship's guns quieted. Kel joined her in the cockpit again. After setting the autopilot, she looked up, met his faint smile, and held out her hand. He took it and squeezed. For a moment, they didn't move. The short space battle had provided the perfect outlet for energy and emotion, but the effort was also draining.

Trina glanced over her left shoulder and checked the charts. They were safely en route to the edge of the galaxy.

"You picked a lovely escape vector," she commented, facing Kel again.

"You said you wanted to find a nice, out-of-the-way planet where we could be ignored," Kel reminded her. "Besides, a few of the nearby Wild planets look habitable."

"I *thought* I wanted that, but now I'm not so sure. And you'd better be right about habitability or this cockpit's gonna get real small, real quick," she warned, leveling a finger at him to emphasize her point.

He smiled roguishly, captured the accusing finger, pulled her to her feet, and kissed her.

"Let's hope so," he murmured when the kiss finally ended.

"We'd better go check on that cargo," Trina said somewhat reluctantly.

Hand-in-hand, they wandered back to the cargo hold where the Rangers had hastily stowed the supplies. Immediately spotting one container marked: fragile, this end up, Trina knelt and pulled the tab at the top. The outer container retracted, revealing a life capsule. Kel disengaged the locks. A flat screen slid out of the top, and soon, Kel and Trina found themselves staring into the cool, pain-filled green eyes of Queen Reia Minstel. A long pause indicated the young queen's struggle to find proper words with which to instruct her son's guardians.

"Greetings. Thank you for coming to our aid. My troubles with our Order notwithstanding, the Rangers have long been guardians and friends to House Minstel. I had hoped to see Reshner through the darkness, but I expect I shall soon join my beloved Terosh in death. Servants have charge of Teven and Rela, but I think it best my children not stay together. As guardians, you have every right to add a surname of your own choosing, but he will always be my youngest child, Tavel, Dulad Prince, third in line to rule Reshner.

"When the time is right, the anotechs will convey my messages to him. They will activate suddenly and most likely distress my son. Hopefully by then, he may return to Rammon to help his brother and sister restore peace. Should he have no desire to rule, I hereby release him from royal duties, provided Reshner has a king or queen either from the Minstel line or duly elected by the Governors Council and the Senate. I would send a Royal Guard with him, but I suspect treachery from somewhere in those ranks. Guard him well, my friends. Queen Reia Minstel, second day of the month of Jira (March), 1547."

The message ended and looped around to the beginning, ready to repeat if necessary.

For several minutes, Trina and Kel clung to each other and stared at the tiny prince.

What do we do?

Despite the panicked thought repeatedly charging through her head, Trina felt herself falling in love with the boy. They had planned to put off parenting for several years, perhaps indefinitely, but it seems the Fates had different plans for them.

"Well, Prince Tavel, looks like you're stuck with us," said Kel.

Chapter 4: Rough Welcome

Jira (March) 2, 1547
Same Day
East Quarter, Streets of Rammon, City of Rammon

Weary, Todd Wellum shivered with anticipation and dread. His mission had been a complete waste of time. They should have been mounting a rescue. Queen or not, Kiata's sister needed to leave the palace soon. He hoped Kiata had sent Nils to meet Kel and Trina Kiren in his stead.

His head hurt from lack of food, and his heart hurt with despair and anger. He growled, remembering the Ashatans' verdict concerning Queen Reia's plight.

It's nothing short of sanctioned murder!

The Ranger High Council had agreed to raise one of the children but immediately quelled discussion of a more direct intervention because the dispute for the throne involved two members with ties to the Minstel line, Reia by marriage and Kezem by maternal blood. Todd suspected Master Liam Deliad wanted Kezem to replace Reia because she'd chosen to marry Terosh against the Ranger code. Todd had arranged for the youngest child, Prince Tavel, to reside in Osem, but without the full support of the Rangers, Lord Kezem would soon rule. If that happened, the young Minstel heirs would be vulnerable to destruction for many years.

This will not end well.

Todd furtively picked his way through the darkened streets.

Malevolent eyes followed his every move from the shadows. Being a Ranger taught him about courage and handling fear but being the father of a four-year-old girl taught him a new kind of fear, one resulting in a stabbing sensation that tightened his chest.

His recent travels confirmed Lord Kezem's firm grip on the planet. Despite the dangers, Todd focused on little else besides completing his new mission of getting his family far away from Rammon. The need to hold his wife and child warred with his judgment and urged his legs to carry him home swiftly. Nearing his house in the East Quarter, Todd traded stealth for speed.

One pace from home, safety, and Kiata, the door swung out abruptly. Finely tuned reflexes saved Todd's nose from a beating, but the head blow would have hurt less than the sight before him. Ceiling lightbars brightened the grim scene. Kiata lay on her left side facing the doorway. The mass of bruises, gashes, and blade marks covering her face represented only a portion of the punishment inflicted upon her body. Todd rushed to her not caring that there were others in the room. Her lifeless eyes pierced Todd's heart, killing the hope he had held for the future. Moaning, he sank to his knees, sick in heart and body. His stomach held nothing to surrender so he choked and retched and sobbed until his strength was gone.

Where's Kayleen? The thought burst through the walls of mental anguish.

Todd's head snapped up.

Kiata must have sent her with Nils, he thought, wishing Ridenspeed to the servant. The hope returned some of his strength.

"Lord Kezem sends his greetings," a familiar male voice announced. "I'm sorry your wife expired before you could see her. Pity. I would have liked to see that reunion."

Todd's body moved before consulting his mind. Screaming, he spun and kicked. His left foot connected with flesh and bone. The satisfying impact brought a smile to his face, but it was short lived. A fist landed on his left cheek and smashed into his nose, releasing a flood of blood. Oblivious to pain, Todd fought with the strength of a man bent on revenge and the courage of someone with nothing left to lose. Strong arms gripped him from behind, but he threw them off, spun, and battered the man's face and neck. More hands grasped him from all sides. He traded punches and kicks with half a dozen young soldiers.

"Enough!" snapped the first man.

Suddenly, the hands let go and everybody backed away, leaving Todd standing near his dead wife. Still dripping blood from his nose, he glared at the speaker who wore a blood-spattered blue uniform filled with fancy rank pins. The man was plain except for his shiny, dark hair which was as well-tended as his ego.

"Kolknir." Todd spat the name like a curse. "What are you doing here? Murdering Royalists seems a bit below your new station. This is Kezem's big night. Have you forgotten everything you learned as a Ranger?"

If the sarcasm irritated the man, he hid it well. Shaking his head, Kolknir glanced down in dismay at his bloody uniform.

"The Rangers are nothing to me. Haven't been for quite some time. You and Kiata were always my favorite students though, so fierce, so competitive," said Kolknir. "You would have been fine allies. Too bad Lord Kezem believed Kiata would never betray her sister, even if they weren't truly sisters."

Blood doesn't make family. Love does.

This second reference to Kiata snapped something inside Todd. With an enraged scream, he launched himself at Kolknir again. Before anyone could draw a breath, Todd's fingers gripped Kolknir's neck and squeezed hard.

To their credit, Kolknir's men reacted in the next instant. Some tore at Todd's iron-like fingers, while others kicked, punched, and cursed him. After much effort, they finally freed Kolknir.

"Do not kill him!" Kolknir shouted.

His men eyed him carefully, clearly confused.

"Don't kill him, my Lord?" a young soldier asked cautiously. His arm was cocked awkwardly above his head ready to deal another blow to their prisoner.

"You heard me!" Kolknir brushed at his sullied uniform, which would forever carry a mixture of his and Todd's blood. "Lord Kezem wishes him to experience the palace prisons."

"Lord Kolknir?" Todd asked contemptuously.

"Yes, Todd, Lord Kezem has made me a sublord," said Kolknir. "You should show me more respect than Kiata did."

Todd had heard of Kezem's sublords. Soldiers, traders, merchants, and even Rangers who supported Kezem's cause through funds, favors, and other traitorous activities were rewarded with high positions in the new government. Todd could tell Kolknir expected a response, so he spat blood at the man's feet. At this point, he cared only about the hope of seeing his daughter again.

***

Jira (March) 2, 1547
Same Day
Merchant Quarter, City of Rammon

She's not dead. She's not dead.

Talyon Keldor silently chanted the phrase, but his eyes argued with him.

This is crazy.

Kiata Wellum certainly looked dead. She lay on a hov sled surrounded by six of Kezem's men dressed in the muddy red uniform of his poorly named Reshner Liberation Army. She was the strongest woman he knew. It pained him to see her so still, pale, and fragile looking. One of the soldiers had the decency to close her eyes. Taly breathed a sigh of relief that Kolknir hadn't bid his men to remove Kiata's head or anything like that.

The queen's plan to rescue her sister was pure insanity, but so far, it seemed to be working as predicted. If anyone else had been asking Taly to go on this strange mission for any other reason than saving Kiata, he would have laughed in their faces, but he owed her his life. He also owed the queen for her treatment of his grandfather. Taly forced down the storm of emotions as he thought of the king's assassination, the queen's danger, her orders, Lord Kezem's hunt for the royal children, the rebellion, and the rest of this mess.

He wished the queen would let him kill Lord Kezem. Taly was realistic enough about his chances of successfully completing that task, but somehow dying in a blaze of glory seemed easier than this shadowy stalking that could go on for years.

The soldiers' steady march brought them in range. Taly eyed them through the scope of his rifle, sent up a prayer for steady hands and clean shots, and fired. The first two dropped before the rest could draw weapons.

Suddenly, the air around Taly and the soldiers lit with energy beams. Some were blue stun beams, but most were the brilliant red color of full-energy, kill shots. Reacting by instinct, Taly fired wildly and dove for cover. The scene before him unfolded in his mind again. As much as he had faith in his own shooting abilities, he could never have released so many beams simultaneously. That left only one explanation: another shooter.

Merisia!

Taly cursed under his breath. He had told her to stay in hiding. He ran to another window two away from the one he'd originally attacked from and cautiously peeked out. Sure enough, a steady stream of beams flooded from a window a few stories up from his current position. A glance down amused and horrified Taly.

The shots from the window were so wild that the remaining four soldiers were firing in several directions, trying to pin down the origin point. They would find it soon, but for now, Merisia's lack of shooting skills gave Taly an advantage. Seizing the opportunity, he shot two more soldiers.

Frustration built in Taly. He needed to get to Kiata soon or one of Merisia's wild shots would kill her. Even as he thought it, one of Merisia's beams struck Kiata in the center of her chest. For an instant, she glowed red as the energy beam washed over a wide area like it had struck a personal shield. Taly blinked but couldn't fathom what was protecting her. The soldiers would have no reason to equip a body with a Personal Shielding Device. Torn between going up to get Merisia and going down to get Kiata, Taly grunted and scanned the area again with his scope.

A fresh squad of soldiers arrived. Their commander pointed up at Taly's building.

Taly shot the commander and then abandoned his rifle and went to find Merisia. He wished he could take the weapon with him, but it wasn't exactly designed as a close-quarter weapon. He and Merisia would be in for the fight of their lives, but perhaps searching the building would slow the soldiers down enough to let them sneak out and rescue Kiata.

"Merisia!" Taly shouted. He had to call her name twice more and put a hand on her shoulder before she dropped the kerlak pistol, turned, and practically tackled him with a fierce embrace.

"I'm sorry, Taly, so sorry. I had to come, had to!" Merisia babbled.

"We've got to go," said Taly, returning her hug. "Kezem's soldiers have entered the building."

A determined look crossed Merisia's face. She scooped up the handgun and held it out to Taly.

"I'll stall them. Go get the Ranger, Taly. Go."

"They'll kill you," Taly argued. "Come with me."

"You don't know that; you can't know that," said Merisia, grinning faintly. "You'd make a terrible damsel in distress, Taly, but they might buy it from me, just might."

Although he hated to admit it, Taly saw that her plan offered him a faint chance. Emotion choked him.

"Merisia, I—"

"You have your mission, Taly, and I have mine," said Merisia, placing a hand over his mouth. "Save the queen's sister." With tears streaming down her face, Merisia fled the room.

Taly wanted to sit down and think about Merisia's words and the million messages in her eyes, but instead, he locked his emotions away, tucked her pistol next to his own, and climbed out the window. The building would be crawling with soldiers by now, so Taly would do the unexpected.

Chapter 5:
The Royal House Falls

Jira (March) 2, 1547
Same Day
Royal Palace, City of Rammon

Governor General Third Lord of Idonia, Kezem Altran—known as Lord Kezem—strode into the Rammon palace at last. He finished clearing the first floor and grunted at the thought of clearing four more floors before reaching the throne room. He'd already passed more guard posts than he could count and each new one irritated him more than the last. Thankfully, many posts were empty, having been abandoned by those enlightened to join the right side before the palace fell.

By the time he reached the two Royal Guards stationed outside the throne room, Kezem's anger overflowed, lending strength to his body. He moved with grace for such a large man. He enjoyed towering over lesser men, and almost laughed at the memory of his scrawny self only a few years prior. Surprisingly, he also missed his mother. After all, tonight was the culmination of her hopes, dreams, ambitions, and years of planning. His movements were quick, decisive, and deadly. He might have let one of his eager soldiers gut the hapless guards, but he figured it would be healthier to vent some anger before reaching Queen Reia. It would be a pity if he skewered the young woman without at least gloating.

Despite their vaunted training, the Royal Guards were no match for Kezem. He wasted little time dispatching them with his electrified banistick and kerlinblade. Although banistick modifications could be as simple or complex as one desired, Kezem had chosen shocks because of the delightful ability to torture people while fighting them. He attacked both guards simultaneously. The banistick in his left hand caught one man in the armpit, resulting in a loud shriek as every nerve fired at once. The thin edge of Kezem's yellow kerlinblade slammed into the other guard's neck, instantly removing his head.

As the guard on the left breathed his last, Kezem casually punched in the code for the throne room door. Ironically, the traitor had rigged the king's hov with explosives for next to nothing but demanded six hundred thousand kefs for the simple code. When nothing happened, Kezem cursed in Resh, Hintle, and Borner.

"I will kill him," he vowed, forgetting that he had already planned on killing the traitorous Captain of the Royal Guard. "I will rip him apart piece by piece! No one betrays me!"

The tone and volume caused his nearby minions to cringe. The soldier stupid enough to be within striking distance paid dearly for it. The banistick slap left him unconscious.

"Deven, get me a prisoner!"

No one moved.

Dark blue eyes blazing, Kezem turned to his soldiers. His high emotional state caused a yellow streak shaped like lightning to slash through either side of his irises. Being one sixteenth Bornovan, Kezem's eye color shifted shades of blue in accordance with his mood. His chiseled face twisted into a fierce expression.

"You struck him, Lord Kezem," a brave soul murmured.

"Then *you* get me a servant!"

The lieutenant bowed and left as fast as his stubby legs would carry him. Luckily, he found a prisoner being led down the hall to the meeting chamber where Kezem's forces were storing servants who surrendered without too much trouble.

Kezem preferred to keep prisoners alive until he was certain he wished them dead. He could always kill them later. He watched with amusement as his youthful lieutenant struggled to subdue the servant girl. Thin but wiry, the servant used her lower center of gravity to spin Kezem's man into the wall.

"Enough! Jorg, Makil, relieve Lieutenant Toft of his burden," said Kezem, recalling that he had a queen to kill.

The twins shared a grin.

"It will be done, Lord Kezem," they answered, moving to follow his order. What they lacked in intelligence, the twins made up for in blind loyalty and delightful cruelty.

Soon, the pale servant was on her knees before Lord Kezem.

"Give me the door code," he ordered.

Fear made the girl's eyes glaze, and Kezem suspected she might pass out.

He deactivated his banistick and returned it to his belt. Then, he changed the kerlinblade settings so that the blade was long and thin before pointing it at her neck.

"Do not faint, or you will never wake."

"Let Atellia go, Kezem. She does not know the code. I had it changed an hour ago," said a calm voice.

Kezem spun on his right heel and stared up at the vidscreen showing Queen Reia's image. She sat erect on her oversized throne, dressed in green and purple ceremonial robes. The hood of the outer cloak touched her forehead, framing her face. Her expression was sad and strained, as if she concentrated very hard on something.

"There has been enough death tonight," said the queen.

"I should slaughter everyone in this palace," Kezem said.

Her expression relaxed ever so slightly.

"But you will not," Reia said with confidence that irked him. She appeared weary, but the coolness of her green eyes helped her maintain the indomitable illusion. "You live by terror, but not even your coldest allies would stand for a complete massacre of the palace staff."

"You believe that? Perhaps this will change your mind." Kezem thrust his kerlinblade at the servant's neck. A scream and curse escaped him as a sharp pain in his blade hand caused him to jerk violently. The blade veered to the left of its target, leaving only a mild burn on the servant's neck.

The girl looked as surprised as he was that she still lived.

Kezem dropped his kerlinblade which suddenly burned in his hand.

"What have you done? Your tricks will not save you! I knew my cousin was insane to marry a Ranger!"

"Why you think me such a threat, I shall never know," Reia commented. "I could never protect so many …" A flicker of amusement entered her eyes, and the right corner of her mouth crept upward slowly. "Perhaps Terosh protects this place."

"It's not possible!" Kezem hated that her mockery could provoke him so easily.

The queen sighed.

"I claim little by way of goodness, but you are evil, Kezem. The easy paths, fleeting wealth, and power promises may sway people for now, but Reshner will come to its senses." Her eyes bore into him. "I promise you. My people will not suffer your rule for long."

He seethed that she momentarily lay beyond his grasp. Snatching his kerlinblade from the floor, Kezem clenched his fists around the weapon and imagined it was her neck. He considered killing the servant for spite but dismissed the thought.

She's not worth the effort.

"Take her away," Kezem ordered. "Jorg, Makil, Toft, break down those doors!" He whirled right to face different soldiers. "The rest of you finish clearing the palace. I want every child, soldier, servant, and other being within these walls rounded up immediately!"

His soldiers rushed to do his bidding, but the battle for the palace raged for two more hours. Eventually, Kezem's soldiers battered through the throne room doors.

Inside, more Royal Guards, Palace Security, and Melian Maidens tangled with his men. Kezem slashed his way through the crowd but only got halfway across the throne room before a dark-skinned Melian Maiden leapt into his path, halting his progress. His red kerlinblade locked with her banistick. He shoved forward, using his superior size and strength to knock her back a few steps. They traded strikes. He added his banistick to the fight. Finally, he smashed the modified banistick under her chin. The blow stunned her and his kerlinblade finished her. Gritting his teeth at the delay, Kezem stepped over the body and continued towards the throne.

Head tilted forward and arms resting at her sides, Queen Reia stood at the edge of the meter-high platform holding the throne. From a distance, she appeared immune to the death and destruction around her. But up close, a steady stream of silent tears spoke her pain at watching good people die in her defense.

Their eyes met and Kezem felt shame, guilt, and grief shoot through him. Her youthful beauty struck him dumb. He despised her for having that effect on him, and the anger drove the feeling away. Kezem wished to possess her, but the people of Reshner would never stand for such dishonor to royalty.

Realizing he had halted, Kezem gathered his courage and marched up to the queen. A triumphant grin spread across his face.

"I am surprised that you have chosen to face honorable death,

Your Majesty."

"There is little honor in this, Kezem," said Queen Reia, waving around them. "I stayed because my people needed me here."

"Your people abandoned you, Reia. You lost them long ago when you considered GAPP for an ally." Kezem shook his head in mock sadness. "When will you learn that people are selfish? They want a strong ruler. They seek money and comfort, and I have promised them both. Their greed makes them easy to manipulate for someone with power, ambition, and—"

"Little respect for life," Reia finished. "You may seize the throne today, but years of war will follow. Are you prepared to fight for it?"

"Do not concern yourself with my well-being, Your Grace. My men will handle the pathetic peasants sympathetic to you," Kezem assured her. "And your children will never reach their destinations. Osem is being destroyed as we speak."

The statement caused a momentary crack in Queen Reia's sad, solemn expression. She closed her eyes to ward off the pain.

"So, the betrayal runs that deep," Reia murmured, blinking back tears.

Kezem's kerlinblade blazed red in his right hand. He contemplated it then made a slight adjustment so that the blade flattened and shone bright green on both sides of a thin, purple center.

"I respect you, Your Grace. Were circumstances different, we might have even been friends. See, I shall even kill you in the colors of your chosen House." A flick of his wrist brought the blade tip to the point of Reia's chin.

She tipped her chin up but did not retreat.

Kezem secretly admired her nerve.

"You know who your betrayer is, don't you? He had hoped to woo you, but your death fits better with my plans. Do not worry. My men will kill him soon enough."

"I do not wish his death. Too much of that has already touched this people," said the queen.

"Well spoken, Your Majesty," Kezem sneered. "Fitting words before you die." He drew his arm back for a killing thrust.

"My death will come but not that easily." Queen Reia twisted to her right and released the clasp securing the outer cloak and robes to her neck. The ceremonial robes flew away from her like living things. Underneath, she wore a comfortable white shirt and plain brown trousers which allowed free movement, clothing more befitting of a Ranger than a queen.

Her clothes reminded Kezem of her humble roots. Without the ceremonial robes, her appearance matched that of any woman, but she was no ordinary woman. A delicate, deadly looking silver blade appeared in her right hand. She saluted, grasping the smooth handle and turning the blade sideways.

One of Kezem's eager men leapt onto the dais ready to strike.

"No!" Kezem roared, fearing his underling might kill the queen.

He need not have feared.

Reia spun away from the clumsy strike, using natural momentum and the flat edge of her sword to beam Kezem's man upside the head.

"I will kill her! All who interfere will die!" Kezem snatched his banistick from his belt and launched his first attack. He struck hard but avoided killing blows, determined to savor the moment.

Their duel lasted untold minutes. Kezem forgot the stress of taking over Rammon. Only this battle mattered. They fought from one end of the throne room to the other and back again several times, dancing over bodies and screaming wounded. His men scrambled out of the way of the desperate duel. The clash of steel on crackling energy mingled with shuffling feet and labored breath. Their weapons met, locked, released, and crashed in a dizzying display of lights and sparks.

Queen Reia drew first blood, catching Kezem's right forearm with the tip of her blade. She smiled radiantly as if that single touch could win back the world he was so bent on taking from her. One of his banistick slashes glanced off her shoulder, but she fought on. Kezem was surprised she could still hold a blade after the shock that must have gone through her. He then poured all his energy into jarring strikes. Her smile disappeared as she concentrated on catching the blows.

Eventually, his brute strength prevailed. He smacked her blade down with the banistick and swept the kerlinblade at her neck. Kezem might as well have struck rock. He pulled his blade back revealing a faint line of blood. His eyes widened.

That blow should have beheaded her!

Queen Reia smiled faintly.

"My friends don't seem to want to let me go."

Though baffled, Kezem redoubled his efforts striking wildly

and with more force. Finally, he disengaged and took two steps back.

"Shoot her!" he ordered.

A dozen shots flew toward them.

Kezem jumped aside as one came too close.

For several seconds, Reia did well dodging the energy beams and serlak bullets, but the sheer number proved too much. Three beams struck her in the back, knocking her forward, and a bullet bounced off her head, leaving her dazed.

"Cease fire!" Kezem shouted.

A few steps brought her within striking distance. He thrust the kerlinblade forward and his blade met real flesh and pierced her heart. She winced but uttered only a sigh. Sinking to her knees, Queen Reia breathed her last.

It was over.

As he watched the light of life fade from her eyes, Kezem waited for the sense of joyful victory to come, but he only felt tired.

Chapter 6:
Linked Fate

Jira (March) 2, 1547
Same Day
Throne Room, Royal Palace, City of Rammon

"Do you like my new accommodations, Sublord Kolknir?" Lord Kezem asked. Having changed into a crisp black uniform and donned a silver cloak, Kezem looked every bit the victorious king he wished to be.

He smiled and gestured expansively. Majestic crimson banners hung from the walls and ceilings approximately every four meters, spanning the throne room's seventy meters length and forty meters width. Each banner featured the silhouette of a man locked in combat with a zalok. The zalok's claws held the man in a bone-crushing grip, but the man's sword was buried in the beast's chest right where the largest heart would be.

"How did your mission go?" Kezem inquired, before Kolknir could answer his first question.

"My mission was a great success," Kolknir said, bowing stiffly, a gesture suggesting familiarity as well as respect.

A big bruise on the left side of Kolknir's face said differently, but Lord Kezem refrained from commenting. After all, the healing wrap on his arm proved even successful missions had their hard edges.

"We cleared the Merchant Quarter an hour ago. The North Quarter will take more time, but I am confident Rammon will fully submit to your rule by tomorrow."

"And what of the young royals?" asked Kezem, pleased that

Kolknir sounded suitably humble. Kezem was not fool enough to believe the heirs would always remain helpless babes. If they survived, Royalist hope would survive, and he would never have a moment's peace.

Kezem had purchased control of the Senate and the Governors Council, but many people clung to the notion that only the Minstel bloodline ought to rule. Technically, Kezem was in line for the throne, but his claim was far less solid than the three, knee-high royals. His mother, Lady Mavis, had been disowned by her father when she'd married his father, Dravid Altran.

Crushing Royalist hopes was why he had struck Osem—stronghold of the Rangers—so hard. Most other Royalists were merchants and peasants, not soldiers, but Rangers could fight rather well and tended to take their vows to protect House Minstel far too seriously.

"No, my Lord," Kolknir said with a frown, "but we are tracking down every Ranger. Despite personal tensions, the queen would seek their aid first. Kiata Wellum is dead, her husband is in our custody, and their child is missing."

Kezem's cobalt eyes narrowed dangerously. A flash of yellow entered his eyes but faded as he clamped down on his anger.

"Where is the queen, my Lord?"

"My plans have changed," Kezem said, rising from the throne and walking to the platform's edge. "She had too many supporters to be spared. Kill the traitor. His loyalty is far too fickle."

"It will be done, my Lord," Kolknir promised. He stepped aside to issue the proper orders.

Kezem nodded absently and paced the dais lost in thought.

What of the girl?

His spies had spoken of plans to smuggle the princes out of the palace, but there had been no mention of moving the princess.

What would Reia do to protect her daughter?

Kezem's cloak swirled as he turned. He fiddled with his banistick and the ceremonial dagger he had taken from a vanquished Melian Maiden. To his knowledge, he had no children, but if he did, the palace would be the last place to leave them. With Rammon's central location, "far away" could mean anywhere.

"The princess must be near." Kezem quit pacing and narrowed his eyes. "Kolknir, seal off Rammon. No one gets in or out until every human child less than four has been killed. Children of other species are irrelevant. Deal with them as you see fit."

"Forgive me, Lord Kezem, but wouldn't it be better to spare the children?" Kolknir inquired. He hastened on before Kezem could object. "Create a camp to sift the youth. The weak will die, and you will be left with strong, impressionable youths to mold into a loyal fighting force."

"Go on."

"It will serve a double purpose, my Lord. The children will become soldiers and their parents will work the weapons factories … for free."

"How would I ensure loyalty?" Kezem wondered, liking the plan. He found it interesting that the people he disliked intensely often proved most useful.

"Fear, power, and rewards. Hold their families hostage. You have done it before, just not on this scale," said Kolknir.

"True," Kezem admitted.

"Turn the Festival of Future Fighters to your own purposes. Compel able-bodied youths to participate in the contests. The top ones could be commissioned as Royal Guards or Melian Maidens and be sent on the Kireshana as usual, and the rest would be given rank and file positions in Reshner's Liberation Army."

"I see. It is a slow plan, but it has promise," Kezem said. Understanding came upon him. Although Kolknir had command of Kezem's invasion force, the power of the rank would soon disappear. "Of course, the Royal Guard would need a new commander," Kezem mused.

"Would you consider me for the honor, my Lord?" asked Kolknir.

"I thought you wished to be Governor of Idonia," said Kezem.

"This sounds more suited to my talents," Kolknir replied. "I have taught many students over the years."

Kezem's deep chuckle filled the space between them.

"That you have. Very well, kneel." When Kolknir followed the direction, Kezem drew his banistick and touched it to the man's shoulders. Even at low power, the electric shocks made Kolknir's shoulders tremble. "I hereby grant you full command of Reshner's armed forces, including the Royal Guard and the RLA. Rise, Supreme Commander Kolknir. Summon Captain Linel so I can promote her to Aster Captain. She will serve directly under you and conduct business pertaining to a new order of the Melian Maidens."

"It will be done, my Lord," Kolknir said.

It never ceased to amuse Kezem to hear the former Ranger address him so respectfully, but he watched the man closely, expecting betrayal someday. "Accept only human candidates of the finest appearance and abilities, Commander," Kezem instructed. "Turn the aliens and the inferior over to Commander Tigert and the factories. I expect your first report in a month."

"As you will, Lord Kezem, so be it," said Kolknir. The new commander saluted sharply and left in a hurry.

Despite the late hour, Lord Kezem ordered the cooks to prepare a celebration feast. The silence in the throne room struck him full force, making him frown. Something was missing. Such a momentous occasion required female company.

"Guards!"

Two of his ever-present, unobtrusive shadows appeared at his side.

"Have the prison guards select some pretty companions. Have them properly attired and send them to the dining hall."

The junior guard nodded, saluted, and stepped back to deliver the order. Kezem looked critically at his outfit and concluded that the military look suited the night. Smoothing back his graying dark hair, Kezem settled back onto the throne and let his mind wander over the glorious evening.

The hard part was over. With Terosh and Reia dead and the Rangers scattered, Reshner was his to rule. Tonight, Kezem would have the political prisoners interrogated and then invite them to join him in building a better, stronger, richer Reshner. He would spare what palace staff he could and have his agents ferret out disloyal subjects. Taking the planet had been a challenge but keeping it would truly test him.

***

Jira (March) 3, 1547
Throne Room, Royal Palace, City of Rammon

Lord Kezem had a splendid night and rose late in the morning, feeling the effects of too much ale. To make matters worse, he received several awful reports as soon as he stepped into the throne room. The squad he had sent after the traitor had returned empty-handed, and pockets of resistance still burned around Rammon.

In a surly mood, Kezem summoned Kolknir for his report, praying it would be good. He could hardly bear more bad news. If things failed to favor him soon, his reign would be extraordinarily short.

"Have the interrogators finished questioning the palace staff?" asked Kezem.

"They have, my Lord," Commander Kolknir replied.

"And?" Kezem prompted, slamming a fist against the throne.

"Queen Reia smuggled the princes out of the palace. One went west with some servants, and one was put in a life capsule and shipped east, most likely to Osem."

"I destroyed Osem," Kezem said. That was an understatement. In hindsight, he admitted the complete bombing had been excessive as well as expensive. The three klipper fighters dropping the bombs had gotten too close and blown themselves to smoky little pieces. "What of the child sent to Osem?"

"No word on that, my Lord. Most of the servants know only rumors. One—"

"You're telling me not one of the royal brats has been found?" Kezem interrupted.

"Most servants claim the princess is still here in the palace," said Kolknir.

Kezem had expected the princess to be within the city limits, but he had not expected her to be that close.

"Bold, even for her," he mused, thinking of the queen. He laughed sharply. "No doubt she believed her Ranger magic would save the child." He chuckled again before issuing his next order. A gleam entered his eyes. "Assemble the palace staff. Seize every female child the princess's age and line them up on the dais facing the crowd. Gather the other children as well."

Within half an hour, Kezem's soldiers had stuffed the exhausted palace staff into the throne room. A couple hundred soldiers had been summoned to guard them and witness the momentous occasion. Kezem would begin his reign by killing Reia's brat. He just had to choose the correct one.

"Welcome to the new order," Kezem announced. A wave of weariness washed over him.

His soldiers laughed nervously, and the palace staff stared silently.

"The princes have been eliminated," he lied, trying to stave off weariness. This was to be a fine moment, and he would enjoy it.

Several people gasped, a few wailed, and most cried.

"I'm told the princess is here. Tell me which girl has royal blood or I shall kill them all," said Kezem.

The large throne room doors swung in slowly, and six soldiers entered carrying sedated toddlers. Another twenty soldiers entered, escorting the remaining children belonging to the palace staff. An outraged cry rippled through the crowd. The lines wavered as Kezem's men held the crowd back. The servants' pleas, threats, curses, and shouts made Kezem smile.

"A hundred and nine children, including six girls the princess's age, were found, my Lord," a young captain reported, saluting.

Receiving Kezem's acknowledging nod, the soldier motioned, and the six toddlers were placed on air cushions. The older children huddled together behind the air cushions, trying to stay as far away from Kezem as possible. Lights ensured that the audience had a clear view of the slumbering children's peaceful expressions.

"There is no reason for these children—your children—to die today," said Kezem. "I will do what I must to protect my people." He stopped speaking and reflected on the Reia-like comment. He dismissed the disturbing thought. "I consider myself a fair man. If someone tells me which child belongs to House Minstel, the others will be spared." Kezem could feel the hatred emanating from the staff and wondered if he had overstepped a fine line. If the staff rioted, he would lose men he could ill-afford to lose. As the silence stretched, his patience waned. Drawing a dagger, Kezem approached the nearest infant.

"Wait!" a defiant voice commanded from within the throng. The sea of people parted, revealing a straight-backed, grim-faced woman with dark skin. Her black eyes pierced Lord Kezem. "You cannot harm her!"

"Bring that woman here," Kezem ordered. The large woman was hustled up to him. "What is your name? Explain your statements."

The woman's glare never wavered.

"I am Sarie Verituse, maiden of Queen Reia Minstel and caretaker of the one you wish to destroy. If you cut her, they will heal her. If you poison her, they will cure her. If you—"

"I get the point. Who?"

"You are powerless against her guardians. Her parents' legacy will preserve her life until you are no more." Her booming voice filled the throne room.

"Her parents are dead!" Kezem shouted. "I cut them down

myself. Her mother died just yesterday. Reia believed herself invincible, but she bled and died, same as the child will!" He circled the air cushion as he spoke and raised the knife over the nearest toddler.

"That is not the right child!" Sarie declared.

Kezem whirled on the woman and lifted her chin with the dagger's tip. The blade drew blood even at the slightest pressure.

"Then, perhaps you'd be kind enough to point out the correct child," he said, dragging the dagger two inches to the left.

"The first child is Princess Rela Minstel," Sarie informed with unsettling calm, despite the warm trickle of blood running down her neck. She locked eyes with Kezem almost daring him to kill her. "Do not harm her, for her pain will be your pain until events transpire to set you both free," she intoned.

Fear and anger shot through Kezem. He had to dispel this Ranger-inspired madness before it spread.

"She is not immortal!" he cried.

"Wound her then, but I tell you now, if she dies this day, so do you," Sarie said.

Without hesitation, Kezem went over to the princess and slit the toddler's left arm. She awoke with a cry, but Kezem's own surprised scream prevailed. He jerked back, dropped the dagger, and gripped his arm tightly, surprised to find blood on his right hand. His arm stung fiercely for several seconds. Then, the pain eased, as the cut on the child's arm closed itself. Kezem retrieved the ceremonial dagger from the floor and sliced off a portion of his black uniform sleeve. The bloody cloth fluttered to the ground. Kezem gaped at his arm which appeared perfectly normal.

"You would do well to keep her from harm," Sarie said.

Kezem ordered the throne room cleared and the servant seized for further questioning. He assigned two guards to protect the child. This turn of events greatly disturbed him. As much as he wished to destroy Reia and Terosh's daughter, he would have to make other arrangements.

This is Reia's fault. Even in death she haunts me!

Chapter 7:
Dark Years

Zeri (June) 3, 1547-Temen (July) 25, 1554
Royal Palace, City of Rammon

Three months passed, and still Royalist rebels harried Lord Kezem's troops. How could they not embrace his vision for Reshner? He had attacked Rammon first, knowing the capital controlled the other cities. Calsola, the nearest city northwest of Rammon, had also fallen quickly, but since then, there had been no clear victories.

At least Supreme Commander Kolknir and Aster Captain Leena Linel's joint recruiting report held good news. Youths from most major cities jumped at Kezem's offer of adventure, fortune, and glory. Unfortunately, they were no match for roaming Rangers and stubborn Royalists.

Rammon had once been famous for its hospitality. A high wall had surrounded the city for centuries, but citizens could boast that the four gilded gates never truly closed to strangers. Friendly gate guards always waited to welcome merchant and traveler alike. Thinking the policy irresponsible, Kezem had soldiers question everyone entering or leaving the city.

The Rammon spaceport was also jealously guarded, and soon, only the foolish and the criminally inclined used it. Kezem welcomed anyone willing to help him maintain power and preferred the cheap, expendable, unsavory types.

Four months into Lord Kezem's reign, the first good news came in. New secret passages had been found in Loresh. The discoverers had looked forward to early retirements, but the payment had come in the form of bullets.

By the first anniversary of Lord Kezem's ascension to the throne, Meritab, Meritel, and Ritten had submitted. Korch stubbornly clung to its independence, despite a lengthy siege. Kezem didn't have the manpower to block each of the underground passages. It irked him that bleeding Royalist hearts in other cities kept supplying Korch, despite their own troubles. He cared not where Ritand stood, for its poor inhabitants could not help him. Supposedly, Huz Mon and Resh were also conquered, but with the pesky Rangers entrenched in and around the Riden Mountains, that assessment was debatable.

Kezem held court for four hours at the end of every week. The ridiculous requests usually amused him, but today, the food shortage complaints, land disputes, and petty disagreements grated upon his nerves. His mind wandered back to his successful sacking of the palace. He was about to cancel the last hour of court when one more peasant slipped into the throne room.

"My Lord, I seek an audience," said the diminutive man. With head tipped forward respectfully, the ragged stranger cautiously approached the throne, not daring to meet Kezem's gaze.

"Speak," he commanded.

"I am Merek, a humble servant. I have traveled far from Terab. Word has spread that you have captured one of House Minstel's heirs. Legends say they possess the power to heal grave wounds and diseases. I seek your blessing to study the child." The stranger held his hands palm-out and slightly in front of him so the guards would know he was unarmed.

"And what would you do with such knowledge?" Kezem asked. He knew of the rumors and had even experienced that odd healing when he'd wounded Princess Rela.

"Sell it," the stranger answered promptly. "I have contacts that would pay a premium for such knowledge."

Kezem burst into laughter. He liked this materialistic stranger. He'd been about to dismiss the little man outright, but the promise of money intrigued him. Planetwide war was frightfully expensive.

"How do you plan on gaining such knowledge?"

"Observation mostly, though when the child is older, more in depth experiments may be performed." Merek's words flowed off his tongue. "A sterile blade could—"

"I forbid harming her. I already know she can heal herself," Kezem broke in.

"You have seen this, my Lord?" Merek asked excitedly, meeting his eyes for the first time. "Remarkable. I had only rumors to fuel my dreams, but you have given me true hope."

When the man fully facing him, Kezem noticed his unusually sharp ears, a sign of non-human blood. Revulsion shot through him, but he determined to hear the being out.

"I will give you access to the princess. She is under guard in the nursery …" Kezem trailed off, noting that Merek wasn't listening.

The small man returned his gaze to the floor and tilted his head thoughtfully.

"A thought, my Lord," Merek began slowly. "Is there one close to the princess?"

"One of the queen's maidens refuses to leave her side," Kezem answered. "Her presence seems to calm the child." He shrugged, wondering where the stranger was taking the conversation.

"The child is still young, my Lord. May I suggest—"

"Do you presume to speak to me as an advisor?" Kezem asked, smiling at the man's boldness. He could use more advisors like this wretch. Keen intelligence could be quite useful; it could also be dangerous. Kezem preferred keeping dangerous people close.

"Raise her like she was your own, and you will gain a powerful ally in your quest to rule Reshner. Mold her mind and control her and those around her."

The wisdom in Merek's words struck a favorable chord within Kezem. His plans for the girl had gone no further than keeping her locked away until he could undo Reia's curse. If Merek could discover her secrets, Kezem might profit. Merek was already correct about Kezem needing more leverage against the young princess. He would give her a few friends to grow close to. Then, when the time came, she would obey him for their sakes. He had a few candidates in mind, including Prince Taytron's brat and the young Meetcher girl. He imagined the rivers of money that would flow if the princess's healing powers could be controlled. Rulers and wealthy people would come from afar just to see her. Suddenly, ruling one planet seemed so insignificant.

Two more years passed. Slowly, the remaining cities recognized Lord Kezem as their ruler. But the fighting continued. Every year a new class of RLA soldiers, Royal Guards and Melian Maidens entered Lord Kezem's service, but despite their enthusiasm, he could not help but compare them to those who had served the king and queen.

Merek's observations of Rela had proven useless, so Kezem's interest in the child waned.

Another four long years slipped painfully by. The annual Festival of Future Fighters replenished the supply of eager young fighters, but the war's length wore on Kezem. He grew weary of putting down rebellions. An uprising in Terab would be quelled just in time for trouble to spring up in Kalmata on the other side of the planet. The joy of vanquishing enemies had long since faded.

One morning, Lord Kezem wandered the throne room feeling trapped. He had known major sections of Reshner would not accept his rule peaceably. He had been prepared to put down several revolts, but he had not been prepared for seven years of civil war. It also irked him that the Royalist influence denied him the title of king.

His thoughts turned to the princess. Anger flowed freely in him, and his eyes turned deep blue with haphazard yellow streaks. He longed to seize Rela's fragile neck and squeeze the breath from her body, but Queen Reia's curse remained upon him. Every captured Ranger, Azhel priest, and dabbling magician had been thoroughly interrogated, yet no one could tell him when his life would cease being connected to that pathetic last link to a vanquished royal line.

Normally, he enjoyed the daily duties of ruling: observing the Melian Maidens and Royal Guards practice, sentencing and executing captured rebel leaders, and watching underlings squirm. However, the times he needed to be alone to think, meditate, and curse the galaxy that clearly hated him were becoming more frequent.

The rage burned within him so hot he shook. A long, loud, and thoroughly satisfying scream escaped him. The mournful, primeval cry echoed in the empty chamber, rattling statues of himself.

"Where did I go wrong?" he roared the question.

Chapter 8: Harmless Defiance, Hidden Heroes

Jira (March) 3, 1547-Temen (July) 25, 1554
Same Years
Royal Palace, City of Rammon

The standing death sentence for anyone who harmed the princess made it so that no hand was ever raised against Princess Rela Minstel. The situation made the young princess bold. Her every whim was answered with pampering and patience. The turnover in the palace staff charged with caring for her was quite high. Eventually, she outgrew tantrums and began perfecting the art of manipulation. Even Kezem's toughest RLA officers could not hide an occasional smile while in her presence.

Although Sarie worked hard to instill a sweet disposition in Princess Rela, the task seemed nearly impossible. Since no hand could discipline the princess, Sarie received ample practice in diplomacy. Though Sarie sometimes felt Rela's sole goal in life was to make her miserable, she deeply loved the child. It fascinated Sarie to watch her young mistress grow, revealing admirable traits her parents had possessed and wild tendencies that were uniquely Rela.

Lorian Petole, a dark-haired, brown-eyed servant child with golden brown skin who was orphaned by the palace invasion grew up with Princess Rela. Even tempered and two years older than Rela, Lorian was a great blessing to Sarie. Sensible and quiet, Lorian had handled weapons from before she could walk. Her parents had even given her a dull dagger to play with, hoping she would join the Melian Maidens when she got old enough.

Lord Kezem encouraged the palace staff to become proficient with weapons. Most children were trained in camps, but Lorian received training at the palace. Anabel and Marc Spitzer, Elia Koffrin, and Kia Meetcher were also encouraged to grow close to the princess, the first two as friends and the second two as guardians.

Lord Kezem forbade everyone from teaching Rela anything beyond rudimentary self-defense skills, but he insisted she learn the basics for his own sake because his few experiences feeling her pain were not pleasant. The annual tradition of letting Merek cut Rela's arm to test healing time was about all he could tolerate. When a glass snake Rela rescued from the food refrigeration chamber bit the princess on the ankle, Kezem felt the bite clear across the palace. Since Lord Kezem had his hands full trying to subdue the planet, Sarie secretly arranged for Captain Peter Estan to give Lorian and Rela shooting lessons.

The young captain pretended to enjoy the small chance at harmless defiance while still serving Lord Kezem, but secretly, his heart always belonged with the princess.

Sarie didn't know whether to be pleased or mortified that by the age of five her charge knew how to hit targets with kerlak guns, serlak guns, crossbows, darts, shootavs, and all manner of other weapons. She feared Rela would one day need such skills.

Merek's constant presence weighed heavily upon Sarie's heart, for she could see what was happening. One day Merek's notes would reach Lord Kezem. Then, she, Lorian, Elia, Kia, Anabel, and Marc would become camarek game pieces. Sarie knew not how exactly Kezem would use them against Princess Rela, so she decided not to worry about the future and devoted her attention to raising the child.

***

Temen (July) 26, 1554

West Detention Block, Prison Level, Royal Palace, City of Rammon

Deep within the palace, a labyrinth of passages hid horrors from the peace lovers still dominating much of Reshner. Supreme Commander Kolknir stood in an observation room on sublevel two looking down on the West Detention Block's combat arena, absently checking his reflection to see if every dark hair was in place. Ever since his Ranger days had ended, he'd become a fanatic about neatness. This was his peaceful spot.

After a hard day's work critiquing Royal Guard hopefuls and handling administrative drudgery, Kolknir liked to come here and listen to riffraff interact. Sometimes he would arrange for the door between two or more chambers to release, mixing volatile occupants. Despite his many duties, Kolknir always made time for selecting someone to fight Lord Kezem.

The prisoners were a filthy, underfed, pathetic lot, but Kolknir made certain they had enough strength to put up a good fight. A delicate balance had to be maintained. Lord Kezem insisted on being tested physically, so Kolknir occasionally gave the combatants stimulant shots to make them more aggressive. He contemplated such a move for tonight's duel. The lucky combatant was none other than his former student, Ranger Todd Wellum.

"Can I help you, sir?" asked a tentative voice.

Startled, Kolknir clamped down on a tide of anger and glared at the young lieutenant. Everyone else knew disturbing Kolknir's thinking time was very dangerous.

"I trust you have a good reason for disturbing me," Kolknir said softly. He considered changing tonight's combatants. Lord Kezem had mentioned that he might not be able to partake in the daily exercise anyway due to an important meeting with Azhel's ambassador. The outlying city was the most recent to sue for peace. "What is the first rule we teach here?"

The young man's eyes widened, but he had the sense to swallow any defensive statements. His pale, thin cheeks flushed as he ducked his head.

"Never disturb a superior officer," said the soldier.

Kolknir enjoyed the game.

"Correct, marksman," he said, a predatory smile forming on his lips. He remembered this soldier. The weakling had barely passed his test to be posted to this prison. He eyed the man contemptuously, recalling how he had trembled after doing his sworn duty in the service of Lord Kezem.

"Lieutenant second class," the man corrected. Realizing his second blunder, the soldier lowered his eyes.

Kolknir glared.

"No, there is nothing you can help me with. Mind your place or join the ranks of the weak below." Kolknir gestured out the window that overlooked the massive empty sandpit filled with gray volcanic ash. The color was just dark enough to be grim and cause bloodstains to blend in. The man nodded vigorously but dared not speak. Kolknir waited to see if he would be foolish enough to leave without permission. He could sense the soldier's stress level rising. "Is the prisoner ready?" he asked, after letting the lieutenant sweat a while.

The boy straightened.

"Yes, Supreme Commander, but I haven't administered the stimulants yet."

"Bring him to me," Kolknir ordered.

The soldier saluted and hurried off to fetch the prisoner.

Kolknir shook his head, amazed that Wellum still lived after seven years in captivity.

The prisoner filed in obediently, wrists bound in front, head down, and eyes fixed on the floor. His thin yet muscular arms held traces of the strength that had once coursed through them. Todd's face bore a dozen marks from shaving with dull prison razors. Kolknir was only mildly surprised that his former student hadn't slit his wrists or attacked a guard.

Kolknir preferred standard cord bindings over stuncuffs because of the marks they left. He half-expected Todd to snap the bindings as Kolknir had taught him to do so many years before. Much had changed since then.

"I don't think this one's up for a fight tonight," said the soldier.

"You're dismissed," Kolknir said. He waited until the soldier was out of hearing range before addressing the prisoner. "Look at me."

Slowly, Todd's head came up.

Kolknir studied him.

The prisoner stared back with intelligent hazel eyes.

Considering their history, Kolknir was surprised to find no hatred in Todd's eyes. He opened his mouth to taunt Todd by mentioning Kiata but changed his mind.

"Can you fight?" asked Kolknir.

"Yes." The answer was clipped but polite.

"Do you need stimulants?"

"No."

"Lord Kezem has an important meeting tonight so you will fight Lieutenant Tayce. Kill him."

That got Wellum's attention, but his only reaction was a clenched jaw.

"What'd the boy do?" he asked.

"He's too weak to be a Royal Guard," said Kolknir. "I despise weakness. There's a good meal in this if you make him suffer before killing him."

***

Todd Wellum worked hard to hold his contempt in check. Not trusting himself to speak, he nodded at the grim order and returned his gaze to the floor. Inwardly, he cringed. He would have to give the boy the dead-man liquor tablet he had saved for so long. The young man's life meant more than a few more months in this wretched place, though not by much.

The fight that evening was swift and brutal. Todd carefully struck the boy in places that would bleed a lot without causing too much damage. He put on a good show, and to his credit, Lieutenant Ethan Tayce proved to be tougher than his boyish features, soft golden hair, and slight frame indicated. Supreme Commander Kolknir enjoyed the bout. As Todd wrestled Tayce to the ground, he slipped the dead-man tablet down the boy's throat and held him in a chokehold until the man went limp.

True to his word, Kolknir had a tretling steak and real fertia wine waiting for Todd back in the two-by-three-meter cell. Todd sighed wearily and sat down on the hard cot. As he ate, he closed his eyes and concentrated on the happier moments of his life. Most featured Kiata and the adventures they had shared while growing up in the Riden Mountains then later as part of the Nareth Talis. The small group of specialized Rangers, whose Kalastan name means Night Torch, dedicated their lives to keeping peace across Reshner. The rest featured Kayleen's birth and the few precious years he had known her.

I will find you, Kayleen. This prison cannot hold me forever.

Chapter 9:
Beautiful Prison

Temen (July) 27, 1554
Princess Rela's Private Chambers, Royal Palace, City of Rammon
The Rammon palace Princess Rela Minstel grew up in differed mightily from the palace her parents ruled. After his invasion, Lord Kezem fortified the walls with guard towers and inlaid glass. Rela's seventh-floor suite of chambers overlooked the east wall, which she privately named Maran, after the Arthuri god of oppression and pain. One of her many tutors had drilled Rela on the three thousand gods of Arthuri before Lord Kezem deemed such knowledge useless and had the man replaced with a historian who specialized in magic and myths.

That one didn't last long either.

When the sun rose, it winked off the glass pieces imbedded in Maran. Rela imagined that each glass piece contained a tiny bit of magic which she could collect if she looked at it a fraction of a second after the sun winked off it. When she collected a hundred, she could make a wish. Soon, the wishes became one wish: to pass beyond the wall.

As the years passed, the game got old. Nevertheless, sunrise was a special time for Rela. Sometimes, like today, Sarie would join her. This morning, seven years into Lord Kezem's reign, Princess Rela sat in her usual spot by the large middle window which offered a generous view of the palace gardens below.

On a clear day, she could see some of the farms scattered about the Kevil Plains. If she used a rifle scope, she could watch the people in the Market District going about their business buying food, selling craft items, or looking enviously at those who could buy or sell. On a really good day, someone would try to steal something, and Rela could watch the soldiers chase the scoundrel. Occasionally, she wondered what became of those criminals, but her innocent mind couldn't yet fathom the horrors that awaited them.

"What's it like out there?" Rela wondered, resting her head against the cool glass.

"Full of dangers," Sarie replied.

Unsatisfied with the answer, Rela sighed. With each passing week, she felt the beautiful palace walls closing in on her. Turning toward her caretaker, Rela looked past the woman to the designs etched into the dansque wood doorframes and let her mind wander.

Who made the carvings? How long did they take? Why did they choose mean creatures like zaloks and goritors? Why not pretty things like wisil, colana, or kyrie birds or strong, noble things like dalagons?

The mental image of the great beasts as tall and wide as hundred-year-old cal trees with three heads, four arms, and a tail strong enough to break through two meters of solid concrete made Rela smile.

Although her tutors showed her countless images of exotic creatures and places, Rela had yet to see most of them, even ones native to Reshner. In fact, the only creatures she saw were those crafty enough to slip into the palace gardens. The glass snake she had freed from the refrigeration chamber didn't really count since it had never been covered in the lessons. Doctor Graven had explained about glass snakes while removing the mild toxins from Rela's left ankle.

"Here, eat something," Sarie instructed, breaking into Rela's thoughts. She gave Rela a riellberry muffin and let her hand rest on her wrist. A gentle squeeze conveyed understanding and sympathy.

The princess took two unenthusiastic bites of muffin before tossing it back onto the tray Sarie had taken it from. She eyed the variety of delectable breakfast treats with disinterest.

Riellberry muffins, blueberry tarts, appola pastries, wheat cakes with fertia jam, and mintas tea, just like always. I bet they don't have to eat the same thing every day out there.

Princess Rela was unaware that most people would attack such a meal like starved korvers. Her thoughts returned to her plight.

"I want to go to the Market District or take a trip outside of Rammon. Can I go, Sarie? Please."

Sarie's compassionate expression disappointed the princess as did her words.

"I am sorry, love. Not today. Lord Kezem has forbidden it."

"I could have some Melian Maidens escort me," Rela pointed out. A desperate note flavored her speech. "They would protect me. Besides, Lord Kezem leaves the palace all the time, and Lorian, Marc, and Anabel have been out lots of times too. Even Elia and Kia come and go as they please. Why not me?" By this time, Rela had abandoned efforts to sound mature. Her whine was pure nine-year-old frustration.

"You will get your chance for adventure, Princess," Sarie assured her.

"When?" Rela demanded. She looked at Sarie with a penetrating gaze, barely noticing the long scar on the right side of Sarie's chin. It had been always been there as far as she knew.

Ignorant of the problems people faced just beyond the palace walls, Rela couldn't understand Sarie's gloomy mood or the undercurrent of anger. Across Reshner, citizens lived in fear for their lives. Lord Kezem's soldiers patrolled the cities and villages with unsettling power. Anyone could be stopped, searched, interrogated, robbed, beaten, or killed any time for any reason. Since the anger wasn't directed at her, Rela shrugged and accepted that Sarie would tell her in her own time.

"We will speak more later," Sarie promised. "Let's walk in the garden."

A thrill rushed through Rela. The gardens were a special place where Sarie often shared stories of a brave, good king and a queen who fought evil beings and creatures to save their people. The stories usually ended happily, but sometimes, the good king and queen had to suffer to defeat the evil.

Rela scrambled out of her silky night dress and into the beige leggings and brilliant blue shimmersilk shirt with golden threads woven throughout that Sarie had chosen for the day. A thin, black goritor leather belt and matching boots completed the ensemble.

Soon, Rela skipped through familiar corridors, down six flights of stairs, and through the main kitchen to the servants' entrance to the royal gardens. The plants and flowers suffered from neglect, but it was easy to picture the stunning place the gardens had once been. Rela raced ahead to her favorite spot, a remote stone fountain with a statue of some unknown ancestor covered in ivy. She climbed onto the outstretched stone arm and hung off by her legs.

"What's the story today, Sarie?"

"You can start the story, Princess. It always begins the same."

Sarie sat on a soft bench near the statue.

"'There once lived a good king and his queen. They were brave and kind and fair,'" Rela recited.

Sarie picked up the story neatly.

"Before the good king became king, he was a prince, and before the good queen became queen, she was a Ranger."

Having never heard this story, Rela's eyes sparkled with excitement.

"Daria said the Rangers are the most troublesome group of terrorists to ever plague Reshner, but Lord Kezem defeated them during the last rebellion."

"Daria is wrong," Sarie replied. "The Rangers are a noble order who stabilize villages and protect important people, including members of House Minstel."

Princess Rela's mouth flew open at Sarie's treasonous words. Lord Kezem hated when people spoke of House Minstel.

"One day, the young prince was sent away on a journey to test his strength. The noble order of Rangers sent a young healer apprentice to safeguard the prince on his journey, for they knew he would encounter many dangers. On the morning of our tale, the young prince awoke surrounded by enemy soldiers from the Restler-Tarpon Alliance."

Rela gasped.

"The Kireshana!" she exclaimed. "Rivira told me all about the Kireshana, but she said it was only for soldiers. Will I ever get to go on it, Sarie?" Excitement and terror mixed in Rela's expression.

Sarie chuckled.

"No, Princess, you are not destined to be a soldier. The prince went because it was a family tradition. His older brother, his father, and all his uncles and aunts—save one—completed their own Kireshana journeys. At this time, his elder brother and father still lived, and everyone expected the older prince to one day be king."

"What happened to the older prince?" Rela wondered. Her head tilted to get a better look at Sarie.

"That is a tale for another day, Princess," Sarie answered. "This is the story of how the younger prince met his bride-to-be. As I said, she was a Ranger."

"Merek said Rangers are bad. Mikel, Plarit, and Wes Vik Iven all said it too," Rela informed. "How could she be a Ranger and be good?" Rela thought she saw pain cross Sarie's face, but it was gone so quickly that she couldn't be certain.

"Do you know why I tell you these stories, Princess?" Sarie asked gravely.

Rela considered the question carefully. Something indefinable whispered the answer into her mind.

"You speak of my parents," said Rela, surprised she had never realized the truth before. "But Merek said they died in the rebellion. He said the people turned against them, but Lord Kezem saved me. How could they be the good king and queen? There were no evil creatures in the rebellion, just people afraid of GAPP."

Frowning deeply, Sarie folded her hands in her lap.

"What else did Merek tell you?" Her voice trembled with an emotion Rela could not identify.

"Lord Kezem is my father's cousin. He stopped the rebels from killing me, but my parents and two brothers died in the attack," Rela answered.

Sarie's hands flew to her face and she started sobbing.

The outburst shocked Rela. She nearly fell off the stone arm but managed to lower herself safely to the ground. She went to Sarie, slipped under her arms for an embrace, and cried, not knowing why her caretaker wept.

"I'm sorry! I'm sorry! What did I say wrong? I'll take it back, honest," she babbled.

With great effort, Sarie composed herself and drew Rela further into a warm embrace. Eventually, she calmed enough to speak.

"The fate of your brothers is unknown, Princess. You mother had them sent away from the palace that dark night. You may not wish to hear—"

"Lord Kezem didn't kill them," Rela protested, knowing exactly what Sarie was thinking. She wriggled out of the hug. "It's a rebel lie meant to undermine Lord Kezem's good work."

Sarie closed her eyes and drew in a deep breath.

"He is smart to have told you his lies early," she admitted. "I am only sorry I had not thought to enlighten you first."

"Who should I believe?" asked Rela.

"At this point, Princess, you must make that decision yourself. But know that your parents were the good king and queen, and that not all evil creatures are enchanted monsters."

Rela disliked it when Sarie got philosophical on her.

"What should I do?" Rela inquired.

"Take this and keep it safe. It belonged to your mother," said Sarie. She opened her right fist to reveal a gold ring with a sizable emerald stone set in purple Nedis crystal. "Search out your past," Sarie encouraged, placing the ring in Rela's palm and curling the child's hand over it. "This palace may be a beautiful prison for you, but your friends are not as confined. Use them wisely and you will discover all you need and much more. The future will come soon enough, and I hope by then your heart will be prepared for the weighty truths."

Sarie steered the conversation away, and Rela quietly listened with half an ear, wishing she could sort out the conflicting stories. As Merek often said, Lord Kezem had been kind to her, how could she think ill of him? On the other hand, Merek was sort of creepy, and Rela felt more inclined to believe Sarie over any of her tutors.

Rela determined to follow Sarie's advice and enlisted her friends' help. They made a game of discovering the facts about her family and keeping her abreast of the current news. Part of her understood that the truth might never shine through the tangled web of lies, but she knew the knowledge would determine her fate someday.

***

Temen (July) 29, 1554
Throne Room, Royal Palace, City of Rammon

Lord Kezem was not in the mood for Merek's complaints, but he listened anyway. It had been a very bad day. A bomb in Kalmata had killed three of his most loyal servants, the settlements near the Crystal Lake reported death from foul water, and a massive fire raged through the Ash Mountains. He didn't care how many people died, but the stream of bad news gave him a sizable headache.

"My Lord, the woman is poisoning the child against you," Merek insisted for the third time in four minutes.

"I do not have time for your petty jealousies, Merek," Lord Kezem said.

"Please, my Lord, it is vital to keep in the girl's good graces!" Merek insisted.

Kezem couldn't fathom what this spineless idiot driveled about, but it taxed his nerves.

"Deal with the woman as you see fit," Kezem instructed, deciding to preserve his sanity.

"Thank you, my Lord, I shall do so at once," Merek prattled.

"If you kill her, make sure it is far from the palace, or Rela will never trust you again," Kezem advised, wishing the man would just go away.

Why do I keep him around?

***

Temen (July) 29, 1554
Same Day
Streets of Rammon, City of Rammon

Sarie Verituse left the Rammon palace with a broken heart. The gutless worm had been quite clear: leave or die. He had been tactful and formal about the whole affair, coming personally to deliver the message supposedly from Lord Kezem. She gritted her teeth. Sarie was no coward, but she could not help Rela if she died. So, she left.

Chapter 10:
Escape from the Mines

Temen (July) 29, 1554
Same Day
Imberg Tosh Mine, Morden Lowlands

Half a planet away, young Teven McKnight struggled to carry a load of tosh out of the dim, claustrophobic mining tunnel. Though only in his fourth month here, he could hardly remember a time when he wasn't stooped over scraping the dingy tunnels of the Imberg Tosh Mines. His thoughts ranged far and wide but did not touch political realms. All the hand carts had been claimed by the time he arrived at work today, despite his extra effort to arrive an hour before his shift started. He tripped on the uneven ground, pitching his load away so he wouldn't land on the bucket. A cloud of tosh dust rose, making his eyes water.

"I can't stay here," he said, choking from the dust.

"No, you can't. It is time you moved on," commented a man.

"Who are you?" Teven demanded, eyeing the man and beginning to scoop tosh back into the bucket.

The plain clothes could not hide the man's powerful presence, and there was something familiar about him. He moved with ease, smooth and balanced, as if ready to dance or fight. His black hair and eyes added to the mysterious air surrounding him. The man hunched to hide his height, but the breadth of his muscles and the strength in his voice told Teven that this man was no miner.

"Leave it. You won't need it, and we cannot stay."

The urgency in the stranger's voice intrigued Teven as much as the promise of escaping the tosh mines.

"Watch it! That wall's coming down!" a man shouted.

A thunderous crash followed as another unsteady tunnel succumbed to Reshner's restless shifting. Teven dashed forward to aid the people inevitably trapped beneath several tons of rock and tosh.

The stranger caught his arm.

"Come with me!"

"I have to help them!" Teven argued, tugging futilely against the stranger's grip.

"You can help them more by escaping," the man said, pinning the boy in place. "Some sacrifices must be made for the greater good. You will understand one day. Now, come!" He picked up one of Teven's arms and tugged.

"Why should I go with you?" asked Teven.

"Because I am a Ranger, and I promised your mother I would train you."

"Why didn't she tell me?" Teven asked, planting his feet.

"I speak of your real mother not your guardian," the stranger replied.

"Why would my mother want me to be a Ranger?" asked Teven, allowing himself to follow the stranger.

How does he know I had a different mother?

"You will be something far greater than a Ranger, Teven."

They emerged from a side tunnel tucked behind some rocks, conveniently out of sight of the mine master's tent. After they'd gone three steps, Teven stopped suddenly.

"I forgot my pay! I should collect—"

"You will not need the money." Sensing Teven's hesitation, the stranger continued, "Your guardian and her son are coming with us to a Ranger camp in the Riden Mountains."

Without further discussion they hurried toward Teven's home.

Teven's head whirled with the rapid changes.

The ten-minute walk to the McKnight ramshackle dwelling turned into a five-minute sprint to beat the rain. They were still a few hundred meters away from safety when the skies opened. Knowing that if too much rain touched his skin he'd get acid poisoning and die, Teven pumped his legs hard. Still, he fell behind the stranger. Teven started falling.

"I have searched too long to lose you now," the stranger muttered.

Teven experienced a brief floating sensation before passing out.

***

Temen (July) 29, 1554
Same Day
McKnight House, Outskirts of City of Huz Mon

Pria McKnight peered out of the shack's only window and idly watched the rain pound the dirt road. She had just finished sweeping and needed to rest. She caught sight of a cloaked man rushing her way carrying a bundle. She frowned. The man's burden looked suspiciously like Teven.

For a heartbeat, she imagined the man was her husband, but that was impossible. Ormek's men had killed him four months ago. She shoved the bad memories aside.

"Nate, get the door!" she shouted to her son who was playing with the wooden animals Teven had carved for him.

"Tev!" the boy shouted, rushing to the door. He flung the door back enthusiastically and some raindrops fell on him. "Owwie! Hot!" he yelped, shaking his small arm about to make the stinging go away.

"Be careful, Nate, that rain could hurt you," Pria warned belatedly, starting a fire to boil water.

While Nate held the flimsy door open, the stranger entered carrying Teven.

"Tev okay?" Nate asked, closing the door and leaning against it.

"It's been a long time, Pria," said the stranger.

Pria turned so fast she nearly knocked the hot pot over.

The man stepped forward and steadied her.

"First things first, let's get the acid off him." His voice carried an edge of command.

As he placed his burden on the bare wooden table, Pria stared at him like he was an apparition. Teven stirred. Nate rushed over to help but only managed to get stepped on and ordered to the corner. He sniffled but obeyed.

"What happened, Captain?" Pria asked.

"He had a rough day in the tosh mines," answered Ectosh Laocer, former Captain of the Royal Guard. "He'll be fine."

Pria flinched when she saw the healed burn marks on his arm but decided not to probe until they finished cleaning Teven. The wooden table over which Pria and Laocer worked creaked and popped in protest. Laocer stood ready to snatch Teven up if the table collapsed. They finished wiping the acid off Teven, who woke up just long enough to swallow some thin broth.

"It's good to see you, Captain," said Pria, once certain Teven would live. "How goes the war?"

"It has been a long time since I was in command," said Laocer.

"Somehow, I highly doubt that," Pria replied, regaining some of her composure.

So much has happened. She glanced around her sparse surroundings. *It's a far cry from the palace.*

One lightbar bravely lit the room but wasn't nearly enough to drive off the gloom. She spotted Nate rubbing his rain-stung arm and watching everything dispassionately.

My brave little sentinel.

Pria waved her younger son over to wipe the acid rain off his arms. The tiny, one-room dwelling perfectly summed up the last few years.

"I have avoided entanglements with Kezem's forces waiting for this day," said Laocer.

A chill shot through Pria, but she ignored it.

"He's too young for the responsibility," said Pria, not bothering to hide the sadness. She shut her eyes in a vain attempt to block everything out. She had trouble reconciling her hopes that Teven would one day save them and her need to protect him and preserve what little childhood he had left. Nate's gentle touch brought her back. She picked the boy up, feeling Laocer's gaze follow her movements.

The captain's expression was unreadable as he gathered Teven up and deposited him on the room's sole sleep pallet.

He seems bitter. Pria knew too well what service to King Terosh and Queen Reia could cost. *What have you lost, Captain?*

"Where do we begin?" Laocer inquired, meeting Pria's cautious stare.

"Should we wake him?" Pria asked, obviously reluctant to do so. She set Nate down to play. Finding her arms suddenly empty, Pria hugged herself.

Laocer looked like he was suppressing the impulse to comfort her with an embrace.

"Not yet. How did you end up here?" asked Laocer.

Grateful he didn't ask about her husband, Pria turned to boil more water for tea.

"A lot has happened since the night we fled." She stopped speaking, not sure how to explain without ripping open deep wounds. "Nathan insisted we stay to defend the palace." Pria smiled even as tears formed. "We had quite a fight over that, but I finally won by reminding him of our vow to the queen. The night was a game of hide-and-seek with Kezem's soldiers, but we made it. We had thought we made it cleanly, but someone must have connected us to the palace because we ended up with a black mark."

"Ah, that explains this," Laocer said, gesturing around at the four close walls.

Pria nodded and sat down at the table, motioning for Laocer to sit as well.

"We couldn't work anywhere but the mines, and the kefs the queen entrusted to us for the care of her son only lasted so long. We did fine for five years, but it got tougher when the money ran out. Even though the mine never paid enough, Nate worked hard to put on a good front for the boys. Then, things got really bad," she said with a thoughtful expression. At the mention of his name, little Nate abandoned his wooden figures and crawled into his mother's lap.

"Who hurt you?" Ectosh demanded. His voice crackled with anger.

You always were perceptive.

"I used to bring food to the mines for my husband and a few of his friends," Pria explained. "Nothing much, just whatever scraps I could gather. The shift master, Ormek, took an unwanted interest in me."

Laocer rose from the chair.

Pria reached over and patted his arm.

Startled, he sat down again.

"What happened?"

Where do I begin?

Pria let her gaze linger on her boys. Nate grew tired of sitting and jumped onto the table and then into Laocer's ready arms. The water finished boiling so Pria got up and made wuzle root tea. She set a cup in front of Laocer, but he only looked at her expectantly.

Knowing she could stall no longer, Pria returned to her seat and fingered her cup of tea.

"The attention grew worse, until I finally stopped going to the mines. I thought that would be the end of it, but one day, about four and a half months ago, Ormek came here with several men."

Laocer tensed again, obviously longing to pound some manners into Ormek's skull.

"Nathan saw them slip off and confronted Ormek." Pria

squeezed her eyes shut but a few tears slipped through anyway. Her right fist crashed onto the table and her left hand desperately clutched her cup of tea. "I will not cry!"

Despite the words, she wept.

"It's okay, take your time," Laocer said quietly. He held little Nate and waited.

Eventually, Pria dried her eyes.

"Ormek backed off that day, but he returned the next day and the next. Each time, Nathan was here, until Ormek's men dragged him outside and killed him."

"Did you see who killed Nathan?"

"I—I don't remember! I was so afraid. I gathered the boys and bolted the door, refusing to come out for three days. If it had only been me, I might have given in or tried some of those defensive moves you taught us." A faint grin flickered and faded. Pria cleared her throat. "By the time Ormek's wife put an end to her husband's harassment, it was too late to save my husband."

"Has anyone else given you trouble?" Laocer's tone said woe to that man.

Pria released her teacup and burst into a fresh round of tears.

"It's okay," he said again, sounding suddenly nervous.

"I'm sorry." Pria smiled through the tears. "You must think I'm—"

"You have nothing to apologize for," Laocer said.

"Yes, I do, Captain. I'm a coward," said Pria. "I let a young boy take on a man's job in a dangerous mine to protect myself. What would Queen Reia think?"

"She would understand," Laocer murmured with an odd expression.

What are you thinking?

Pria didn't know he was thinking of the last seven years preparing for this meeting. He'd dreamed of teaching a tall, strong, vibrant adolescent not a boy traumatized by the tosh mines.

"He's so young," Laocer commented.

"He will grow into a fine man, like his father," Pria said. "I have cared for him like I promised. You will train him like you promised, and somehow, this planet will be set right." She was on a roll now. The words flowed from the deep place where she had hidden hope under years of worry and hardship. "It is more than a promise made to our beloved queen. Riden has placed you here at this time for this time."

Nate slipped away. Laocer folded his hands on the table and stared at Pria.

As she watched his shoulders straighten and his posture adjust to exude confidence, Pria realized he could only be here for one reason.

"I'm coming with you," said Pria.

"Where are we going?" asked Teven. Black hair tousled, sleepy-eyed, and still looking exhausted the boy staggered to his feet.

"Some place safe," said Laocer.

Pria felt him watching her but paid no attention. She was too busy packing. Fortunately, the diminutive dwelling didn't hold many possessions. Pria stripped the coverings off the sleep pallet and used them to wrap up the few food stuffs left in the house.

"We're ready," she announced.

Food bundle tucked under her left arm, Nate strapped to her back, an ancient dagger clipped to her waist, and a bewildered Teven in tow, Pria left the shack she had called home for seven years and never looked back.

Chapter 11: Ambush

Allei (August) 2, 1554
Restler Campsite Near Riden Mountains

In a desolate part of the planet west of Rammon, some mercenaries sat around a dying fire.

"Remember, under no circumstances are the boys to be harmed. We are getting paid good money to take them alive," Gareth Restler warned his men.

"Are we going to keep the woman?" Coleth Timmer asked. His gaze stayed fixed on his infopad which bore images of their targets. The Chermesh's long ears wiggled with suppressed hope.

Gareth shook his head and thought about how much he hated lengthy stakeouts.

"I tried to bargain for her, but the client wants her dead so that's the way it goes." Internally, he wondered if he should have pressed the issue of the woman's life harder.

"What's so special about these mine rats?" Tyron Hither asked, looking up from the blade he was sharpening. His fangs glinted in the bright moonlight. "The fee's generous, but you've got to admit the request's very unusual."

"I don't question orders," Gareth replied.

The others nodded and continued to clean their weapons. Most of his people were still at Base Camp near Kalmata, but Gareth had chosen four of his best to handle the Riden Mountains job. The job was typical for these days. Sometimes they would be hired to rescue rich brats that wandered off. Other days they would carry out an assassination for one side or the other.

The Restler Raiders had existed long before the ill-fated Restler-Tarpon Alliance, even before Lord Kezem set his heart on Reshner's throne. Gareth fully intended to carry on the family tradition. He hired professionals, but occasionally, he had to remind his people of the top three mercenary rules: get paid, never question, and remain emotionally detached. He had once broken the third rule and paid for it dearly.

As the sun began its descent, Gareth stretched to prepare his muscles for the coming hike and subsequent fight.

"Let's go," he said.

***

Allei (August) 3, 1554
Riden Mountains

The McKnight family and their guide traveled for four days bundled up in rain cloaks provided by Ectosh Laocer. By sunset the fourth day, the storms had passed, but the air still hung in a thick layer over the Riden Mountains. Despite this, Teven McKnight felt lighter with every step he took toward the nearest peak, Mount Palean.

I'll never have to step in a tosh mine again.

"Tired, Momma," Nate complained.

"You're tired?" Teven asked incredulously. "Who's been lugging you around the past week?"

"Tev tired too, Momma," Nate added.

Teven smiled down at his little brother. Nate could be annoying, but he had a heart of gold.

"Be brave, boys, when we reach the mountains we can stop to rest," his mother encouraged.

"Here, let me take him," Laocer offered.

Teven gratefully surrendered his burden and continued to follow Captain Laocer. They traveled with this arrangement for several kilometers. When they came within twenty meters of the mountains, Nate got a second wind and challenged Teven to a race.

"I beat you to big rock," Nate stated, squirming from Laocer's grasp and taking off.

"Oh, no you don't. I'll catch you running backward!" Teven jogged along behind his brother, letting the younger boy have a solid head start. The thrill of the race brought a broad smile to his face.

"You boys be careful," Pria admonished.

For several meters, Teven concentrated on the race.

"I win!" Nate shouted, triumphantly jumping on a flat rock in front of Mount Palean. The mountain walls rose up sharply on either side of the rock.

Teven didn't see the well-muscled, furry being rise from behind the rock Nate had claimed, but his mother's scream said something was amiss.

The attacker's responding shriek slammed into Teven's back.

Teven whirled. His feet tangled, and he landed flat on his face. He coughed, sputtered, and spat dirt. Looking up, Teven saw a cargo sack swallow his brother. Fear drove Teven to his knees, but the travel cloak hindered his efforts to rise.

Four more shadowy figures separated from the nearby rock walls. One man pointed a heavy serlak gun over Teven's head and fired.

More screams followed.

The crack of the serlak gun crashed across Teven's senses as a bullet tore through the air and struck Pria full in the chest. The impact threw her back almost a meter before her body collapsed.

Teven's breath fled as shock claimed his mind. He stared at his fallen mother, waiting for a bullet to strike him and end the burning ache twisting inside his stomach.

It never came.

Suddenly, Laocer filled Teven's vision. He was everywhere at once, driving the attackers back with swift, sure blows from a flat yellow blade of energy. Teven had heard the miners speak of kerlinblades and dreamed of holding one, but no fantasy—or nightmare—could have prepared him for this fight. Laocer's blade meted out justice to one attacker after another so fiercely that the three left alive fled.

A whistle from the leader signaled the retreat.

For a moment, Teven could imagine his mind had conjured the attack, but Laocer's grim expression and torn clothes convinced him this was real. Struggling to his feet, Teven teetered and focused again on his mother's crumpled form. He rushed to her and would have embraced her lifeless form had Laocer not grabbed his shoulder and held him fast.

Rage and despair rose in Teven. He knew people died every day, but there had always been a distinction between danger and safety. Home was always safe. Four months ago, that illusion had been severely assaulted. Now that both guardians he loved and regarded as parents were gone, the illusion shattered.

"We should leave," Laocer said, releasing Teven's shoulder.

Teven didn't say a word. Instead, he fought off his grief long enough to gather brush for a fire to burn his mother's body. He would not let either beast or acid rain lay further claim to her.

His eyes fell upon the broken pieces of the two dead attackers. He consciously turned his gaze away.

Scavengers can have the murderers. They deserve no better.

***

Allei (August) 3, 1554
Same Day
Eastern Edge of the Riden Mountains

Tired, hungry, and frightened, three-year-old Nathan McKnight bawled inside the sack. Had he lain still, the bag would have seemed much less confining because it was designed to allow air to flow freely. But fear drove him to thrash until utter exhaustion overtook him. The frantic rocking motion of someone carrying him made his stomach hurt. Nate threw up inside the sack. The combination of sudden stench and burning throat made him scream, cry, and thrash with new energy.

"What's that smell?" a male voice asked. He followed the statement with a long stream of angry words.

The sack carrying Nate sailed through the air and crashed into something hard and bony. Vomit splattered all over this second being, eliciting more curses. With the mission a solid failure, tempers were short.

The Restler Raiders had not expected any opposition, so the fierce counterattack surprised them. The big man who fought back certainly knew how to handle a kerlinblade.

Nate tumbled from the sack and landed in a dusty heap. He caught a brief glimpse of his captors before passing out.

"Coleth, dump the boy in that stream we passed a few minutes ago," Gareth instructed. He glared at the filthy wretch, but he could not afford to kill him. They had already lost too much on this mission. "We'll take him to the slave market in Fort Riden."

"We won't get much for him," Coleth commented, hating his current assignment.

"We'll get something. Supreme Commander Kolknir always wants children for the production lines," said Gareth.

Nate heard none of this conversation that would greatly alter his life.

True to their word, the mercenaries took him to Fort Riden's slave market where Captain Glaiser of the Reshner Liberation Army bought him. Glaiser, a widower with no children, determined to raise Nate as a son.

Chapter 12:
New Recruit

Allei (August) 7, 1554
Ranger Camp, Riden Mountains

Sky watching, as much a survival technique as a hobby, helped Aveni pass the time. Patrol duty bored him.

Roughly every three months the Talmeth Volcanoes, located on the southwestern coast of the main continent, spewed molten metal and chemicals most life forms found toxic. Soon thereafter, the acid storms would begin. Only the first would be potent enough to melt spaceship paint. The next two would sting, and the last few would only cause harm on rare occasions. Most of the days between these cycles would be sunny and fair, but sometimes, the planet got moody. That's what sky watching was all about, seeing the subtle signs of Reshner preparing to make life interesting for her inhabitants.

At such times, it was best to find a hole or a tavern and hide until things calmed down again. Despite the instinct to dig, Aveni preferred taverns. The chairs and benches usually adjusted to accommodate his bulk. With two arms and two legs as thick as dansque tree trunks, Wirshers made remarkable fighters but lousy scouts. Still, when a Wirsher could be convinced to play guard for a while, one could rest easy.

As the sun plunged behind the mountains farther to the west, Aveni noticed the white clouds multiplying rapidly.

"Uh oh, we in for it now," he wheezed. "Oy, Bova!"

"What?" snapped the surly Ranger. A day night sneaking around enemy posts had put the Rorgen in an especially foul mood.

Bova—whose real name no one seemed to remember—crashed onto the planet seven years ago, just in time to run afoul of Lord Kezem. His nickname came from those first days when frequent trips to the tavern usually ended with him being locked up for lifting kefs from other patrons or fighting.

"Storm coming," Aveni said cheerfully. "Gonna be nasty."

Bova grunted then trudged off into the labyrinth of tunnels and caves where he knew food awaited. Had this been Rorge II, Bova could have hunted stelberg rats all night. This was not Rorge II, nor would he ever see the beautiful caves of his youth again. The exploding sun had made certain of that. When his home had disappeared in one terrible instant, Bova had lost his sense of humor. The thought of each perished loved one was like a thousand paralyzing bites from voracerflies, ironically one of the few life forms Rorge II and Reshner shared. These thoughts shadowed Bova, wrapping so closely around him that he didn't hear Aveni's frantic, lumbering steps until the cave vibrated behind him. He whirled, preparing a scathing response to the brute's intrusion on his thoughts.

"Visitors," Aveni announced.

Bova narrowed his eyes, somehow managing to look down his nose at the two-and-a-half-meter-high Wirsher filling the tunnel behind him.

"Who?" he asked.

"Don't know. Not dangerous, I think," said Aveni.

"I'll judge that," Ranger Knight Bova muttered. "Go meet them and see what they want. If they're friends feed them. If not, try to take them alive but don't let them escape. Think you can handle that?"

Aveni squeezed himself around and went back to the main entrance. Wirshers made excellent interrogators due to their natural ability to measure a being's intent. Countless centuries hunting brizer panthers at night on moonless Wirsh had taught them to feel which way their prey would leap. It also produced excellent night vision. Aveni saw a figure he recognized.

"Captain? Captain! Wayward lost Captain Laocer back!" he bellowed.

"I see you're still faithfully guarding the last stronghold of the Rangers," Laocer commented. Catching Aveni's questioning glance, he started on introductions. "This is—"

"The one," Aveni finished. The Wirsher's calculating gaze swept over the young shell of a human more thoroughly than any sensor.

The dark-haired ten-year-old wore a vacant expression.

Aveni sensed that Captain Laocer had yet to explain things to the boy.

"Apologies. Apologies. I mean not say too soon," said Aveni.

"Everything will be explained in time," Laocer assured him. "We were ambushed near Mount Palean. His family did not survive. We didn't stop for much rest along the way. I'm going to make arrangements for the boy now."

"Food do good," Aveni agreed. "Go see Bova or he yell."

"Long day?" Laocer asked, knowing the surly knight's moods well.

"Very long. Very grumpy," Aveni said, bobbing his head left and right in the Wirsher version of agreement.

***

Kayleen Wellum slumped against a tunnel wall by an air vent listening to a storm beat the mountains. With one leg propped against the opposite wall and the other tucked under in a position most would consider extremely uncomfortable, Kayleen idly sucked a mintas drop while counting the seconds between claps of thunder. She thought of the day's training. The duels had gone well until she faced Cloat, and then, as usual, she lost. With eyes open and head bowed so that her shoulder length, wavy, red-gold hair hung in her face, she let her mind replay every move of that last hand-to-hand duel. She frowned at the memory.

"I thought I might find you here," said a voice she recognized.

"Captain!" Kayleen cried, dropping to her feet. She waited in a glowlamp's tiny pool of light for Ectosh Laocer to reveal himself. Excitement coursed through her, making her come alive. Laocer filled a void in the orphan's heart. The unpredictable times between his visits were always too long for her.

"Hello, Kayleen. Agile as ever I see. Good. You're going to need that when we start giving you real assignments," Laocer said. Although he held no official rank among the Rangers, Laocer had lent a stabilizing authority during the war. Most Rangers below the rank of knight would follow his orders without question.

"I'm ready. I'm always ready. Can I go on a mission with you?" Kayleen knew the answer would be negative, but the tradition of asking had to be maintained.

"You get bigger every time I see you," Laocer commented,

sidestepping the question. "Have you beaten Cloat in a duel yet?"

"Almost," she muttered. A frown crossed her face. Her silvery-blue eyes gazed into empty space as she recalled the duel again.

"Uh oh, what happened?"

"I had him, Captain! I had him in a chokehold, and then, I lost the will to fight. He slipped away wearing that stupid grin of his," Kayleen complained. "Before I knew it, I was staring up from the ground trying to catch my breath."

"Ah. I thought as much," Laocer said. "Cloat's mildly telepathic; it's not unusual in his species."

"His species?" Kayleen repeated. She braced her arms against both walls and pushed until she could move her legs into position to help her climb. "I thought he was human," she added, once she'd reached a satisfactory height. Kayleen placed one foot on an air vent's narrow ledge and the other on the opposite tunnel wall. Exercise always helped her think.

"He's actually Danatesh," said Laocer. "They age in spurts and live to be four or five hundred years old. Cloat may look thirteen, but he's probably seventy."

"Seventy? I want to be Danatesh too," Kayleen said with an easy smile. "That telepathic power could come in handy."

"There are other ways to gain power," Laocer reminded her.

"Practice and hard work," she recited, her voice muffled by the height. Having done this hundreds of times, she conquered the wall easily. Kayleen possessed her own powers, pure grit being one of the most potent. Higher up where the distance was greater, Kayleen performed a few flips. She kicked off one wall, somersaulted in the air, and kicked off the other wall. Finally, she caught the right wall and clung to it.

"I'd sap Cloat's will, throw him to the mat, and squash him like the dung beetle he is," she declared.

Her voice floated down in a dainty way that made Laocer chuckle.

"I have an assignment for you, Kayleen," Laocer said casually.

Next instant, she stood before him, still as a statue, waiting for him to continue.

"I thought that might grab your attention," Laocer said with a laugh, "but don't get too excited until you've heard what I want you to do."

"I'm ready for anything," Kayleen said, echoing her earlier

sentiments. "Walk ready, stand ready, and live through the fight." The words proved she had paid attention in her survival classes. Even if she didn't enjoy the task, she would do it to please him. It was the least she could do for her mentor and friend.

"I've brought a boy about a year younger than you. He's as a guest, and he's going to need a friend."

Her excitement changed to a mixture of curiosity and disappointment.

"He will train here with you, but eventually, I'd like to send you both to the palace for a very special mission."

"Really? When can we go?" The girl bounced up on her toes, brimming with energy.

"When the time comes," Laocer promised, telling her nothing.

***

Allei (August) 7, 1554 – Allei (August) 11, 1554
Ranger Camp, Riden Mountains

The Ranger cave system in the Riden Mountains reminded Teven too much of the Imberg Tosh Mines for him to feel comfortable. Luminescent rock and scattered lightbars could only brighten the area so much, and the effect was quite eerie. Despair ate at him. Then, anger flared bright and hot, making his eyes sting with unshed tears. He growled and clenched his teeth until his jaw ached. His posture was such that a slight nudge would have laid him out flat.

Somewhere on the road between the ambush site and the Ranger camp a wall had formed between Teven and his mysterious companion. He didn't want to live anymore, not without his mother and Nate. He dug his fingernails into the flesh of his palm. It hurt and that was good. Physical pain could be controlled. The emotions flowing through him made him queasy and lightheaded. His knees started to buckle so he leaned heavily against the nearest wall. His anger spiked again for no other reason than his body and spirit were both tired of fighting numbing emotional pain.

A breeze from a vent column coursed through the dim tunnel carrying shiners. The bugs created their own light, rode the wind current, and twirled around Teven's legs. He reached for them instinctively. Several dozen perched on his hand. Had the last few days not transpired, he might have been charmed by their peaceful glowing.

Several minutes later, Teven forced himself to stumble to a large, semi-deserted cavern where he picked at a flavorless meal.

Captain Laocer showed up as he finished eating.

"I have acquired quarters for you," Laocer announced.

The small room Teven shared with two other boys made him feel lonelier than ever. Laocer left him there to unpack and grieve in peace. Teven curled up on the assigned bed and cried. By this time, four days after the attack, the salty taste of tears was familiar to him.

Teven spent two days mourning while conversations with his mother played over and over in his mind. He remembered the day she had spoken to him about his real parents. The conversation had started simply enough with him saying, *"I love you, Momma."*

Pria McKnight had finished tucking baby Nate into his makeshift crib. Then, she turned and leveled a warm, serious gaze at him that sent a shock of fear through him. Kneeling before him and gathering him into a comforting embrace, she had whispered, *"Teven, I could not love you more than I do. You will always be my son, but once upon a time, you had a different mother. One who gave you life and breath and loved you just as much as I do."*

"Who was she? Why didn't she keep me, if she loved me?" he had asked.

Her answer played in his mind like soothing music.

"She was someone I greatly admired: beautiful, brave, kind, and selfless to a fault. Evil people killed your father and then threatened her, but she did not fear to face violence or death, only that these might befall you. She gave you to me, so you would be safe from her enemies."

"Who was my father?"

"An honorable man, noble and brave," his mother had answered. Her eyes had twinkled with amusement. *"Both your parents possessed such strong personalities, it's a wonder they didn't kill each other over a petty disagreement."*

Teven had laughed with her even though he didn't really understand. Then, he turned the conversation serious again.

"Who killed them? Why would someone kill them?" he had asked.

Recalling those questions released new waves of hurt, pain, and anger.

"The reasons are complicated, but part of it was that they possessed great power and used it to help the weak. Some people despised their benevolence."

Subsequent conversations had slowly revealed more about his parents, but Teven knew there was much more to be learned. The McKnights spoke well of them but would tell him nothing about what sort of power they wielded.

Teven slept the third day straight through and awoke on the

fourth morning with a ravenous appetite. Sick of fighting despair, Teven determined to fight back. He would let the Rangers train him, but he would never truly be one. He would learn enough to exact revenge for his murdered parents—all of them. In due time, he would find the murderers, and they would pay for their deeds in full.

Chapter 13: Trainers and Teachers

Allei (August) 11, 1554
Ranger Camp, Riden Mountains

Before the sun rose, the Rangers attended to various chores. Morning guards hastily finished meals and trudged to their posts, expecting boredom but ready for excitement. Night guards retreated to their quarters for much needed naps before afternoon training sessions. The Ashatan Council members prepared for a day of making weighty decisions and issuing orders. Masters put finishing touches on lectures and knights—including Talyon Keldor—prepared for missions. Healers scrambled about on various errands. Older apprentices began lessons or corralled young recruits.

Teven McKnight found himself in the Grand Assembly Chamber with a group of apprentices. Feeling the stares of his peers, he hoped no one would try to talk to him. He wasn't in the mood. He kept his stance slightly hostile, but something brushed his left sleeve anyway. Looking up, Teven found himself staring into silver-blue eyes tucked in a youthful face with friendly challenge written all over it.

The girl leaned closer, further invading his space.

"Captain Laocer sent me to fetch you. It's not time to train you with the group yet," she whispered.

Teven liked her gentle, vibrant voice. The girl wore a tan tunic over dark trousers. A leather belt held a variety of pouches whose contents Teven could only guess at. An empty belt loop marked the place where a banistick would hang one day.

"Follow me." Without waiting for a response, the girl turned and walked swiftly through the small crowd.

Teven made a split-second decision and followed the girl, admiring the way the tunnel lights highlighted her reddish-blond hair. He jogged to match her rapid pace.

"Where are we going?" he asked.

She turned a corner and either didn't hear him or refused to answer.

Teven rounded the corner and stopped abruptly. Four tunnels converged at this point. He had come from one, another curved sharply left, one stretched out in front and a fourth branched right. Lost and feeling silly, Teven muttered something he had heard miners say and turned to return the way he had come. Two steps back toward the familiar, he stopped again.

She's down the middle path.

The knowledge entered his head like a whispered thought. It seemed like a crazy stab in the dark, but every instinct drew him down the center tunnel. Taking a deep breath and preparing a few questions for the girl, he stalked down the tunnel after her.

"You're walking like a herd of Terabian elephants," the girl's pleasant voice scolded from behind him. "We're going to have to fix that if you're going to be a Ranger."

"Who said I wanted to be a Ranger?" Teven demanded, whirling on her. "I didn't want to come! I want to go home! I want my mother and brother!"

"You're not the only one who's lost family. Deal with it," snapped the girl.

Her voice cut deep into Teven's strung out emotions. Tears formed, but he refused to let them fall. His teeth clenched so hard his head hurt. He wanted to punch something, even her—especially her—but he could do nothing more than stand there helpless and miserable.

"Your brother is probably still alive," said the girl, placing a hand on his tense forearm. "Kezem pays mercenaries for children he can brainwash and turn into soldiers or factory workers. Only the Rangers stand between him and more kids like you … and me."

"Who are you?" Teven asked, jerking his arm away. He didn't want to think about his family.

Instead of replying right away, the girl jumped, placing one foot on each tunnel wall and climbed higher.

"Kayleen Wellum," she said finally. "Nils, the man who brought me here, was murdered at the start of the war. I should have died with him that day. Master Ekris said she didn't know how I survived my wounds. I must have been about four, but I don't remember anything about that or my parents, except that they sent me away." The girl paused to let the words sink in. "So, you see, Teven, we have more in common than you might think."

"Like what?" he demanded.

"Losing family," Kayleen replied softly.

"What does it matter?" asked Teven.

"I don't know," Kayleen answered, "but Captain Laocer has special plans for you. He came here at the start of the war too, but he left four years ago to go on a personal mission. Since then, he's come and gone every few months. This time, he returned with you."

Teven's neck hurt from peering up into the darkness where Kayleen had disappeared. Then, she appeared before him, face to face, only upside down.

He retreated a step, eyes wide.

"Why would he look for me?" Teven inquired, curiosity replacing frustration.

"Does it matter? You're here," Kayleen answered. "Captain Laocer asked me to train you." She disappeared again into the unknown heights, reappeared directly behind him, and struck the center of his back.

The blow drove Teven forward. He clumsily dropped into a defensive position.

Kayleen serenely observed him, crossing her arms.

"We have a lot of work to do," said Kayleen.

"He'll learn," said Captain Laocer from behind Kayleen. If Laocer's presence surprised her, she hid it well.

Teven guessed her casual, almost bored, stance could be changed to combat readiness in a heartbeat.

"What's going on, Captain?" asked Teven.

"Your home is here now," said Laocer. "The Rangers will teach you to fight, and when you are ready, you will be given a mission which will answer questions you have yet to ask."

"Why should I do anything you say? You got my mother and brother killed!" Teven shouted.

"You will one day have the power to overthrow Lord Kezem," Laocer said quietly. "He destroyed everything I held precious. That makes for a rather large score to settle. Kayleen is right. Your brother is alive, but you must learn to fight if you want to rescue him."

"Glad to know I have a say in my future," Teven said, glaring.

"Deep down, we want the same thing," said Laocer. "Listen to me. Learn from me. Join the Rangers and then the Royal Guard. From there you can destroy Lord Kezem."

"Why me?" Teven asked. "What makes you think I want to destroy Lord Kezem?"

Teven expected a vague, unhelpful answer. Instead, Laocer met his eyes and spoke in an unexpectedly tender tone.

"It's in your blood. You are Crown Prince Teven of House Minstel, son of Queen Reia and King Terosh, and for your mother's sake, I will help you reclaim the throne."

The title landed on Teven like a crashing spaceship.

"He's the lost prince?" Kayleen's words mixed question and statement.

"What happens if I don't want to take the throne?" Teven asked, crossing his arms defiantly.

"Then, we had better hope your brother and sister still live," said Laocer, "because a royal from House Minstel must take the throne or this planet is doomed."

"Doomed. Right," Teven muttered. "Well, I guess training beats mourning forever."

Teven sensed a deep, almost ominous, sense of satisfaction rolling off Laocer. He dismissed the observation and let Kayleen lead him back to the chamber they had started in. The silence between them was deep but not necessarily uncomfortable. Teven spent the rest of the day idly watching hand-to-hand duels. His mind kept repeating the conversation with Kayleen and Laocer.

If that's normal Ranger recruiting, they're pretty lousy at it.

***

Allei (August) 12, 1554
Ranger Camp, Riden Mountains

On the fifth day at the camp, Teven McKnight dragged himself to the morning training session. It certainly beat working in a tosh mine, but he felt out of place. Most of the other apprentices had been born to this life or trained from a very young age. They possessed faster reflexes and stronger muscles than he did. They could quote Ranger codes, tell a hundred legends, and survive for weeks in the Riden Mountains with nothing but a banistick and a travel cloak. He wasn't sure whether to envy or pity them. Most were war orphans.

"Relax. You're tenser than a coiled Porit viper," Kayleen said.

"That's what happens when one might get hit," Teven said with a scowl.

"It wasn't personal," said Kayleen. Her tone lacked apology. "I had to check your reflexes. You did rather well."

One of the largest beings Teven had ever seen lumbered in and conversation ceased. Lightweight armor protected the figure's broad chest while a chitin carapace protected his back. His two arms waved about madly, but Teven attributed this to excitement rather than psychosis. He looked familiar. Teven eventually remembered the guard who had spoken briefly with Captain Laocer when they first arrived.

The being's voice boomed across the chamber.

"Good. Good. Young ones learn fast. Aveni teach weak points. Pressure weak point and opponent fall. First, I teach Rorgen weak points. Young ones greet volunteer Ranger Knight Bova!"

The class clapped politely. Teven craned his neck to see a lithe, muscular being sidle into the chamber. The being walked upright but each limb looked the same, indicating that all four could be used to run. Golden fur covered his arms, legs, and lean, shrewd face. Sharp yellow eyes glared at the bumbling giant who had summoned him.

The short lecture fascinated Teven. Aveni methodically walked the apprentices through each of Bova's weak points, occasionally jabbing the Rorgen. Finally, as expected, Bova leapt at Aveni, aiming for the throat, giving the latter a chance to demonstrate firsthand how weak points worked. Two well-placed punches drove Bova to the ground, quivering.

"Brilliant, Aveni, but you'll be the first guest for my lesson." The irritation in the yellow eyes melted into glee.

Next, they covered human, Elish, and Danatesh weak points. After a quick review, the youths paired off. As Teven had suspected, Kayleen pulled him aside. She repeated the key points before inviting him to strike her. His hand shot out but not swift enough to overcome her finely tuned reflexes. After five fruitless tries, he grunted, eliciting a smile from his self-appointed trainer.

"Quicker," Kayleen urged. "Anticipate my moves. Make feints, pretend, catch your opponent off guard. Distract them."

"What do you mean?" Teven asked, straightening out of his defensive position.

Automatically, she followed suit.

Then, one quick step forward brought him in range.

"I mean—" A split second later, her right arm was twisted

behind her back with both his thumbs digging into her elbow. "You did it! Excellent!"

Teven had never heard someone so happy about having an elbow tweaked. For the first time since his arrival, he genuinely smiled.

"You're ready for a match," said Kayleen.

His smile disappeared.

***

Masquerading as one of the recruits, Jalna Seltan worked hard not to hurt her opponents. Carefully orchestrating convincing falls and clumsy maneuvers took some serious concentration. Still, centuries-worth of practice had taught her something about judging beings. In addition, the anotechs fed her information on heart rate, brain capacity, pulse, temperature, and temperament. Most of the adolescents were human and thus easy for her anotechs to read.

Everyone except the newest boy had normal readouts, but a few spikes in his brainwave activity intrigued her. The anotechs acted as if they had found old friends within the boy. This warranted further investigation. He fought well enough to tell Jalna that one day he would be a great fighter, but his troubled green eyes spoke of deep, distracting pain. He was pale with a round young face, lean build, and curly, jet black hair that needed cutting. Jalna watched him duel a red-haired girl. His movements were stiff but swift, yet there was no doubt about the duel's outcome. Within a minute, the girl threw the boy to the training mat and then helped him up again. Jalna brushed some brown hair off her forehead and approached the pair.

"Greetings. I am Jalna. Would you like to duel?" she asked the boy.

"No," the girl replied. "He's not ready yet."

Jalna smiled politely and focused on the girl.

The anotechs reported: ***Kayleen Wellum, possessive of subject.***

"Sure," the boy said, ignoring Kayleen. "I'm Teven, by the way," he added, offering his right hand to shake.

As soon as their hands touched, information flooded into Jalna's brain. Chemical composition, percentage sweat, firmness of grip, and other signs became character clues.

"You don't like it here," Jalna commented, brows knit together. "Why do you stay?"

"I have no choice." Teven looked away.

"There's always a choice!" Jalna said, tempted to emphasize the statement with a smack upside the head. Too many times had she uttered that admonishment to deaf ears.

"What would you know about it?" Kayleen demanded.

Jalna detected an undercurrent of strong emotion in Kayleen's question. She eyed the pair with renewed interest. Something, besides rumors, had led her to this camp, and she got the impression that the boy might have something to do with that.

"The lesson is over," Jalna said. "I suggest we continue this conversation in private."

The youths exchanged surprised glances at her sudden authoritative tone.

"No way," Kayleen declared. "You can't order us around, and none of this is your business anyway." With that, Kayleen seized the boy's arm and hauled him out of the chamber.

Jalna considered following them. They had absolutely no chance of avoiding her if she chose to pursue. The girl walked softly, but the anotechs would sense the boy's footfalls practically anywhere, even in a crowd.

She let them go. Nothing would be gained by pushing them today. If anything, Jalna Seltan knew how to wait well.

***

Allei (August) 19, 1554
Royal Palace Roof, City of Rammon

Heart aching within, Ranger Knight Talyon Keldor crouched on the palace roof and considered his next move. He had spent years as Captain Peter Estan searching for news of Merisia. Officially, he was in Rammon to observe Lord Kezem and protect the princess, but personally, he needed to know what happened to his friend. To search so long and so hard and learn that he had missed rescuing her by mere months caused crushing pain that stole his breath.

As he silently mourned his friend, Taly thought of everything that brought him to this roof tonight.

Who am I? What am I doing?

His career had started in the Tarpon organization because his father worked for them. When the Restler-Tarpon Alliance formed partly through the marriage of Merisia Tarpon to Gareth Restler, he had traveled with them as an Alliance agent. Then, when Merisia had gotten pregnant with Gareth's child, she'd talked Taly into helping her flee her husband, so the child would not become an Alliance hostage.

That didn't end well.

Honestly, Taly had never expected it to end well. Jumping to a logical but completely inaccurate conclusion, Gareth Restler had sent RT Alliance agents after Taly and Merisia. The pursuit had started in Meritab and ended in Terab where they had both been captured. Taly almost wished to go back to that time and face Gareth's misplaced retribution, for at least then Merisia had been alive.

A pair of Rangers, Kiata and Todd Wellum, had rescued Taly from the Deegan Estate in Terab, placing him in Kiata's debt a second time. The first time Kiata had rescued Taly from a Porit viper's poison when he was just a child, despite his father's mistreatment of her over some firfe spice. The Rangers had smuggled Taly into Rammon then out to a farm on the Kesler Plains owned by Todd's older brother, Terik.

I owe them so much.

After about a month, Taly learned his grandfather was about to be put on trial for murdering the last queen, so he snuck back into Rammon and sought help from Todd and Kiata again. They had arranged for him to meet with Queen Reia so he could plead for his grandfather's life.

The trial was a horrible, nerve-racking time for Taly who knew that Niktrod Keldor had indeed poisoned King Terosh's mother, Queen Kila. At first, Taly had merely feared his grandfather might be assassinated by a citizen too eager for justice, but he'd soon learned the danger was greater still because King Padric Creston of Gardan—Queen Kila's father—had claimed the right of execution. The best King Terosh and Queen Reia could do for Taly's grandfather had been to offer him a peaceful end before King Padric could torture him to death.

After the colored crossblades disaster that left the king half-dead, Taly had begun to repay his debt to the queen by escorting Lady Akia Zelene on an herb gathering mission through the Riden Mountains. That was the first time he'd experienced what life as a Ranger might be like. After that, he spent some time helping Lady Zelene with her duties as royal ambassador for King Terosh to the people of Ritand.

From time to time, Taly had discretely inquired after Merisia Restler. When Lord Kezem had the Restler-Tarpon Alliance destroyed, Taly feared for Merisia's life once again. With Lady Akia's blessing, he left her service to seek his old friend. For years, Lord Kezem kept her in prisons Taly couldn't hope to breach, so he watched, waited, and honed his fighting skills. Finally, the day came when Kezem used Merisia to bait a trap for King Terosh. Taly hadn't realized what was happening until the only thing he could do was take Merisia and run.

Not a day went by without him questioning whether he should have gone back to rescue the king.

He ordered us to go.

The reminder did nothing for Taly's sense of guilt. Right or wrong, they had fled, hiding in Estra for a few days then slipped across the Asrien Sea to Chara where they waited out the beginnings of Lord Kezem's rebellion. Soon after the king's death, the queen had contacted Taly about saving her sister. At the time, the instructions seemed cryptic and crazy, but then Kezem's forces moved in precisely the manner Queen Reia predicted. It was eerie.

Merisia, why couldn't you listen to me?

Despite Taly's pleading, Merisia had followed him in search of Kiata Wellum. Once again, Taly had been faced with an impossible choice: complete his mission or stand with his friend. He completed his mission and safely stole Kiata from Kezem's lackeys, but the price had been very high. Merisia's crazy plan failed because one of the soldiers recognized her. Had Taly stayed with Merisia, they would likely have both been killed and Kezem would have tormented the queen by showing her Kiata's body. Still, Taly wished things could have gone differently for Merisia.

What good are the gods if all they grant good people is a life of captivity, heartache, and pain? Taly knew the question was inherently unfair, but he hurt too much to care.

After reviving Kiata and delivering her to Father Morgivesh Niktol in the Temple of Marishaz in Chara, Taly had returned to Rammon to seek Merisia. The gate guards had been showing people infopads with his description, so instead, he went into the Calsol Forest until things calmed down. Wandering aimlessly worked for a few days, but somehow, he'd ended up in the Riden Mountains seeking the Rangers.

Life goes in strange circles.

If anyone had told his childhood self he would one day be a Ranger, he would have thought them the worst sort of insane. Now as a Ranger, his orders to keep an eye on Lord Kezem's plans and guard the princess from afar were very vague. He enjoyed his work with Princess Rela, but every time he became Captain Peter Estan, he took a grave risk. He wasn't egotistical enough to think nobody else capable of teaching the princess to shoot, but few else would dare.

Do I stay or do I go?

Chapter 14:
Farm Country

Allei (August) 26, 1554
Ranger Camp, Riden Mountains

Two weeks later, Jalna spotted her quarry right where she had arranged for him to be. Anotechs could be quite persuasive when they wanted to be. At her bidding, they had suggested the boy explore this side tunnel. He looked uncertain, but then, his brows knit together, and his jaw tightened with determination. He clearly braced for a surprise. When he drew near, Jalna used anotechs to light the path leading to a dead-end chamber.

"Where is your lovely bodyguard?" asked Jalna from the shadows. On a whim, she modified the tone to reflect both age and wisdom. Even as the words left her mouth, she molded her features to match that of an elderly woman she had met more than two centuries ago.

"She's not my bodyguard. She's a friend," said Teven.

"Whether either of you intended it, she has tasked herself with guarding you," said Jalna. "Surely you have noticed she hardly leaves your side."

"Who are you and what do you want?" Teven asked, rubbing his temple.

"You sound weary, which I find worrisome at this stage."

"Stop!" Teven's shout bounced around the chamber.

Jalna silently thanked the anotechs for dampening the sound.

"I'm sick of it! No one speaks to me normally. I'm not blind! I see how they watch me. I can feel their hope, but no one tells me what

I'm supposed to do! All I ever get is riddles. What am I training for? What am I fighting for?" He sounded decades older than his ten standard years.

Jalna smiled. Her previous observations had revealed only an eager student. Today, she heard the boy's determination and knew he needed her direction.

"My name is Jalna Seltan. We met some time ago, though I was much different then," Jalna said, flashing him a memory of the occasion.

"You're the girl—the one who wanted to duel," Teven said.

"Correct, and you are Teven McKnight, prince and scion of a fallen Royal House. I confess to knowing little more than you concerning your past, but I offer my services as a teacher. Such a thing will require much trust, so I will tell you and your companion about my past when the time comes."

"What could you teach me?" Teven's question was laced with suspicion. "And what will it cost me? I have nothing."

"You are marked for greatness, and many will suffer under—or be saved by—your hand," said Jalna. "Since you have that fate and power, I wish to guide you to good purposes."

"Why?" Teven stood with his hands at his side, feet slightly apart, chin lifted defiantly.

"Because I could not save my planet," Jalna said softly. "I spent decades fighting greed and corruption before being banished. Now, I take up the causes of people I come across."

"How do you decide which side is right?" Teven wondered.

"Everyone knows what is right. As thinking beings, we respond to stimuli, such as pleasure and pain, and take steps to achieve or avoid these. But it is deeper than that. We know kindness, compassion, and love are good, but they constantly war with malice, cruelty, and hatred. Though we know what is right and good, we fulfill selfish desires first, often to the detriment of weaker beings."

"Great, another philosopher, as if Aveni wasn't enough," Teven muttered.

"Enough talk. It is time for lessons." Jalna instructed the anotechs to fully light the chamber.

The sudden bright light did not faze Teven.

"First lesson, do not trust your eyes or ears, for they are easily fooled," Jalna said, switching to her youthful voice. She modified her features to match the voice.

Teven's lips parted, but he said nothing for several seconds.

"What can I trust?" he asked finally.

Jalna's face and voice melted back to the elderly woman.

"Instinct. You were born with strong will, which shall serve you well. Strengthen your mind. Learn everything you can, even your enemies have much to teach you."

"I don't have any enemies," said Teven.

"You will," Jalna promised. Sadness clung to both words.

"Oh … okay. Anything else?" Teven wondered.

"The second lesson for today is confidence."

"Confidence?" Teven repeated. "Confidence in what?"

"Your walk is heavy because you seek to please the universe, but the core of you doubts your ability to accomplish such. Drive doubts from your mind and your heart, soul, and body will be lighter." Teven's mouth opened to protest, but Jalna held up a hand and continued, "That is the chain one way, but let us work the other way. Walk with me and concentrate on placing your feet instead of letting them punish the earth you tread. Don't speak. Just walk."

Rolling his eyes, Teven attempted to walk as she described.

Jalna suppressed a chuckle at his enthusiastic but very clumsy gait which reminded her of one of Porit's bow-legged stilt birds.

"Relax and glide," she suggested.

"I feel like an idiot."

"That will pass with time. Try turning it into a dance."

"I don't know how to dance," Teven objected.

That is apparent.

"Place your feet, as if stepping too hard would break some barrier separating you from a pit. Good. Slower now. Left foot lift; left foot place. Right foot lift; right foot place. Just like that. Repeat that same process slightly faster now … and faster still. Good. Now try side to side. It's the same smooth motion in a different direction. See, you can dance. You may rest now. We will continue later, and someday your footfalls will be graceful and sure."

***

Elsewhere in the compound, Kayleen spent the afternoon beating wooden dummies to burn off the unexplained anxiety caused by Teven's absence. For some reason, she kept picturing the pretty girl who had tried to duel Teven a few weeks back. The girl's face had been flawless. That perfection irked her.

By the time she finished with the dummies, the time for the

evening meal had long since passed. She headed to the dining chamber and found Teven contemplating a half-finished bowl of stew.

Tretling stew again.

She tried not to wince. Mountain herders traded tretlings for protection from korvers, panthers, bears, and zaloks. The late hour explained the lack of others but not Teven's presence and unfocused gaze. She glared at the top of his head and took a seat opposite him.

"Hello," he greeted.

"Where have you been?" they asked simultaneously.

"You first," Teven said, politely deferring.

"Stop that!" Kayleen ordered.

"What?"

"That—that *noble* thing," Kayleen sputtered.

"If my manners offend thee, fair lady, I do apologize," Teven quipped. His green eyes teased her.

Kayleen threw a playful punch at him.

Teven ducked right into his bowl of thick brown stew. At first, he looked annoyed, but seeing Kayleen's face contort with suppressed laughter made him laugh. Then, she too lost her battle, and their laughter filled the empty room.

"You deserved that." Kayleen said, handing him a cloth to clean his nose.

"Agreed," Teven replied, just to bother her.

She threw another punch which he caught easily.

"You've been working on that," said Kayleen.

"It beats getting hit every day," said Teven with an infectious grin.

Kayleen blushed. She couldn't understand him or herself when it came to him. Teven's boyish charm and compassionate spirit intrigued her.

"So, where have you been?" Teven asked again.

"Training," Kayleen answered. "Speaking of which, I have a special training mission for you, but it requires a six-day commitment. Want to take a trip with me?"

"Where are we going?" Teven asked.

"I'm not telling you until we get there," answered Kayleen. "That way, you can't back out on me."

***

Allei (August) 27, 1554
Riden Mountains to Riden Flats

The next day, Teven and Kayleen set out early. They started with a shortcut through a series of tunnels snaking under much of the central Riden Mountains. Ranger Knight Bova escorted them for much of the way. Then, they hiked alone over the remaining mountains, reaching the last by late morning.

Teven gasped for breath.

"Don't die on me yet," Kayleen called over her shoulder.

Teven didn't have the breath for a comeback, and Kayleen wouldn't have heard him anyway for she jumped the last three meters of the perilous descent. She landed lightly and smiled a challenge up to Teven.

He narrowed his eyes and leapt, landing with a loud grunt.

"We'll rest, eat, and then hike the last distance," said Kayleen.

Teven groaned.

"You said six-day commitment, not tunnel trekking, mountain climbing, endless hiking, feet hurting, six-day commitment."

"No whining. Besides, it'll be good for you."

After a brief rest and some food, Teven had enough strength to plod on.

"We're going to help some relatives of mine with the harvest," said Kayleen, once they'd gone too far to turn back.

"Meaning …"

"Meaning I'm going to hand you a long stick with a really sharp blade attached and teach you how to use it on wheat, barley, and polata plants," Kayleen said cheerfully. "Besides providing much needed help for my aunt and uncle, it should strengthen your arms and teach you to control heavy weapons. Just don't cut your hand or head off. They're hard to reattach."

"I'll try to remember that, but I thought you said you didn't know much about your parents."

"I don't," Kayleen said. "Uncle Terik is my father's brother. Both he and Aunt Nala refuse to talk about my parents. All I ever get is 'Too dangerous to discuss, lass' or 'You'll know everything when you need to know, dear.'" Kayleen's voice dropped then rose in pitch as she imitated first her uncle and then her aunt.

They continued their journey through the Kesler Plains toward the Riden Flats, passing many bright, golden grain fields, stretches of rich, green grass, and patches of countless wildflowers. Here and there tiny fossa trees and scruffy looking pora bushes broke the utter flatness of the plains. Near the end of the day, they arrived at their destination.

"Kayleen!" cried a voice.

Teven felt the air move as a small girl flew past him and crashed into Kayleen.

"Owww. Watch the ribs, Chloe," Kayleen said, returning the hug. "Teven McKnight meet my cousin, Chloe Marie Wellum. Chloe, this is Teven."

"Hello, Chloe," said Teven.

The child's return greeting got muffled against Kayleen. When the girl finally released Kayleen, she turned and studied Teven.

"He's handsome, Kaylee," she whispered loudly, causing Teven and Kayleen to blush. "I have to show him to Momma." With that declaration, Chloe grabbed Teven's hand and hauled him into the tiny farmhouse.

Soon, Teven found himself the center of attention, but eventually, things settled down. Fresh bread and appola juice were set before the guests. As the family exchanged greetings and news, a brief pang of jealousy pierced Teven. Kayleen's young cousins chattered incessantly. Their craziness reminded Teven of Nate, causing a dull ache in his chest. Nevertheless, he forced himself to smile and answer the many questions flung his way.

That night, Teven shared a tiny bed with two of Kayleen's cousins. The younger boys didn't seem to mind, and Teven was too tired to care. He slept soundly until somebody shook him awake. His eyes snapped open. Kayleen stood at the foot of the bed grinning sympathetically. Chloe knelt on the bed beside Teven, leaning forward so that her face hovered a few centimeters away.

"Up!" Chloe bellowed into his face. "Sun's been out for a half-hour. You're late. Momma left biscuits for you, so get dressed while I go get your food." With that, Chloe scrambled backward on her knees and leapt off the bed.

After consuming the delicious biscuits, Teven and Kayleen set out for the fields. It didn't take Teven long to get a feel for the heavy staff with its built-in blade. Following Kayleen's instructions, he methodically swung the scythe back and forth across the ripe fields. His arms became tired and his breath grew labored, but he continued swinging. Small insects buzzed and chattered near his ears, adding their voices to the laughter bubbling forth from Kayleen's cousins. Their carefree attitude made Teven feel ancient inside, but he chose not to worry. Instead, he relaxed into the rhythm of the work. A gentle breeze cooled the sweat on his brow, as he breathed deeply of the fresh, earthy scent of the he Kesler Plains.

"Let me see your hands," Kayleen said, after about an hour.

Glad for the rest, Teven complied. He liked the feel of her rough hands on his.

"No blisters, that's odd," said Kayleen.

"Some of the miners had blisters, but I've never gotten one." Teven shrugged and hefted the scythe. "I want one of these. It'd probably go through those nasty mountain creatures pretty easily."

Kayleen nodded and returned to binding the loose stalks of grain Teven felled. She didn't speak for a full minute.

Teven watched her work, admiring the smoothness of her movements.

"When I'm here, I almost forget about the war," she said softly.

Teven nodded, understanding the feeling.

"Me too. I could stay here forever." Teven continued working but stole glances at Kayleen.

The sun bounced off her hair, making the red sections flicker like flames.

The next three days passed quickly, and as promised, they undertook the return journey on the sixth day. Much of the harvest still lay in the fields, but a good portion had been brought in and bound. Part of Teven didn't want to return to the Ranger compound or continue his training. This simple life felt right to him, but cruel reality would not be put off.

Chapter 15:
Daughter of the Maker

Pirua (September) 3, 1554
Ranger Compound, Riden Mountains

After listening to Teven and Kayleen explain their farming adventure, Jalna took advantage of their exhausted state to share her story with them. She brought them to the same obscure cave where she had first taught Teven how to walk softly and bid the anotechs to seal off the chamber and direct others away.

The anotechs native to Reshner had finally shared some of the recent past. She figured the young prince and his sister ought to know the whole story someday, but for now, she would ease the prince and his Ranger companion into knowledge of the anotechs' history. They also told her of the severe restrictions concerning everything related to the anotechs.

That needs to change.

Jalna had waged quite the word war with the Reshner anotechs. They still weren't fully persuaded, but at least they were being civil about the disagreement.

"What do you want from us?" asked Kayleen.

"Nothing yet, dear child. For now, I wish only to give you a proper introduction to me," said Jalna. Once again, she adjusted her features to match those of a thirteen-year-old girl.

Kayleen's eyes widened in surprise, but she only nodded, waiting for Jalna to explain. Teven had already seen this transformation, so his expression remained passive.

"Would you like me to tell you the story or shall I let the

anotechs show you?" asked Jalna.

"What are anotechs?" asked Teven.

Suppressing a sigh, Jalna explained that anotechs were microscopic machines that could adapt, learn, change, and grow like living beings. Certain protocols kept them dependent upon humanoid species, but a subsect of anotechs called Dalonos, literally "Dark Ones," had been trying to sow seeds of chaos across the galaxy for many centuries.

"The best way for you to understand anotechs is to experience them," said Jalna. "Are you ready for this?"

Both children nodded eagerly and exchanged nervous smiles. Impulsively, Teven reached out and held Kayleen's hand. Jalna held her left hand out to Teven and her right hand out to Kayleen. Once their hands were connected, Jalna guided them to a sitting position and instructed the anotechs to start the scene.

The children fell into a trance-like state.

Jalna didn't need to see the scene. She had experienced it hundreds of times over the years and lived it once upon a time.

*****

Enis (April) 19, 730
Over Eight Hundred Years Ago …
Headquarters of InGeneus Designs, Planet of Kalast

Once I leave here, I'm never coming back. Ever. I will infect your precious system and turn the mockeries of humanity against you.

The words filled the air then left a heavy silence in their wake.

Dodging a small metal table, Jalna's father, Sebastian Seltan, approached the unconscious form strapped to the wall. He was an undisputed genius, but also a madman. Hate or revere him, everybody feared the man who, through decades of careful engineering, had perfected the anotechs. Through these tiny machines, he controlled the mysteries of life. Those he wished dead suddenly died. Those he wished alive miraculously recovered from deadly wounds or illnesses.

"Come now, Jalna, be reasonable," said Sebastian, as if he could control her through will alone. Normally, he would use anotechs for such a task, but she was currently using hers to protect her mind against such assaults. "I'm your father. You know I only want what's best for you."

"You're my father. You should have seen this coming," Jalna said, from behind him.

Sebastian whirled and saw a full-sized, translucent representation of his thirteen-year-old daughter. His glance flitted back to her still form then back again to the hologram.

"I didn't teach them that," said Sebastian. "Interesting."

The near-perfect representation of Jalna studied the body fixed to the wall. Life support machines kept the heart beating, blood flowing, and lungs breathing. Despite the wicked-looking straps, the living corpse wore a peaceful expression.

The child's translucent essence walked through the small table, stepped around Sebastian, and stood protectively in front of the physical girl. She regarded Sebastian coldly.

"Best for me, best for Kalast, call it what you will, Father." Bitterness dripped from the girl's words. "For years, I deluded myself into believing you truly had good intentions, but one can only believe fabricated dreams for so long."

"You're like your mother: beautiful, brilliant, and stubborn," Sebastian said in an even, reflective tone. He ran his left hand through his light brown hair. His synthetic skin looked as fresh and clean as it had decades ago when Proyles, a nasty skin disease, prompted his anotech research.

"I have decided I am more like mother than you, which is why I trust myself with the anotechs." The corners of Jalna's mouth quirked upward.

"You cannot win," said Sebastian. "There are thirteen billion people waiting to be healed of their problems. Would you deny them that?"

"Healing I don't mind, for its own sake. But at what cost? Would you have them sell you their souls?" Jalna asked. Her voice flowed with passion. "I know the masses wait for your delusions, but I also know they mean less than nothing to you … like me." A note of real pain crept into her voice. "They think you're a god, but I know better. You don't care what—"

"I *do* care. Don't you see? Godhood is finally within our grasp. We must seize perfection and superiority, to end disease, crime, poverty, and—"

"And everything that makes life worth living besides," Jalna finished. "Being alive isn't about the winning or losing. It's about fighting. Population control failed years ago, Father. Imperfection, rising above bad circumstances; these things are at the core of life."

"Where do you get your crazy ideas?" Sebastian wondered, shaking his head. "I'll have to modify the genes next time."

"There will not be a next time," said Jalna. "I destroyed your samples of my genes."

"What's to stop me from taking new samples?" Sebastian asked.

"Everything that can be created can be destroyed. The anotechs you gave me as a baby are only machines. They obey their masters. In this case, me."

Sebastian growled and cursed Jalna's long-dead mother.

"I knew she would rig the anotechs!"

"Of course, I did, Bastian, no one in their right mind would let you completely control anything," replied a mature female voice from Jalna's young holoform.

Sebastian nearly jumped out of his synthetic skin.

"Meria!" He tried to back up but bumped into the table.

The holographic figure stepped forward. With a seductive expression totally unbefitting of a teenager, Jalna's translucent form gently caressed Sebastian's left cheek. The skin there tingled.

He shivered.

"Hello, darling, I won't ask if you've missed me

since you wouldn't have murdered me if you were planning on feeling bereft," Meria Seltan said through Jalna. "Do not worry. Our daughter is safe, despite your best efforts to perfect her into oblivion."

"Meria," Sebastian repeated, dazed. "How—"

"Since you cannot stop the changes now, I shall explain things. This insane affair with perfection must cease," said Meria. "When reasoning with you failed, I took matters into my own hands."

"But you're dead!" Sebastian protested.

"Anotechs are wonderful things, aren't they? You're not very good at hiding murderous intentions, Bastian," said Meria. "I knew you would succeed in destroying my body, so I transferred to Jalna in a dormant program. She is still here and quite fine, but it seems both of us might be out of bodies if you have your way. I have learned to live without, but I will not let you harm our daughter. I'm going to reprogram your anotech files."

"That's impossible." Sebastian wanted to shout, but the protest came out weak and raspy.

"You keep telling yourself that. It might help you sleep."

"Wha—"

"Shhhhhhh. Let the anotechs take over."

Following orders from Meria, the anotechs flowed from Jalna's fingertips into Sebastian. They conquered the brain first then the body by systematically surrounding and rupturing each cell. Sebastian collapsed, writhing as his cells exploded. Aware that she doomed herself as surely as she had her husband, Meria, through Jalna, spent the next three days destroying the rest of Sebastian's dangerous technology. Then, she broke the cruel bonds binding her daughter and set the child free to live in the chaotic universe.

*****

Enis (April) 19, 730-Allei (August) 8, 1554
Kalast and many other Planets

At least that's how the anotechs portrayed the story.

Jalna herself had been unconscious. Her mother had not been completely successful in confining the problem. Although Meria debugged the system, destroyed the anotech makers, and obliterated every file pertaining to the malevolent technology, several ships piloted by thieves and idealists alike had already left Kalast carrying anotechs.

After the confrontation with her father, Jalna tried to save her world but not even the anotechs could save Kalast from the damage her father had inflicted. She spent seven decades working tirelessly to establish a strong government, but greedy politicians thwarted her efforts. Finally, she lost heart and went into exile.

In a rickety old ship, Jalna left her home planet to follow the anotech trail. She felt burdened to control the rogues among them. Her anotechs allowed her to mimic nearly any humanoid feature, even horns if necessary, but Jalna preferred the face she had once possessed as a young woman.

She needed little sustenance, but natural curiosity often propelled her to local taverns and other common meeting places. She could have done anything. The anotechs could regenerate themselves. They made her impervious to disease, untouched by age, practically immortal. But she could still be harmed. She learned the hard way that anotechs didn't react well to bullets or energy blasts. One or two holes could be repaired in time, but she could bleed to death if she sustained too many wounds at once.

At any time, she could command the anotechs to shut down and let Fate have her body, but something drove her on. She spent seven centuries traveling the galaxy. Eventually, hope of finding the other anotechs faded, but Jalna found solace in aiding people she came across. Some welcomed her help, others scorned it, but everybody feared her. As much as people fight to gain power, they fear it in others. They also fear things they do not understand, and few understand the anotechs. Inevitably, Jalna's secret always came out. Then, no matter how much people revered her, she became an outcast.

On the remote planet of Porit, the guardians of the semi-sentient vipers had once suffered greatly because they stood between crystal hunters and untold fortunes. Although viper crystals could be safely extracted through careful surgery, few hunters considered that option. Many hunters fell to toxins, but the triumph of a few ensured a steady stream of adventurers.

Upon landing, Jalna was attacked with poisoned darts. Although she avoided most darts, a few struck her, and when the poison failed to kill her, she became like a goddess to them. She organized the viper guardians, called the Gedenia, under a respected leader and helped beat back the invaders and establish profitable trade agreements with nearby planets.

Porit had been a success, but like all successes, it came to an end. Jalna considered staying there permanently until the Gedenia tried to build her a temple. Then, she left in a hurry. Exhausted, Jalna chose nearby Reshner as her next home.

*****

Pirua (September) 3, 1554
Same Day
Ranger Compound, Riden Mountains

"Upon arrival, I took a job in a tavern to gather information," said Jalna as the scene ended. "Eventually, the anotechs led me here, to the two of you."

"Why to me?" Kayleen wondered. "I get why Teven. He's a prince, but I'm just a Ranger orphan."

"The anotechs from this planet have yet to share everything with me, but they are never wrong," said Jalna. "They tell me you're very important, so I have decided to invest myself in your training. Is that acceptable to you?"

Kayleen and Teven exchanged puzzled yet excited glances before accepting the aid.

Chapter 16: Strike Hard

Kest (October) 23, 1559
Ranger Camp, Riden Mountains

Five years passed like nothing to Jalna Seltan, but Teven McKnight and Kayleen Wellum changed significantly. Kayleen slowly blossomed into a young woman, losing none of her agility yet gaining more strength and grace. The wisdom burning behind her silvery-blue eyes further enhanced her pretty features.

Teven transformed from boy to young man seemingly overnight. He flourished in the crisp mountain air, which liked to toss his wavy black hair around. His nose sloped gently downward toward the wide, mischievous grin that often brightened his face, and his intense green eyes glittered from beneath the neat, dark strips of his eyebrows. Teven's thin, wiry frame gave way to confident muscles, but he hesitated to use this newfound strength.

"Blast it, Teven. There's nothing gentle about combat!" Kayleen scolded. "You know the moves, and you have the strength to hurt your opponent. Use it!"

"I'm trying!" Teven snapped.

"She is right," Jalna said. She was in her elderly woman form today, a persona she was growing attached to because it aptly portrayed her feelings about Reshner. In short, the whole planet seemed aged by the constant fighting. "Strike harder. She is trained for this."

"If you don't hit me harder, I *will* hurt you," Kayleen said. Her petite nose flared, and her lips pressed firmly together, causing her jaw to slide forward in a downright stubborn expression. Her long, red-gold braid whipped over her left shoulder as she swung a strike that would have seriously hurt Teven's right shoulder had he not twisted out of the way.

"Fine." Teven circled Kayleen, waiting for an opening.

As she had done for years, Jalna studied the combatants. She wished Teven would get over his fear of hurting Kayleen. Their fighting styles, though different, complimented each other. Teven measured his movements, flowing back and forth, dancing in to strike swiftly, and then fading out of reach. Whenever he could, Teven would dodge a strike rather than meet it. Kayleen was more direct. Though just as light on her feet, she was efficient about her movements, choosing to let Teven draw near, catching his strikes, and then unleashing a series of lightning swift strikes to drive him back.

Jalna expected the match to go on for some time. Teven had greater size and strength, but Kayleen had more experience. Furthermore, Teven failed to press his advantages, a weakness both Jalna and Kayleen tried to correct. Kayleen repeatedly knocked Teven down but his energy seemed limitless. Each time, he leapt to his feet and continued the match. Their banisticks met with loud satisfying cracks but neither was willing to land a finishing blow.

"Would you prefer to fight me?" Jalna asked, silently berating herself for not thinking of this solution sooner. "I can't be seriously hurt," she reminded them. The statement stretched the truth, but they didn't have to know that part.

Kayleen and Teven stopped sparring.

"Sounds good to me, but lose the old lady look," Kayleen said, walking to the combat ring's edge.

Jalna smiled and complied, stepping into the ring as the girl they had first met.

"Better?"

"Much. Thanks," Kayleen replied with a satisfied smile. She tossed Jalna her banistick. "Fighters begin when ready," Kayleen instructed, taking over as match moderator.

Teven shook his head in amused exasperation.

Jalna bowed to Teven, feet together and arms held at her sides. The bow showed that trust existed between the combatants. Opening ritual over, Jalna and Teven assumed ready stances and began the bout. Again, Teven dashed in and out with surprising fluidity. At first, Jalna simply deflected his blows. Her eyes followed his movements carefully, waiting for the right moment to strike. The fight continued in this manner for several minutes. Then, Teven launched a right-to-left slash at Jalna's knees. Instead of jumping away, Jalna jumped toward him and thrust her weapon at his left shoulder.

Caught off guard, Teven stopped his attack mid-swing, stumbled back a step, twisted his upper body to the left, and whipped his banistick up to meet hers. The force of the weapons crashing together sent Teven spinning further left. He used the twisting motion to his advantage by spinning and kicking simultaneously. His foot grazed Jalna's side. The small hit was inconsequential but bolstered Teven's confidence. He intensified his attacks. Blows rained from every side, and Jalna was hard-pressed to catch them.

After several minutes, Jalna disengaged and bowed again, ending the match.

"Well fought. Your strike quality is much improved," she said.

"See, you can fight hard." Kayleen glared at Teven. "You were holding out on me."

"Am I interrupting?" a familiar voice asked from the entrance to their little dead-end cave.

"Captain!" Kayleen exclaimed, stepping forward and embracing Captain Ectosh Laocer. "You're late. You said you'd be back by the tenth of the month. That was thirteen days ago!"

"Good to see you, too, kid," Laocer said, returning Kayleen's embrace.

Jalna watched an amusing flash of jealousy flashed through Teven's eyes. No doubt the boy would deny it. Jalna had paused a moment so Kayleen could greet her old friend, but now she stepped forward.

"Greetings, Captain Laocer. It has been quite some time," she said.

"Jalna Seltan, I don't know how you do it, but I like the young look."

Jalna felt the intensity of Laocer's gaze, and something in his eyes said he felt differently. The look faded in a heartbeat, and Jalna didn't dwell on it.

"But that's not why I came. The Festival of Future Fighters approaches, and I think it's time these two joined the Royal Guard and Melian Maidens," Laocer announced.

"Are we ready?" Teven wondered. He idly flipped his banistick from hand to hand.

"Of course, we're ready," Kayleen said. "Some derringers go on the Kireshana as young as eight or nine, at least they used to. Wait. You don't think we're ready?"

"I didn't say that. It's just—" Teven began.

"We must intensify our training, if you are to do well," Jalna commented, cutting off the rest of Teven's defense. "The Kireshana has killed many a candidate before you."

The anotechs had been very detailed in their reports of Kireshana deaths from the recent and ancient past.

"We'll be fine," Kayleen assured her. "It's probably no more difficult than a level seven apprentice trial."

"We've not been on our level seven yet," Teven pointed out. "As I recall, we had a bit of trouble on last month's level five trial."

"Trouble we handled nicely, as I recall," Kayleen replied, crossing her arms smugly.

"Trouble we *could* have avoided," Teven said.

"Hey, they were holding out on us," said Kayleen. "I just called them on it. We rescued the hostages, didn't we?"

Teven snorted but ruined the effect with a smile.

"Two on seven are not good odds," he pointed out. "Next time, we should try something less confrontational first."

"I am curious as to what lies ahead," Jalna said before Kayleen could continue the argument. "I too may try this Kireshana. Besides, someone has to watch your back while you two argue." Jalna shifted her facial features, arranging them into that of a young man about Kayleen's age of sixteen.

"That is so creepy," said Kayleen.

Jalna could feel the girl's eyes travel over every millimeter of her new body. The anotechs shivered under the scrutiny, causing a tickling sensation.

Calm down! she commanded the tiny machines.

Captain Laocer nodded with approval.

"A male persona will allow you to stay closer to Teven," said Laocer.

"That and it'll give me a chance to exercise my powers," Jalna said, placing her right fist into her open left palm. "No offense to my gender, but when it comes to cracking heads, males certainly have more fun."

Despite freely demonstrating a few anotech tricks and letting them see pieces of her past, Jalna had never fully explained her father's invention to Teven or Kayleen. She wasn't about to do so in front of

Captain Laocer. Something about the man made her cautious.

"What will we call you?" Kayleen asked. "We certainly can't call you Jalna. It means 'delicate flower' in Kalastan. Though that certainly would earn you the fights you're looking for, that kind of attention could be bad."

"How do you know that?" Teven asked. "They didn't teach that in the code class."

"Oh, I know many things," Kayleen said, lifting her chin imperiously. "To be honest, I don't know how I know. I just do. I guess it's just one of the odd facts floating about in my head," she continued with a shrug.

Jalna added a note to her mental log on Kayleen.

Memory flashes.

The mental list of intriguing details concerning Kayleen was growing quite long. Beyond the surface beauty, too often hidden by dirt, Kayleen had proven herself to be thoughtful, impulsive, athletic, intelligent, loyal, and dangerously fearless.

"You are correct. Call me Jal then," Jalna said, after a moment's thought. "It means 'wanderer,' a fitting title for our purposes."

***

Kest (October) 24, 1559
Wellum Farm, Kesler Plains

Captain Jairis Selok locked gazes with the defiant farmer.

"Terik Wellum, you have fallen behind with taxes and contributions to the cause. We are here to collect them." He resisted the urge to sigh and kept his voice stiff and even.

He lost count the number of farmers who had died protecting their pathetic pieces of property. Still, he admitted this land was remarkably beautiful. Golden fields of wheat stretched for kilometers around, interrupted by green and red rows of polata plants.

I wouldn't mind owning this, he thought, though knew it would ultimately go to one of Lord Kezem's pet governors or senators.

"I refuse to be robbed any longer!" the prisoner declared, interrupting Captain Selok's thoughts. "I cannot meet the quotas without starving my fam—"

A muffled crash and a sharp female scream came from inside the house.

The farmer's face drained of blood.

"Nala!" He turned to enter his home again, but two soldiers each caught an arm and held him firmly while a third applied stuncuffs.

The man flinched as a shock coursed through his arms.

Captain Selok glanced sideways at his aide.

"Lieutenant Surin, help Dobbin retrieve the family."

Within five minutes, Terik Wellum, his wife, two sons, and daughter were lined up outside of their tiny home. There was no need for this much ceremony, but Selok enjoyed exercising army authority. He rotated the men performing executions, and it was currently Lieutenant Surin's turn. Captain Selok watched dispassionately as Surin positioned himself and the men.

The farmer and his wife wore expressions that wavered between outrage and fear, with fear having a distinct edge. The boys, Jacob and Jared, twelve and thirteen respectively, stood to either side of their younger sister. Each young man had his body angled to intercept any threats to Chloe. For her part, the ten-year-old child glared at Lieutenant Surin.

"Leave us alone!" Chloe said, stamping a foot.

Jared's hand shot out and covered Chloe's mouth. A brief but distinct shake of the head further stressed the need for silence. The movement also placed Jared firmly in front of Chloe so that any retribution would fall to him.

The child's outburst caused most of the soldiers to tense. Selok casually held up a hand, signaling his men to relax. Lieutenant Erid Surin and Lieutenant Aaron Kaelo—on loan from the Coridian Assassins—were the only two, besides Captain Selok, who didn't flinch.

Twenty seconds passed, then Surin spoke.

"Terik and Nala Wellum, you are charged with failure to pay taxes, supporting subversive causes, and—"

"That's a lie!" Terik shouted.

Kaelo slammed a fist into Terik's face. The blow drove the man against the house and unleashed a steady stream of blood from his nose. Nala screamed and tried to go to her husband, but the sharp prick of Kaelo's kamad dagger halted her. Most soldiers preferred energy weapons, but Kaelo preferred the traditional weapon of Coridian Assassins. The boys protested the rough treatment but fell silent as the blade moved from Nala's shoulder to her throat.

"Steady, boys," Kaelo murmured, keeping his gaze on Nala.

Selok wondered if he would have to step in.

"Be silent while the charges are listed," Surin instructed, staring each of them down before returning his attention to Terik. "Your relation to Rangers casts doubts on your loyalty. The decrease in crop production proves your guilt. You have also failed to register your children for service to Lord Kezem."

"My production rates remain steady, but the quotas keep rising," Terik said bitterly. "What do you want me to do? I cannot keep up with unreasonable demands!"

"Take us to Rammon," Nala said suddenly. "Let us appeal to Lord Kezem. There must be something we can do to—"

"There is," Kaelo assured her. With a swift flick of the wrist his dagger opened the right side of her neck.

The woman's husband and children screamed. Her body stayed upright for one long second before slowly sinking to the ground.

Lieutenant Surin shot an angry glare at Kaelo but didn't dare reprimand the Coridian Assassin.

Captain Selok cleared his throat, breaking the stunned silence that had fallen thickly over prisoners and soldiers alike.

"That was … unconventional, but the penalty for these crimes is indeed death. Terik, you have been informed of the charges against you. Lieutenant Kaelo will now carry out your execution. Do you have any last words?"

Terik's eyes riveted upon his wife's body. Tears mingled with the blood on his face, but his features hardened.

"Riden bless House Minstel."

The treasonous words sealed his fate. At a nod from Selok, Lieutenant Surin drew his serlak pistol and shot Terik in the face. The three children collapsed together in a sobbing mass. Selok ordered them separated and bound so they could await transportation to a manufacturing plant.

When it was over, Selok retired to his private tent and took notes on the incident. He wasn't one to play favorites, but both Kaelo and Surin would bear watching.

***

Ferrim (December) 26, 1559
Ranger Camp, Riden Mountains

Another two months slipped by as Teven threw himself into his training. He would soon need endurance, strength, and courage in abundance. First, there would be the Festival of Future Fighters, which would determine his place in the Kireshana. Then, he would face the long journey itself. If he survived the race's seven trials he would be commissioned as a Royal Guard. High Commander Torent expected perfection from those undertaking the Kireshana. At least, Teven wouldn't have to go through the trials alone. Kayleen would be there trying to impress Melian Maiden High Commander Leena Linel.

"You're not listening to me," Kayleen said, clearly annoyed.

They sat facing each other in a narrow hallway practicing the honor codes.

Teven shrugged and nodded agreement, earning a playful swat on the shoulder.

"Ouch! All right, I'll listen but this is so boring," said Teven.

"You'll thank me later, when you know the Royal Guard code of honor backwards and forwards," Kayleen said.

"I know," Teven said. "But is it really going to help?" The question hung in the air. He didn't want to admit that he already knew the code because learning it had almost been too easy.

"It is time," Jalna answered in her Jal tone.

Teven and Kayleen were on their feet in an instant. Teven rocked back on his heels to avoid smacking heads with Kayleen who turned her head so fast that he caught a mouthful of her long hair. She had given up on shoulder length hair a few years back because long hair could be braided easier.

"Why are you dressed like that?" Kayleen demanded, gathering and re-braiding strands of escaped hair.

Jal wore beige slacks with brown boots and a dark shirt. The ensemble was cinched with a bright red belt, which declared the wearer a hopeful in the Festival of Future Fighters. When they made it to the Kireshana, they would trade the red belt for a more functional brown leather one.

"It is time," Jal repeated. She had made a conscious decision to speak as little as possible while being Jal. Listening would provide many more learning opportunities. She still felt something dangerous lurking in the shadows surrounding this planet. Before long, he, she, or they would reveal themselves.

The trio withdrew into their own thoughts.

First to stir, Jal said, "Don't let me interrupt. I'm just here to listen."

"This boring exercise is going to be the death of me," said Teven.

"Quit complaining and recite the seven Royal Guard codes of honor and the pledge to Reshner's Slimy Sovereign Ruler." With an attractive smile, Kayleen eased herself to the ground with natural grace.

"The abuse I take," Teven said. He grinned and reclaimed his patch of dusty ground.

Jal watched the two friends with lazy interest.

Teven cleared his throat grandly.

"From the top, if you please," Kayleen prompted.

Clearing his throat, Teven launched into the pledge first.

"This day, I pledge my service to Reshner's Sovereign Ruler, Lord Kezem of Idonia. I will serve, protect, and honor him all my days, forfeiting life if necessary to fulfill this duty." He paused.

"Code of Duty," Kayleen encouraged.

He made a face at her but started reciting the code.

"The Code of Duty—serve, protect, and honor Reshner's Sovereign Ruler, Royal Guards, and Melian Maidens. This requires strength. The Code of Strength—mind, heart, and spirit must be strong enough to carry the burden of truth. Strength comes in many forms; to overcome one must persevere. The Code of Perseverance—should someone threaten Lord Kezem, infinite space cannot hide him from me, yet I shall employ wisdom when seeking my foes."

He paused thinking, *I'd rather just lock Kezem in a korver den.* The thought's vehemence surprised him.

As if she had heard the thought, Kayleen's grin widened.

"The Code of Wisdom—to possess great wisdom is a rare gift," said Teven. "I will share my knowledge with Lord Kezem and his agents. Courage, the companion of wisdom, will walk with me always. The Code of Courage—I fear neither battles of word nor sword nor blazing blade. My enemies will flee or fall. While courage strengthens my heart, my feet will swiftly pursue justice. The Code of Swiftness—justice must be swift, yet stillness may best catch my enemies. The Code of Stillness—silent, vigilant, and alert, I await evil, so I can strike it down with word or sword. If I fall in this service, my life will have been well spent."

By the end of Teven's impassioned recital, Kayleen's mouth hung slightly agape.

"You read that once. How did you do that?" asked Kayleen.

"I'm just that good." Teven shrugged and smirked.

Kayleen threw the code book at him.

He laughed and caught the projectile.

"Is that any way to treat a genius?" he wondered.

"Only if he deserves it," Kayleen replied. "We'd better hurry up and get you into the Royal Guard. Maybe they can knock some humility into you."

"Yeah, Kezem's men are always good for violence," Teven agreed.

Immediately, a chill settled over the threesome.

"Sorry," Teven whispered.

Tears welled up in Kayleen's eyes, but she held them back.

"Not your fault." Kayleen's tone held all the weariness and frustration they had both felt since hearing of the attack on the Wellum farm. She wiped at her eyes, even as her left hand formed a fist at her side.

"I know, but that's why we must join the Royal Guard and the Melian Maidens," Teven said. "They were once noble orders dedicated to protection and peace. Something's gone terribly wrong at the highest levels of government." He picked up Kayleen's left hand and squeezed. "We're going to set things right. I promise."

Chapter 17:
Dangerous Good Deeds

Ferrim (December) 26, 1559
Same Day
Princess Rela's Private Chambers, Royal Palace, City of Rammon

Princess Rela Minstel sensed her companions' unease. She endured almost a quarter hour of strained chatter and half-hearted banter before she had to know what bothered them.

"What's wrong?" Rela's eyes scanned slowly from left to right, studying Lorian, Marc, and Anabel in turn.

No one said anything, but their faces spoke volumes.

"We're leaving tomorrow," Marc said at last.

"The Festival of Future Fighters begins in a couple of weeks," Anabel explained.

"Captain Titus is running a pre-festival camp out on the Balor Plains for the candidates from the palace," Lorian added, seeing no change in Rela's perplexed expression.

"Why was I not made aware of this?" Rela asked, irritated.

"Tell her," Anabel said, elbowing her brother in the ribs.

"What good would it do anyway?" Marc Spitzer frowned and glared at Anabel.

"She deserves to know," Anabel insisted.

"Tell me what?" Rela's attention flickered between her two friends, but she settled her attention on Marc.

He lowered his eyes and swallowed hard.

"If you won't tell her, I will," said Anabel.

"We discovered that your uncle is locked in the prison below the palace," said Lorian. She placed a calming hand on Anabel's arm.

A few hundred questions vied for Rela's attention. She could voice none of them, but her friends knew most of them and tried to give her answers. At first, they spoke as one and nothing made sense, but finally, they agreed to let Marc be the speaker.

"His name is Todd Wellum," said Marc. "I found his name when I was poking around the prison records. It meant nothing to me until I broke into the vid logs for Lord Kezem's daily fights. I was testing a new program to—"

"Get to the point," Anabel snapped.

"My program filters out background noise, so I can focus on one conversation at a time," Marc explained.

"What did you hear?" Rela asked, folding her hands to remove the temptation of throttling her friend. A thought struck her. "And does Lord Kezem know about your program?"

"I don't know if Lord Kezem knows about it, but if he knows, he hasn't done anything about it," Marc said shrugging. "Anyway, I heard Supreme Commander Kolknir boasting to Ambassador Ilidan that the entertainment would be provided by Ranger Todd Wellum, husband of the late queen's sister. Since you're—"

"She gets it. You can shut up now," Anabel said. She nodded to Rela who was lost in thought.

Marc reached out and gently touched Rela's hand.

Unused to being touched, Rela stiffened, but before Marc could pull his hand back, she clasped it with both her own and squeezed desperately.

"We didn't want to tell you because there's not much we can do," Lorian said, keeping her voice cool. "The Kireshana can take a year or more to finish."

"There's always something to do," Rela murmured, releasing Marc's hand. She didn't know what she would do, but the challenge lit the first flickering flame of rebellion within her. She would free her uncle.

"What are you thinking?" Marc asked.

Rela's mind raced. She needed help, new friends to be her eyes, ears, and voice.

"What do you know of the new kitchen boy?"

"Nicholas Riggs? Nothing special," Lorian said, shrugging. "His parents are Governor Nolan and Senator Katarina Riggs of Ritten."

"He wants to join the Royal Guard, but he's too young," Marc added.

"No, he's not. His mother forbade him from entering the Kireshana," Anabel clarified.

An idea came to Rela, causing her to smile.

"Before you go, I have one last task for you," said the princess.

***

Ferrim (December) 30, 1559
Palace Gardens, City of Rammon

Princess Rela reached out and touched the statue, remembering the last time she had come here with Sarie. She smiled at the memory of hanging upside down from the statue's strong arm. She wondered what had become of Sarie.

Even Lord Kezem wouldn't dare harm her, Rela thought, knowing it was more wish than declaration.

The sound of footsteps interrupted her thoughts.

"You summoned me, Princess," said the servant boy, bowing respectfully. "How may I serve you?" His warm brown eyes and slight frame gave him an air of innocence.

Doubts crowded Rela's mind. The temptation to send him away and forget the whole thing tormented her, but the memory of her uncle's plight gave her courage. Straightening her shoulders, she studied the boy. He shifted uncomfortably, and Rela realized she should say something.

"I have a task for you." She paused. If she had misjudged Nicholas Riggs, the consequences for her uncle would be dire.

You must do this!

"I will do my best to please you, Highness," the boy promised. The reserve in his tone told her next to nothing, but he leaned forward eagerly.

"It will be dangerous," Rela said, staring into Nicholas's eyes. "Can I trust you?"

"What must I do?" Although he controlled his emotions admirably, Nicholas's eyes gleamed with a craving for purpose.

"Deliver this infopad to RLA Captain Tayce, former Royal Guard, assigned to Fort Vik," Rela instructed.

The light in Nicholas's eyes dimmed.

"No one else must know of the correspondence. Your parents are visiting your brother at Fort Vik in a few days, are they not?" Urgency drove Rela's words out with speed.

"They are, Highness," said Nicholas.

"I have encrypted the infopad such that Captain Tayce should be the only one able to access the data, but the RLA possesses resources I do not. You must deliver it into his hands directly without anyone else knowing." Rela considered adding a vague threat about what Lord Kezem would do if Nicholas got caught. Seeing she had the boy's full attention, she rejected the idea. He was idealistic, but the threat of actual danger might harm her cause more than help.

***

Idela (January) 10, 1560
Captain Tayce's Office, Fort Vik

Lieutenant Ethan Tayce survived the surprise duel thanks to Todd Wellum's dead-man pill. He deserted the Royal Guard that night and fled to his sister's house in Meritel. Two weeks later, after three hours convincing both of his sisters he was still sane, Tayce enlisted in the RLA. Hard work brought Tayce up the ranks from derringer to marksman to lieutenant to ventor to paladin and finally, captain of Fort Vik. As captain, he finally had time to think. The more he thought; the more he frowned.

What do I have to show for my life?

His uniform finally fit well around the upper arms and his boyish features had hardened. Unfortunately, he had no time for romance, and he certainly wasn't out to impress his men, or the political prisoners housed at the fort. He frequented taverns for the rumors soldiers spread freely, but his position and an aversion to burning brain cells left him few friends there. His younger sister, Elena, a mother of three, also kept him abreast of the current news.

The years of ignoring injustices weighed heavily on Tayce.

Lord Kezem's a madman and I've spent years serving him!

He didn't know when seditious thoughts first entered his mind, but once they did, he could not shake them. Shortly thereafter, he received his first encrypted letter from Princess Rela.

The depths of her knowledge initially frightened him. If she wanted to get him killed, she had only to breathe a few words to Supreme Commander Kolknir. Her first letter explained what she knew and why she was contacting him. Since then, he had done his best to fulfill her orders. Most were small deeds, but sometimes, he altered lives for the better in more significant ways. Rescuing slaves, feeding refugees, and conducting prison breaks paid only part of the debt he had built up over the years.

Tayce's thoughts turned to his darkest memory. After

completing his Kireshana, he'd been so fired up with patriotic pride that he had immediately transferred to the Rammon palace prison. He had no idea his commanders expected him to beat a woman to death to prove his loyalty. His hands shook as he remembered the political prisoners being marched into the combat arena. All had been terrified women. Their hands were bound in front with chains connected to their waists and ankles. They wore only minimal clothing, but they appeared clean and groomed. Only later did Tayce realize they'd been kept in such pristine condition so that the horrors of the night would be clearer.

The five new recruits had each been given a number corresponding to a prisoner. Supreme Commander Kolknir had relished introducing each woman and her crimes. Tayce didn't remember much about the others, but his prisoner was Merisia Restler. Her crime was aiding enemies of Lord Kezem and escaping lawful custody. The sentence, of course, was death. The longer Tayce could make her execution last, the more bonus pay he would receive.

Phantom screams echoed in Tayce's mind. When he had refused to torture the woman, Kolknir brushed him aside, telling him to learn well. Defiantly, Tayce had killed the woman as soon as possible, but he felt nothing but shame for the whole incident.

A knock startled Tayce back to the present. Grateful, he pushed the memories away, stood, and squared his shoulders as the door swung slowly in.

"Marksman Cory Tiridan reporting, sir," said the soldier.

"Tiridan, good to see you. Please, have a seat," Tayce said, gesturing to the chair.

The marksman hesitated briefly before lowering himself onto the chair.

"What would you say to a transfer to the Royal Guard, marksman?" Tayce inquired, choosing his words carefully. He hoped he had judged the young man correctly. If not, he probably wouldn't be around long enough to fully realize the consequences.

Surprise and resentment flashed across Tiridan's features.

"As you wish, sir," Tiridan said, starting to rise.

Tayce waved for the younger man to remain seated. To avoid appearing imposing, Tayce took his own seat.

"You are a conscript, correct?" he asked.

"I am," Tiridan said. His mouth pursed, as if holding back more words.

"I have watched you for some time, and I think I can trust you," Tayce said, trying to gauge which way Tiridan's anger would blow. "By speaking this way, I place my life in your hands. One word to the wrong person will land me in prison or worse. You see, I owe a great debt to someone, and I'm far behind with payment."

"I'm sorry, sir, but I don't see what that has to do with me," Cory said.

"The man I am indebted to is a prisoner in the Rammon palace. Supreme Commander Kolknir had me fight Ranger Todd Wellum, thinking he would kill me, but the Ranger helped me fake my death. I fled here, so you see my predicament. Honor dictates that I help Ranger Wellum, but I cannot return to the palace."

Tiridan straightened.

"How can I help, sir?"

"I can transfer you to the palace prison's third watch," Tayce explained. "It would be your job to deliver a packet of stimulants, an infopad containing instructions, and food to Ranger Wellum. My sister, Elena, will give you the supplies upon request. Here is her Rammon address," Tayce said, holding out a small scrap of paper.

The marksman stared at the paper then slowly reached for it.

"She will give you some last-minute instructions and two hundred kefs for your troubles," Tayce added.

Tiridan tucked the paper into his pocket.

"Thank you, sir. The money will help my family. They've been having a rough time of it since I got conscripted. My pa's health is failing, and the Kala Mountains show no mercy to the weak."

Standing face-to-face with a young man concerned about his family moved something inside Tayce. He walked to the safe tucked behind the large, ugly painting of Lord Kezem and retrieved the hundred and fifty kefs he'd been saving for a new kerlinblade.

I despise that painting!

His old trusty blade would have to do for another month.

"Take this for your family. It's not much, but I hope it will go to better use than my ale fund. I will write the transfer orders effective tomorrow." As he handed Cory the money, his heart felt lighter.

Cory Tiridan bowed, saluted, and retreated to pack his bags.

"Ridenspeed to you, marksman," Tayce murmured.

Chapter 18: Anotech Upgrade

Idela (January) 12, 1560
Path to Festival of Future Fighter's Camp, Kesler Plains

Gazing back at the long stretch of road behind them, Kayleen Wellum let a faint grin cross her weary face. She leaned back against a rock, tired but happy to be outside. Having spent much of her life in tunnels and caves, Kayleen had developed a deep appreciation for fresh air, even if it was occasionally tinged with metals or ash.

After traveling thirteen days on borrowed horses and three more on foot, Kayleen eagerly anticipated their pending arrival in Rammon. A hov could have covered the distance in a few hours, but these days, most vehicles were RLA controlled.

Only scattered farmlands on the Kesler Plains, Balor Plains, Resh Grasslands, Riden Flats, Kevloth Plains, and Kevil Plains could boast safe grasslands. Besides these, a few poor villages, the ruins of Osem, and some cities composed the rest of inhabited Reshner. It amused Kayleen to know that maps show the inhabited section of Reshner in grand detail and relegate the rest to a narrow strip, when in fact most of the planet is solid ice.

Kayleen had studied the major cities of Rammon, Korch, Azhel, Ritand, Ritten, Korch, Huz Mon, Kalmata, Meritab, Meritel, Terab, Chara, Estra, and Idonia, but she had never visited any of them. Each city had a governor and at least five senators, but most cities had many more senators, depending on how closely they ingratiated themselves with Lord Kezem.

As they passed more open land, Kayleen enjoyed the peaceful

beauty. She knew the peace was an illusion, but she grasped it anyway. She silently thanked Master Kelsa Celdin for teaching her to recognize various wildflowers and other plants vital to the healing arts. Kayleen wondered if she possessed the mental endurance to become a healer master. She dreamed of living out under the stars and walking past seemingly endless fields.

She winced. Thoughts of beautiful fields reminded her of Uncle Terik and Aunt Nala's execution. Their fields and house belonged to Senator Elosh of Meritab now, and her young cousins belonged to the RLA Manufacturing Corps.

I doubt I'll ever see them again. The depressing thought weighed on her and turned her musings to the parents she couldn't remember.

Nils, a good friend and caretaker, had been killed bringing her to the Rangers.

Love is dangerous.

Kayleen steered her thoughts away from that black hole of despair. It would never work anyway. She loved helping people too much to withdraw. She also had an important mission to complete.

The weather the past few days had been unusually pleasant, but that was about to change.

Kayleen watched the sun steadily lose ground in its valiant battle against dark clouds.

"We should hurry," she murmured, regaining her feet. She looked at Teven who merely nodded, not bothering to rise. "We need to get there before the acid rain catches us."

Jal nodded.

Teven rose, picked up his pack, and mechanically walked past his companions wearing a vacant stare.

"Is he okay? What's wrong with him?" asked Kayleen, drawing Jal close.

"He is feeling the collective pain for the first time," Jal explained, studying Kayleen for a long moment. "Remember the special machines I spoke of before? The ones my father invented many years ago? Teven already has access to the anotechs because he is royal. They give him great empathy, but he cannot control them right now."

"Why would he need to control them?" Kayleen asked.

"Anotechs have many uses," Jal said. "Some uses can be learned through experience, and others may be taught. But I had not expected them to keep him quite so in tune with this world."

"What do you mean?" Kayleen asked, alarmed. "Will they hurt

him?"

"It's complicated," Jal said.

Kayleen glared.

Jal made a placating gesture.

"They are as much a burden as they are a blessing. And they are in you as well, though not to the extent they are in him."

"What?" Kayleen let her frustration come through the question.

"Do you truly wish to help Teven?" asked Jal.

"Of course," Kayleen answered.

"Then hold this." A small, glowing orange orb materialized in Jal's hand.

Kayleen accepted the orb with her left hand.

"What—ouch!" Kayleen released the ball and shook her hand but small spikes held it tightly against her palm. Instinctively, she used her right hand to try and free her left. Spikes sprang out of the other side, snagging her hand. Against her wishes, both hands closed, driving the spikes further in. She bit back a cry. A wave of something like acid and fire rushed through her, spreading up from her hands and traveling every millimeter of her body. Too busy fighting the anotechs to scream, Kayleen groaned. Slowly, the orb disappeared, as the anotechs flowed into her.

"Do not fight them," Jal said with maddening calm. "Be strong, Kayleen. The pain will pass soon. The anotechs must create the passages through which they will travel in you."

Kayleen's eyes sparkled with a mixture of shock, anger, and pain.

"I will explain further shortly," Jal promised.

Kayleen desperately cast her gaze upon Teven who had stopped ten paces in front of them. His back was to her; his shoulders slumped. Though paralyzed, every fiber of her cried out for help. Contrary to Jal's order, Kayleen fought the invaders. Her face flushed with fever. Though her eyes remained open, her concentration stayed focused on the strange entities traveling through her body.

***

Teven's pack slipped from his shoulders and hit the ground with a thud. He had started the trip feeling excited, but now, he felt strangely drained. His limbs refused to move. A hot pain shot through him and disappeared in an instant. Then, he heard Kayleen's cry echo within his mind. Anger welled up and rushed out of him like a breath held too long, snapping him from the lethargic state. He whirled, drawing his banistick.

"Wait," Jal commanded. "She will control them."

"This isn't right," Teven said through clenched teeth. His heart beat so fast it pressed painfully against his ribs. "She didn't choose this, and neither did I. I—"

"You are stuck," Jal said, with a sad, knowing expression. "And now, so is she. The anotechs have chosen her, as they chose you. They will help you save this planet, but they only help the worthy. You have broken their hold over you, gaining their respect. They will serve you forever."

"I don't want them! I want to be left alone!" Tears of self-pity slipped down his face. "I can't do this!"

"You must, Teven. The people need a strong prince," Kayleen stated. "Lord Kezem's reign has been far too long as it is."

Teven whipped his head left to look at her. Kayleen stood serenely, as if nothing had happened.

Seeing her unharmed, Teven willed himself into a calmer state. He returned the banistick to his belt, rushed to Kayleen, and picked up her left hand.

"Do you trust them?" asked Teven.

"I'm fine. See, they're already repairing the damage," Kayleen answered. She held out her right hand palm up and wiggled her fingers as proof.

He turned her left hand over and watched the wounds close. Then, he gazed into her eyes.

"You didn't answer my question."

"Yes, I trust them," said Kayleen with a wry smile. "We've come to an understanding about who gets to run my life."

Kayleen's smile melted the icy anxiety around his heart, so Teven reluctantly released her hand.

"Now I know where you get your I-am-invincible-and-have-a-death-wish attitude," said Kayleen. "I have half a mind to bust down the palace doors and have it out with that usurper right now."

"Kezem is a petty tyrant, but even petty tyrants have the nasty habit of drawing unsavory people to their sides. We must be cautious," Jal said.

Chapter 19: Festival of Future Fighters

Idela (January) 13, 1560-Idela (January) 16, 1560
Linderberg Inn, West Quarter, City of Rammon

Teven's churning thoughts kept him awake that night. He felt strangely free. Since his mother's death, a cloud of despair had clung to him like a suffocating blanket, even during the happy times with Kayleen and Jalna. Everything changed in the brief, agonizing moment of feeling Kayleen's pain through the anotechs.

Eventually, he slipped into an uneasy sleep. Sometime during the night, a beautiful woman filled his mind. Other thoughts fled. She wore flowing, deep purple robes which had generous green swatches around the sleeves and sides. He knew her.

"If you hear these words, my son, then I am gone." The woman smiled faintly, tipped her head forward, and slowly shut her striking green eyes. *"I can picture you looking just like your father. You are sixteen today, a man by custom and tradition, but I remember the first moment your father held you. Terosh was so proud to have a son."* Her smile faltered, and her eyes opened, glistening with unshed tears. *"You are my eldest child, Teven, and as such, it falls to you to save this people from Lord Kezem. Listen to Pria and Nathan, but never forget you are the Crown Prince of House Minstel. Your sister, Rela, will stay in the Rammon palace. I fear for her. The Ralose Charm will preserve her life but do little to protect her mind. Your brother, Tavel, should be with the Rangers in Osem. Seek him out. He will help you reclaim the throne."*

Then, just as suddenly as she had appeared, his mother vanished.

Despite the disturbed sleep, Teven rose ready to begin his

trials. He dressed in dark brown pants, a beige shirt, and the red belt of a Kireshana hopeful. Anyone with the twenty-kef entry fee was a hopeful, but most candidates wore a red belt to signify their status anyway. Anyone who made it to the Kireshana earned the right to be considered a derringer, the lowest rank of Royal Guard or Melian Maiden, even though technically you had to pass the trial to join either order. The rank only existed for the Kireshana though since survivors gained a rank upon completion.

The vision of his mother returned, making Teven pensive.

How will I reclaim the throne? Do I even want to?

He considered discussing the dream with Kayleen or Jal. Both would certainly have something to say, but Teven wasn't ready to invite advice. With effort, he pushed the thoughts aside and descended the stairs to the common area where he found Kayleen and Jal waiting.

The innkeeper served a morning meal of wheat cakes and lila juice. The food barely touched their tongues for the haste with which they ate. Thirty kefs passed into the innkeeper's hands to settle their account. Then, they were off to the Balor Plains where the Festival of Future Fighters would give the high commanders a good idea of who would make it in the Royal Guard and Melian Maidens.

Teven divided his attention between navigating the crowded Rammon streets and thinking of what lay ahead. He thought he could win three of his first five duels and become a first-class derringer. There would be twenty each of first, second, third, and forth class derringers. The Royal Guard and Melian Maiden hopefuls competed within their orders, but overall rank was scored against every candidate. Those not earning a rank could still compete in the Kireshana, but they had to wait two days to start. That was a change from the past.

Rising to marksman status required surviving the Kireshana. The journey started in the Balor Plains, ran through the perilous Calsol Forest, into the Huz Mon salt mines, and over most of the Riden Mountains before dumping candidates at the coastal city of Resh. From Resh, roughly the halfway point, one would turn south to Fort Riden for return supplies.

Before Teven knew it, the tournament grounds stretched before him. Excited shouts of hopefuls mingled with merchant cries and drunken laughter, forming a festive atmosphere. The scent of cooking meat, strong perfumes, and the sweat of thousands of beings assaulted Teven's senses. The merchants remained confined to a few neat rows on the southeastern corner. Ten dueling squares dominated the northern half, and tents for the combatants decorated the southwestern corner. The city of Rammon provided the southeastern border while other borders were marked with fences.

"Snap out of it," Kayleen said. "You're going to have your head bashed in if you daydream during a duel."

"I'll be fine," said Teven. "You worry about beating your opponent without breaking something on her."

"But I am such a gentle spirit," Kayleen protested. She flashed him an innocent grin.

"We should split up for now," Jal said, before slipping off into the crowd.

Teven exchanged a weary glance with Kayleen, nodded, and walked toward the registration tables.

"Quit now while you're still alive," said the corpulent man behind a rickety wooden table. He rumbled with laughter.

Teven ignored him and placed the entry fee on the table.

"Don't mind Rither here, lad, he's just sore his boy couldn't cut it in last year's duels," said the man next to the one who had spoken.

"It's your blood to be lost, boy. Have at it," Rither commented taking the money and putting it in the collection bin. "Now, I just need your name."

Teven gave the man his name, watched him punch it into an infopad, and wandered through the merchant stalls pretending to study the wares. He let his ears investigate the competition.

"Lorian Petole will win in the Melian Maiden contests hands down. I've never seen anyone move that fast," a woman insisted. "She may even win overall!"

"Aww swiftness won't save her out there," replied the woman's companion. "Darien Torrington will do fine though. That boy could take on a Driden lion with his bare hands."

The woman scoffed.

"Slow as a night creeper, he is. Some unknown's bound to beat him."

Teven scooted to the next stall.

"I heard they're changing the rules this year," a young man commented to a merchant man selling healing packs and herbs. The boy's voice was high with excitement. "The top female and male duelists receive a weapon of their choice from any merchant, a hundred kefs, and a two-day head start on the Kireshana! Two days, and that's on top of the two days the no-ranks have to wait!"

"Only if they survive," said the merchant, waving a healing pack in the youth's face.

"The prize money for the other first-class derringers ain't bad neither," piped up a boy, obviously related to the other young man. "They'll get something between twenty-five and ninety kefs. That could buy a whole lot of kertcha jelly or blaze bug taffy." The child sounded wistful.

"They ain't gonna spend it on no bug taffy," the brother scoffed. "They need to buy weapons to kill the wild korvers and other creatures they're gonna face."

"More important, they also get an extra one-day head start on the rest of the hopefuls," the merchant added. "A day behind the top two, but three days in front of the pack. My money's on those first-class derringers to win it."

Teven had heard enough. He and his companions would have to be in the top twenty to gain good position. He wanted to refrain from getting too much attention though, so winning the tournament was out of the question, even if he thought he could do it. The head start would help, but really, all that mattered was surviving the Kireshana with enough points to earn the rank of marksman. Only the high commanders, supreme commander, and respective councils for the Royal Guards and Melian Maidens knew exactly how points would be granted, but Teven had a basic idea of how the system worked.

A series of trumpet blasts announced the opening of the Festival of Future Fighters. After a small parade and a few long speeches, High Commander Torent directed the candidates to check the screens scattered about to see when they were scheduled to fight.

Teven's name appeared next to challenger, Treve Baringer, challenged, square two, and duel six. It took him ten minutes to locate the correct box. Excitement filled him as he watched two young men engage in hand-to-hand combat. As challenger, Teven could choose a weapon to fight with or declare the match a weaponless one. Despite the added risk of injury by using banisticks, Teven decided it would be best to fight with the weapons. There would be very few hand-to-hand duels during the Kireshana itself. He reported his decision to the announcer's assistant and turned back to the current duel.

One young man finally triumphed. The combatants bowed, the victor was announced, and two young women took their places.

"Lorian Petole, challenger, will face Anabel Spitzer, challenged, in weaponless combat. Hopefuls step forward," said the announcer who doubled as match moderator.

One girl had light brown skin that reminded Teven of a plains rabbit. The other girl's complexion ranged closer to creamed tretling milk. From the looks the combatants exchanged, he figured they knew each other. The duel that followed seemed to be a vicious battle, but Teven saw the fleeting smiles the girls exchanged.

They must be friends.

Each girl anticipated the other's moves, and for a time, it seemed neither would win. Finally, Lorian landed hard on her right side. Anabel moved close to deliver one final blow, but Lorian whipped her legs around and back so fast they blurred before sweeping Anabel's feet. Teven didn't even see Lorian get up, but suddenly, she had Anabel pinned to the ground.

The next three duels were sorely mismatched and ended within the first minute. Then, it was Teven's turn.

"The challenger, Teven McKnight has opted to face the challenged, Treve Baringer, with a banistick," said the announcer. "Stand back, people, this could get violent."

An excited murmur rippled through the small crowd around box two.

Teven felt like he'd spent every day of the last five years preparing to step into this dueling square. Kayleen, Captain Laocer, Jalna, and many Rangers had personally invested hours in him. Nothing would stop him from earning a place in the Royal Guard and coming one step closer to Lord Kezem. Not much thought had been given to what he would do once he made it into the palace, but that didn't matter now.

Only this duel matters.

Teven bowed, saluted, and opened the banistick. He did nothing, daring his opponent to attack. Through force of will, Teven waited a hair longer than he should have to block Treve's strike. The blunder gave Treve a false sense of security, which fueled the fires of overconfidence. Mindful of his footwork, Teven led his opponent around the dueling square. The area provided for the duel was more than adequate for hand-to-hand matches, but the introduction of banisticks quickly cut down the space. Teven conserved his energy by letting Treve hack away. Then, when he sensed his opponent tiring, Teven maneuvered the other boy into the corner and out of bounds.

"Penalty! The challenged has violated the arena bounds. The challenger is declared victor!" shouted the match moderator.

Teven stepped back and grinned at his stunned opponent. Treve glared murderously at him. As Teven tipped his head forward to bow, Treve's banistick snapped up. Only well-tuned reflexes saved Teven's chin from the devastating blow. Still, the banistick's rough tip grazed Teven's right cheek, drawing blood. The two young men locked gazes. Teven shook his head, sighed, and left the dueling square. He felt the anotechs begin knitting the torn flesh back together but stopped them. It would not be wise to let anyone know the anotechs could heal wounds.

The competition passed quickly. Teven fought four more duels over the course of several days, two with banisticks and two hand-to-hand. He won them but made certain that the fifth win was on a technicality like the first, resulting in him getting sixth place overall and third place for Royal Guard hopefuls.

Kayleen scored high enough to earn third place overall and second place for the Melian Maiden hopefuls. Kayleen and Lorian Petole initially tied, so the officials arranged one more duel between the two young women. After four rounds, Lorian prevailed, earning first place both overall and for the Melian Maiden candidates.

The closing ceremonies consisted of more speeches and a recitation of the codes of honor, first the Melian Maidens and then the Royal Guards. Teven, Kayleen, and Jal stood on stage, interspersed among the other top candidates. The prize money was determined by place, and in addition, all twenty winners received a ceremonial dagger that marked them as first-class derringers. After the ceremony, the commoners left and derringers of every class gathered for debriefing.

High Commander Leena Linel's voice boomed through the crowded tent. Teven noted that her mouth barely moved when she spoke. She spoke very fast, but he had no problem following her.

"Welcome ladies of the Melian Maidens and gentlemen of the Royal Guard. You have surmounted the first phase of integration into these fine orders. Soon, each of you will begin the Kireshana, a true test of character and strength. If you pass the seven trials laid out for you on the journey, you will earn the ranks given to you today. If you fail any test, you will be stripped of the rank. You can then try again next year or accept a post in Reshner's Liberation Army. Supreme Commander Kolknir could not come today so High Commander Torent will explain further." She stepped back and surrendered her spot in front of the voice amplifiers.

A powerfully built, swarthy man strode to center stage.

"Hand in 1000 kefs at the Kireshana's end and quote the honor codes to fulfill your duties. Obtain the kefs any way you wish."

Teven worked hard not to shake his head in disgust.

"Get a purple scale from a queen zalok to prove you have courage. Show your strength and endurance by scaling Mount Palean in a day. Guides waiting at the foot of the mountain will monitor your progress. Outwit, outmaneuver, and otherwise thwart those who come behind you, but do not kill them. And be patient when you reach the Lotrian Fields. If you rush through them you will die." With that, High Commander Torent stepped away from the voice amplifiers, and High Commander Linel took his place.

"Remember, loners travel faster but also die sooner. Expect to take anywhere from six months to a year to finish the Kireshana. In fact, a few derringers from two years ago reported in last week. This is rare but not unheard of. And one more thing … be mindful of the fact that other elements of our orders train during this time. Good luck. You are dismissed."

Teven felt the commander's sharp gray eyes upon him. The noise level in the room rose, but Teven pondered High Commander Linel's last warning.

Kayleen will know what she meant.

He went in search of his friend.

"Teven! Over here!" came Kayleen's voice through the babble of the crowd.

He waded against the press of people.

"Let's get out of here!" she shouted into his ear.

Once outside, Teven drew a sweet breath of cool evening air. A mild wind whispered of coming rain, but for now, the night was peaceful. He walked silently beside Kayleen for several minutes, enjoying the sense of calm streaming off her.

"What do you think High Commander Linel meant about other elements training?" asked Teven.

"There are rumors that Coridian Assassins hunt derringers," replied Kayleen. "I don't know if it's true, but I wouldn't put it past them. We can debate that point later."

Teven accepted this. He didn't know much about Coridian Assassins, but he could bet Jal would have quite a bit to say about them. Pushing the issue from mind, he wandered the tournament grounds with Kayleen conversing about everything and nothing. Neither wished to end the night.

Chapter 20:
Head Start

Idela (January) 17, 1560
Kireshana Starting Point, Balor Plains

Next morning, dark storm clouds hung over the Calsol forest, northeast of the Balor Plains and right along the path of the Kireshana. Nevertheless, the mood remained festive. The crowd cheered the top two duelists who had earned the right to start today. The rest of the derringers took a short break from their final preparations to watch Lorian Petole and Bari Aleron step up to the starting line.

"So long, suckers," Bari Aleron muttered, idly slapping dust from his dark blue travel cloak.

"Good luck," Lorian Petole offered with a thin smile.

"Don't need it, but thanks," Bari replied, looking at Lorian for the first time and scrapping his plan to sprint ahead. He imagined her light brown skin touching his own, warm and inviting.

Her dark brown eyes held a depth and sincerity not found in many. The bulky rain gear could not hide her feminine figure, a fact he fully appreciated.

Her smile broadened slightly.

"See you at the finish," said Lorian.

At that moment, High Commander Linel's sidearm spit a green flash of energy across the starting line into the padded target put there for that purpose, signaling the start of the race.

Lorian shot forward, kicking up some dirt which landed on Bari's immaculate black boots.

"Hey!" Bari protested, smiling despite himself. He hitched up his heavy pack and trotted after her, thinking he liked the view fine from here.

She won't be able to keep that pace long, Bari thought.

Nevertheless, Lorian's figure kept getting smaller and smaller in the distance. When she disappeared into the Calsol forest and Bari was still a kilometer behind, he realized his error. Tightening his pack straps, Bari sprinted full tilt toward the forest.

***

Back at the starting line, Teven and Kayleen walked slowly to Kayleen's tent to check on their supplies.

"That girl sure can run," Teven commented.

"Yup," Kayleen agreed. "One of the girls I fought yesterday, Vania something or other, said Lorian came from the palace where she does nothing but run and train."

"Sounds like someone I know," Teven said, turning and staring down at her. He straightened his shoulders which had broadened nicely. He liked the way the stiff wind played with Kayleen's hair.

The cool humidity caused her reddish-gold hair to curl more than usual.

"Look who's talking," Kayleen said, meeting his critical gaze.

"Did I imply something?" Teven asked innocently.

"It is way too early to jump on my nerves, boy," Kayleen said. She had more to say but a mouthful of hair delayed her long enough for Teven to speak.

"Must you say it like that?" he asked, wincing. "What's wrong with my name?"

"Say what?" Kayleen asked. "Would you prefer something more endearing, like Tevvie?"

"Point taken."

"I kind of like 'Tevvie,'" Kayleen continued with an evil grin.

"I shall say no more. Round one goes to the fair lady," Teven said, reaching past her and flinging the tent flap aside with a flourish. Bowing from the waist, Teven waved Kayleen in.

It took them all morning to gather various supplies. In addition to weapons, they would need camping, climbing, swimming, and emergency gear. Flashfloods, korver clans, windstorms, and graveground were just four of the life-threatening challenges they could face. Despite the danger, Teven sort of wanted to see a wallay.

The tiny creatures responsible for graveground had the nasty habit of digging their tunnels dangerously near the surface. When they moved to a different area, nothing was there to put fresh cradul onto the tunnel walls. Eventually, the walls grew brittle and collapsed. The depressions—depending on size—could do anything from twist an ankle to swallow a herd of tretlings.

Jal stopped by early afternoon and invited them to share the midday meal. Their conversation was guarded, but Teven gathered that Jal had some interesting information to share. After the simple meal of peri juice and tretling meat in wheat wraps with lettuce and tomatoes, the trio continued with Kireshana preparations.

Throughout the morning, the storm clouds had thickened. The wind picked up, buffeting the tents.

After lunch, Teven and his companions rushed back to Kayleen's tent. A steady rain fell. The howling wind and the rain's enthusiastic cadence eased their fear of being overheard.

"I had forgotten how crude young men could be," Jal commented, referring to the rowdy group in the mess tent.

Teven shrugged.

"Manners aside, did you learn anything?" he asked.

"A little about our competition." Though still speaking as the youth, Jal's tone slipped into teacher mode. "Bari Aleron hails from Idonia. His parents are Senator David and Lady Anna Aleron. He's strong, hardy, and knows how to handle a banistick and a kerlinblade. Lorian Petole is an orphan raised as a servant in the Rammon palace. I imagine she knows how to use any weapon."

"She's got a nasty right uppercut, too," Kayleen added, gently touching her chin.

"Oh, and Lord Kezem has standing bounties on information leading to anyone connected to House Minstel," Jal added.

"It's been more than a decade since he took over," Kayleen commented. "The man sure knows how to hold a grudge."

"In any case, it will make our trip more interesting," said Jal.

Teven didn't say anything because the vision of his mother sprang to mind. He thought so hard he became lightheaded. As he began falling, Kayleen caught his left arm and steadied him.

"Are you all right, Tev? Teven, answer me," Kayleen said, squeezing his left arm.

"No, wait. The anotechs are working," Jal said.

Teven heard the conversation faintly, as though it took place across a great distance. He felt himself being lowered to the ground.

Once he was down, his mother appeared again.

"Do not fear, my son. This strangeness will pass. Let the anotechs work, but also, learn to divide your attention between them and the world around you." She vanished.

Teven found himself staring up at Jal and Kayleen who were kneeling over him.

"You'll be fine in a few seconds," Jal promised.

"I saw her," Teven whispered. "Twice now."

"Saw who?" Kayleen asked.

"My mother. The first time was in a dream I had a few nights ago."

"Why didn't you share this dream with us?" asked Jal. "I might have been able to explain sooner and prevented this. You're lucky it didn't happen in public. That would take some explaining."

"You *do* have some explaining to do, a lot of it. What are the anotechs? Besides tiny machines. What do they do? Why do I keep seeing my dead mother?" Teven's voice rose until he practically shouted the last three words.

"The anotechs are guides and guardians," Jal explained. "My father invented them before losing his mind to some of the nastier personality twists of rogue anotechs. They call themselves Dalonos, which means Dark Ones in Kalastan. Although I hunt these dark anotechs, most are neither good nor evil, only what you make of them. Someone like Lord Kezem is not to be trusted with anotechs."

"Will the visions continue?" Teven wondered.

"Will I have dreams, too?" Kayleen inquired at the same time.

Jal thought a moment.

"Teven, I think the dream is a start to more detailed messages your mother gave you before she died. If so, I can teach you techniques to streamline them. They are probably triggered by certain phrases or events. And no, Kayleen. You need not worry. I doubt you will have dreams of this nature. Most of your anotechs came from me, and I certainly didn't plant any messages in them."

"That's a relief. Well, I think you two have some anotech controlling to discuss, so I'll finish packing our supplies," Kayleen said, climbing to her feet. "I also wanted to do a little browsing at the merchant stalls."

With a short break for an evening meal, the lessons continued long into the night. From time to time, Kayleen would join them. Teven listened with rapt attention as Jal described the various advantages that came with anotechs.

Jal cautioned Teven against becoming too dependent upon the machines. If used properly, they could provide protection from acid rain, various insects, and even some diseases. Most of the benefits were limited to the anotech's current master, but a few of the generalized healing benefits could be bestowed upon others.

"Why didn't they protect me from the acid rain before?" Teven asked, having stuck his hand outside the tent at Jal's bidding. The water flowed off his hand easily without leaving red, irritated marks.

"They probably did protect you from most of the poison, but they rely on you for direction as much as you depend upon their aid. Like small children, they only perform complicated tasks when instructed how to do so. Tell me, have you been sick much?"

"No," Teven admitted. "Never really."

"I thought not. They must have general instructions to guard your life. Once you learn to wield them yourself, you will be able to stand against anything the Kireshana can throw at you. Now, I think it is time we retire. It is nearly morning, and we will need the rest."

"Goodnight then," Teven said. He hauled his weary, stiff self off Kayleen's bedroll and staggered from the tent.

That night, he had no trouble sleeping.

Chapter 21: Danger in the Calsol Forest

Idela (January) 17, 1560
Calsol Forest

Tryse steadied his breath with two different calming techniques. Almost ten when Lord Kezem came to power, Tryse had been raised in the RLA youth camp based in Korch. When his aptitude for hand-to-hand combat caught his commander's attention, he found himself transferred to the Royal Guard camp at Azhel.

Now, more than twelve years later, Tryse frowned into the semi-darkness created by the thick canopy of cal and dansque trees. His thoughts tried to wander, but he forced them back to the mission, mentally reviewing the list of twenty targets that would start the Kireshana ahead of the others. His assignment was simple: kill three derringers.

Tryse cocked his head to the side, wondering how he felt about the mission.

It is a great honor to get the Kireshana trial.

So far, he had performed admirably. Despite starting a half-hour behind the first two derringers, he had surpassed them. Anxious to test them, he decided to swoop down upon them like a bird of prey and attack with his kamad dagger. As a trainee, his blade was not poisoned, so his blows would have to have force behind them.

The sound of heavy footfalls echoed in the quiet forest. He concentrated and picked out two different pairs of feet approaching him with all the subtlety of the Azhel Grand Percussion Band. Tryse shook his head with disgust.

You'll have to do better than that if you want to survive.

Pity touched him. Perhaps their steps faltered from weariness.

Fatigue is no excuse for faulty technique! The remembered admonishment came fully charged with Kelp's voice. Tryse almost flinched, expecting to feel the sting of a whip.

The derringers were suddenly below him. Tryse waited for them to pass and dropped to the ground with a muffled thump. He covered the two steps to the female derringer and thrust the dagger at the back of her neck.

At the last second, she threw herself forward and spun to face him.

"Bari!" the girl cried.

In that instant, Tryse saw her raw fear, and it shook him. Having missed his first target, Tryse switched direction and propelled his kamad dagger toward the second derringer. The boy twisted aside and caught Tryse's weapon hand. Grunting, Tryse dropped the weapon to his other hand and threw it at the female derringer. By this time, she had a banistick in hand and used it to swat the dagger away. His dagger lodged in a cal tree with a loud thump.

Suitably convinced these two were worthy enough to continue, Tryse shoved the young man into the girl, straightened, and bowed. They watched him warily. Instead of renewing his attack, Tryse retrieved his dagger and used a low branch to haul himself higher. Within seconds, the bewildered derringers were far behind, and Tryse began planning his next attack.

Knowing the others would not be along for a day or so, Tryse settled down in a tree to sleep. The battle rush faded, and his emotional state calmed. He pictured the recent fight and noted several places where a different move could have altered the battle.

I won't make those mistakes again.

As often happened during quiet moments, Tryse wondered what killing someone would feel like. His friends from the first camp had probably already shed blood, but Coridian Assassins trained significantly longer than others. The Kireshana trial was the last test. Those who passed gained power and honor, and those who failed never bothered returning.

My dagger was a centimeter from a living being!

The thought thrilled and frightened him. Part of him knew he should not be so pleased to kill. Eventually, he forced his mind to his old life in Korch with his parents and two brothers. It gave him enough peace to fall asleep.

***

Idela (January) 18, 1560
Kireshana Starting Point, Balor Plains

The next morning, as they stood amid controlled chaos, Kayleen practiced using anotechs to glean information from her surroundings. At first, the information overflow left her disoriented, but slowly, her mind accepted the influx of information. She stiffened when a hand touched her shoulder and relaxed again upon realizing the hand belonged to Teven.

"It's about to begin," Teven warned in a whisper.

Kayleen shut off the sensory anotechs.

"That is definitely going to take some getting used to," she murmured.

Teven answered with an understanding nod.

"Where's Jal?" asked Kayleen.

"Back there somewhere," Teven said, waving a hand toward the back of the small group.

Soon, eighteen first-class derringers, including Kayleen, Teven, and Jal, would begin the Kireshana. They would not see Rammon for months. Some would never see it again. Everyone would be changed by the trials ahead.

A wave of sadness touched Kayleen as she studied the faces around her. Most were around her age of sixteen, almost seventeen, but a few appeared as young as nine or ten. Their faces radiated excitement, but she could easily picture those same faces twisted in pain or still in death. A powerful desire to protect them came to her.

Kayleen categorized them by needs. Each had proven he or she could handle single opponents and direct attacks, but the enemies on the Kireshana would include fatigue, hunger, and cold. Growing up in a Ranger camp in the Riden Mountains gave Kayleen a slight advantage, but she knew this journey would greatly tax her reserves.

There are no rules out there.

The living enemies would not strike one by one. Before the end, teeth, guns, banisticks, daggers, and kerlinblades would draw more than their share of blood from the young derringers.

High Commander Linel fired her pistol. Again, a flash of green zipped past the derringers, tracing the starting line before slamming into the padded target. Under less pressure to start the race strongly, most derringers began with a steady trot. Kayleen set off at a gentle pace, enjoying the coolness of the morning. Her thoughts turned to Teven who jogged beside her. A few kilometers down the path, well out of sight of the cheering crowds, everyone slowed to a brisk hike. Steps waxed increasingly cautious as they approached the Calsol Forest.

If everything went well, it would take a few weeks to traverse the Calsol Forest. They could walk or rent horses in Calsola for three hundred kefs each. For those, like them, who could not afford a horse, the benevolent masters of the Huz Mon salt mines had a credit system set up with the Calsola stables. On horse, it would take a week to cross the Riden Flats. Kayleen fully intended on renting horses so she counted a few extra days to pay off the debt. Three more weeks would see them through the northern Riden Mountains. A month or two after that they should be past Fort Riden and to the foot of Mount Palean. These were rough estimates based upon educated guesses on how fast their group could travel.

"Planning ahead?" Teven asked. They had dropped behind the main derringer pack, so it was safe to talk.

"This is going to be one long trip," Kayleen said.

"Just think, in another year we'll be inside the palace ready to bring justice to Lord Kezem," said Teven.

"How will we bring justice to him?" Kayleen asked, genuinely curious.

"Kill him, I suppose," Teven answered. His tone betrayed doubts.

"What do we really know about him? Does he deserve death?" It surprised Kayleen that this conversation hadn't come up earlier. They had never questioned Captain Laocer's orders. "Besides usurping the throne … and killing your mother … and condoning the murder of my aunt and uncle … and stealing their farm and shipping my cousins to manufacturing plants and starving half the people. Okay, I'm convinced; he's got to go."

"Life in the mountains has left us a little naïve," Teven admitted. "The people at the Festival of Future Fighters seemed happy enough, but … there was fear there, too."

"The thought of starving will do that to you," Kayleen said dryly.

"Maybe it's Lord Kezem's fault, maybe not," said Teven. "He can't control everything, right? He's only one man, but he is the man in control. This is confusing! I just don't want to create more problems if Reshner's in good hands."

"You wouldn't want your throne back?" Kayleen asked, shocked. "I haven't known many royals, but I know enough to know that that's definitely odd."

Teven smiled and adjusted his pack.

"Thanks." He shook his head, struggling to explain. "I've never tasted the power attached to the throne, so I don't miss it, but from what little I know of my parents, they would have risked everything to right Reshner. There are enough problems to warrant righting. I can do no less."

Kayleen turned her head to hide a smile. She kind of liked this philosophical Teven who argued himself in circles.

***

Idela (January) 18, 1560
Calsol Forest

Midmorning the next day, Tryse resumed his stakeout refreshed and ready for anything. He heard the next group of derringers crash through the forest three minutes before he saw them. Tension wound his muscles tight. Adrenaline pulsed through him, giving him the euphoric rush that could only be experienced before and during combat.

Like the day before, Tryse fell upon his unsuspecting victims like a windstorm. They screamed and scrambled for weapons, but it was too late. Tryse's kamad dagger found a target. He felt the blade sink into a boy's chest and watched blood bubble from the wound.

Cerulean eyes widened, then deadened.

The picture burned into Tryse's mind. Had his body not been aware that death awaited him if he stayed, Tryse would have stared at the body for ages.

He couldn't remember the fight after that. He came back to himself shivering in a cal tree. A dark stain on his left sleeve reminded him of the spilled blood. A shudder coursed through him.

This isn't right! It's not supposed to feel like this!

Before he knew it, Tryse sobbed, not caring if anyone or anything heard.

The bloodstain mocked him. With a frustrated cry Tryse attacked his sleeve with his clean dagger. Even distraught, he had remembered to clean his weapon after the battle. The offending portion tore free and fluttered to the ground. Gripped by a strong sense of futility, he stared hard at his dagger and pondered slicing his wrists.

I can end this pain.

A strange, slippery memory stopped him. When he was a boy, his father, a representative for Korch farmers and merchants, had taken him to Rammon to request royal aid for recent crop failures. Tryse had not been allowed into the meeting, but later, his father had presented him to King Terosh and Queen Reia. Their faces returned to him clearly. He relaxed into the memory. Both had been elegantly attired in green and purple ceremonial robes.

Tryse couldn't recall much of the conversation, but he remembered the queen's words.

"Your father speaks very highly of you, Tryse. I hope you will one day exceed his expectations."

Tryse gritted his teeth.

Father would be ashamed of a murderer. I will never serve Lord Kezem again.

"I'll start again," Tryse vowed. Then, reality crashed on his head. He could not give the boy his life back, but he would not return to his masters. That left him halfway to nowhere.

I can't go back.

Tryse spent the rest of the day and much of the night planning his next move. He worried about the other two Coridian Assassin candidates. Plian, an ill-tempered coward, favored poisoned flingers stolen from the armory. He would probably sit in a tree and rain death from above. Stealing the flingers would stop Plian. Gia preferred to become friends with her targets, but she wouldn't have that luxury on the Kireshana. Most likely, she would strike at night while the derringers camped. Tryse could claim a camp for himself, but that would only force her to change targets. Maybe he could talk to her. A chill settled on him. Gia's reputation for manipulation was well founded. If Tryse didn't watch it, her dagger would one day be lodged in his chest.

***

When they reached the edge of the Calsol Forest, Kayleen set up the tents, Jal prepared a meal, and Teven gathered some fire fixings. Afterward, Teven sat on his bedroll and fiddled with the used kerlinblade he had bought with his winnings. The handle was old and worn, but the blade worked well.

"Have you practiced with it yet?" Kayleen inquired.

"Nope. You up for a sparing match?" asked Teven.

"Sure."

It took them two minutes to reach the Balor Plains again. Even after the long day of walking, new energy coursed through Teven as he squared off against Kayleen. They set the blades to the lowest shock setting to avoid killing each other. Kayleen saluted. Teven returned the gesture, stepped forward, and threw himself into the duel. When their blades crashed together, his blade turned from yellow to green, and her blade changed from red to orange.

"That's odd," he muttered.

"I think it's meant for a colored crossblades game," Kayleen said, swinging at his head.

"It's distracting," Teven grunted, catching her blade. They fought for several minutes with the colors changing until Teven called a halt. "Bothersome color changes," he muttered, inspecting the handle. After a few seconds, he finally noticed a series of tiny black panels lining the bottom and sides of his kerlinblade handle. He fiddled with the panels, having Kayleen test the changes by knocking her blade into his.

Within five minutes, they figured out how to keep the blade a steady color. Teven chose a blue blade, and Kayleen chose a purple one. Then, their duel resumed.

Kayleen faked an overhead strike. The violet blade descended but stopped short of Teven's raised guard. A turn of her wrist slipped the blade under the guard to the point of his chin.

"I win," she said.

"Draw," he challenged, raising his blade slightly so she could see it in her peripheral vision.

She sighed.

"Draw it is. Time to eat?"

"Always," said Teven.

They held the blades at each other's throat for a second longer, neither wanting to back down first. By mutual agreement, they lowered and deactivated their weapons at the same time. An awkward silence and stillness settled between them, as they stood at arm's length regarding each other. Teven wasn't certain where their relationship stood. He cared for her deeply but feared revealing his feelings might destroy the five-year friendship. If it was true friendship, it could withstand the blow, but he hated to take the risk. He caught her eye.

"Good match," she said, boldly stepping forward.

Something fired in his brain, telling him to make a move. Wildly clutching his fleeing courage, Teven attached his kerlinblade to his belt and wrapped his arms around her. The warm embrace felt right. Had she hesitated, he would have backed off, but he felt the strength of her affection compressing his ribs. He was about to follow the embrace with a kiss when a keen sense of danger took control of his body. Pushing away from Kayleen, Teven stumbled back and twisted, narrowly missing a silver flinger.

The sharp little weapon would not have done much damage had it struck him, unless it was poisoned, but Teven didn't want to take a chance. Kayleen's kerlinblade flared to life. Teven followed suit. A zinging sound alerted him to more flingers. He crouched, holding the blade across his body to provide the most protection. A flinger sailed past his left ear. Another flew at the center of his chest. He raised his blade and made a slight adjustment so that it was wider and flatter than normal. Suddenly, there were two blades for Kayleen had crossed hers with his. The flinger hit dead center of their blades and dropped harmlessly at their feet.

They braced for more, but none came. The usual music of early evening resumed as if nothing had happened. They stood ready for a tense minute longer.

Finally, Teven took a cloth from his pocket and wrapped the weapon inside.

"We should get back to Jal," he said.

Returning to the campsite, Teven and Kayleen reported the incident to Jal.

"Judging by the traces of gully fish poison on the tips, it's probably from a Coridian Assassin," Jal commented, examining the weapon's sharp points. "They're earlier than I had anticipated."

"What will we do?" Teven asked.

"Stay alive," Jal replied.

Teven couldn't argue with the logic, but he had been hoping for more detail to the plan.

"We should take turns watching the camp," Kayleen suggested.

"We should pick up more traveling companions," Jal offered.

Teven nodded to both suggestions.

"I'll take first watch tonight. I'll wake Kayleen in three hours, and she can wake you in six."

During his watch, Teven practiced accessing his mother's messages and letting the anotechs do most of the watch work. He had finally been able to shut the dreams out, but then, he had not been able to find them. After following several convoluted mental trails, Teven imagined a plain, bare room with only a table and a chair. In the chair sat his mother, wearing a purple shimmersilk gown and her usual smile.

"It might surprise you to see me as I was the day I died. I hope you will continue to listen to me long after you are older than I." Her smile dimmed. *"As I ponder my impending death, I find myself at a loss to share wisdom with you. Terosh always was the better thinker. I wish you could have known him better. Never be afraid to love, Teven. To lose is a part of life, but to love is to gain the universe. Despite the pain, you will be a better man for the experience."*

The woman and the room faded.

Teven's watch passed, but he continued to think. He became aware of eyes watching him but received no anotech warnings. Eventually, he woke up Kayleen. The anotechs could keep watch while they slept, but for the sake of appearances, they would have to get used to watches.

Chapter 22:
A Quiet Escape

Idela (January) 23, 1560
Todd Wellum's Cell, Prison Level, Royal Palace, City of Rammon
The unmistakable sound of the lock disengaging roused Todd Wellum from his peaceful slumber. More than a decade in this hole had taught him to sleep lightly. One could never tell when the locks might suddenly release, allowing the prisoners to roam freely and abuse one another. Todd knew better than most people that changes could happen in a heartbeat. It was always best to be prepared. Kezem's prisons below the Rammon palace were extensive.

Todd rose and dropped into a defensive position ready to defend his meager possessions. The crude comb, a pack of cards, and other trinkets were probably worth less than a few kefs, but they were amenities that eased the painful boredom between carefully regulated exercise sessions. His neck popped, reminding him of the unkind years that had passed.

"What do you want?" he whispered in a tone somewhere between curiosity and hostility.

"I am here to set you free," a young guard announced quietly.

It took a moment for Todd to recognize the newest addition to the prison regiment, a conscript if prison gossip could be trusted. The young man spoke softly and swiftly, but Todd heard every word.

"Your benefactor arranged for a sick form saying you've contracted yellow fever. I'm supposed to give you these and escort you out of the prison." The man slipped a small pouch around Todd's neck. It bulged slightly. "Maybe you should turn it the other way."

Todd nodded and twisted the string so that the pouch hung over his back.

"Do you have bindings?" he asked.

The young man nodded and slipped stuncuffs onto Todd's arms, activating the energy bindings.

"Once we're outside, you're free to go, but you have to attack me first. The infopad has further instructions. Go to the house indicated and wait for the manhunt to end." Saying such, the soldier turned around and strode out of the cell.

Todd followed with a mixture of elation and trepidation that made his head spin, but each step he took toward freedom strengthened his limbs. His initial clumsy steps became more graceful until he glided along behind his escort. Hope of seeing his daughter further spurred him on and his instincts slowly came to life again.

She will be a woman by now.

As they neared the first checkpoint, the young man straightened his shoulders and marched confidently up to the two guards.

Remembering the cover story, Todd stumbled and leaned heavily against the wall, keeping his head bowed so the guard couldn't see his alert eyes.

"This man has yellow fever. I have his quarantine orders here," said his escort, thrusting some papers forward.

"Sure, whatever," said one guard.

"Rookie," muttered the other with disgust.

They were through.

The second checkpoint proved a bit more harrowing.

"Look at me," demanded the gate guard.

Todd lolled his head to the side and rambled something unintelligible.

"He can't understand you, ma'am," Todd's guard explained.

Todd felt the woman's eyes heat the top of his head. He silently prayed to Riden, Kala, and Resh that the explanation would satisfy her.

"Get him out of here," she finally ordered.

"Yes, ma'am."

As he stepped outside, Todd glanced up; the sight froze him in place.

"Beautiful!" he said, referring to the millions of twinkling stars. Some were far off worlds with problems of their own, some were balls of hot gas lending life to those worlds, and others were reflective rocks hurtling toward those worlds bent on destruction, but all possessed a majestic beauty Todd had not seen for untold nights. He smiled up at the three moons, Gemuln, Corid, and Marishaz, each present only in partial glory but adding a gentle glow to the night.

"This is no time to stargaze!" the guard hissed, drawing Todd back to the present situation.

"You're right," Todd replied, prying his eyes away from the night splendor.

They hurried in the direction of the quarantine cells.

The guard stopped suddenly.

"Here's good enough. I'll release the bindings now. How will you incapacitate me?"

"I'll put you in a chokehold. It will be quick and painless," said Todd.

To his surprise, the guard shook his head.

"It's got to leave a mark."

"What's your name?" Todd asked.

"Marksman Cory Tiri—"

Todd swept his hand out and brought it down on the young man's neck. The guard's surprised scream was muffled but loud enough to convince any possible witnesses that an attack had taken place.

"Thank you, Cory," Todd whispered to the fallen soldier. He slipped away from the prison to view his new instructions, anxious to meet his benefactor.

***

Idela (January) 23, 1560
Elena Carpan's Home, Merchant Quarter, City of Rammon

Aware of the late hour, Captain Ethan Tayce slipped into his sister's home, feeling like an intruder. His stomach twisted.

"Ranger Wellum?" he called softly.

A search of the first floor turned up nothing. A thousand thoughts of the plan going wrong flooded his mind as he climbed the stairs to the second floor. Instinctively, he clutched the weapons he had brought for his guest.

"Right here, Captain," Todd said from behind Tayce.

Ethan whipped, pistol coming to bear on the unseen voice. Flicking on a lightbar to banish the oppressive dark, Tayce saw the man who had saved him years ago.

The men regarded each other.

Relief and worry silenced Tayce for several seconds.

Despite the smile, the former prisoner was a shell of a man. The prison rags hung from his lean frame. The regular exercise regime kept him in shape, but poor diet and abysmal sanitary conditions had left their marks. His light brown eyes bore the haunted look of having seen hope rise and die too many times. The small spark found in those eyes could easily be lost or mistaken for insanity.

"I'm glad you made it," Tayce offered awkwardly.

"Thank you. Your aid means more to me than I could ever express or repay," Todd said.

"It is a small thing compared to what I've done in Kezem's name," Tayce said.

"Kezem's will is far reaching," said Todd. "You cannot undo everything but standing against him now should help."

"I wish I could do more for you," Tayce said.

"I will be fine. Return to your post, wherever that may be. I do not wish to know it. Todd assured him. "You have endangered yourself enough on my account. I will return to my Order with all possible speed."

A cautious look crossed Tayce's countenance.

"The Rangers may not be the noble peacekeepers you remember."

"What happened?" Todd demanded.

Tayce motioned for Todd to sit, buying time to choose his words.

"Rangers still inhabit camps in the Riden Mountains, but they have new leaders, including some who condone terrorist activities." He held up a hand to ward off Todd's protests. "Hear me out. The Captain of the Royal Guard gave Kezem access to the throne room then disappeared shortly before the invasion. One of my older brother's first missions was to hunt down the queen's betrayer, but his men lost the fugitive in the Riden Mountains."

"Laocer," Todd breathed the name like a curse. Prison whispers suddenly made sense. "He always regarded Reia strangely."

"You knew the queen?" Tayce asked, clearly shocked.

"She was once a Ranger, a friend, and my wife's younger sister as well," Todd said, chuckling at Tayce's expression. "But please continue. I must know everything."

"A man like Aster Captain Laocer does not simply disappear

forever," Tayce said. Every few months, I hear of him leading a raid or showing up in a village where a bomb explodes. It could be that the captain is long dead and merely a convenient excuse, but that doesn't change the fact that many of the attacks are senseless. It seems the noble Order has sadly declined."

"Your concern is noted and much appreciated, Captain Tayce, but I must seek them out anyway."

A thought occurred to Tayce.

"The Kireshana began a couple of days ago. The Coridian Assassins also train during this time. They will pick off the weaker derringers. I have always detested the practice. Why don't you protect them like the Rangers of old? It will help you hone your skills and give you time to gather information on the new Rangers. If the rumors are unfounded, rejoin them, but if they are true, be cautious."

"Your plan is wise, and I will consider it," Todd promised.

Tayce remembered the weapons meant for the Ranger.

"These items no longer exist as far as the army is concerned," he said, handing Ranger Wellum a serlak pistol, an outdated kerlinblade, a personal communications unit, and a handful of flingers. "The comm links directly to my own, but it's possible for listeners to gain the frequency. Use it when you need me most. I may only be a captain, but I have some useful connections in other branches of the military and government." As an afterthought, he added his own kerlak pistol to the pile.

"I couldn't take that," Todd protested.

"You will need every advantage possible," Tayce said. "Now go, I will return to my post and look for more ways to help your cause."

"Then it is your cause, too."

"Yes, but I have little time to devote to it," said Tayce. "I'm concerned for Princess Rela's safety."

"Do what you can, and I shall do what I can. Riden willing, we will meet again, Captain."

The men shook hands. Then, Tayce supplied Todd with a tent, bedroll, blanket, some kefs, and food enough to see him on his way.

As dawn lightened the streets, Tayce watched the Ranger slip into the early morning shadows.

Chapter 23:
Huz Mon Salt Mines

Idela (January) 19, 1560-Lanolin (February) 21, 1560
Kireshana Path, Calsol Forest to the Huz Mon Salt Mines

Kayleen pondered Teven's tale of someone watching them. They broke camp and continued their trek. Late afternoon, they stumbled across the body of a young derringer. A deep gash in his chest marked a blade's trail. It struck her heart to see a child so violently dead.

"We should bury him," she whispered.

It took them several hours to burn the body and bury the ashes. The young derringer's traveling companions had stripped his body of supplies except the clothes he wore and the small derringer dagger. Kayleen watched Teven finger the handsome blade handle. After laying one final handful of dirt over the remains, he reverently placed the dagger over the grave.

The small group was exceptionally quiet that night. It is one thing to know danger exists around every tree and quite another to touch flesh recently rendered lifeless. Kayleen had seen bodies before, even ones that met violent ends, but this was different. Those bodies had been carefully prepared by someone else. This time, she had prepared the body, touched fire to the sticks beneath it, and helped dig the small hole for the ashes.

The encounter did much to dispel Kayleen's remaining romantic notions about the Kireshana. As the days slipped by, she too became aware of the watcher. Sometimes she would feel malevolent eyes but then the sensation would fade and calm would take its place.

Kayleen's seventeenth birthday on Lanolin (February) 3, 1560 dawned bright and clear. Teven surprised her by giving her a simple necklace made with sturdy wistril weed wound through the tiny carved figure of an astera flower.

Upon reaching Calsola several weeks later, Teven and Kayleen watched Jal skillfully barter with the horse master. Finally, the grumpy old man rented them three horses for five hundred kefs. One hundred was paid up front and the other four hundred would be worked off in the Huz Mon salt mines. The Riden Flats flew past in seven days. Kayleen was pleased with their progress. On foot, the same journey could have taken a month.

Conditions in the mines were horrendous. Kayleen worked hard to control her rising anger at the poor treatment of the workers. The outrage burned hotter still, knowing she was powerless to change things. They steadily scraped salt off the mine walls for five days. To gather their quota faster, Teven and Kayleen climbed the rock walls to reach untouched salt reserves.

Word spread and soon the mine master dragged his corpulent self down to where they worked.

"Fine work! Fine work! And who might you young ones be?" he asked.

"Teven McKnight, Kayleen Wellum, and Jal Seltan," Teven said succinctly. A small tick above his left eye betrayed deep irritation.

Kayleen silently willed him to hold his temper. She swiftly descended and stood by his side, resisting the urge to physically hold him back.

"I am the master of this humble mine, Gavrie Jeriton, and I hope I can convince you to stay on. There's good money to be made."

"I'm afraid that is impossible, sir," Kayleen said.

"Your debt is almost paid off, but I could offer you four hundred more for half a week's work," Gavrie said a bit too eagerly. His shifting eyes declared him a liar. If they agreed, they would never leave the salt mine.

Reading the thought process happening inside his thick skull, Kayleen removed the heavy salt pouch from around her neck and thrust it at him. "That should settle our account, Master Jeriton," she said in a frosty tone.

Panic entered the man's black eyes.

"But see how much good you can do? These poor workers could use the break."

"Then give them one," said Teven.

Gavrie had them on his playing field now and Kayleen knew it. Her dislike for the man increased tenfold.

"We all do what we can, young sir, but there are quotas to meet," said Gavrie.

His cold attitude grated on Kayleen's nerves. She briefly considered offering their services in exchange for a day of rest for the workers. It would be a small price to pay if they could momentarily ease the despair. The idea came and went in a flash, as Gavrie opened his cavernous mouth again.

"I find you too valuable to let go," Gavrie said apologetically. His massive hand clamped around Kayleen's right forearm.

"That was dumb," noted Teven.

Gavrie apparently didn't hear him.

"Why don't you two gentlemen get a couple of pouches and gather some of that precious salt? Your lady friend and I will wait for you in my office."

As soon as Kayleen felt the slightest tug, she threw her arms into Gavrie's ample gut, eliciting a rush of foul breath. She would have choked, but the smell vanished almost as soon as it began. Kayleen grabbed her assailant's right hand and bent the fingers back until she felt them about to snap.

Meanwhile, Teven's arm swept out and pressed Gavrie's sweaty neck against the wall. It pleased Kayleen to see Teven could hit hard when it counted. Jal stood out of the way.

"First of all, Jal doesn't climb mine shafts," Teven began. "Second, never threaten a lady or a derringer and especially not a lady who *is* a derringer. Third, learn some manners. Our debt is paid so we will take our leave now. Do *not* follow us." A bit more pressure caused Gavrie to gurgle and fall unconscious. Teven let him slip down the wall, looking entirely too pleased with himself.

Uncomfortably aware of the audience forming around them, Kayleen started toward the exit. A desperate voice stopped her cold.

"Take us with you!" called a young female voice.

Turning, Kayleen saw a girl with skin a few shades darker than her own pale complexion.

The child's expressive blue eyes pleaded her case.

"I am Jenell, and this is Karric," said the girl, gesturing to a stout youth at her side.

"We're derringers, too," the boy insisted. "Take us with you. We can help," he offered. His dark face made his white, toothy smile that much more brilliant. "We got here a few days ago. We had enough kefs to pay off our debt yesterday, but Gavrie wouldn't let us go."

"We were afraid to fight him," Jenell admitted.

"Come on then," Teven said.

"Me too!" shouted a boy. "I've got to get out of here!"

"We can't take everyone," Kayleen said. More shouts and requests followed as they fled up the tunnel to the surface. Kayleen figured anyone bold enough to follow deserved to come. She would not encourage it, but she didn't have the heart to turn anyone away either. As surely as she knew her own feelings, she knew Teven felt the same way.

"We should not make a habit of this," Jal commented, jogging along beside Kayleen.

"Which part? The fleeing for our lives or picking up strangers?" Kayleen fired the questions and stole a glance over her shoulder at the three mine urchins they had acquired. They grabbed their packs, and then, ran for four kilometers without stopping. Slightly winded, Kayleen took a good look at their younger companions who gasped for breath. "Tev, hold up a minute, or we're going to lose our new friends!"

Teven stopped running, looking none too pleased with the delay.

"Can we ditch them in Huz Mon?" he asked.

"Not likely," said Kayleen. "They'll just end up back in the salt mines or worse."

"I don't like taking responsibility for them," Teven complained.

"Oh, a fine, princely attitude that is," Kayleen teased, trying to lighten the grim mood. "I don't like it either, but they're safer with us than without. No one ever said right things were nice things."

They whispered so the others, who stood a respectful distance away, would not be able to hear.

Just then, Jal and the last salt mine clinger arrived.

"This, my fleet-footed friends, is Quasim. He has quite a tale to tell," said Jal.

"I want to go home," Quasim declared, holding his chin high and pressing his trembling lips together. He looked no more than seven years old. "My family lives in Ritand. Bad men stole me and sold me to the soldiers in Fort Riden. A Ranger bought me."

Kayleen's mouth gaped. As far as she knew, the Ranger policy stood firmly against slavery.

Hiding his shock better than Kayleen, Teven shot her a look that said they should hear Quasim out before responding.

"The Ranger sold me to Master Jeriton," said the boy.

"What did this Ranger look like?" Kayleen asked, dreading the answer.

"He was sort of tall with dark brown hair, dark eyes, and skin a little lighter than his," said the boy, pointing to Karric. "I don't know much more. He didn't speak much."

Kayleen suppressed a groan.

Lots of men answer that description.

Teven looked like he wanted to continue the conversation, but Kayleen didn't want to pursue the thought any further.

"We should continue," she said. To Quasim, she added, "We'll take you to Resh at least. That's not far from Ritand."

No one argued with her. The weather darkened to match their mood. Each trudged on lost in thought. The torrential downpours of acid rain stuck to a regular pattern, but one could never quite predict Reshner. Surprise storms were also common.

"We need to hurry," Jal urged, spurring the group forward.

Hurry to where? Kayleen thought, quickening her steps. The wind caught her travel cloak and slammed her to a halt.

"Get the tents out!" Teven ordered. He threw his rain cloak over Quasim's shoulders. "Stay down!"

"What about you?" the boy shouted.

Kayleen didn't hear him but read the message on his lips. She whipped off her travel cloak and draped it over Quasim's head. Then, she ran to help Teven unpack the tents. They couldn't set up the tent beams for fear the wind would turn the poles into skewers, but the hardy fabric would protect them. Once the rain hit the ground, the dirt would neutralize the acid, but if it landed directly on skin it would feel like a million ravenous **voracerflies** having a feast. She futilely wished the younger derringers had their equipment packs. There had been no time to retrieve them during the hasty retreat from the salt mines.

Teven's tent was thrown over the two derringers. Next, Kayleen's tent was opened. Before they could get under its protection, the gray skies loosed their arsenal. They dove under the cover but not before getting soaked. Kayleen groaned and leaned over to Teven.

"We're going to have to explain this!" she shouted.

He shrugged, settled onto the quickly soaking ground, and motioned for her to join him.

Hoping Jal had Quasim safely tucked under the third tent, Kayleen sat down next to Teven and rested her head on his shoulder. His left arm wrapped protectively around her. Content to listen to the rain pound on the tent, she didn't speak. Teven was a little soggy but comfortable.

I could get used to this.

The hectic day slowly faded from mind. Kayleen let her thoughts wander to the trials ahead. The first pass through the Riden Mountains would begin in a day or two followed closely by stops in Resh and Fort Riden where most derringers earned kefs doing odd jobs. Then, they would scale Mount Palean.

"We'll make it," Teven said, surprising Kayleen. The rain had slowed to a gentle flow, allowing them to speak. "The anotechs said you were agitated," he explained. "It doesn't take much to read into 'agitated' on the Kireshana."

"I suppose not. How are we even going to find a zalok queen, let alone get close enough to take a souvenir?" Kayleen asked.

"You're the Ranger; you figure it out," he teased.

"Most Rangers have enough sense to avoid zaloks they aren't assigned to protect," she shot back.

"Well, derringers don't, so we'll find out soon enough," said Teven.

When the rain ceased, they continued their hike toward the mountains. Many hours later, they finally set the tents up properly and prepared to spend the night. It was a little tight, but Kayleen shared her tent with Jenell and Teven squeezed in with Jal, having surrendered his tent to Quasim and Karric.

We'll need to pick up more supplies when we get to Resh.

Chapter 24: Lair of the Zalok Queen

Lanolin (February) 23, 1560-Jira (March) 14, 1560
Entrance to Zalok Cave, Northern Riden Mountains

Staring down the gaping, teeth-lined mouth of a four-and-a-half-meter-long young zalok, Teven McKnight almost wished he hadn't known exactly where to find the beasts. After two uneventful days of travel, it was time things got interesting again. He just wished there was such a thing as interesting without involving death.

"Watch the tail!" Quasim cried, staying well behind Teven and Kayleen.

Teven was grateful that Jal had a firm grip on the boy's shoulder.

"Do you have a plan?" Kayleen asked tersely. Her kerlinblade was raised in a guarded position that would do very little if the zalok's swinging tail connected with her.

"Not getting smacked with that spiked tail," Teven replied.

The young zalok reared back on its hind legs and loosed a shriek that cut through Teven, rattling his bones.

"And shutting that thing up."

"A serlak rifle would come in handy right about now," Kayleen said wistfully. She danced away as the flailing tail came her way.

"How's your aim?" Teven inquired

"What am I shooting at?"

"The zalok's left eye," Teven responded. "It's got a heat sensor right above it. An energy blast there should blind it long enough to let us slip past." As he had no intention of further involving Kayleen, so by *us* he really meant *me*. If he died in the cave beyond somebody had to live to see the younger derringers through the rest of the Kireshana.

"Should?" Kayleen's voice was incredulous, but she traded her blade for their only energy pistol, an ancient-looking thing that hadn't been worth the scrap metal it was made of until Jal's technical genius and a fresh energy pack breathed new life into it. It took Kayleen three shots to hit the eye sensor, a fact the zalok did not appreciate. Louder, longer shrieks came from the depths of the massive creature. Its black bulky body shivered with pain and rage. The tail swung faster and harder. "Go!"

Teven scrambled under the creature's legs and into the short tunnel that led to the zalok queen's lair. The tunnel was plenty wide for him but would be a tight squeeze for a zalok. The anotechs had been right so far. It didn't take him long to find the queen. Slightly larger than the zalok Kayleen had temporarily blinded, the queen had a black, leathery face, a back covered by row after row of purple scales, and a broad powerful tail. Teven paused to consider how to extract the prize. He had no desire to kill the beautiful creature.

"Let me talk to her," Kayleen suggested.

"What are you doing here? Who's going to let us out of here?" His heart beat faster. He didn't like her being so near to danger, a ridiculous notion considering their mission.

"Relax, Jal has the pistol," said Kayleen, holding out her empty hands as proof. "Besides, the anotechs say the warrior zalok should be disoriented for another twenty minutes or so."

"Just stay back," said Teven. "If you fail, she's going to brain you with that tail."

"Thanks for the vote of confidence," said Kayleen.

Teven crept to the left wall and waited. His movements gave him a good look at Kayleen who, to his horror, sat cross-legged right in front of the zalok queen. The creature eyed Kayleen carefully then suddenly snapped her head in Teven's direction.

"Kayleen, what are you telling her?" asked Teven, feeling the full weight of the queen's stare.

"He does not intend you harm. We seek scales to give to our masters," Kayleen explained to the zalok. She fell silent, but the expression of fierce concentration said the communication continued.

She's crazy.

Several long minutes later, Kayleen climbed to her feet and bowed to the zalok.

"Thank you. With your permission, we would like to collect more scales than we need so we can leave some for the many others who come behind. Then, they will have no reason to disturb you."

Teven shifted his concentration to the zalok. He sensed her reluctant approval. The zalok settled to the ground and tucked all six legs beneath her large body. He approached cautiously.

"Hurry, Teven, she has eggs to lay and young to feed," Kayleen said.

Teven shook his head in bewilderment but did as requested. Four swift steps brought him close enough to touch the zalok. He hesitated. Warmth radiated from her body.

"Take as many as you can carry but not all from the same spot, and she requests that we seal the entrance when we leave."

"Don't they need to get out?" Teven asked. He carefully began pulling scales from the creature's body. The scales pulled off easily with muffled pops. Teven selected an even distribution of deep purple scales and slipped them into a soft pouch at his waist.

"The half-year hibernation approaches," Kayleen explained. "Besides, zalok claws are especially well-suited for carving through rock. Whatever barrier we can erect won't be a problem for them."

Ten minutes later, Teven and Kayleen stepped back into the fresh mountain air. A sharp bark from the queen's cave caused Teven to jump. The zalok warrior they had wounded to gain entry glared balefully at them but made no move to harm them. More barks followed and the young zalok trundled toward the opening.

"How are we going to seal that?" Teven wondered.

"With a charm," Kayleen said.

"What charm? You don't know any charms."

"They don't know that," she murmured with a grin. "We're going to sacrifice a tent, and you're going to write about the horrible death that awaits those who enter the cave unbidden."

Teven grunted but understood the direction of her thoughts.

"Why am I doing the writing?" Teven didn't really mind; he just wanted to argue with her.

"Because you have such pretty handwriting," Kayleen answered. "Besides, this is my brainchild so you get to do the grunt work." The silly grin came back, making her appear younger than her seventeen years. She unpacked her tent, and together, they attacked it with their daggers.

"What are you doing?" asked Quasim, voicing the question

written in every eye.

The corner of Jal's mouth twitched up. No doubt the anotechs were telling Jal quite a tale.

"Placing a curse on this cave," Teven replied.

"A curse," Quasim repeated. Doubt filled the two words.

"Help or stand aside," Kayleen said.

"Stand aside," Teven amended. "In fact, go get some stones to make a container."

Quasim, Karric, Jal, and Jenell gathered small stones and fashioned a small container out of them. By the time they had finished, Teven and Kayleen had the tent cut in roughly the right shape with several strips and poles to use as anchors. The broadest, cleanest side was placed face up on the ground. Teven ground up some soft rocks and a few purple scales. Then, he added water to make a paste and wrote his message.

Death beyond to the mortal who dares breach this portal.

"Lovely," Kayleen commented. "Please don't become a poet."

"Is it that dangerous in there?" Jenell wondered. Her crystal-blue eyes widened, and her chin length black hair framed her face, despite the mountain breeze.

"How are we going to get our scales?" Karric demanded, scratching his short, dark, fuzzy head hair.

"I have enough for all of us," Teven said, removing the pouch from his belt and dumping the contents into the stone box. "Take whichever one you want. We're going to need a few more stones to make this a little higher. I don't want the wind to catch any of the scales." He reached in and selected a scale for himself and Kayleen.

"Thanks," Kayleen said, tucking the purple scale into a pouch on her belt.

Teven put his scale back into the bag he had upended and refastened the pouch to his waist. His knees cracked as he stood.

"You'll sleep well tonight," said Kayleen.

"Are we camping here?" Quasim wondered.

"That would be wise," Jal said. "Night will fall within the hour. We have the favor of this zalok queen, but the others may not be so kind to strangers. We will need to seek shelter in the cave if rain comes."

Teven shot Jal a warning look, catching Quasim and the others looking curiously at him. Jal shrugged as if to say that at this point the charade hardly mattered. Teven wasn't so sure but said nothing.

Quasim and Kayleen wandered off to forage for mountain herbs. Jenell and Karric tackled the task of making one big tent out of the two remaining ones. Jal built and attended a small fire. Teven perfected the stone box, shoring up the sides with more layers. He also put several slits in the tent blocking the cave so fresh air could enter and fierce winds could blow through without ripping the cover away.

The herb-seeking expedition yielded a bit of mintas, corlia, and yelcha to add to the three ration packs they could afford to use for the evening meal. They still had a week or two of mountains to traverse and another two weeks or so to Resh. Teven reasoned there must be a small village or farmhouse along the way where they could seek aid, but conserving food was still necessary.

The evening passed pleasantly. Kayleen sang an old ballad about Kolpec Rinn, a Ranger who fell in love with the daughter of a sea captain. Not approving of Ranger Rinn, the girl's father took her with him as he sailed on the North Asrien Sea. Kolpec swam twenty-one days through icy waters until he caught the ship. His devotion won the hearts of father and daughter, but Ranger Rinn died the next day from an illness brought on by the Asrien Sea. The distraught woman vanished into the air the same night her lover died. Although she was never seen again, it is said twenty-one stars were born that night.

Jenell and Karric shared a local dance from their small village of Kerimia. Jal weaved several tales of adventure on far-off planets. Though Teven had never heard of any of the planets, he detected a ring of truth to the tales. Quasim described how to properly gut a gully fish to avoid the poison glands. He explained that bones became utensils, poison was sold, normal oil became fuel, and most other parts became food. No part went to waste. Teven showed off a few of the minor anotechs powers under the guise of silly magic tricks. He stacked rocks, made his skin light up from within, and created a small dust devil.

The six travelers squeezed into the makeshift double tent to sleep.

They rose when the sun's first rays shined over the mountains to the east. The morning and afternoon hikes went smoothly. Kayleen shot a cannafitch to supplement their supplies. The tough meat was bland but provided a passable midday meal. The evening meal once again came from ration packs and random herbs.

The days slipped by much the same: eat, walk, eat, and walk some more. With the slightly larger group, they could only travel as fast as the slowest member, Quasim. Teven didn't mind much, until supplies dropped to a dangerously low level. On the other hand, his feet had ceased to ache, and his lungs again adjusted to the thin mountain air.

Despite still feeling someone watching them, Teven began to enjoy the Kireshana. Since they had come across very few dangerous predators, Teven concluded the watcher must be friendly.

Occasionally, they stumbled across a korver or panther shot cleanly through the neck, no doubt gifts from their mysterious protector. They had one close encounter with a small korver clan but escaped without a fight. The bloodlust and excitement in the korver shrieks fascinated Teven as much as his first encounter with them so many years ago.

Nine days after collecting the scales from the zalok queen, Teven led his small band down the last mountain onto the Resh Grasslands.

"We'll reach Resh in a couple of weeks. Perhaps someone there will be able to escort you home, Quasim."

"I don't want to go home," Quasim stated.

Teven said no more but spent the rest of the afternoon thinking of ways to convince Quasim to stay in Resh. The frail boy had held his own on the trip through the Riden Mountains, but Teven had enough to worry about protecting Karric and Jenell. Jal and Kayleen could defend themselves, but he still felt responsible for them.

"We'll figure something out," Kayleen said.

Teven felt better knowing that someone understood him. Jal did most of the corralling and prodding of the younger derringers and Quasim. The length of the Kireshana wore on Karric and Jenell. Nevertheless, Teven and Kayleen pushed the group to keep a steady pace. The longer they stayed out on Resh Grasslands, the more time they would spend vulnerable to Coridian Assassins. They had no idea how many assassins roamed, but a bone here and a body there kept the sense of danger powerful.

Chapter 25:
Priest's Good News

Lanolin (February) 27, 1560
Laocer's Safe House, City of Ritten

Ectosh Laocer had spent many hours coaching Benali in Azhel priest mannerisms. The actor knew the script solidly. A few wrong gestures might be lost on Lord Kezem, but too many mistakes would lead to failure.

As Captain of the Royal Guard, Laocer had been to Loresh several times, but only royalty were allowed into certain sections.

Such secrecy must hide treasure!

If Lord Kezem could be lured to Loresh, Laocer would kill him and force the princess to open the forbidden chambers, winning both the treasure and the throne. The legends were ambiguous about what age the royal must be to open the chamber, but even if the princess was too young, Laocer could still send for Teven. Terosh and Reia's eldest child was sixteen now and legally considered a man.

Timing was crucial. Laocer had paid his mercenaries only a quarter of the amount promised, relying on Loresh's treasures to make up the difference. They would go to Loresh according to a very specific timetable, but if Benali messed up, the timetable would burn.

Deep worry lines covered Laocer's face, as he paced the small dwelling. He had lived here ever since betraying the main Ranger compound several months back. Most Rangers had escaped, but hopefully, they would be too distracted to care much when he launched his bid for the throne. He hated depending so much upon others, but he needed the mercenaries. The strain of passing years had begun to tell on his body, showing up mostly in his dark expression.

Laocer threw himself into a series of training moves, imagining his opponent was Lord Kezem. The sweet sensation of approaching revenge made his movements frantic. The wooden dummy shuddered under several devastating blows. By the time Laocer had finished, the dummy's head hung sadly to the side and one arm lay on the floor. Laocer silently swore that one day Kezem would resemble the broken dummy.

***

Lanolin (February) 27, 1560
Streets of Rammon to Royal Palace, City of Rammon

Benali practiced his lines and priestly gestures during the hov ride from his employer's safe house to Rammon. It had been no small feat to gain a pass into the palace, but even Lord Kezem was loath to snub an Azhel priest.

Benali had only been to Rammon twice, but he noticed the difference in the atmosphere. Part of him missed the majesty and beauty of the old Rammon. While the old city had many buildings with beautiful, rounded architecture, this new Rammon boasted block after block of ugly, square, gray monstrosities.

There had always been poor people walking about in drab clothes, but they had always been balanced by a sea of bright colors representing the middle and upper classes. What Benali saw today definitely favored somber tones, except where the dark red uniforms of army soldiers dominated. The soldiers roamed the streets at will, collecting protection fees and generally causing more trouble than they prevented.

Benali instructed his driver to go near the Merchant Quarter. Maybe his mind was being selective, but he could clearly recall the beaming faces of children and merchants from the old Rammon. Today, the market hummed with activity, but a desperate air hung over the crowd. The shouts sounded angrier and the bartering sounded cutthroat.

"My heart aches for these lost souls," Benali said, trying to stay in character.

The driver laughed; it was not a pleasant sound.

Benali had the driver stop three blocks from the palace so he could jog the rest and appear suitably exhausted. The strictest Azhel priests abhor technology. Benali personally thought the belief ridiculous, but he didn't have to agree with the cult, just pass for one of the wackos. Rounding the final corner before the block leading to the palace, Benali slowed to a walk. Although slightly late for his noon appointment with Lord Kezem, Benali wasn't worried. Such would be expected of a man who had supposedly crossed the Kala River, climbed the Ash Mountains, ridden many days on horseback, and walked the length of Rammon. He grew tired thinking of the trip.

The Royal Guards at the palace gates waved Benali by with hardly a glance at his pass, which was good because he could barely breathe let alone talk to them.

Must exercise more.

He wandered down several wrong passages before asking a servant girl for directions to the throne room. He figured a servant would be the least dangerous person to ask. She gave him a strange look but kindly pointed him in the right direction.

On the way up to the fifth-floor throne room, Benali passed statue after statue bearing Lord Kezem's likeness. He snorted with disgust. Noticing several guards lining the walls, Benali turned the snort into a hacking cough. Now approaching eyes and ears that mattered, he began his routine of priestly movements, waving his arms about slowly and muttering blessings.

The stoic throne room guards were a bit more cautious than the other guards. They stopped him and studied his pass carefully while an automatic sensor scanned him for weapons. Once he was cleared, they signaled someone inside who disengaged the dozen locks keeping the throne room door shut.

Someone's a bit paranoid.

The heavy doors swung slowly inward powered by two identical young men throwing their whole bodies into the task.

Lord Kezem sat perched on Reshner's throne, staring down his nose at Benali.

Been practicing the look, have we?

The expression made Kezem appear simultaneously powerful, important, and omnipotent.

And idiotic.

Benali approached with a careful limp and briefly nodded. Azhel high priests did not fully bow to any man, even the planetary ruler.

"Greetings, Lord Kezem, keeper of Riden's flock," Benali said, being mindful to move his mouth slowly. He kept his tone wavy and inserted convincing cracks here and there to keep Kezem concentrating on the voice instead of the actor.

"State your business," Kezem snapped. "I haven't the time or patience for word games."

"Reshner's three moons align with the Lady's favor four months hence. Riden's consort, the goddess Zaria, knows you seek her treasures deep in Loresh but takes pity on your mortal soul. In exactly four months, take the young princess there, and she will unlock the hidden chambers."

With his heart trying to escape his chest, Benali struggled to keep his voice slow and grave. Kezem's expression was hard to read, but Benali saw a gleam at the mention of Loresh. He wasn't quite sure where he stood with regards to the ancient tale, but obviously, two very powerful and ambitious men believed it to be true.

"Why do you not seek the treasures yourself and donate the money to the poor?"

Benali knew he was being mocked. For someone who claimed to not like word games, Kezem did a fine job of throwing words around. Benali clamped down on an un-priest-like retort.

"The servants of the gods merely worship and deliver messages, Favored One. I was bid to tell you what I have; my part is finished." At this point, Benali figured less was more.

Lord Kezem would form his own plans, which were hopefully in line with Benali's employer.

"And what if I command you to tell me again?" Kezem challenged. He spoke with the cool confidence of a man used to getting his way.

Benali grew tired of Kezem's pettiness, but he let none of his impatience reach his expression.

"Then, I would repeat myself, Favored One," he answered with all the graciousness he could muster. "In four months, Princess Rela of House Minstel will be able to unlock the secret halls of Loresh."

"How will she find the door or doors to unlock?"

"The gods know all, but they do not always tell mortals every secret, Favored One." Benali enjoyed placing the imaginary ball back on Kezem's side of the playing field.

"Is her presence enough or are the rumors true, will the gods require her blood at Loresh's hidden gates?" Kezem asked the question with a straight face, but Benali knew he must be quaking at the thought of having to hurt Princess Rela. More specifically, Kezem feared the pain he might have to endure to reach the treasure. It was common knowledge that Queen Reia had somehow linked her daughter's life to Lord Kezem.

Benali thought very carefully about his answer. Upsetting Lord Kezem would not be wise, but not encouraging him enough would also be bad.

"Sacrifice may be required, but with the Lady's favor, the power of the moons should augment any power the princess lacks. Assuming, of course, she is willing to help."

"What do you mean by *willing*?" Kezem demanded.

How should I know? I just made that up!

"If the princess does not wish to find the secrets, the treasure will not call to her," said Benali, struggling to keep his voice steady. "Without the call, her steps could forever wander Loresh." Benali knew he was rambling, so he consciously stopped talking.

One look at Lord Kezem convinced him he had succeeded in his mission. Then, everything went wrong.

"Thank you for your time, Father Benali. You have been very helpful. In fact, I'm going to invite you to stay with us until we see your vision come true."

Kezem's tone was benevolent, but Benali sensed two Royal Guards flanking him.

"Jorg and Makil will escort you to your quarters," said Kezem.

Benali's head spun. He nodded dumbly as the Royal Guards led him from the throne room. He ran the conversation over and over in his head. Not once had he messed up. Every inflection and word had been perfect. Then, it hit him; he'd been too good. Never, in all his life, had a flawless performance been a negative thing. He had no choice but to continue with the charade. Worse still, Azhel priests shun strong drinks, so he couldn't even drown his misery in a tall tankard of ale.

***

Lord Kezem slumped on the throne, rubbing his temple with both hands. The priest's words about Rela's willingness to find the secret chambers disturbed him. He had ways to make her willing, but it would be difficult. The child had an exasperating stubbornness about her.

Probably from her mother.

Equally disturbing was the part about wandering Loresh forever and never finding anything, for it had proven true so far. His men had been up and down Loresh's tunnels hundreds of times to no avail.

Rela was his key to the treasure. He grew more certain of this every day. He had been nothing but benevolent toward her for years, yet she snuck around behind his back trying to aid dissident fools! Fine gratitude indeed. It was high time she started paying back the debt she owed him. Leading him to the treasure would be a good start.

Chapter 26:
Princess Rela's Near Escape

Lanolin (February) 29, 1560
Princess Rela's Private Chambers, Royal Palace, City of Rammon

Life for Princess Rela Minstel was not unduly hard, but her frustration at being confined to the palace grew as the years passed. She only ever felt real pain during the annual ritual of letting that fool, Merek, slice her left arm with a dagger, but she gradually became aware of Lord Kezem's crueler side. She spent much time studying history and politics, practicing shooting, exploring the palace, and aiding marked people. For a while, she had Sarie Verituse and her friends to tell her how the commoners fared.

Oppression and corruption ruled, and she was powerless to stop it. Lorian Petole and Anabel and Marc Spitzer went to train in the Kireshana, leaving only a bitter Nicholas Riggs behind. The instructors said Nicholas wasn't ready for the Kireshana, but Rela knew the truth had more to do with his mother's wishes than his readiness. Since having him deliver the infopad to Captain Tayce, Rela had sent Nicholas on a few errands, but she couldn't really confide in him. Still, she knew enough to suspect Nicholas would be in danger if he stayed after helping her escape.

Several years back, Rela realized she barely had two kefs to her name. It had started with Lorian selling some trinkets they had found in storage rooms and morphed into a tidy network of business contacts and private trade deals. Slowly, the pile of kefs grew. The money meant little to her except that it would pay off some corrupt guards.

After agonizing over where to flee, Rela chose Idonia because her favorite geography tutor, Dasel, had described it as the place where the richest land met the matchless beauty of the South Asrien Sea. In truth, Rela wished to visit every part of Reshner, even the Felmon Desert and the Frozen North, but she would go to Idonia first.

"Princess? Are you in there?" called Nicholas.

She hesitated then remembered she had sent him on an errand. Rushing to the door, she threw it open.

Nicholas stepped past her holding a tightly wrapped bundle.

"Thank you, Nicholas, set it on the chair over there. Did you get everything?"

"Are you still going through with this crazy scheme?" asked Nicholas.

"We've been through this," Rela said with infinite patience. "I can't spend the rest of my life trapped in—"

"A palace," Nicholas interrupted. "You're in a palace, Princess. Half the planet's crammed into community housing and you're complaining about being trapped!" He threw her package onto the chair with disgust, a flush breaking out over his pale cheeks. His servant's robes had a few dirt smudges from his recent errand.

Rela marveled at how much Nicholas had matured in the last few months. Part of her knew he had a point, but it didn't change her mind. Feeling very weary, she sank onto the edge of a fancy chair and sighed.

"I'm sorry, Nicholas. I wish I could do more for the people, but I must escape. I have to break this link to Lord Kezem, and I cannot learn how to do that from here."

"I know," said Nicholas. "That's why I'm helping you. It'll probably be the death of me."

His joke fell flat, hitting solidly upon her fears.

"Don't say that!" Rela cried. "That's why you have to come with me."

"I can't. Lord Kezem will never let me be a Royal Guard if I run away," said Nicholas.

"Forget the Royal Guard. This is your life we're talking about!"

"No," Nicholas said, dragging the word out. "We're talking about your plan to leave the nicest place on this planet."

Rela snorted and wondered how dense her friend could be.

"Lord Kezem can't harm me, but he has placed good people around me so I'd remember how much I have to lose." Rela had never realized how much she cared for Nicholas.

"What could Lord Kezem possibly want with you?" asked Nicholas.

"I have heard my family has special powers, but those who tell me that already know more than I do," Rela said with a self-deprecating grin. She thought of her mother. Several dreams had brought messages of encouragement and love, but so far, none had explained what Rela could do for Kezem. Perhaps she was only alive because of the curse linking her to the man. Sarie used to speak of the Ralose Charm as a blessing, but after hearing Lord Kezem refer to it as a curse, Rela had come to consider it a curse as well.

"I've heard only royals can unlock the secrets of Loresh." Nicholas said, surprising Rela. "But it's just a fable. No one in their right mind believes the story."

"What story?" Rela demanded, wondering why Sarie and her tutors had never mentioned Loresh. "Tell me."

"As you wish," said Nicholas. "Loresh is a series of caves in the Frozen North, southeast of Estra. The legend says that the first cave system has an enchanted door to another series of caves. Supposedly, only members of House Minstel can unlock the door and reach the treasures beyond."

"What treasures?" Rela wondered.

"No one knows," Nicholas answered, making his voice extra mysterious. "Some say room after room of gold and gems, but I doubt that's true. House Minstel would never have fallen if it possessed that kind of wealth."

"Why do you say that?" asked Rela.

"If even half of what the legends say is true about the Loresh treasures your parents could have surrounded the palace with a wall of mercenaries for fifty years!"

"They wouldn't do that," Rela argued, shaking her head. "Besides, it's pointless to speculate about what they should have done. What I *am* going to do is get out of here, and you're going to help me."

Nicholas bowed deeply.

"Yes, Princess, I will help. I have paid the guard half of his fee, and the rest is still in the pouch. In one hour, you will be walking the filthy streets of Rammon in glorious freedom."

"You're coming too, remember?" Rela's sharp blue eyes dared him to disagree.

"No one is leaving," said a chilling voice from doorway.

Both youths gasped. Rela glanced at Nicholas and knew some

of his surprise was feigned. Her heart stopped beating, and her breath caught in her throat. Her thoughts slowed. Rela could only stare at Lord Kezem with dumbfounded horror.

"Greetings, Lord Kezem." Nicholas bowed from the waist.

"You are lucky to have such good friends, Princess," said Lord Kezem, ignoring the boy.

"Am I?" Rela whispered, tasting the bitter betrayal. She sucked in sharply, trying to hold back frustrated tears.

Princesses never let people see them cry!

"I see you've been busy," Lord Kezem commented, waving at the bundle on the chair. He strode up to her, flanked by a dozen Royal Guards in splendid dark blue uniforms.

Her spacious front room suddenly felt crowded.

Kezem's hand shot out and caught her neck, spilling the tears that had formed. His hand tightened enough to make breathing difficult.

"My Lord, the Ralose Charm!" cried Nicholas.

Rela couldn't tell if the warning was meant to protect her or Kezem. The hand at her throat loosened. Her hands hung at her sides, rendered useless as much by emotion as physical predicament.

"I will deal with you later, Lieutenant. Get in uniform and go arrest that greedy fool," Kezem ordered. "You're on watch tonight."

The mention of Nicholas's new rank shot anger through Rela and gave her back her voice. She twisted her head enough to look at her former friend.

"Congratulations on your commission, Lieutenant Riggs." Rela squeezed each word through clenched teeth.

Avoiding her piercing gaze, Nicholas hastily exited the room.

"The sooner you understand you cannot escape, the sooner your life will be easier, Princess," Kezem lectured, releasing her. "You may think you hate the boy, but his life is still in your hands, as are the lives of those on the Kireshana. Since you cannot be trusted to behave, I am assigning some Melian Maidens to watch over you."

Rela stared at the doorway, wishing the floor would swallow her and end the misery. Silent tears continued falling as she listened to Kezem. With effort, she choked down sobs.

"What do you want from me?" she asked at last.

"You will know when I wish it so," replied Kezem. "Until then, consider my words concerning your friends." He left the threat hanging in the air and marched out with the Royal Guards on his heels.

Rela collapsed onto the plush carpet and sobbed, letting her emotions run their course. After several minutes, she calmed down enough to notice the others. A woman knelt in front of Rela, flanked by five more spread in a semi-circle at her back. Rela sat up and wiped away the tears.

"We are the Melian Maidens assigned to protect you, Princess," spoke the woman closest to Rela. She had a pleasant face with smooth features and a lithe body that spoke equally of grace and strength. Her voice calmed Rela's frazzled nerves. "I am Kia Meetcher. With me are Linnea Price, Jola Westin, Clara Argnon, Elia Koffrin, and Nalana Vastel. Lord Kezem bids us watch you constantly, but you have nothing to fear from us."

Rela regarded each woman carefully. The leader appeared to be in her mid-twenties, and the others looked in their late teens or early twenties.

"Can you teach me to fight?" asked Rela.

A flicker of amusement crossed the head maiden's face.

"You wish to challenge him one day," she stated.

Rela nodded.

"The charm works both ways," Kia gently reminded her. "If you harm him, you will feel the pain you cause, and his ability to sense your injuries will make practice difficult."

"Lord Kezem has trained for years and sustained many injuries I have shared," Rela argued. "It's time I returned the favor."

"Hand-to-hand combat should be fine, but we're going to have to be very careful with kerlinblades," said Kia, thinking aloud.

"There is a way," Jola offered.

"Explain," Kia ordered.

"Train when he does," Jola said.

"It will take some coordination, but it should work." Kia nodded approval of the plan.

"I have had a little training but not nearly enough. The instructors have taught me all they are willing to, but I fear I must one day confront Lord Kezem," said Rela, mostly talking to herself. "If I kill him and die in the process, I will count it a fair price for freeing this people."

The speech came easily to Rela. Though she was trapped in the palace, she understood that the situation outside was grim. Perhaps the maidens would be willing to act as her emissaries to the marked people in her friends' stead. The prison could certainly use more of the medical supplies Lorian had smuggled in. Rela would take them to the prison herself if necessary, but there were many other tasks to be done outside the palace.

The head Melian Maiden looked deep into her eyes, searching for something. Rela endured the pointed stare and gave the maiden one of her own.

"We will teach you what we can," Kia promised.

Relief rushed through Rela. Perhaps this constant guard would be a good thing.

Chapter 27: Rescue Mission

Jira (March) 15, 1560
City of Resh

After weeks traveling through mountains, fields, and forests, Resh's hard structures seemed strange and foreboding to Teven, Kayleen, and their companions. The city, highlighted by a series of centuries-old elegant spires, possessed an austere beauty. Used to the annual influx of Kireshana travelers, many merchants gathered in the main square to sell them anything, legal or otherwise. Some people offered legitimate work for the derringers, but just as many sought to take advantage of them.

The first day in Resh, Teven tracked down suitable living quarters. The overpriced small housing unit in a rough section placed them in close quarters, but Teven clung to the optimistic notion that they would not be there long.

Each day, the group went out in pairs to query the locals about work. There was never a shortage of menial labor opportunities, but more often than not, such opportunities merely taxed the body, numbed the mind, and paid pathetically.

A week passed, then two. Among the six of them, they made enough to continue renting the small housing unit and eat decently, but the point of staying in Resh was to earn the kefs to pay the price required to rise from derringer status. As he watched their resources dwindle, Teven gained a new sympathy for mine workers and tenant farmers. Preoccupied with worry, Teven barely registered the agitated conversations taking place around him.

"We've got to do something!" a distinguished elderly man shouted. That statement alone would not have caught Teven's attention but the next one did. "Kezem's men are becoming bolder by the second!" The man gestured angrily with a walking stick.

Teven slowed his steps, and Kayleen followed suit.

"It's Lord Kezem, Father. Show some respect, or the RLA will cart you off to prison!" admonished a younger man. The man's shiny tunic and gold lined trousers spoke of money.

Teven paused. They had nowhere pressing to be anyway.

"Pretty soon there will be no one left to work the fields," a woman lamented, possessively clutching the younger man's arm. "How will Brana make me sweet frolers if all the farmers get conscripted or killed?" Her tone indicated more distress over the loss of the treat than the farmers' plight.

"It's all right, my dear. Lord Kezem's army will crush the rebellion soon," said the man, patting the woman's arm.

"Don't think you've escaped this thing, Gavin," the father warned, shaking the walking stick in his son's face.

The younger man leaned back to save his nose.

"Abiel may be too young for them now but in a year or two they'll come to claim him. Mark my words!"

Teven exchanged a glance with Kayleen. He didn't care if the family knew they'd been eavesdropping.

"Excuse me. Is there some trouble, sir?" he asked.

"Mind your own business," Gavin snapped.

The older man drew himself up. He was not dressed nearly as finely as the young couple, but he wore his plain attire with dignity. Fire burned brightly in his eyes.

"Trouble! I'll say there's trouble, and it's got Kezem written all over its ugly self!" said the man.

"Father!"

"Hush, Master Niklos, that's treason!" cried the woman. "Hurry now or we'll be late for the performance." She detached herself from her husband and placed a placating hand on the older man's arm.

Master Niklos softened his tone but not the resolve in his steely gray eyes.

"You two go on ahead, my dear. I'll only slow you down."

"But you're the one who wanted to see the Kalmata String Quartet," the woman protested.

"Old men and women of all ages have a right to change their

minds," said the man.

Shaking their heads, the man and woman continued down the busy street. Teven watched them walk away then looked back at the older man and found himself pinned in place by a probing stare.

"Etoni eva alaeris!" Master Niklos exclaimed under his breath.

Teven recognized the exclamation as Kalastan, but the man spoke too swiftly for him to guess at its meaning until the anotechs provided a translation: ***By the stars, there is hope.***

"Come with me!" The man took off down the street in the opposite direction from the young couple. His steps suddenly had a youthful spring to them.

Teven and Kayleen struggled to match his pace.

"What's this about?" Kayleen demanded, when they finally halted three blocks from the start of their frantic dash.

Teven suppressed a grin. He could always count on Kayleen to not mince words. He took stock of his surroundings. They were in a nicer section of Resh. The streets were clean but cold and devoid of joy. The neighborhood boasted single family housing units packed tight enough for plains sparrows to spread their wings and touch two walls.

Master Niklos waved his hand in front of a security sensor on a door midway down the street. A triumphant chime announced success. The lock disengaged, and their host waved them in.

Teven hesitated briefly but sensed no danger. He strode through the door into a receiving room which favored the colors green and purple. Master Niklos motioned for them to continue into a comfortable side room to the left of the receiving room. Teven walked into the room and tensed when Niklos touched a button at his belt. An energy field buzzed to life across the doorway.

"Do not be alarmed," said Master Niklos. "That is a sound damper which will allow us to converse freely."

"About what?" Kayleen demanded. As usual, she beat Teven to the question by a fraction of a second. Her hands crept toward the inside of her cloak where she had stashed her kerlinblade.

Teven twitched his head negatively and willed her to be patient.

"We're listening," he prompted, taking a seat.

Kayleen remained standing.

For a while Master Niklos just stared at Teven. He opened his mouth several times but always closed it again.

"I knew my feelings were not wrong," he finally said in a rush. "They said to go to the square during the Kireshana, and I have for the past five years."

"Who are you?" Kayleen asked.

"I am a former Ranger turned tosh merchant. My name is Niklos Mikhail McGreven." The man's tone told Teven he did not like the direction his life had taken. "When I was a Ranger, I taught many students and had many apprentices. Though I grew close to most of them, two orphans, sisters in name but not in blood, became like daughters to me. You are are the son of the younger one." He spoke the words with deep emotion that rang true.

"You knew my mother?" Teven asked, torn between caution and the need to know more.

"Queen Reia Minstel was not always queen," Niklos said tenderly. "She was once a Ranger and my student, one of the best. Young, idealistic, headstrong, impulsive." He smiled as he said it. His gaze turned from Teven to the floor, deep and unseeing as he stared into the past.

"Please go on," Teven begged, hardly daring to breath. The few scraps of information he had heard about his past only whet a ravenous appetite to know more. Although the Kireshana consumed his energy and ability to puzzle out his past, that did not remove the desire to know.

Niklos's cloudy gaze cleared a little.

"Your parents met on your father's Kireshana, as he battled Restler-Tarpon Alliance soldiers. At the time, Prince Terosh fully believed the Royal Guard was all life could ever offer him, so he spent happy months traveling with Reia Antellio. The Blood Harvest changed everything. Your grandmother, Queen Kila, had been dead for ages by this time, but King Teorn and Prince Taytron went to Mitra to secure a wife for the crown prince. They were assassinated along with the Mitran royals."

"And suddenly my father was king," Teven said sadly.

"Soon thereafter, yes, but Prince Terosh was away from the palace when the news about King Teorn arrived. RT Alliance soldiers had lured your mother into a trap to draw out the prince, and it worked."

"How did they escape?" Teven wondered.

"I do not know for sure. However, I do know that they married soon after being reunited, before receiving news about the king and elder prince. See—"

"She wasn't supposed to marry him," Kayleen finished.

"What? Why not?" Teven asked, surprised that Kayleen knew some obscure Ranger rule he did not.

"Reia was forced to choose between her love and her life as a Ranger," said Master Niklos. "The prohibition against marrying into the royal family has existed for centuries, but it is not something all Rangers believe in."

"How come I never heard of this?" Teven asked, feeling left out.

Kayleen shot him a *think-about-it* look.

"You're the prince. The only royal you'd be eligible to marry is you sister."

"Oh."

Lost in thought, Master Niklos winced.

"The situation was sorely mishandled."

Silence stretched and Teven feared he would never go on, but Kayleen came to the rescue with a timely prompt.

"Mishandled, Master Niklos?"

"Yes, gravely. Reia chose to love her prince, and the Ashatan Council stripped her of her rank as a healer and banished her. It broke her heart and split the order. Many prominent Rangers thought the council unjust. I did not know what to think. She had spurned our codes, which forbade loving a royal, but should ignoring an unjust rule have earned her our ire?"

Another long pause ensued. Teven waited this one out.

"I left the Rangers soon thereafter but stayed in touch with Reia during her time as queen. From time to time, she would seek my counsel. Your parents faced many a crisis with wisdom and boldness. Then, your father was murdered, and this business with Kezem began."

"How did you know I'm her son?"

"I have eyes and ears, boy," Niklos said. "I have heard the whispers surrounding Reshner's lost princes. So many stories swirl I no longer know what is true, but I see you here and know there is hope. Lord Kezem's fist has been hard on this people for far too long. Join the rebellion. Fight for your throne!"

"It is not yet time," Teven murmured, surprised at how calm he sounded.

"Then at least right some wrongs," Niklos insisted. "You are a derringer. You seek jobs, do you not?"

Teven and Kayleen nodded, but Niklos paid no attention to them.

"Of course, you do. Yesterday, a troop from Fort Riden came to collect the young as they do annually. The salt mines, the weapons plants, and the RLA training camps await the captured. Did you not feel the pain of the bereaved mothers in Resh? My own wretched son and his fool wife think themselves immune from the suffering, even after seeing the soldiers seize my daughter's son. But their son will soon be old enough for the mines. Then, they will know. Save my daughter's son and as many of the others as you can. Five thousand kefs are all I can spare, but they're yours if you can rescue those doomed souls."

Teven's jaw dropped. He had never seen that much money, but he knew they desperately needed it. The only remaining question was how five derringers and a salt mine survivor were going to find and defeat a detachment of RLA soldiers.

Before he could voice his question, Kayleen spouted off a stream of questions.

"How far ahead are they? How many are there? How well-armed are they?"

"They are headed back to Fort Riden. The troop is twenty-three strong including officers, and they should be moderately armed. But they are also unsuspecting and lazy. I followed them once, but I could never fight so many by myself. They took about thirty captives. The boy you will be looking for is Garrett Rimton. He is about a head shorter than you with blond hair and brown eyes."

Teven's heart sank.

A quarter of the planet answers to that description!

"Won't the soldiers just return and take the children again?" asked Kayleen.

"Leave that to me," said Niklos. He gave them a thousand kef advance and some tamitin powder to knock out the soldiers.

After a few final instructions, Teven and Kayleen returned to the tiny housing unit and convinced Jal to stay behind to look after the others. They needed to move swiftly and silently to succeed in a rescue. They packed a few supplies, picked their way through Resh to the outskirts, and followed the road south and slightly west.

***

Two days later, they caught up to their quarry. The first sighting was midmorning. They spent the rest of the day shadowing and carefully observing. Thankfully, Niklos had been right about the sloppy soldiering. Twice they spotted prime opportunities for the captives to slip off unnoticed. Throughout the day, Teven and Kayleen bounced possible rescue plans off each other.

When night fell, Kayleen slipped close to the camp. Teven waited thirty seconds for her to get into position before using the anotechs to imitate a korver's hunting call. At the same time, he took a thick stick and beat the nearby bushes. He repeated the eerie call, catching the attention of the two guards closest to the prisoner tent.

"Should we tell the captain?" asked one guard.

"He's got ears. It's just a bunch of mangy korvers; nothing to worry about," replied the second guard.

Teven changed tactics. Taking the sturdy stick, he stepped on one end and hauled up with all his might. As the satisfying snap filled the air, he cried, "Ahhhhh! Help! They're everywhere! Help!"

That worked, perhaps too well.

Sputtering curses, the guards grabbed their rifles and charged toward Teven. He didn't stick around to see how many followed.

***

Jira (March) 17, 1560
Temporary Camp, Morden Lowlands, Path to Fort Riden

Teven's cry for help froze Kayleen's heart, but the anotechs assured her he was fine. It was not part of the plan, but it made a weird sort of sense and worked well. Most of the guards rushed toward the disturbance. Shaking her head, she poured tamitin powder into any container she thought the guards might use. She smiled when one jug marked water emitted the sharp stench of ale. A generous portion of powder found its way into the jug. She had to be careful not to knock out the prisoners, but she doubted they would be treated to the ale.

When the last of the powder had been poured, Kayleen considered slipping away to wait. Then, she had a better idea. Quickly, she found the supply tent and started searching. She found some nice blankets and spare tents. She thought about donning a spare uniform but dismissed the idea. Kezem's armies weren't big on assigning female soldiers escort details. After dumping a sack of potatoes, Kayleen filled the bag with several tents, kerlinblades, kerlak pistols, and serlak pistols. She forwent the bulky blankets.

Finding a bunch of ration packs, Kayleen threw the whole stack into her bag of purloined goodies. On second thought, she opened a grain bar and ate it as she waited for Teven. They would have to wait until most of the guards were neutralized before looking for Garrett Rimton. She finished the bar and tossed the wrapper into the corner.

To her surprise, she felt some of the anotechs leave her and move toward the wrapper. She watched it disintegrate then felt the anotechs re-enter her right hand.

That was weird. Point taken. No more littering.

Part of Kayleen felt guilty for stealing, but she reasoned that the supplies had probably been stolen from good people already. She was merely redeeming what had already been lost. The more she thought about the mines, taxes, raids, fear, graft, and thousands of other wrongs with their roots in Kezem's government, the less guilt she felt.

Something rustled behind her. Kayleen whipped her head around but not before a hand covered her mouth and nose. She stiffened. Her heart slammed into her throat.

"It's me! Don't scream. It's okay. It's only me!" Teven spoke into her ear.

Anger replaced her fear, but relief overpowered both emotions. Kayleen relaxed, leaning back against him. Slowly, his hand released her mouth and nose. He continued to hold her.

"Teven, you scared a year off my life!" she scolded in a loud whisper.

"I'm sorry. I couldn't think of a better way to quietly get your attention."

The deed was done so she let it drop. They sat in silence, enjoying each other's company and waiting for the grumbling soldiers to go to sleep.

An hour later, a strange silence settled over the camp.

"Naptime for all the good soldier boys," Kayleen whispered. She struggled to her feet and rubbed her legs to regain some feeling.

Lacking a better plan, they resorted to direct interrogation. They settled into a pattern. Kayleen would poke a prisoner, while Teven held his hand over their mouth.

"Are you Garrett Rimton?" Kayleen would ask. At a negative head shake, she would ask her second question. "Do you know who is?"

Teven would cautiously lift his hand to hear the answer. The interrogations were not as quiet as they had hoped, but the fourth prisoner questioned shook his head yes and looked at her with wide eyes.

"Your grandfather sent us to fetch you," Kayleen quietly informed. "Let's go."

"I can't!" Garrett said, visibly upset. "They've got us chained together."

Kayleen hissed in frustration. That would hinder things.

"Teven—"

"I'm on it. One key coming up."

While Teven searched for the key, Kayleen roused the other sleepy prisoners. A confused babble rose, threatening to grow exponentially.

"Quiet!" she ordered. "We're getting out of here. Anyone who wants to go home is welcome to come along." She cocked her head to the side and listened hard. The anotechs were trying to tell her something.

"I'm not going!" one boy announced, breaking her train of thought. "I'm going to be a Royal Guard and protect Lord Kezem from those Ranger terrorists." Superiority dripped from every word.

"Then you're headed for the wrong camp," Kayleen retorted. "The Royal Guard is based in Rammon and Azhel. Anyone who wants a career in or near the palace must compete in the Festival of Future Fighters and finish the Kireshana. Fort Riden recruits go to the Huz Mon salt mines, Azhel energy plants, Idonian glass factories, or some obscure army post. Trust me. It won't be the glorious life you're picturing." She didn't know why she was arguing with the child. He seemed like a nice fit for the RLA.

"I'll scream," the boy threatened. "Then, they'll capture you and take *you* to the salt mines!"

Scream and I hit you, Kayleen silently promised. *On second thought, why wait?*

Holding out her hand out in a non-threatening manner, Kayleen said, "Hey, take it easy. Not everyone wants to join the RLA. They at least deserve the chance to choose." With each soft word, Kayleen stepped closer to the troublemaker. Her movements were fluid and graceful. The swift crack of her right hand across the side of his neck barely rustled the air.

The kid dropped unconscious.

No one spoke.

Teven returned and surveyed the scene with grim amusement.

"Well, that ends that discussion," he said cheerfully. "I'll just release you all and you can choose. Except you, Garrett, your grandfather made your choice. Your mother's worried sick."

The last statement convinced Garrett it was for the best. Kayleen was grateful for that. She didn't think her nerves could take much more excitement. As Teven unlocked the chains holding the last prisoner, Kayleen finally heard what the anotechs were trying to tell her: ***Touch chains to unlock.***

"Oh!" Kayleen exclaimed. Everyone looked at her confused. "No keys next time, Teven."

He nodded.

Twenty-eight of the thirty-one children left with Teven and Kayleen. They stopped by the supply tent for the pack she had readied. The sheer number of escapees forced them to grab extra food and tents. They split the group in half to increase the chance some would make it back to Resh. The tamitin powder would work for several hours, but that was a small window to rely upon, especially since their pursuers knew their destination.

Chapter 28: Ritand Refugees

Jira (March) 20, 1560-Jira (March) 21, 1560
City of Resh

Fear prompted them to move quickly. By some miracle, both Teven and Kayleen safely guided their charges back to Resh within three days. Returning them to proper families proved a bit chaotic, but it was a task Niklos Mikhail McGreven undertook happily. He explained that the children would be sent to safe houses scattered around the western half of Reshner where they would be shielded from Lord Kezem's wrath. Teven wasn't surprised when the former Ranger announced he had another job for them.

Tired but still experiencing intoxicating success, Teven listened to Master Niklos.

"I have gathered more funds from the parents of those you rescued," Master Niklos began. "By all rights, the money should be yours, but please, hear me out. The Ritand Quarter on the west side of Resh is sorely in need of help. Twelve more community shelters need to be built soon. Winter is coming. The government has dragged its feet for months. Governor Zelene would have set it right promptly. Governor Luvak speaks of freeing funds, but he doesn't care. There's no food and scarcely any medicine."

"And you want to use the money to help them," Teven concluded, nodding his head.

"And you want us to build the shelters," Kayleen added. She sounded less than ecstatic about the idea but that was most likely the exhaustion showing. Dark circles and bloodshot eyes attested to the fact that she had had little rest on the return journey to Resh.

Niklos nodded, looking guilty. He frowned.

"Here are the four thousand kefs I owe you for rescuing Garrett plus the five hundred from his parents. The other families put forth another three thousand. I will give you the money if you ask it." His eyes begged them not to ask, and his hand hovered protectively over the pile of kef notes.

Teven looked to Kayleen for support. Her approving nod was almost imperceptible.

"Keep the money, Master Niklos," said Teven. "We will help as long as we can, but I want to reach Mount Palean before the winter storms."

"Thank you." Master Niklos solemnly bowed his head.

"There's just one catch," Teven added. "One of our companions, Quasim, is from Ritand. Help us search for information on his family or a family willing to take him in."

"You ask much, Prince Teven, but you give much as well," Niklos said, bowing from the waist. The title flowed easily from his tongue.

"You might want to be careful about saying that name," Kayleen cautioned. "I know, you know, and Teven knows, but if Lord Kezem finds out there's going to be big trouble."

"Your words are wise, Kayleen." He looked like he wanted to say more but stopped himself. "I pray the day hastens when such caution will be unnecessary. Until then, I will be careful. Now, if you will excuse me, I will go order concrete and wood for the shelters."

Thus dismissed, Teven and Kayleen stumbled to their rented unit. A wonderful shower and a few hundred questions later, Teven collapsed onto his bedroll and fell into a deep sleep.

He opened his eyes the next morning to a vision of his mother. She wore the same exquisite robes of purple and green he had seen her in the first time.

"Greetings, Teven, I apologize for placing such responsibility upon you. House Minstel has been granted great power. With that power comes the duty to care for the people. They are stubborn and foolish at times but good at heart. Misused power leads to tragedy. The truth of the anotechs awaits you in Loresh. Go there if you need a more thorough lesson on abuse of power." She smiled that sad smile he had come to expect. *"Lord Kezem seems bent on reliving the past. I am tired now and must go face my destiny. May Riden watch over you, my son."*

The vision disappeared, leaving Teven feeling empty. The

finality of his mother's message tore at his heart. He could replay the message of course but that would only twist a blade through the pain. His emotions ran the usual course of anger, despair, resolve, and pain. Silent tears fell, and he mentally railed against the universe that left him alone in so many ways.

Kayleen sat down beside him. Along their Kireshana, a vision would come to him with some word of wisdom. Before, she had let him deal with the pain as he saw fit, but this time, she drew near and embraced him.

"Another dream?" she whispered into his dark hair.

A wave of embarrassment washed over Teven. Tears were unbecoming. He drew in several ragged breaths and willed the stream to a stop. There must be some unwritten rule that princes shouldn't cry, especially in front of their friends.

"A vision, of my mother … just before she left to face Kezem," he said.

Kayleen nodded.

"A last message," she said, sensing his fear and embarrassment. "Don't be afraid, Teven. Tears are natural; don't fight them."

"I want to do what she expects of me, but I don't know what that is!"

"What did she say?" asked Kayleen.

Teven repeated his mother's message word for word.

"That's it; her last words to me," he finished.

"Savor them, Tev," Kayleen encouraged. "They're gifts. Not many mothers get to say goodbye."

He knew she was right but couldn't shake the grief. Then, it hit him that she might mean more by that statement.

"Did your mother or father say goodbye?" he wondered.

"No, my earliest memories are of the Ranger camp." Kayleen gave him a weak smile. "But sometimes I dream they're still alive somewhere, searching for me. It's a foolish notion, but it gives me something to cling to."

"It could be true. We both know what happened to my parents, but not knowing about yours leaves room to hope," Teven said.

"Speaking of hope, we have some to bring to the Ritand refugees," Kayleen said.

Her words spurred him to action.

Within ten minutes, Teven was dressed in dark brown pants and a beige shirt. Suddenly, it dawned on him that he and Kayleen were alone. Jal must have taken the others out to the site early. He hesitated before adding his belt with the banistick and resisted the urge to take one of the kerlinblades. He didn't want the refugees to feel threatened. Kayleen wore her travel cloak so she could take a kerlinblade and a pistol. Teven preferred the banistick anyway.

As they left, Kayleen handed him a large chunk of wheat bread and a small flask of appola juice. He swallowed the bread whole and poured the juice down his throat with such speed he almost choked. Kayleen just shook her head at him. They hurried down block after block until they came to the grim gates surrounding the refugee section.

A grumpy man dressed in a rumpled, rusty brown RLA uniform stood stiffly at his post. He sniffed with disgust.

"Turn back or be prepared to smell like filth for a week!" he warned. "Gotta keep watch or these wretches will pollute the whole city."

Teven didn't trust himself to speak properly, so he said nothing. As if the high fence was not enough of a change, the concrete stopped and the dwellings turned to rickety shacks at best, tarps thrown over half-rotted sticks at worst. It was like stepping into another world. Their steps automatically slowed.

"I don't smell anything strange," Teven whispered, as they hurried further into the dismal wreckage of broken lives.

He felt eyes watching them and let his gaze wander from one shack to another. Dressed in rags, a few of the younger children played with the dirt. The older ones stared blankly, having lost interest in that small joy. Several children coughed. Many of the refugees were short, bipedal creatures with flat ears, three large black eyes spaced evenly across their faces, and smooth olive skin. A fair number were human of varying skin tones.

Teven cast a glance at Kayleen's troubled expression. Her walk stiffened as she concentrated on something. Then, she stopped walking altogether, drew in a quick breath, and paled.

"Wait," she said, reaching for Teven's arm. "Tell the anotechs to stop filtering your sense of smell for just a moment."

He did so. The stench of a thousand rotting things hit him at once. He let the anotechs continue their wonderful work.

"I see what he means," said Teven.

"I don't think there's a good sanitation system here," Kayleen noted. It was an understatement. Rotten cores of unidentifiable things lay in the streets covered with flitnits and the grubs of many other insects.

"Can we do anything?" Teven asked.

"We'll find out," Kayleen said, continuing down the street. "Let's find Master Niklos and the others."

At Niklos's name, an older boy looked up.

"He's down Hope Street planning the new shelter project." The boy struggled to his feet. "I'll take you there." He swayed a moment, and Teven thought he might fall over.

"Are you okay? When was the last time you ate anything?" Kayleen asked, stepping to the boy's side and reaching out to steady him.

"There are six others in my house," the boy responded, glaring at Kayleen. He raised his head defiantly and removed his elbow from her grip.

She gave Teven a bewildered, pained look. He shrugged and followed the boy.

"Ah, Crispin, I see you bring the young benefactors," greeted Master Niklos. "Come, come, I am eager to show you the plans."

Crispin said nothing but looked at Teven and Kayleen with a little more respect.

Niklos put them to work pounding nails into boards arranged to form walls. It was early afternoon before Jal and the others made an appearance.

Karric and Jenell bowed in greeting.

"The midday meal will be ready soon. Master Niklos says you can stop now," Karric announced.

"I'm glad we have his approval," Kayleen said with a grin.

"Come outside," Jenell said. Her excitement seemed a bit much for a simple meal.

Teven hefted the wall section they had just completed. Stepping outside, he was surprised to see a large crowd. He froze, holding the wall in front like a shield.

"Don't just stand there," Niklos snapped, eyes twinkling. "Greet the grateful people."

Teven tried to retreat into the doorway but was blocked by Kayleen.

"Wrong way, hero." Kayleen pointed the other way.

"Traitor," Teven shot back, setting the wall section down.

After the morning of hard work, the midday meal led into a

celebration of thanks for the much-needed supplies. Teven and his friends were stuffed with many Ritand treats. Part of him felt guilty for eating their food, even if he did help buy it, but he had enough sense to know the cultural affront it would be to refuse. He vowed to work harder for these people. Winter was coming, and many would perish if the shelters were not finished in time.

***

Jira (March) 22, 1560-Zeri (June) 1, 1560
City of Resh

Despite Teven's wish to reach the mountains before winter, the small band returned to the refugee section of Resh every day through the rest of Jira (March) and through the months of Enis (April) and Retsi (May) until the beginning of Zeri (June). The shelters hastily erected before the first snowfalls in the middle of Enis (April) proved to be just the beginning of a long list of projects that needed doing. The labor kept their muscles toned, and daily practice duels and shooting contests kept their fighting skills sharp. It also entertained the refugees, especially the children.

In the few spare hours, everyone but Kayleen performed a variety of tasks to scrape together kefs to continue their journey. Kayleen spent her time planning and directing a waste management system. By their fourth week of work, the air around the refugee section smelled much cleaner. She had wrestled funds for proper pipes and contractors from the stingy governor and the city council. The trick had been to keep pushing the idea that the sections which bordered the refugee sector would be less prone to disease and free of the awful stench.

Master Niklos kept his promise to seek information on Quasim's family. Eventually, he tracked down an older sister who agreed to care for the boy, despite a growing family of her own. Quasim was harder to convince, but the weeks among his people had endeared their simple life to him.

As Teven walked Quasim to the sister's shack in the southern portion of the refugee sector, he noticed the boy was unusually quiet.

"What's wrong?" asked Teven.

"You don't want me to travel with you!" Quasim complained.

Teven stopped and looked down into the boy's hurt eyes.

"It's not that, Quasim. We enjoy your company. You're a great help, but we want you to be happy. The rest of the Kireshana will be rough. I don't want to put you through that."

"I would be a burden," said Quasim sadly.

Teven said nothing; he struggled to sort the swirling feelings inside him. A sense of foreboding had been on his heart for several weeks now.

"You are a fine traveling companion, Quasim, but there is danger ahead," said Teven. "Danger I must face alone."

"You're leaving the others?" Quasim asked, sounding part pleased and part upset.

"I don't know," Teven answered honestly. "Jenell and Karric aren't ready to go on yet."

"You'll come back, right?" Quasim asked with some concern.

"If I can," said Teven.

They came to Quasim's new home and said goodbye. A lump rose in Teven's throat. He swallowed hard.

The simple conversation weighed upon him until he returned to the small rental unit. He didn't bother greeting his friends.

"We have to leave," he announced.

"Jenell has a cold," Jal commented with a frown. "She shouldn't travel right now."

A deep, wracking cough came from the back corner as if to confirm Jal's words.

"I know," Teven said calmly. He hadn't really known Jenell's cold had worsened, but it confirmed his guess that he and Kayleen would travel alone. If it got any worse Jal might have to use the anotechs. "Stay here with Jenell and Karric. Master Niklos insisted on giving us four thousand kefs for our labor. That should be enough to pay the rent for another few months. Kayleen and I will take some weapons and supplies. Follow whenever you can."

Loud protests answered his plan from everyone slated to stay behind.

"I'm fine!" the half-delirious Jenell insisted.

Karric's firm hand on her shoulder kept her in the bedroll.

"No, you're not," Karric said. "But I am; I'm going."

"Something's not right. Our friends are nervous," Jal said cautiously. They had never explained the anotechs to the younger derringers and now did not seem like the best time to start. "Karric, stay with Jenell. I must talk some sense into Teven and Kayleen." That seemed to mollify Karric and the sick one.

"Jal, you know we travel faster alone," Teven began, once they were outside.

Jal raised a hand to wave off more reasons.

"I don't like it," said Jal. "Lord Kezem's plans will reveal themselves soon, and you are walking into a trap."

"He doesn't even know about me," Teven protested.

"Doesn't matter—" Jal began.

"They need you," Kayleen interrupted. "You have trained us well, but Jenell and Karric will not survive the Kireshana alone."

"I suppose not," Jal admitted, letting Kayleen switch the subject.

"Trap or not, Jal, we've got to go," Teven said.

The argument continued in circles for an hour. Eventually, Kayleen slipped away to pack. Finally, Jal insisted they take three thousand kefs with them and gave them some last-minute instructions on handling the anotechs.

Karric reluctantly helped them finish packing. Teven took him aside and spoke words of encouragement, reminding him to take care of Jenell and Jal. Kayleen slipped over to Jenell's bedroll and whispered similar encouragements. The hardest farewell was to Jal. Knowing the separation would only be temporary did not lessen the pain of parting with their friend.

Teven and Kayleen left Resh a little after dawn. They traveled down the familiar road south toward Fort Riden.

Chapter 29:
Trouble in Fort Riden

Zeri (June) 8, 1560
Entrance to Fort Riden, Morden Lowlands

After about a week, Teven McKnight and Kayleen Wellum finally reached Fort Riden, Lord Kezem's northwest stronghold. The fort was a city unto itself, complete with a small theater, barracks for up to four thousand soldiers, four taverns, and a prison capable of holding a few hundred captives.

As soon as they arrived, a gate guard directed them to an imposing set of heavy doors to their left. There, they checked in with the marksman manning the desk.

"What brings you to Fort Riden?" he asked, attempting to be friendly but coming off as bored. He didn't even bother looking up. A series of random circles across the paper in front of him also attested to boredom.

"We're derringers," Kayleen offered, stepping in front of Teven. They had agreed that the less people knew about him, the better.

Hearing a female voice, the marksman's head snapped up, and he shoved his drawings under a stack of official looking documents.

"You're late," he commented with a frown. "Most of the derringers were through here weeks ago."

"Our business in Resh kept us longer than expected," Kayleen explained, carefully telling him nothing. She gave the man a coy grin and leaned close as if to whisper a secret. "We've never been here. Where's the best inn? Is there anything we should know? Who's in charge?"

"That'd be Commander Arnold Glaiser, ma'am. You probably won't see him while you're here though. How long are you going to be here anyway?"

"A few days," Kayleen said vaguely, standing up straight. "Enough to rest up for the finish."

"Perry's Palace has the best rooms, and the tavern attached to it serves the best ale and wine," he informed, glancing about furtively. "And twenty kefs gets you a detailed tour of everything Fort Riden has to offer. Most derringers find the tour *very* interesting." His dark eyes lit up as he mentioned the tour.

Kayleen got the impression the man had a side business going on. She queried her anotechs for Teven's feelings on the matter and got a warm sense of approval.

"We'll take the tour, marksman …." Kayleen trailed off as she placed twenty kefs on the desk in front of the man.

"Weldon. Clive Weldon."

Kayleen worked hard to keep a straight face.

"And the tour is twenty kefs *each*," Weldon added.

"You'll get the other twenty when we get our tour," Kayleen assured him.

"Fine. Meet me outside this tower in an hour. That's when my shift ends."

They went to Perry's Palace and arranged for a room. There wasn't much to unpack so they spent the remaining time in the tavern listening to the off-duty soldiers chat. They wanted to learn the latest news from the palace but welcomed rumors as well.

"The commander's too easy on that boy of his," complained a mostly drunk lieutenant.

"I heard he tried to run away with one of them derringer dames that came through here last month," his drinking companion added.

"Aww, he didn't really want her," said the lieutenant. "The kid's not even ten! He just wants out of this blasted fort. Not that I blame the boy."

The conversation seemed mundane to Kayleen, so she focused on another. She only caught part of the conversation because the soldier and his two buddies were on their way out the door.

"—tried to put a hov engine fire out with water from Crystal Lake last week. Blew 'imself to bits."

Kayleen tuned in to a third conversation.

"I heard Lord Kezem's closing in on Gordon's band of misfits," a short, fuzzy creature commented.

Kayleen did not recognize the species, but that was nothing unusual considering her lack of experience with the wider universe. Most Rangers were humans, and Kayleen had grown up interacting with less than a half-dozen species.

"Alexi Gordon's a fine soldier. He could have had a great career," the being's drinking companion lamented. "Now, he'll just be another corpse on the Kesler Plains."

Kayleen continued scanning conversations. Her gaze fell upon a woman serving drinks to a surly looking man who sported a colorful left eye.

"I warned you to keep those paws to yourself," the woman chided. "Prisoner or not, that girl can pack a punch. Don't fret, dearie, Lord Kezem's personal guards will be here late tomorrow to pick her up."

Kayleen's ears perked up at the mention of Kezem's guards. Teven's expression also reflected interest.

"Shut up, Maybel," the man muttered, staring into the black ale swirling in the clear container he had clenched in his fists.

The woman shrugged and went away. She drew up to the table Teven and Kayleen had chosen.

"What can I get you dearies?" she asked in a syrupy voice.

"Do you have appola juice?" Teven asked.

"Ah, a good boy, very rare these days. She's got you whipped, don't she, love?" she said, winking.

"I'll have the same." Kayleen raised an eyebrow and gave the woman a cool stare.

Maybel bustled off to get their drinks. At this early hour, the tavern was sparsely populated. She returned in a moment with their order.

"What's got him down?" Teven jerked his head at the customer with the black eye.

"Who Jake? That's nothing. He'd been bothering a pretty derringer for a while. Then, last night, Commander Glaiser sent him in here to arrest her and her friends. She didn't take kindly to the arrest or his wandering hands and walloped him good."

"What were they arrested for?" Kayleen asked, trying not to sound too interested.

"Now, I don't like to tell no tales," Maybel hedged. She slid into the booth next to Teven and spoke in a whisper loud enough to be heard clear across the room. "But rumor has it the orders came from the top—the way top—as in Lord Kezem himself. The Commander's orders to arrest the derringers even say Royal Guards are coming to collect 'em."

"What did they do?" Kayleen pressed.

Maybel shrugged and waved her hand across her face like the question was a bad smell.

"It could have been anything, dearie. Lord Kezem's word is law. I don't ask no nosy questions. It's much safer that way."

"That's smart," Teven agreed.

Kayleen had the sudden urge to kick him but resisted when she realized he was trying to squeeze more information out of Maybel.

Suitably encouraged, Maybel continued to jabber.

"Some say these derringers hail from the palace. The one that gave Jake what he had coming arrived a few weeks ago but waited for the others. She obviously knew them. Criminals usually stick together, don't they? They probably killed someone or some such."

Subsequent theories were only more outlandish.

Kayleen sipped her drink. The tingling sensation on her tongue said there was more than appola juice in her glass, but the distraction it provided helped her control her tongue. Besides, it didn't taste too bad, just a little strange.

When the time for their tour approached, Kayleen rose.

"Excuse us. We have a meeting to attend now. You've been very kind." She tossed a few kefs onto the table, not waiting for a response.

Teven slipped out the other side of the booth to avoid Maybel.

"What do you think?" Teven asked quietly, once they had exited and were striding toward the tower where they would meet Clive Weldon.

"I think the prison just became part of our tour," Kayleen replied.

An extra sixty kefs added the prison to the Fort Riden tour. The first half-hour consisted of Clive Weldon listing off troop strengths and showing them the barracks and the supply rooms. In the armory, Clive hinted he might be able to sell them some fine weapons. Their last stop was the prison, which was in the same building as the armory.

What idiot planned that? Kayleen wondered.

She charmed Clive into letting them walk by the cell she sensed the derringers in. Fortunately, Clive was conceited enough to have several days' worth of good things to say about himself. All she had to do was get him started and fake interest. Their conversation allowed Teven to talk to some of the prisoners.

***

Zeri (June) 8, 1560
Same Day
Prison Block and Armory, Fort Riden, Morden Lowlands

Since they were conveniently in the same cell, Teven quickly located Lorian Petole and her companions. He remembered seeing the other two at the Festival of Future Fighters, but their names escaped him.

"Do you stand with those against Lord Kezem?" whispered Teven.

Lorian's dark brown eyes searched his. She got to her feet, approached the bars keeping her from freedom, and gripped them firmly.

"My loyalty will always be with Princess Rela Minstel," said Lorian evenly.

Teven gasped.

"You know her! She's alive?" His mother had said the Ralose Charm would protect Rela, but he had hardly expected the thing to work. Besides, knowing she should be alive and hearing as much from someone who knew her were two very different things.

"Of course, she's alive. Lord Kezem's life is linked to hers. He wouldn't dare harm her," said Lorian. "Hence our predicament," she added, gesturing to her friends. "We were raised with the princess to be hostages whenever Lord Kezem decided he wanted something from her. I guess that time approaches."

"Then you are my friends," Teven said, pushing down his anger and raising a hand to touch the lock. The lock obediently clicked open. He swung the heavy gate out.

Clive Weldon spun at the noise. Kayleen's eyes widened, but she reacted with characteristic swiftness. Before Marksman Weldon could utter a word, her right fist crashed into the back of his neck. He sank to the ground with a groan.

Kayleen peered down at him, hoping she hadn't caused permanent damage.

"Teven, tell me why I just knocked out our guide," said Kayleen.

"Because we're causing a small prison break," he replied, rushing up to Weldon and relieving the man of his kerlak pistol and their kefs. Then, setting the kerlak pistol for high stun, Teven systematically put the four prisoners he wasn't interested in down for naps. "Here," he said, tossing the pistol to Lorian. A plan formed as he spoke, "Try not to use it. We want to leave without having half the RLA after us."

"That's going to happen anyway," said Kayleen.

"Where are we going?" Lorian inquired, checking the pistol.

"You two are crazy," the other young woman remarked.

The anotechs identified her as Anabel Spitzer.

"I'll take crazy if it gets us out of here," the young man pointed out.

Marc Spitzer.

"We'll continue with the Kireshana until we get to the Kesler Plains. Then, we can head south to Meritab. We should be able to get a hov there to take us back to Rammon," Kayleen said.

"What will we do in Rammon?" Lorian asked, growing more skeptical by the second.

"We'll figure that out when we get there," Teven said, forcing confidence into his voice.

"Shouldn't we be moving *away* from the palace?" Marc asked. "Just a thought, but isn't the point of escaping to deprive Kezem of hostages to use against Princess Rela?"

"We have to help her, Marc," Lorian insisted.

"Argue on the road," Kayleen hissed.

"Sorry. Oh, this is Marc and Anabel Spitzer. Who are you?"

"Kayleen Wellum. That's Teven McKnight. Now, if we're done with introductions, we should be on our way."

"We should wait until evening," Teven suggested.

They had a brief argument via the anotechs.

Kayleen looked at him impatiently but finally agreed.

***

Not wanting to risk going back to any of their rooms, they raided the armory and a supply room for new weapons and equipment. While the others packed supplies, Kayleen poked around the armory, hoping to find the special weapons Marksman Weldon had alluded to. She concentrated hard and let the anotechs search. They found nothing from a preliminary scan but admitted there was too much metal to get an accurate reading.

Practicing some of Jal's last-minute instructions, Kayleen stretched out her fingertips and gently touched the wall. Then, she imagined the anotechs flowing from her fingers. When she pushed too fast her right index finger began bleeding. The anotechs immediately repaired the small tear, but from then on, Kayleen proceeded with more caution.

Fifteen minutes later, Kayleen crouched on her haunches browsing the selection of special weapons. She took the few dozen flingers, ten shock nullifiers, two flash grenades, and several kerlinblade upgrade packs. The shock nullifiers would clamp onto the ends of banisticks and counter any energy influx.

After distributing the new toys, Kayleen made everyone eat a ration pack. They would have to run most of the night to put distance between themselves and the Fort Riden troops. She didn't want anyone fainting from hunger along the way.

Soon after they finished eating, a pair of guards entered with the evening meal. Lorian stunned them with the kerlak pistol and took their weapon belts. Then, she locked them in the cell she and her friends had vacated. The group forced themselves to eat the prison fare, in addition to the ration packs, knowing it might be their last warm meal for a while. They spent two more tense hours waiting for Fort Riden to settle down for the night.

Kayleen used the time to modify the banisticks and update the newly acquired kerlinblades. The chores provided a pleasant distraction.

A glance out the window revealed the sun's dying rays.

Patrols are still wandering around, but if we don't do something stupid, we should be able to stroll out the back checkpoint.

***

As Teven rounded the last corner before leaving the prison, he crashed into a boy who looked strangely familiar.

"Nate!" he said with wonder, elation, and fear.

"Teven? Is it really you?"

"What are you doing here?"

"I live here," his brother replied, grinning. "I came to see Marksman Weldon. One of the guards said he saw him going this way."

After a brief hesitation, the brothers awkwardly embraced. The rest of the group hung back to watch the exchange. Teven pulled back to study Nate. The six years had made quite a difference, but Nate was still just a boy. Teven's heart ached to see the hard look that came so easily to his little brother.

"What are you buying from Weldon?" asked Teven, protective instincts on high alert.

"Just a little Nespin spice." Nate's posture stiffened with defiance.

"Nate! That stuff will kill you," said Teven.

"No, boredom will kill me," Nate responded. It was then that Teven noticed Nate's pretty maroon uniform. It was obviously custom made for him. Feeling Teven's scrutiny, Nate pulled at a rank insignia. "Instant lieutenant, who'd have thought? It's the privilege of being Commander Glaiser's son."

"Don't rush it, Nate," Teven said gently.

You're nine!

"But I'm missing so many adventures!"

"Teven, we need to leave," Kayleen said. She moved to a position behind Nate.

"I'd drink to that if my father would let me drink. What's your hurry?" Nate asked, casually leaning against a cold wall and crossing his arms.

A torrent of emotions threatened Teven's ability to function. He forced himself to breathe regularly.

"Nate, promise me you'll forget you saw us." He didn't want to hurt his little brother, but they couldn't afford to be caught.

For the first time, Nate noticed the others.

"Hey! You're those derringers they arrested yesterday!"

Kayleen didn't wait for him to shout a warning. She grabbed his mouth and neck and applied pressure until he passed out.

Teven watched with horror, unable to move.

Gently lowering Nate's unconscious form to the ground, Kayleen apologized with her eyes.

"He'll be fine, but we should go," she said.

The small group dragged Teven out of the prison where the cold night air slammed into them and brought him back to his senses. They strolled casually toward the back entrance to Fort Riden, which would place them on a southeast road to Mount Palean.

Once out of sight, they broke into a swift trot. They needed to place as much distance between themselves and the fort as possible. Their initial pace was slower than Teven would have liked due to the need to conceal their trail. He felt hunted.

Less than a day from Fort Riden, the small band of fugitives began dodging search patrols. Teven had not expected the commander to be happy with the escape, but he hadn't expected him to empty Fort Riden either. News must have reached Lord Kezem that his prisoners had escaped. Occasionally, Teven felt their mysterious guardian watching.

Even Lorian sensed it.

"Someone's watching us," said Lorian.

"We know," said Kayleen.

"We don't know who it is, but someone's been protecting us for months," Teven clarified.

"That's odd," Marc commented. "Same thing happened to us."

"I don't care who he is as long as he's not shooting at us," said Kayleen.

Twice, they got caught by small patrols, and twice, they fought their way free.

Teven learned to appreciate Lorian's kerlinblade skills. He was also relieved to know that the fair-haired siblings could hold their own in a fight. It gave him a keen sense of satisfaction to know that Lord Kezem's finest instructors had taught his new companions how to fight. The third patrol they came across were dead, victims of their own explosives. Teven shuddered to think of Kayleen or one of his other friends stepping on a mine.

Once they were two days away from Fort Riden, Teven began to breathe easier. On that second evening, they risked a small fire to have a warm meal. Exhausted, Lorian, Marc, and Anabel went to sleep immediately after the three plains rabbits were devoured. Teven and Kayleen sat by the fire and listened to the chatter of various insects and small creatures that populated the Morden Lowlands.

"Listen," Kayleen whispered.

"To what?" Teven's hand automatically reached for a weapon.

"Life," she said softly.

He did as instructed and found it beautiful. The twittering, clacking, buzzing, and screeching created a lovely natural symphony. Teven's hands stopped searching for his weapons and found Kayleen's left hand. He gave it a reassuring squeeze, before leaning back against his pack. He closed his eyes and concentrated on identifying the creatures.

Chapter 30: Conquering Mount Palean

Zeri (June) 17, 1560
Morden Lowlands

For more than a week, they struck a convoluted path to throw off pursuit. Finally, they arrived at the foot of Mount Palean. Lorian Petole stared up at the steep slopes.

A long, low groan came from Kayleen.

"My feelings precisely," Lorian remarked.

Sunlight bounced off the white mountains, causing Lorian to shade her eyes, but Kayleen seemed unaffected.

"One day's not a very long time," Lorian said.

"At least we have good motivation," Kayleen replied, waving toward the long road behind them. Distant smoke announced patrols preparing their morning meal.

"Agreed," Lorian whispered.

They checked in with the man living at the foot of the mountains.

He warned them to watch for falling ice and other dangers, urging them to reconsider attempting the climb.

"This is a very bad time of year to be doing this," said the guide.

"It's more exciting this way." Lorian flashed him a tight smile.

The man grunted and proceeded to supply them with spike strips for their boots and thick gloves to aid their climb.

"You'll have to climb straight up on three different occasions. I suggest you choose a leader wisely. There should be a row of small flags on the top, but if there aren't any left, hand this cloth to Kladder when you get to the other side." The man gave Anabel a blue and green handkerchief.

They tied themselves to each other with ropes through their belts. Kayleen was chosen to lead, since she was the only one with significant climbing experience. Teven had been dragged out to climb short cliffs several times, but Mount Palean was on a completely different level. If they had had three days to do it, the climb would have been simple, even enjoyable, but a one-day deadline called for unsafe haste. The challenge was designed to conquer those who had the strength for the Kireshana but lacked cunning, endurance, or courage.

The first hour of ascent was easy, the second grew arduous, and Lorian found herself gasping by the third hour.

Kayleen called for a short break.

"I can't … feel … my feet," Anabel complained. She began to remove her left boot.

"Keep those on," Kayleen instructed.

Lorian felt there was something odd about the way she said it. After a few seconds, it occurred to her that Kayleen sounded completely normal.

"But my feet hurt!" said Anabel.

Kayleen concentrated, weighing the consequences of an unmentioned plan.

"Give me your hand," she commanded Anabel.

"What?" asked Anabel, looking baffled.

Instead of repeating herself, Kayleen reached out and touched Anabel's gloved hand.

"Ouch! What was that?" asked Anabel.

"They're called anotechs, and they'll help your blood circulate better. Be nice to them; I want them back later," Kayleen said with a teasing grin.

Lorian opened her mouth to request a more thorough explanation.

"It's a long story," Teven warned. "We should continue. I'll tell you on the way." With that, he reached out and touched her arm.

She felt a sharp prick. Then, she felt a rush of warmth spread through her body.

"Whoa! No, no, no. None of that for me thanks," Marc protested, as Teven reached over to touch his arm.

"It's okay, Marc; it really works," Lorian assured her friend, amazed at how good she felt.

They began climbing again. As they did, Teven explained what he knew about anotechs, which wasn't much.

Marc held out for another twenty minutes, but as they approached the first vertical climb, he broke down and let Teven give him some anotechs.

"I can barely feel my arms," he said.

"Serves you right for refusing help," Lorian said unsympathetically.

Kayleen started the vertical climb. Marc followed then Anabel, Lorian, and Teven.

Lorian felt her arms tremble when she was a third of the way to the top. The supply pack strapped to her back grew heavier every second. She reached carefully for a more suitable handhold so she could rest a moment. A cry from above drew her attention.

"Look out!" called Kayleen.

A rock the size of Lorian's head came barreling down the mountain. Without thinking, Lorian threw her body to the left and scrambled for a new handhold. Just as her hand closed around a sturdy rock, Lorian felt Anabel's full weight on her belt. A surprised cry escaped her. More confused shouts came from above, but Lorian's eyes were clenched shut as she concentrated on gripping her rock. She fervently hoped her belt wouldn't break or pull her pants off. The few seconds it took Anabel to get a new hold on the mountain seemed like a lifetime to Lorian. When the danger passed, she willed her hands to release the rock. Ten minutes later, she gratefully took Marc's hand and let him haul her up onto the small plateau.

"Let's not do that again," Lorian said, when her breathing returned to a semi-normal rate.

"Sorry, we've got to do it twice more," Kayleen said, "but I vote we eat before taking on this next stretch." She placed a gloved hand on the rock wall rising straight up into a cloud in front of her.

Over ration bars, Lorian, Marc, and Anabel talked about their life in the palace.

"It's got its hardships but we poor, humble servants survive," Marc concluded.

"What's Princess Rela like?" asked Teven.

Lorian detected more than mild interest in his tone, and his deep green eyes looked hungry for information. There was also a buried pain that Lorian could not explain. She pushed these observations aside to answer him.

"She's frustrated."

"Has been for years," Marc added.

"What does she look like?" Kayleen asked, though Lorian got the impression the question would have come from Teven sooner or later.

"She's pretty—"

"Oh, Lorian, you do our princess a great injustice!" Anabel exclaimed. She spoke directly to Teven. "She's gorgeous. Her crystal blue eyes are like rare jewels redeemed from the depths of the South Asrien Sea. Her light brown hair's so soft that—"

"I'm sorry," Marc interrupted. "My sister reads too much romantic sappy stuff."

"You know I'm right, Marc. I've seen the way you look at the princess," Anabel teased.

Marc shrugged and nodded agreeably.

"How does he look at the princess, Anabel?" Teven asked slowly. A muscle in his right arm twitched.

Detecting a shift in Teven's demeanor, Lorian defended Marc.

"Like any man with eyes. Princess Rela is indeed beautiful like her mother." Lorian could swear Teven flinched at mention of the former queen. "I was only a child when Lord Kezem claimed the throne, but I saw Queen Reia once or twice. Her image is forever etched in my mind."

"I know the feeling," Teven replied dryly.

The shadow of a grin touched Kayleen's face.

Teven rose, and everyone took that as a sign to move on.

There were no more mishaps on the next vertical climb, but it was a good fifteen meters more than the last one and left everyone short of breath. It also contained fewer handholds. At one spot near the top, Lorian couldn't find any place to hold. The wind picked up, whipping through her clothes and touching her with its cold breath. She clung to the rock surface and endured a barrage of tiny ice flakes. A few tears escaped and froze, further adding to her misery.

The next segment consisted of a slippery slope at a forty-five degree angle. Teven and Kayleen both took the lead, practically dragging the others along by the rope. Lorian held her own during this part, but her legs shook with fatigue.

"We've got four hours of daylight left!" Teven shouted. "We've got to move faster!"

It was not pleasant news. Thinking of the constant danger Princess Rela faced, Lorian found the strength to push on. Being confined to the palace had made Rela naïve but not stupid. Lorian admired her friend's easy affection. For as long as Lorian could remember, Sarie had charged her with keeping Rela safe and informed. She had done her best so far, and she would not let the princess down now.

Were Lord Kezem's fate not linked to the princess, my blade would have been buried in him long ago.

Lorian was pulled away from her thoughts by the third and final wall standing between them and Mount Palean's peak. With her resolve fortified by warm memories, Lorian scaled the wall like she had been climbing her whole life. She knew exactly where to place her hands and feet. This time, she was a half-step behind Anabel in reaching the plateau.

They ate the next meal while climbing to the peak. At the top, they took a moment to enjoy the view. The Riden Mountains stretched out to the north as far as the eye could see. Behind them, to the west, Fort Riden looked like it could fit in an infant's palm. Smoke rose from the southwest where the Imberg Tosh Mines and processing plants belched smoke into the air. To the south, the city of Ritten appeared as an ungainly bump on the vast flatness of the Kevloth Plains. To the east and northeast, the gorgeous, colorful Kesler Plains and Riden Flats seemed to go on forever. In between, Lake Ceree showed up as a glittering strip of blue.

Lorian found no words to capture the beauty.

"I've got one!" Marc exclaimed triumphantly. He held up a frozen stick with a piece of red cloth tied to it.

"Great, Marc, great. Make me deaf while you're announcing your wonderful discovery," Anabel said, rubbing her left ear. The move brushed some frost crystals from her short, blond hair. "Besides, we don't need it since we have the blue and green cloth."

The descent was more harrowing than the ascent. Several times, one or more of the group slipped, pulling everyone down the slope at unsafe speeds. The most terrifying moment for Lorian came when Marc slipped and fell sideways into Kayleen and Anabel, tossing both young women from the mountain. Their surprised screams were drowned out by Lorian's own scream as she, Marc, and Teven followed them headfirst. Fortunately, they landed in a snowbank five meters below the cliff they had tumbled from. Despite the danger, they remained tethered together.

The sun had weakened the ice on this side of the mountain. As they neared the bottom, a solid crack split the air. Lorian's heart stopped and she looked up to see a wall of ice and snow headed their way.

"Run!" Kayleen, Marc, and Teven cried simultaneously.

They took off, but Anabel tripped on the rope, slowing progress. By the time everyone had regained their feet, the wall of snow slammed into them. The five friends flew a good six meters before landing one by one. Anabel landed hard on her left arm, which responded with an audible crack. Tears flowed freely as she clutched her left arm and opened her mouth in a silent scream. Everyone gathered around her.

"Oh, no, now we're in for it," Marc commented. "She doesn't do pain well."

Anabel gritted her teeth and glared daggers at her brother. Blood started seeping through Anabel's sleeve and dripped onto the snow. The shock of seeing blood brought on bone-wracking sobs that shook the wounded arm, which increased the pain and resulted in more sobs.

Lorian felt helpless. She could set a simple fracture, but this one was far from simple.

"Calm down, Anabel," Kayleen commanded. She removed her gloves, touched Anabel's right arm, and closed her eyes to concentrate.

Anabel passed out.

"What did you do to her?" Marc grabbed Kayleen's right shoulder.

"I put her to sleep so she wouldn't feel the pain," Kayleen answered, shrugging off his grip.

"Get me a thermal blanket," Teven ordered, already loosening Anabel's travel cloak and slicing the sleeve of her shirt away. "Lorian, see if you can set up a tent around us. It's going to be dark soon, and the wind will pick up."

Marc ripped into his pack trying to find a thermal blanket. It took him a moment to find one and tear it open.

Teven took the blanket and wrapped it tightly around Anabel.

"Marc, take the flag to the cabin and tell Kladder we're going to be here for a while. See if he has a bed he can spare for her," Kayleen ordered, knowing they needed to get Marc away from the sight of

Anabel's injury.

Lorian built a tent around Teven, Kayleen, and Anabel. It was difficult because she had to work without moving them. With her task done, Lorian entered the tent to watch Teven and Kayleen work. Kayleen had started a small fire by the door and was filling a pot with snow to make water. While the water warmed, she added a packet of sterilizing chemicals.

"Can I help?" Lorian inquired.

"Hold her still. I think she's waking," Teven answered.

Lorian rushed to Anabel's side and held her shoulders down. She watched Kayleen dip a cloth in the sterile water and toss it to Teven. He braced himself, used the cloth to cleanse the wound, and slid a bone back beneath Anabel's skin. The sight of blood seeping out of the wound turned Lorian's stomach. She tried to look away but couldn't. A muffled cry came from Anabel who suddenly fought Lorian's grip. Kayleen lent her weight to Anabel's legs so she wouldn't kick Teven while he worked. Lorian looked down and noticed the makeshift gag for the first time. Poor Anabel was as pale as the snow around her.

"Ssshhhh, it's okay; it's over," Lorian murmured, stroking Anabel's sweaty hair. She moved her head so tears wouldn't fall on her friend.

"Kayleen, are the bandages ready?" Teven asked hoarsely. He looked pale as well.

"Yes, but they're still hot," Kayleen replied.

"Well, cool them down fast," said Teven. "The anotechs are slowing the blood flow, but they can't stop it. She's bleeding all over the place here."

Lorian watched fascinated as Kayleen gathered several strips of a former shirt that lay on the snow beside the pot in which they had been sterilized. A minute later, she handed the strips to Teven who wrapped Anabel's wound tightly. Then, Teven and Kayleen placed their hands on Anabel, bowed their heads, and closed their eyes. Lorian remembered how the anotechs had helped her climb Mount Palean. She peered down at her poor friend through tear-filled eyes. Anabel's face flushed a bright pink then turned a deeper, frightening shade of red.

Lorian's alarmed cry brought Teven and Kayleen back to the present.

"She's burning up!"

"Let the anotechs fight for her," Kayleen said.

"Will she die?" A lump of fear lodged in Lorian's throat.

"Hard to say, but I don't think so," said Teven, shrugging wearily. "The anotechs are helping her fight the infection. She should be okay in the morning."

"How is she?" Marc asked, entering the tent.

Teven repeated his prediction. Kladder did have a bed to offer Anabel, but at this point, no one wanted to move her. Instead, all five weary travelers crammed into the tiny tent and huddled for warmth. Marc fell asleep holding Anabel's good hand. Lorian settled herself on Anabel's other side. Teven slept in front of the tent's entrance, and Kayleen squeezed in between Lorian and the tent wall. Aside from Anabel, nobody slept well that night.

Chapter 31:
Terrible Truth

Zeri (June) 18, 1560-Zeri (June) 25, 1560
Kesler Plains

Next morning, Teven and Kayleen collected some of their anotechs.

Anabel awoke looking pale but much better.

"What happened?" she asked, lifting her bandaged arm and studying it curiously.

"You don't remember flying through the air, landing on your arm, snapping it like a twig, bleeding all over the place, and scaring me half to death?" Marc stared at his sister incredulously.

She shook her head.

"Was it bad?" asked Anabel.

Lorian chuckled first, then Marc, then everyone.

"Yeah, it was bad," Marc answered, rubbing his stiff neck.

"Squeeze," Teven ordered, taking Anabel's left hand in his.

She grimaced but managed a weak squeeze.

"Good; it's healing," said Teven. "The anotechs have reinforced the bone, but it'll take some time to completely heal. I suggest you use your other arm as a landing pad for a while."

"Thank you, Doctor Teven. I'll try to remember that," said Anabel.

They ate a hearty morning meal of fried eggs and korver jerky, courtesy of Kladder and his wife Nora. Then, they packed their tent and continued their journey into the Kesler Plains. The weather on this side of the Riden Mountains was much nicer. Winter on the Kesler Plains could be very brutal but was usually mercifully short.

A week later and well into the Kesler Plains, Kayleen grew weary of seeing one gorgeous field of grain after another. A sea of fresh purple flowers made her recall something her father had said. She frowned and concentrated. Since when was she able to remember anything about her father?

Kayleen could almost hear his voice saying, *"When in come the iras, out goes the winter."*

"Iras," Kayleen murmured at the memory.

"Did you say something?" asked Teven.

"My father used to talk about iras," Kayleen said, gesturing to the pretty purple flowers. More of the memory returned to her. "We used to take a hov from Rammon to my uncle's farm on the Kesler Plains. Sometimes we would stop to watch small animals hop in and out of the iras."

"I thought you couldn't remember your father," Teven said.

"I couldn't but now I can. Strange," Kayleen said with a one-shoulder shrug.

"Very strange," echoed Teven.

"Where are you from?" Lorian asked.

The anotechs unlocked new information every second, and a deep longing to know her parents swept over Kayleen.

"Rammon, I think. My parents had connections to the palace, strong connections."

"What kind of connections?" Teven wondered.

A phrase popped into Kayleen's mind and wouldn't go away.

"Enuli asanti rimnula," she murmured.

"Which means, what exactly?" asked Marc.

"I don't know. It just came to mind. I think my mother said it once," Kayleen said, shutting her eyes. "It was important to her." She concentrated so hard that she broke out in a sweat. A cool breeze sprang up and gave her a chill.

"Easy now. Don't think about it. It'll come to you when you need to know," Teven said.

Ignoring him, Kayleen opened her eyes.

"The words sound vaguely Kalastan, but I've never heard of them before."

"What language is that?" inquired Anabel.

"An old language used by the Rangers," Kayleen replied. "They're the ones who raised—"

"Not to be rude but those clouds look odd to me," Marc

interrupted, waving a hand behind Teven and Kayleen.

Kayleen whirled and saw a long line of fluffy white clouds hurtling toward them. Her heart picked up its pace.

"He's right. This is not going to be pleasant. We should head for that farmhouse," she said, pointing to their right. About four hundred meters away, a small house shuddered against the swiftly rising wind.

"I don't know about that house. It looks like it wants to swallow us, shake us around, and spit us out again," Marc commented.

Everyone ignored him.

"What's wrong? It's just a storm," Anabel said. "We have equipment to handle rain courtesy of the Fort Riden troops."

"Don't bother with rain gear. It won't protect us from that," Kayleen said, shaking her head. "And there's never just a storm out on the plains!" she added over her shoulder as she dashed for the tiny house.

They sprinted as fast as they could with their heavy packs. Teven caught up to Kayleen but stumbled to his knees because he was off balance from the added weight of Anabel's pack.

Kayleen paused to heave him to his feet again.

"Leave the packs!" she shouted, whipping off the shoulder straps of her own pack. "We'll get them later!"

Seeing she was serious, Teven, Lorian, and Marc dropped their packs.

Anabel ran with her left arm tucked across her chest, trying to keep the recently broken bone from moving. The anotechs had done wonders with it so far, but it still had a long way to go for complete healing. Each jarring step sent a stab of pain shooting through it.

"I can't! It hurts!" she cried, halting suddenly.

Kayleen ran back to Anabel.

"I'm sorry, but you can't stay here!" She shouted to be heard above the rising wind. "This is a windstorm!"

"Please, just leave me!" Anabel begged.

The others stumbled on with Marc in the lead.

Kayleen shook her head.

"These fields are going to be alive with flying debris soon! We need shelter now!" She grabbed Anabel's good arm and dragged her along in her wake.

As they approached the house, they heard a piercing woman's wail above the wind.

"Mika!"

The shriek of the wind grew louder in response.

Kayleen spotted a woman running back and forth in front of the house wringing her hands and shouting. Next instant, Kayleen's sharp eyes picked out a boy about forty meters beyond the left side of the house.

"Get that woman to shelter!" she ordered.

Teven and Marc ran for the woman.

"Get her inside!" Kayleen screamed. She shoved Anabel at Lorian and didn't wait to see if Lorian obeyed.

Kayleen analyzed the situation as she ran toward the boy standing in a sand patch kicking his legs and screaming as particles pelted him from every direction. Small stones cut into his bare legs. A branch snapped off a nearby tree. Controlled by the massive, unseen hand of the wind, the branch bucked first one way then the other before hurtling at the child. Kayleen urged her legs to pump faster. With a desperate cry, she flung herself at the boy, caught his waist in her arms, and yanked him along her flight path.

The branch struck her back with enough force to beat the breath from her body. Midair, she twisted to land on her back, biting her lower lip in the process. Another branch ripped a hole in the shirt sleeve protecting her left forearm and a stone scraped along the exposed skin. Feeling the sting of flying dirt, Kayleen launched to her feet again, still cradling the boy. Running with Mika in her arms was awkward but desperation strengthened her legs. Kayleen ran harder than ever. The wind buffeted her left then right then from above, trying to rip the boy away. She fought it, determined not to lose him. Twenty seconds later, she pounded on the door to the basement shelter. The doors swung open, and Kayleen allowed a dozen hands to ease her and her burden to safety.

"Nice job," Teven greeted cheerfully.

Kayleen looked up. He was upside down from her perspective. The hands lowered her to the floor.

"Ugh, I feel awful," moaned Kayleen.

"Complain; complain. Well, this time you have a right to," Teven said. His smile didn't quite mask his worry. "Next time, warn me when you're going to do something like take on a windstorm."

Teven's face was replaced by the boy's mother.

"Thank you! Thank you for saving Mika! He's my only child! I'd be lost if I didn't have him!"

Kayleen sat up. The sudden shift in position made her lightheaded. Tiny sparkles of light danced around her vision.

"Glad I could help," Kayleen mumbled, speaking slowly so as not to further upset her stomach which was already fully prepared to rebel. She wiped blood from her bottom lip. "Where's Anabel?"

"I'm here," Anabel said, not sounding happy about being alive.

"How's the arm?" asked Kayleen.

"Still there," Anabel replied. Her tone spoke of incredible pain.

The wind howled above them, drawing every eye to the rattling shelter door.

Teven knelt beside Kayleen and used his derringer dagger to cut away the tattered lower half of her left sleeve. A thin line of blood marked the path the rock had taken.

"Don't worry. It's just a small cut," Kayleen said.

Teven frowned, but she silently reassured him that the anotechs had everything under control.

It struck Kayleen that there was no father with the family. She pondered ways to bring up the question, but the woman saved her the trouble.

"I'm sure my husband would thank you if he could, but he was conscripted into the RLA last year." The woman's voice trembled with a mixture of sadness and anger.

Kayleen's heart went out to her.

"Have all the farmers in the region been taken?" Teven wondered. He settled into a more comfortable position on the floor.

"They have. My husband, Marcus, was among the last to be taken to serve that beast!" the woman spat. She yelped, realizing the consequences her words might have. "Oh, please don't tell anyone I said that!"

"We're not exactly in the good graces of His Excellency," said Teven.

"Who are you?" Mika asked with childlike innocence. He sat on the dirt floor in between Teven and Kayleen.

Introductions went around. Everyone who was still standing sat down, resigned to the fact that it could be a very long night. Outside, something heavy smashed into the shelter doors, startling everyone.

"How long's it going to last?" Marc questioned.

"Hard to say when it comes to windstorms," said Kayleen. "They can last minutes, hours, or days, but most commonly they're only a few hours in length."

"I wonder why we never heard of windstorms in the palace," Anabel said. "One would think the tutors would mention something like that."

"You work in the Rammon palace?" Carla Etan asked. "Marcus and I did as well. He was a cook, and I was a serving maid. Before that, I was an indentured servant who sang under the stage name of Lady Gianna LeCross. The queen's Safe Service Act rescued me from my abusive master."

"How long ago was that?" Kayleen queried.

"Oh, years ago," Carla said with a dismissive wave of her hand. "We left about a year before Lord Kezem took the throne. We didn't agree with King Terosh and Queen Reia's move to align Reshner with the Galactic Alliance of Populated Planets. It's nothing but a tax burden and a headache." Her tone turned thoughtful. "Still, I wonder what would have happened if the king and queen had not been murdered."

She lies, said the anotechs.

What do you mean? Kayleen kept her expression neutral even as she grilled the tiny machines.

This woman was among those the queen urged to flee just before the palace invasion.

Why would she lie to us?

The anotechs stayed silent for several minutes while they subtly searched for the answer. Finally, they returned to Kayleen.

She does not mean to lie, but this is the story she has told for years. Those who fled as the palace fell were the closest allies of House Minstel. The lie is all that has saved her family for years. She believes it now.

"Can you tell us what happened? When the palace fell, I mean," Teven said eagerly.

"Where have you been, young man?" asked Carla.

"We've been away a long time," said Kayleen.

Teven shot her a grateful smile.

"I will tell you what I know," Carla promised. "King Terosh was lured into a trap and assassinated. The Captain of the Royal Guard delivered his body to the palace a couple of days later. The queen did not take the news well. Most of Reshner spent months in mourning while Lord Kezem urged rebellion. Finally, he moved against the palace."

"Who was the Captain of the Royal Guard?" Teven's tone indicated he could guess but dreaded being right.

That got Kayleen's attention, and she waited anxiously for Carla's answer.

"A fine soldier who disappeared about the same time as the palace changed hands," said Carla. "He was probably killed."

"What was his name?" Teven asked.

"Captain Laocer, of course. You must have hidden in a box for the last thirteen years not to know that," said Carla.

Traitor, whispered the anotechs.

What do you mean? Kayleen demanded, dazed.

Aster Captain Ectosh Laocer conspired to kill King Terosh and betrayed the throne room codes so Kezem could capture the queen.

Why? Every instinct in Kayleen argued with the anotechs.

He loved the queen and wanted to marry her, but Lord Kezem betrayed him.

Kayleen's mind reeled. From Teven's expression, she could tell a similar conversation was taking place in him.

"I heard he escaped that night," Lorian said helpfully.

"I *know* he escaped," said Kayleen hoarsely.

"What's wrong?" Anabel asked. She placed her good hand on Kayleen's arm. "You look like you've seen a ghost."

"Not just any ghost, *that* ghost," Teven said, confusing everyone but Kayleen.

She felt ill.

"He's alive!" Anabel exclaimed, still not understanding. "We should find him. He can help us fight Lord Kezem."

"He would help us, but we're *not* seeking his help," Teven declared.

Every eye turned to him.

Mika inched away from Teven and closer to Kayleen.

"Captain Laocer betrayed the queen," Kayleen explained in a whisper. She knew the words in her heart, but saying them aloud drove the emotional dagger deeper. The image of the man who had been a father figure to her shattered, destroying a treasured piece of her childhood.

"How can you know that?" Carla demanded.

Because I believe the anotechs, thought Kayleen. She searched her mind for a logical explanation to give the curious crowd without betraying the anotechs' full powers.

"Because Laocer is very much alive." One look at Teven's deep green eyes said things were swiftly clicking into place.

"I guess that makes sense," said Lorian, understanding slowing entering her eyes. "Everyone knows he was in love with Queen Reia."

Teven stiffened, and Kayleen placed a calming hand on his arm.

"He also conveniently found King Terosh's body," said Lorian, either ignoring or not noticing Teven's reaction. "If he was truly protecting the king during the assassination, he would be dead. His survival must mean something, and he disappeared the night the palace fell."

"He arrived in a Ranger camp in the Riden Mountains with several wounds. He gained their respect and made many friends." Kayleen was surprised at the depths of bitterness rising inside of her. "He searched many years until he found the lost prince."

"He murdered the prince's guardian and trained him to fight Lord Kezem," Teven added, spitting the words out like poison.

"You speak of yourself," Lorian said with awe.

Anabel and Marc gasped.

Teven looked away.

"Couldn't the captain have earned his wounds defending the queen?" Carla asked.

"He could, but he'd be dead," Lorian answered. "No one of significance who stayed survived that night. Only servants and children lived to become Kezem's slaves. He must have run. At the very least, he's a traitor by cowardice."

"I still don't believe it," Carla argued. "That doesn't sound like the man I knew."

It didn't really matter what she believed. They still lacked many pieces to the past, but this one terrible truth about Laocer's betrayal created a new bond among the five fugitives.

The tiny cellar fell silent save for the distant sound of rushing wind beating the fields and trees. Kayleen sat surrounded by her friends, wondering what she would say to Captain Laocer when she saw him. There would certainly be angry words, but what did she seek from him?

An apology? A confession?

What did she wish upon him?

Retribution? Revenge?

Until now, he had never done anything to hurt her, but this pain tore deep. She became aware of Teven's smoldering presence. She needed to speak with him alone but worried that the others would misunderstand such a request. The more she wondered, the less she knew, and the larger that ball of frustration grew within her.

Chapter 32:
New Perspective

Zeri (June) 26, 1560
Etan Wind Shelter, Kesler Plains

The windstorm carried on throughout the night. They shared a meal of dried tretling meat and grape juice. The conversation was kept purposefully light and meaningless, but the weight of the first conversation left Teven McKnight tossing and turning, tormented by bitter feelings. A small part of him questioned the conclusion he had drawn. He wished that his mentor was a righteous man, but his instincts told him otherwise. The anotechs, with their endless logic, calculated the odds of other scenarios and always came back to the first, most painful one.

When sunlight finally blazed through the tiny crack between the double doors of the shelter, Teven got up. He cast a brief, jealous glance at Mika who had fallen asleep in Kayleen's arms. His friend seemed so peaceful that he hated to wake her.

Anabel began to stir and moaned.

Teven crept over to her and squeezed her right shoulder gently.

"Wake up, Anabel. We need to change the bandages," Teven whispered, trying not to wake everyone.

The jostling during the windstorm had caused Anabel's wounded arm to bleed.

"I have some sterile wrap around here somewhere," Carla offered, already wide awake.

"Thanks. That would help," said Teven.

Carla searched the small shelter and finally found the sterile wrap.

Teven wasted no time in changing the bandages around Anabel's arm. The wound looked fairly clean. A thin layer of anotechs formed a protective barrier over the place where the bone had pierced the skin, but most of the anotech efforts concentrated on knitting the bone fragments back together or fighting off infection. The frantic flight for shelter had undone some of the previous healing efforts. The anotechs cut down on some of the aching pain, but they could do nothing for the sharp pains which struck whenever the arm was moved.

Everyone worked to lift Anabel's flagging spirits. Then, they hastily ate a meal of preserved ira petals and bid farewell to Carla Etan and little Mika. Pushing the shelter doors open took a lot of effort because a heavy branch had fallen across them.

Outside, the sun shone brightly, but fallen trees and disheveled ira fields testified to the windstorm's destructive power. Teven surveyed the damage as they retrieved their packs. As they continued along the correct path, Teven and Kayleen fell behind the others.

Lorian hesitated a moment and then nodded when Teven waved her on. She ushered Anabel and Marc along at a slightly faster pace.

Kayleen said nothing, giving Teven time to gather his thoughts.

"I've thought about the discussion last night, and I've gained a new perspective on the matter," Teven began.

"Which one?" Kayleen asked. "The war, Lord Kezem, Captain Laocer, us?"

Teven was surprised she had included them in that list, but he had pondered their relationship too.

"All of it," he said, tipping his right shoulder up in a half-shrug. "I began my training because Laocer told me to, and I had nothing else to do. But then Jalna showed up and introduced the anotechs, and I met you and learned practically everything else." He halted suddenly and placed a hand on her right forearm. "I've come to realize, I have more than Laocer's dream to fight for. It's become *my* dream, Kayleen. A dream of taking down Kezem, righting every wrong he's done to the people, and spending the rest of my days with you."

"You dream big." Kayleen smiled broadly but sadly.

"What's wrong?" Teven asked, taking her left forearm and tenderly tracing the cut she had earned during yesterday's rescue. At his touch, the anotechs in his fingers healed the wound.

Kayleen stood still with her head bent forward and her eyes closed for the few seconds it took to fix the cut. Then, she looked up with tears in her eyes.

"Teven, I—" she broke off and drew in a shaky breath. "I can't love you!" The words broke the dam holding back the tears.

"But you could love me!" Teven protested, mistaking her meaning. Confused, he stepped closer and wrapped his arms around her.

She answered the embrace willingly. Her voice was muffled because her head was buried against his chest.

"I don't know what it is! It's just something inside me that says we can love each other but not be *in* love! And I do love you and want to be in love with you. That's what hurts so bad!"

She wasn't making much sense, but he didn't feel right telling her that while she was so distraught.

"It's okay. We can take it slow. We're still good friends," Teven said, wishing he had a better rebuttal. He held her tightly to prevent himself from leaning down to kiss away her distress. He feared saying the words aloud, but his mind shouted *I love you!* After a few moments he reluctantly said, "We'd better catch up with the others before they get themselves into trouble."

Kayleen sniffled and stepped away, wiping tears.

Teven's arms felt empty.

"I'm sorry," Kayleen whispered, as they slowly began walking after their friends.

Me too, Teven thought.

After half a minute of silence, Kayleen cleared her throat.

"I really don't know what it is … it's just a cold feeling that says any commitment of love we make will shatter before it's realized."

"We're both confused right now, that's all." Teven didn't want to think about what she'd just said.

Kayleen attempted a weak smile.

"More memories returned to me last night. The anotechs can tell me many things but not how to react to their information overload. I asked about my parents and they answered, but I'm not sure I trust them."

"Why not?" asked Teven.

"They said my parents were Rangers. It makes sense, but there's something more—some fact I'm missing—and it's driving me crazy!"

Teven happily noted that she sounded more like the fiery Kayleen he loved. A smile started forming but froze at a man's harsh voice.

"Whom do you serve? Are you friend or foe?" the stranger demanded. He emerged from the tall grain to their left and pointed a kerlak pistol at the side of Teven's head.

Teven weighed the odds of answering the question and attacking the man. They were at a slight disadvantage because their opponent already had his weapon out. He concluded answering the question would be the best start.

"The answer to the first is reserved for friends, and the answer to the second depends on whom you serve," said Kayleen.

"Do you serve Kezem?" demanded the man.

"No," Teven answered instantly, noticing the absence of title. He waited for an energy beam to burn his head open.

It never came.

Instead, the man lowered his weapon.

"Then, you are friends, and we are in sore need of friends right now," said the stranger.

Teven studied the man who had the careworn look of someone who had lost much. A hard glint in the man's black eyes promised he would fight until death claimed him. His brown hair was shaggy, but his beard was neatly trimmed.

"Kezem's forces gather around us," said the stranger. "I think it best if you join us. We can offer you some protection."

Teven held in a laugh but could not suppress a smile.

"You have a strange way of asking for help," Kayleen said, voicing Teven's thoughts.

"I do not ask for aid," said the man, drawing himself up proudly. "I offer it."

The weight of the man's gaze settled squarely on Teven's shoulders.

"What did you do to get on Kezem's bad side?" asked Teven.

"I was an RLA captain who found his conscience," the man replied. "And you?"

"I was born," Teven answered.

The intensity of the man's scrutiny increased tenfold.

Teven offered the man his right hand in a gesture of friendship. He didn't know whether he could trust the man or not but figured the truth would be the best course of action.

"I am Teven McKnight, and my friend is Kayleen Wellum. We travel in the company of several derringers from the palace, people Lord Kezem would like to reclaim."

"My people should have spoken to them already," said the stranger.

"You must be Captain Alexi Gordon," Kayleen said.

Gordon nodded stiffly.

"Fort Riden rings with tales of your impending destruction," said Kayleen. "When will Kezem's forces arrive?"

"We don't know for sure, but my scouts reported Commander Perit's troops gathering near the Lotrian Fields yesterday. They have hovs and could be on top of us at any moment."

"How many strong are you?" Teven questioned.

"Forty-seven, counting you," said Captain Gordon.

"It is a hopeless battle then," said Kayleen.

Gordon flexed his jaw.

"I do not enter hopeless battles! We will drive them off!"

Teven had no doubt Alexi Gordon believed the words, but he personally agreed with Kayleen. Commander Perit would easily commit a thousand soldiers to the battle. This small band of rebels would probably be wiped out, but Teven refused to abandon them to such a bleak fate.

"Well, Captain Gordon, we are at your service," Teven said, tipping his head respectfully. "Take us to your camp so we can talk strategy."

On the dash to the tiny rebel camp, Captain Gordon explained the situation.

"We've been lucky so far. Commander Perit split his division into four sections and spread them out over the Kesler Plains. Unfortunately, my forces are also scattered to draw Perit away from our main force. Perit's a fool I had the misfortune to serve under once upon a time. He prefers overkill."

"Is that why you left?" Teven asked. Months of conditioning and mild anotech augmentation allowed him to keep up the conversation while they ran.

"Yes, we stumbled on a group of seven Rangers while on a recruiting mission. Perit ordered my entire command to attack them. My men killed more of each other than the Rangers. The man may be a fool, but he commands many soldiers. What's worse is that I don't want to kill those wretches. They're children, farmers, and miners, not killers."

Teven let the man rant before steering the conversation back to the current situation.

"How many soldiers will Perit commit here?" he wondered.

"Best estimates say four hundred, but it could be more," said Captain Gordon. "Perit's an idiot, but I'm worried that Captain Renith and Aster Captain Selok may have formed their own plans. They are definitely not fools."

"Are they friends of yours? Would they let you slip away?" Kayleen inquired.

"No. They may have been my friends long ago, but they've gained too much under Kezem to let friendship get in the way," Gordon replied. "Selok's men especially worry me. Some of them have a reputation for being unpredictable, hot-headed, and cruel."

They arrived at the small camp hidden in a collapsed graveground depression. For as much as the position protected them from sight, Teven could easily picture it as a death trap. Most of the tents and supplies were packed. No one spoke but adults nervously fingered weapons or frantically rounded up children.

"I thought you said there were only forty-seven of us," Teven said.

"Forty-seven fighters," Gordon clarified. "Most of the children are too young to hold a gun."

"We cannot fight here!" Teven declared.

"We don't have a choice," Kayleen announced. As she spoke, her kerlinblade came to life in her left hand, and her right hand pointed a pistol over Teven's left shoulder.

A danger sense told Teven to move. He dove to the right as an energy beam sizzled through the space he'd just vacated.

Chapter 33:
Battle on the Kesler Plains

Zeri (June) 26, 1560
Alexi Gordon's Rebel Camp, Kesler Plains

The pitched battle on the Kesler Plains raged out of control. The red-clad enemy separated from the surrounding fields and swept into the depression like a flashflood.

Kayleen Wellum twisted away from a young soldier's lunge. His kerlinblade sailed past her so close she felt its heat. Dropping her kerlinblade and pistol, she grabbed the soldier's right wrist and squeezed until he dropped his blade. Then, she wrenched his right arm up behind his back and buckled his left knee by stomping on it. They hit the ground as three energy beams flew over their heads. The soldier threw her off and tried to roll away, but her right foot lashed out and caught his chin, ending the fight.

Kayleen scooped up her weapons, scrambled to her feet, and frantically looked for Teven. Another soldier slashed at her with a steel sword. There was something simultaneously cruel, crazy, and cocky in his expression, but she had no time to ponder what it could mean. She caught the strike with her kerlinblade and disarmed the man with a deft flick of her left wrist. He stumbled to one knee. Her blade hovered near his neck, but she hesitated to land a killing blow, wanting him to yield and live. A child ran past, and before she could react, the man whipped a dagger from his boot and grabbed the boy.

"No!" Kayleen cried, knowing it was already too late.

The man's dagger struck the child above his right hip. Kayleen didn't hesitate this time. Her blade bit deep into the soldier's neck. She didn't enjoy killing, but there was no way to prevent that now. She tried to block out the screams, curses, cries of pain, and sickening thuds of serlak bullets slamming into flesh. Holstering her kerlak pistol, Kayleen rushed over to the screaming boy.

"Mommy! I want my mommy!" the child wailed, clutching his bleeding side.

"Calm down! Hold still!" Kayleen instructed.

An energy beam zipped toward them, and Kayleen knocked it out of the air with her kerlinblade. She debated herself briefly before shutting the blade off and tucking it back on to her belt. More beams came at them. Kayleen yanked the child aside, letting the beams pass harmlessly and find other victims in the crowd around them. She wrapped both arms around the boy's split side and willed the anotechs to stitch the gaping wound closed.

The boy fainted.

A nearby rebel screamed as one of Perit's men thrust a kerlinblade into his chest.

The stench of charred flesh struck Kayleen's senses until the anotechs took over. Horrified, she grabbed her kerlak pistol from its holster and put a hole in the soldier's back. She hated to leave the wounded boy, but she was attracting too much attention to adequately protect him. She shot two soldiers advancing on her from the left, ran five steps, and shot another three.

Several beams and bullets came her way. Kayleen back flipped to avoid some of them and retrieved her kerlinblade from her belt to deal with the others. Suddenly, something slammed hard across her shoulder blades, throwing her forward. Kayleen tossed her weapons away so she could land without killing herself. As she hit the ground, she rolled to face her attacker. A banistick beat the dirt next to her head. She lashed out with her feet, catching the assailant across the knees, dropping him. Propelling herself to her feet, Kayleen planted a fist in the man's face.

Flexing her painful right hand and squinting against the dust clouds being raised by the battle, Kayleen rolled twice and reached for her kerlinblade. Her shoulders throbbed, but adrenaline gave her the strength to regain her feet and swing the violet blade up in time to block a blade closing in on a little girl.

The man behind the blade rocked back on his heels and eyed her with amusement. His biceps nearly burst from the strained uniform shirt, and he towered over her by a good half-meter.

They locked gazes.

A few other soldiers looked like they wanted to enter the duel, but Kayleen's opponent stared coldly at them until they chose different targets.

Kayleen gently pushed the girl aside and behind her.

"Put down your blade, and I'll kill you quickly," promised the massive soldier.

"Sorry, but I like my chances with the blade better," Kayleen retorted, sucking in some deep breaths. A bullet whistled past her right ear. She half turned to check on the child.

The man struck at her head quicker than she thought possible.

Kayleen ducked and took two stumbling steps backward to keep her head.

"Come, let me kill you," the man taunted. He took a few casual swipes at her. His swings rapidly got harder and faster. Then, he took a small step forward. "If we capture you, Lord Kezem will crush every bone in your rebel body."

"That's reassuring," Kayleen replied, backing up, reluctant to have her arms snapped in two by the force of his blows. A massive swing struck the ground where she had been standing.

"Stand still!" roared the solider.

"Not likely!" Kayleen danced out of the way of three more thrusts, suddenly glad for Teven's example on the importance of dodging. She pivoted on her left foot and nearly tripped over the child she was trying to save. "Get out of here!"

The girl turned to run, but a wall of fighting soldiers blocked her way. Kayleen jumped back to avoid a slash. She backpedaled, whirled, and cut a hole in the line so the girl could scramble away. A young soldier yelped with pain as Kayleen's blade batted him aside to make way for the child. She paused to watch the girl slip through.

"How noble!" mocked the large soldier directly into her left ear.

Shock coursed through Kayleen, and she expected to feel a blade burning through her chest. Instead, a hand slammed into her back, flinging her into the wall of soldiers. She bounced off someone and sprawled on her back in the dirt. Somehow, she managed to keep a grip on her kerlinblade without taking her legs off.

"Get up so I can skewer you properly!" said the soldier, standing to her right. His dusty boots were even with her waist, and his white blade blazed inches from her neck. His dark eyes widened with the unholy gleam of battle lust.

"Kayleen!" called Teven.

She looked out of the corner of her right eye and caught a glimpse of Teven rushing her way, fighting through a crowd of soldiers. Suddenly, she realized a line of maroon uniforms encompassed her.

"No, Guidan! Lord Kezem wants them alive!" someone shouted from the crowd.

The man blinked, confused by the interruption. He frowned with disappointment but pulled his weapon back slightly.

"Get up!" he snarled. "You're now a prisoner. Your unconditional surrender begins now, or pain will pave your way to the palace. Do you understand?"

There's no way I'm surrendering! Kayleen's mind screamed even as she nodded slowly and climbed to her feet, glad that the child had made it though the line. She stared up into the soldier's face.

Dirt and blood showed up as dark splotches on his pale face, lending to his ruthless appearance.

"Let's get this over with," Kayleen muttered, whipping her blue blade up and tipping it in a salute. She flicked the switch to keep the blade color constant.

A dull thud reached her ears.

The man grinned but didn't advance. A line of blood trickled out of his nose.

Kayleen stared at him in shock but had little time to ponder her extended leases on life and freedom.

A soldier tackled her from the side.

The kerlinblade flew from her hand. Kayleen threw an elbow back into man's head, but he held on tightly. She wrenched her body back and forth, loosening his grip. Once free, Kayleen took two running steps. Seeing a dagger descend toward a familiar fallen form, she stopped short and tackled the man about to stab Lorian. He went flying to the left, and she bounced off his bony shoulder gasping for breath.

Groaning, Kayleen rolled over and half-rose. A kick caught her in the ribs nullifying her efforts to rise. She rolled onto her back too tired to continue fighting. Her vision clouded, and her thoughts turned to Teven. Another kick to the ribs brought an explosion of pain. Her body curled reflexively. More blows followed in rapid succession before she mercifully passed out.

***

After dodging the first energy beam, Teven yanked his banistick from its clip and flung it out. It opened directly into a man's head with a nice thud. The soldier fell over wearing a stupid grin. Teven flowed through the crowd of RLA grunts, swinging his banistick back and forth. He ducked behind a dueling pair to avoid an energy beam, and it hit Gordon's man, ending the match prematurely.

Teven slammed the banistick into the dueling victor's stomach and brought his left hand down on the man's neck when he doubled over. A sharp shout behind him drew his attention. He spun to see a man with a hole in his head topple over. A group of four soldiers charged, and Teven raised his banistick defiantly, ready to meet them. Much to Teven's astonishment, they were cut down by serlak bullets while they were still a few paces from him.

My protector is still watching.

A kerlinblade sliced toward Teven's left leg. He knocked it away with his banistick, grateful Kayleen had modified the weapon to resist electricity. The young woman wielding the attacking blade grinned and swung at his neck. His eyes widened. Women were rare in Kezem's army. Teven moved without thinking, stepping close to her. His feet moved swiftly and surely, sweeping him into and out of danger several times during each heartbeat. Blade met banistick several times in rapid succession. Finally, a wild light came to the woman's eyes, and she swung with all her might. Teven dodged and brought his banistick up under her chin, knocking her out.

He turned and saw another soldier three meters away mercilessly pounding on a fallen rebel. Remembering the flingers Kayleen had given him, Teven whipped out three and hurled them at the soldier. The man straightened with an enraged scream as the flingers bit into his shoulders, back, and butt. The flingers didn't kill the man, but the distraction allowed the rebel to scramble away.

As Teven moved to engage the soldier, an exasperated cry reached his ears.

"Just die already!"

He turned to see a young rebel repeatedly slamming a body with a banistick.

"Stop it! He's dead!" Teven grabbed the young man's arm but was immediately thrown off.

"He killed my father!" the boy wailed.

"Then you won't do your father any good by sticking around to die!" Teven retorted. He traded his banistick for his kerlinblade and opened it as wide and flat as it would go. "We're falling back! Get out of here!" He caught an energy beam on his blade, directing it away from the distraught boy.

Though it hardly seemed possible, the boy's voice held more panic when he spoke again.

"Where's Anna? My sister! I've got to find my little sister!" The boy drove his banistick into a soldier's chest and began a frantic search.

"How old is she?" Teven asked, trying to follow the boy's erratic search pattern. The sooner they found the sister, the sooner the boy would leave the battlefield. Teven had known the rebels would lose this fight before they entered it, but he was determined to help them cut their losses.

"Six!"

"What's she—"

"There! Behind those soldiers!"

As they fought their way in the child's direction, Teven saw Kayleen disappear into the roiling mass of fighting soldiers.

"Kayleen!" called Teven.

With a wild cry, an enthusiastic soldier barreled at Teven, kerlinblade cocked over his head to strike.

Teven made the mistake of meeting the blade with his own. The blades trembled with the impact, and Teven went flying off balance to the right. He landed on his feet and traded his blade for his kerlak pistol. Three beams stopped the crazy soldier then Teven turned the pistol against others, systematically taking out enemy after enemy. He pulled the trigger one more time and a faint whine resulted. Tossing the useless gun aside, Teven reached again for his kerlinblade.

Get to Kayleen!

The thought burned through his brain on loop as Teven again rushed toward his friend, beating people aside with his kerlinblade. A little girl slipped through the line of soldiers, and her brother scooped her up and took off. Teven caught another glimpse of Kayleen brawling with some soldiers. Then, she disappeared again beneath a swirling mass of enemies. He tried to reach her, but something caught his shoulder. He whirled and swung.

Captain Alexi Gordon ducked.

"It's too late! We've got to retreat!" The rebel leader held a wounded child in one arm and Teven's right arm in the other.

"I'm not leaving her!" Teven declared, shrugging off the hold.

"Yes, you are!" said Captain Gordon firmly. "You're going to protect the children during the retreat."

Teven felt himself spinning around and being propelled away from Kayleen. His heart nearly tore in two. His mind demanded he return to her, but he knew Captain Gordon was right. Commander Perit's troops had her, and if the rebels stayed much longer, they would die. He muttered Kayleen's name over and over as he fled. His despair turned to anger, which he took out on all who dared to follow Gordon's rebels.

Once they were safe, Teven looked about for Anabel, Marc, and Lorian.

I hope they're safe.

***

Zeri (June) 26, 1560
Same Day
Tryse's Camp, Kesler Plains

Tryse used a high-powered sniper rifle borrowed from Fort Riden to take out RLA soldiers. Like most sniper rifles, this one shot projectile bullets. He'd been following this rebel band for some time but hadn't revealed himself. Captain Alexi Gordon had once taught a kerlinblade class Tryse had taken.

Four soldiers approached a young rebel who waved a banistick boldly. Tryse took them out. He shot until the twenty bullets were spent. Then, he slammed in another cartridge and shot some more soldiers.

Tryse briefly mused at how far he had fallen from the ideal Coridian Assassin. Most in the special branch of the Royal Guard tended to scorn sniper rifles. Over the past few months, Tryse had come to appreciate the sleek weapon. He had followed derringers through most of the Kireshana, but then, he had taken to ambushing Fort Riden patrols. Hearing of Captain Gordon's plight caused him to seek out the rebels.

It helped that Tryse didn't much like Commander Perit. The opposing groups broke apart. Tryse continued to take out Perit's men. Shooting required some concentration, but he was still able to observe that the split had not been clean. Perit's men had prisoners. Tryse cursed. Kezem never had his men take prisoners unless he wanted something from them, and Tryse was determined to deprive Kezem of everything he wanted. He briefly considered shooting the prisoners but dismissed the idea. He would just have to follow Perit's men and hope he could help the prisoners escape.

***

Zeri (June) 26, 1560
Same Day
Kesler Plains

Hidden in a flimsy nalga tree two kilometers from the battle, Todd Wellum contemplated helping the rebels. He knew they were doomed, but he hoped they would defy the overwhelming odds. Knowing he would learn more by watching, Todd decided against interfering. He was curious. Commander Perit had committed an awful lot of men to destroy one tiny band of rebels.

Todd recognized one of the young rebels as a derringer. Although Todd had never bothered drawing close to those he protected, he knew he had seen this one before. The boy glided smoothly over the battleground, leaping into and out of danger. Then, another man stopped the young man from fighting and urged him to leave. Todd frowned and adjusted the field glasses for a close look at the young man's face. The enhanced view revealed a stream of tears and two syllables. It looked like a name. Todd's hand froze then trembled. He denied what he thought the boy was saying.

Kayleen.

Todd trained the field glasses over the boy's shoulder to a tangled mass of maroon uniforms that matched the color of the battlefield. A flash of red-gold hair floated among the soldiers. Todd's heart soared with hope, but the figure receded so quickly he doubted his eyes. He widened the field of vision, hoping to catch one more glimpse of her but found nothing.

The battle was over, and to Todd's amazement, Commander Perit's soldiers began to gather the prisoners. Miners and farmers were often pressed into joining the RLA, but whenever the rebels clashed with the RLA, the result was death to one side or the other.

Two soldiers lifted the young woman with flowing reddish blond hair from the depression. Todd focused the field glasses on her. The girl looked exactly like Kiata.

"Kayleen," Todd whispered in awe. A cry lodged in his burning throat. Every muscle strained to leap to his feet and fight for his daughter, but if he charged in now, he would only end up dead.

He had waited more than a decade to see his little girl again. A few days would not make a big difference, but they would certainly hurt. Silent sobs shook his body, as he watched the scene unfold.

The soldiers dropped Kayleen's limp form on the depression's edge and returned for more prisoners. A stab of pain and anger urged Todd to fly to the battle and kill every one of Perit's soldiers. Todd fingered his energy pistol but managed to keep his senses. Another young woman, this one with light brown skin, was dumped beside Kayleen.

Finding the sight of Kayleen too painful to face right now, Todd scanned slowly sideways, right to left. A visibly upset young man was yelling at a soldier placing stuncuffs on a pale young woman with a heavy layer of white cloth around her arm. A bright red stain indicated that the battle had reopened the wound. If the soldier activated the energy fields, the girl would probably faint from the shocks. The boy threw off the arms restraining him and punched the man hurting the girl. A stun beam ended his violent protests.

Todd shook his head and squashed another urge to help the rebels. He would never make it in time anyway.

A picture of the other young man, the one who had uttered Kayleen's name came to mind. Todd determined to have a chat with him. They would both be seeking a way to rescue Kayleen, so it was time to work together. Then, it struck him that he knew the young man.

Hello, Teven. You look like your father.

Chapter 34:
Hov Troubles

Zeri (June) 26, 1560
Same Day
Commander Perit's Camp, Kesler Plains

Kayleen felt sick when she woke up. She breathed slowly for several minutes and took mental notes on her condition. Her stomach ached, her head hurt, her ribs and back throbbed, and most of her muscles felt like they'd been pulled from her body and slapped back on haphazardly. She forced her eyes open and found herself in a tent. She lifted her right hand and was only mildly surprised to find it attached to her left arm. She let both arms flop back onto her stomach where they had been resting. A sore muscle in her abdomen twitched in protest, eliciting a groan from Kayleen.

"You have a way of expressing my feelings," Lorian Petole's voice said from somewhere to her right. "Thanks for the save, by the way. I'm sorry you got kicked for it."

Lorian's words brought the dull throbbing in Kayleen's lower right ribs to the forefront of her mind. She moaned again and rolled her head right to peer over at Lorian.

"No problem. Glad I could be of service," Kayleen muttered. She tried to sit up, but only managed to lift her head two inches before a wave of nausea flattened her again. She squeezed her eyes shut and willed her stomach to settle.

"I'd stay down if I were you," said Lorian. "You took quite a beating."

"Did anyone get away?" Kayleen asked, taking the good advice.

"Teven did."

Kayleen sighed with relief.

"Thank goodness. What about Marc and Anabel?"

"Right here," Anabel called from Kayleen's left. "Marc's unconscious because he tried to play hero when they arrested us."

Kayleen shook her head and immediately regretted it. Colorful spots floated behind her shut eyes. She felt the anotechs repairing some of the damage her body had sustained, so she stayed still to let them work.

"You talk in your sleep," Anabel said.

Kayleen grunted.

"You kept repeating that phrase from the other day," said Marc.

"Enuli asanti rimnula," Kayleen supplied with her eyes still shut.

"Right, that's the one, only this time you added 'edolin cumani' to the beginning," Lorian said.

"It is some sort of curse?" Anabel wondered.

Kayleen detected a note of pain in her voice.

"No," she said, making it a long word. She rolled the words over in her mind. *Edolin cumani enuli asanti rimnula*. "It's a healing charm, I think, but I don't know what it's for because I still can't make sense of the words."

She asked the anotechs for an explanation, but they remained suspiciously mute on the subject.

"Then, how do you know it's a healing charm?" asked Anabel.

"I just do," said Kayleen, knowing it was true but unable to explain why.

"It's hardly a useful charm," Anabel complained. "I could use a little healing here."

"Can you reach my hand?" Kayleen asked.

"Sure. Why?" said Anabel.

"I'm going to give you some more anotechs to help your arm heal faster," Kayleen explained.

A moment later, Anabel's cold hands wrapped around Kayleen's right hand.

Kayleen shut her eyes tighter in concentration. A brief inner battle ensued as the anotechs protested leaving their work on her aching muscles to go mend Anabel's arm. Kayleen won just as she heard the tent flap snap open.

"On your feet!" shouted a male voice. "Commander Isaac Perit present!"

Reluctantly, Kayleen opened her eyes but she didn't bother standing. She didn't think she'd make it anyway.

"Never mind formalities," Perit said gruffly. His stiff posture, gray hair, and grim expression spoke of a military background.

Perit appeared tall, but Kayleen attributed that to the deceptive view from the ground.

"Step away from the other prisoners!" barked the soldier who had announced Commander Perit. A swift stride brought him in striking range.

Instinctively, Kayleen shut her eyes and tensed, but the sound of a smack brought them open again. She caught a glimpse of Anabel collapsing next to her. The short, wheezing gasps hissing through Anabel's teeth told Kayleen that the soldier had struck the bad arm.

"Stand down, marksman," ordered the commander.

The young man looked disappointed but complied. He glared at the captives like it was their fault he got reprimanded.

"The hovs will be here within the hour to take you to the palace," said Commander Perit. "I'd like some answers before they get here."

"Good luck getting them," Kayleen challenged, drawing the hint of a smile from the grim commander.

"Your attire and kerlinblade claim you are a derringer, but my men say you fight like a Ranger," said the Commander. "I have orders to capture these three," he continued waving toward Anabel, Marc, and Lorian, "but you were never mentioned. That makes me curious."

He paused.

"Was there a question for me?" asked Kayleen, forcing a flippant tone. Having her head cocked to the side at an odd angle made it especially difficult to maintain a casual tone.

"Are you a Ranger?" Perit sounded impatient.

Kayleen felt it was useless to deny the accusation but wished to offer the commander no more help than she absolutely had to.

"I was raised by them," she answered carefully.

"Where is their hideout in the Riden Mountains?" asked the commander.

A flash of inspiration came to Kayleen.

He's testing me.

This was followed by a rush of anxiety for her friends in the

Ranger camp. Captain Laocer came to mind and cold anger replaced anxiety.

"You already know the answer to that question," said Kayleen.

"Indulge me," said the commander.

"No."

Shock flashed across the commander's face. Obviously, he was not used to having his requests denied.

"If you have no information for me, then I have no use for you," Commander Perit said.

The marksman smiled and gave Kayleen an icy smirk. His hand rested lightly on his kerlinblade.

"But Lord Kezem does, and he would be displeased to know you killed a prisoner," said Kayleen.

"He would never know," Perit growled.

Kayleen knew, as he did, that Lord Kezem's spies were everywhere. A report of the entire battle had probably already reached him.

"You're a very bad liar, Commander," said Kayleen. It was time to go on the offensive. "Why were you ordered to capture my friends?"

Commander Perit regarded her cautiously. He must have concluded the information would do no harm for he answered. Something in his expression said he found the situation distasteful.

"Trouble at the palace. Lord Kezem needs to coerce Princess Rela into cooperating."

His statement made sense but didn't tell Kayleen anything new. She felt the vibration of approaching hov engines before she heard them. When she did hear them, it sounded like more than a few.

"Our ride approaches," said Kayleen.

At that moment, Commander Perit's comm unit beeped and spoke.

"Commander Perit, the Royal Guards have arrived to escort the prisoners to Rammon."

The commander nodded to his soldiers.

Kayleen and her friends were roughly hauled to their feet. Still disoriented, Marc leaned heavily on his guards.

"Watch the arm!" Anabel protested.

The marksman who held Anabel squeezed her arm cruelly, making her grimace.

Propelled from behind, Kayleen had little choice but to exit the tent. She looked left and drew in a sharp breath. Twenty splendidly dressed Royal Guards stood at attention around four hovs arranged in a line. Their navy-blue uniforms stood out against the fields of light grain around them. Two klipper fighters hung in the air behind the line of hovs. Fear gripped Kayleen.

Lord Kezem really wants Lorian and the others.

Several kilometers into the journey to Rammon, Kayleen grew desperate. If they reached the palace, bad things would happen. The foursome had been split up. Marc and Anabel Spitzer had been taken in the first hov, and Kayleen and Lorian Petole had been tossed into the third. The second and fourth hovs each carried six soldiers, forming a small caravan. Sleek klipper fighters darted back and forth above them. The black and silver machines thrummed with angry-sounding power. The tinted windows made it impossible to see inside the cockpit.

Kayleen's arms remained bound in front of her. They had been traveling for four minutes now. At this rate, they would reach Rammon in a little under three hours. A gust of wind buffeted the speeding hov, throwing Kayleen into the side. As she reached out to steady herself, a crazy idea came to her. Willing some anotechs to slip through her fingertips, she sent them to the hov's engine compartment. A half-minute later, they returned reporting success. She silently cheered.

"What are you so happy about?" Lorian asked in a whisper.

The engine coughed and died, sparing Kayleen the obligation to answer. The surprised driver cursed and wrestled the steering stick. At Kayleen's bidding, a few straggling anotechs stung the pilot's arm. He jerked the steering stick back and to the left crashing into the fourth hov. Both hovs came to a grinding halt, pitching prisoners and soldiers against safety restraints.

Kayleen ignored the questioning glance Lorian cast her way.

"Hov Three, why are you stopping?" called a male voice through the hov's speakers.

"Don't you know how to drive?" fumed the irate pilot of the fourth hov.

"Why do you think I'm stopping?" muttered the pilot of Kayleen's hov, before activating his comm. He ignored the other pilot. "Engine difficulty, Predator One," he informed, managing to keep his tone civil.

"Well, fix it!" snapped Predator One.

The four soldiers, including the pilot, got out to inspect the damage.

"It's done for," the pilot of Kayleen's hov concluded.

"What just happened?" demanded the fourth hov's pilot.

"How should I know?" snapped Kayleen's pilot.

Kayleen sent anotechs jumping from her hov to the fourth one. She tuned out the rest of the argument to focus on directing the anotechs from afar. Thirty seconds later, smoke began rising from Hov Four. She worked hard to keep a straight face.

Seeing smoke out of the corner of his eye, Hov Four's pilot whined.

"Aw, now my hov's down too!"

Retrieving her anotechs, Kayleen bit her lower lip to hide a grin.

The rest of the convoy stopped and came back to join the two disabled hovs.

Predator One's annoyed voice came over both pilot's receivers.

"Move the prisoners to Hov Two, squeeze an extra soldier into each, and double bind the prisoners. Half the squad will stay here and wait for help to arrive from Meritab. The rest will finish the mission."

The soldiers obeyed. Kayleen winced as a second set of stuncuffs settled to the left of the first, giving her a solid line of metal for forearms. It was a pity she couldn't smack the nearest soldier with all that metal. A wave of guilt washed over her for the extra pain Anabel would suffer from the second set of stuncuffs.

Crammed in the back of Hov Two with a soldier between herself and Lorian, Kayleen waited impatiently for another fifteen minutes. She could have had the anotechs release her at any time, but that would not improve the situation. She needed to free Lorian, Marc, and Anabel and wanted to be well out of the range of any reinforcements before making another move. When she felt it was safe, Kayleen sent the anotechs to work their magic on Hov Two's controls.

"What the—" said the pilot.

"Hov Two slow down!" commanded Predator One. "You're flying erratically!"

"The panels are flashing, Captain! I have no control!"

"Well, get some control!" said the commander in Predator One.

Kayleen ordered the engine disabled but warned the anotechs not to break something vital. The hov sputtered and slid to a stop, so Kayleen recalled the anotechs.

A stream of curses came from the pilot's neck where the

receiver was imbedded. The pilot grumbled and got out of the hov. Instead of going to the engine, he stormed up to her door, yanked it open, grabbed her by the collar, and pulled her close.

"What did you do to my hov, Ranger Witch?" growled the pilot.

Though she tried, Kayleen couldn't stop the smile that answered him. Her safety restraints were removed, and the pilot dragged her from the hov. A shove sent her flying toward Marc and Anabel's hov which had returned to help. She used the momentum to stumble into it, thrusting out her bound arms so her head wouldn't smash against the hov. The metal stuncuffs made a satisfying crunch on the hov's hull. Two strong shocks ripped along her arms, but she ignored the pain. Kayleen considered sending anotechs to bite the man who had pushed her, but she refrained. He had done her a favor. Knowing she wouldn't get another shot at this, Kayleen sent the anotechs zipping onto the final hov.

"Get her away from that hov!" screamed Predator One. The tortured cry came from a half-dozen comms at once, making it eerie and amusing.

The anotechs were back in seconds, duty done. Something akin to a machine sigh came from Hov One which gently settled to the ground.

Silence reigned over the Kesler Plains.

Kayleen straightened, turned, and smiled serenely up at Predator One. Her crossed arms made her appear smug. The Royal Guards eyed her with fear and respect. She could feel the intense glare Hov Two's pilot leveled at her back.

"What are your orders, Captain?" inquired a soldier.

A sigh came from the comm receivers.

"Predator Two, report our troubles to Rammon in person. The rest of you get out the emergency tents. We're staying the night. And someone restrain that Ranger!"

Predator Two hesitated, and Kayleen almost pitied the man who had to report failure to Lord Kezem.

"She already has two sets of stuncuffs on her, Captain Holeth," noted the soldier who had asked for orders.

"Restrain her feet, too," said Captain Holeth peevishly.

"That won't hold her, sir," the soldier lamented.

"Are you questioning my orders, Danub?" snapped the captain.

"No, sir, but Rangers are notoriously difficult to keep captive," said Danub.

"Separate her from the others and stun her. If she tries to escape, kill her."

Touchy, touchy.

Kayleen had no intention of escaping without her friends.

"Danub, hold her friend, the one with the broken arm," Captain Holeth ordered. "Reed, place your kerlinblade against the girl's neck. Meeks, restrain the Ranger. Ranger, you do anything stupid and your friend gets a very large hole in her neck."

Danub and Reed hurried to carry out their orders.

Kayleen's heart thudded in her chest and she watched helplessly.

Danub stood behind Anabel with his left hand around her waist and his right hand on her forehead, tilting her head up. Reed whipped out his kerlinblade with a flourish and pressed the tip against the side of Anabel's exposed neck.

Both men stared stonily at Kayleen.

She returned their gazes steadily but didn't fight as Meeks released both pairs of stuncuffs. She let her arms fall at her sides. Meeks walked behind her, grabbed her right wrist, twisted it, and wrenched the arm up behind her back. A hard boot slammed into her right calf just below the knee, causing it to buckle. Hot pain shot through her right arm and shoulder.

Meeks laughed. It was not a pleasant sound.

"Not so tough anymore, are you?" he mocked in her ear. "I'm gonna ask the captain for some quality time with you later. I love red heads."

Kayleen gritted her teeth, trying to hide the pain. Since two pairs of stuncuffs would not fit on Kayleen's arms while they were behind her back, one pair was reapplied and turned up high enough so that even slight movements set them off. As if that weren't enough, Meeks pushed Kayleen onto her face, so he could fit her ankles with restraints. As she fell, she instinctively twisted her head to the right to avoid breaking her nose. Kayleen winced as a shock coursed through her whole body.

"Is that really necessary?" Lorian demanded.

Kayleen shook her head and silently begged her friend to stay quiet. The soldiers picked her up, causing small electrical charges to run up and down her arms, making her teeth tingle. The failsafe mechanism stopped the charges just as the soldiers roughly deposited her in a hastily erected tent. She shifted position to something halfway comfortable before a stun beam helped her sleep.

***

Zeri (June) 26, 1560
Same Day
Throne Room, Royal Palace, City of Rammon

"The prisoner transport has been delayed, my Lord."

Kezem shook with rage.

The pilot in front of him, designation Predator Two, trembled with fear. Not knowing what else to do, the man rushed to explain.

"One of the prisoners is a Ranger. She disabled two of the hovs by crashing them into each other and then got the other two by …."

"By what?" Kezem asked.

"I d-don't know, my Lord. Magic, I think. D-dark magic," Predator Two stammered.

Kezem growled and made a violent slashing motion, which caused Predator Two to wisely fall silent.

"Kolknir!"

"Here, Excellency." Supreme Commander Kolknir looked annoyed that Kezem had neglected to include his title, but he stepped forward obediently.

"Send Captain Quedron and four more squads to fetch the prisoners. Sedate the Ranger until I can question her, but do not harm her. Leave that to me. Take the prisoners to Estra. I will meet them there." Kezem wanted to study the Ranger, question her, and discover more about this strange ability to conquer hovs. Once satisfied, he would kill her.

"Yes, Your Excellency. It will be done." Kolknir bowed and left to issue the proper orders.

Lord Kezem pondered his next move and wondered if he really needed those prisoners. Princess Rela was helpless to resist. He could have stuncuffs placed on her, and she would have to obey him. On a whim, he summoned the Azhel priest.

When the distraught man was brought before him with his robes not quite on straight and his hair mussed, Kezem felt nothing but contempt for him.

"The four months are almost over," said Kezem. "Tell me, priest, is it truly necessary to have Princess Rela's full cooperation in the matter of finding the treasure chambers in Loresh?"

"Oh yes, Favored One, if she does not wish to find the door, she will block its cry from her heart and mind," replied the priest.

"Where does this call come from? Why can only she hear it?"

The priest lifted a hand and stroked his chin. His gaze became distant. For a moment, Kezem thought the man might be stupid enough to ignore him. But at last, the priest spoke, "The cry comes from the departed spirits of House Minstel. They only call their own."

"Then, I will give her reason to hear that call," said Kezem darkly.

They could fly into Estra but would then have to hike the five kilometers to Loresh for fear that the heat from the hovs would collapse a vital tunnel. The quickest way to the Frozen North would be to go directly south from Rammon across the Kevil Plains and the Ash Plains. When they reached the coast, they would have to fly a hov over the South Asrien Sea or spend hours on a boat.

Kezem grunted. Neither option appealed to him. He disliked trusting hovs over water and outright despised boats.

Chapter 35:
An Ally Revealed

Zeri (June) 26, 1560
Same Day
Temporary Rebel Camp, Kesler Plains

The rebels certainly have amazing stamina, Todd Wellum thought after following them for almost six hours.

Relief flooded his weary limbs when the rebels finally stopped to make camp just as the sun began to set behind the Riden Mountains. If they traveled a little farther, they would run into the Lotrian fields. Todd could have gone a few more kilometers, but they would not have been pleasant ones, especially if they involved the Lotrian Fields.

He stopped about ten meters from the group, leaving the distance to avoid hastily released bullets. Todd waited for the rebels to finish setting up tents in a protective circle. When they settled down, he called to them.

"Hold fire! I am a friend!"

Immediately, a dozen weapons swung in his direction.

"Put your hands up and step closer!" ordered the leader.

"Tell your people to put down their weapons!" Todd called back.

A tense moment passed before the leader spoke again.

"We seem to be at an impasse!"

"I want to ask the boy next to you about one of his companions," said Todd.

"Kayleen?" the boy asked, perplexed.

"Yes! May I step closer?" asked Todd, voice trembling.

The leader nodded to his people who reluctantly lowered their weapons.

"Come slowly," he warned.

Keeping his hands well away from his weapons, Todd covered the distance between them as swiftly as he dared. His composure lapsed momentarily when he came within a meter of the boy who knew his daughter. He staggered forward. The boy recoiled.

The rebel leader's pistol snapped up.

"Stay where you are," said the rebel.

Feeling his knees giving way, Todd knelt. He didn't care that the pistol was still trained on his face. He stared desperately at the young man.

Tell me of my daughter!" he cried.

The young man nodded, and a flash of understanding entered his green eyes. The eyes were Queen Reia's, but the wavy black hair and finely structured features reflected King Terosh. Todd could almost see the thoughts whirling through the young man's head.

"Welcome, uncle," the boy greeted with a calm that reminded Todd of the queen.

"What's going on?" Confusion and anger were equally present in the rebel eader's tone, but he lowered the kerlak pistol.

Todd ignored him.

"Captain Alexi Gordon, meet my uncle, Ranger Todd Wellum," the boy announced.

Todd couldn't fathom how the boy had conjured his name or their family connection, but his next statements shocked him even more.

"He's been protecting derringers throughout the Kireshana," said Teven. "I … felt him watching."

"Prince Teven!" Todd said hoarsely. "I thought Lord Kezem had killed you!"

"He tried," Teven said with a faint grin.

"Your Highness, forgive me for not recognizing you," said the rebel leader, dropping to his knees before the boy.

"There's hardly a need for that out here," Teven noted, gesturing to the wide-open plains surrounding them. "I need to recover my friends before Lord Kezem gets them."

"We will help you," Captain Gordon promised.

"Thank you, Captain. We must cross the Lotrian Fields and get to Meritab. Then, we can take a hov from Meritab to Rammon."

"I'm coming with you," Todd said.

Teven nodded like he had suspected as much.

"Come, have a meal with us," Captain Gordon invited Todd. "Pitch your tent nearby. We'll start out in the morning."

Todd made no move to gather his things. Instead, he said, "Tell me about Kayleen. I've not seen her for more than thirteen years."

Chapter 36:
Shifting Loyalty

Zeri (June) 27, 1560
Princess Rela's Private Chambers, Royal Palace, City of Rammon

Kia stood perfectly still and watched Princess Rela Minstel sleep. Lord Kezem had not been joking when he said he wanted the Melian Maidens to watch over the princess constantly.

Whom do I serve?

The question came to her unbidden, as it usually did in these quiet moments of the night watch. Lord Kezem demanded weekly reports on the princess, and as head maiden, it fell to Kia to compose these reports. She didn't like spying on her young charge.

She thought over the last few months and found herself drawn to the princess by more than the need to protect her. One could hardly help liking the vibrant young woman who, despite the unseen chains, found ways to ease the suffering of others. Several times, Kia and the other Melian Maidens had found themselves conduits of good will, secretly carrying food, medicine, and clothes to families marked by Lord Kezem. A mark made trading nearly impossible and could be earned by offenses as small as wearing green or purple in support of House Minstel.

A soft thump brought Kia out of her reverie. Her bound brown hair whipped as she snapped her head around to glance at Jola who stood ready for battle with her hands hovering over her kerlinblade and banistick.

She must have heard it, too.

The assurance made Kia draw her banistick. She favored the

weapon over kerlinblades because of its versatile nature. The lightweight piece of gilded metal could be snapped out in an instant to its full meter-and-a-half length or be made to partially unfurl for close quarters combat. Kia flicked her weapon out to its full length and slid the handle to the middle, so she could bat away any projectiles.

Peering intently at the corner where she heard the noise, Kia suddenly sensed danger from behind. She spun to see a black-clad figure drop noiselessly onto the end of Princess Rela's bed. Without thinking, Kia leapt onto the bed and interposed her body between the princess and the assassin.

Four in three weeks!

Kia couldn't believe the princess could have made so many enemies during her fifteen years of life. She didn't have time to dwell on that.

The assassin raised a pistol, but Kia's twirling banistick knocked it away before he could fire. The assassin cursed, tucked his right hand close to his body, and took out a throwing dagger with his left hand. Movement to Kia's left caught her attention. Relying on instinct, she closed her banistick and hurled it at the figure in the shadows. Then, she rushed the first assassin, throwing him from the bed. A clunk followed closely by a groan told her the banistick had struck her target. The one she had thrown leapt to his feet, but Jola was there to slam a hand across the back of his neck. He slumped in Jola's arms with a small, feminine cry.

Jola ripped the black mask from the assassin, releasing a mass of golden hair.

The prisoner moaned.

Jola stuncuffed the young woman and lowered her to the ground.

"Move and I kill you," said Jola.

"I am already dead," muttered the girl. Bitterness soaked the words.

Kia couldn't blame her for the attitude. She was correct. The attackers were as good as dead. After scanning the room for further signs of danger, Kia turned on the lights and moved to place restraints on the being she had beamed.

Princess Rela woke up and stared around her room wide-eyed.

"Again?" she asked. "Don't these people have anything better to do than try to kill me?" She threw off the blankets, revealing her shimmering purple night dress. It was one of the few items Kia had smuggled into the palace for the princess. Kezem had practically banned all forms of the royal colors.

A dagger flew toward Princess Rela. Kia watched helplessly as it whipped through the air. Rela threw herself to the left, but the dagger scraped along her right forearm. Kia flinched as Princess Rela winced. If the blade was poisoned, the princess would be dying right about now.

Jola flew across the room and dove behind the bed. A fierce wrestling match ensued. Kia rushed around the bed in time to hear a loud crack as Jola's boot met the man's lower right leg. His pained cry was cut short by a blow to the head. Jola dragged the limp man toward her first prisoner then returned for the attacker Kia's banistick had subdued. She added him to the line of prisoners and reached for her comm.

"I'll call Palace Security," said Jola.

"Wait!" Princess Rela and Kia shouted as one.

Kia's hazel eyes flew to the princess whose expression radiated pity. Intuition told her the princess would object to punishing the prisoners. Kia retrieved her banistick from the floor and braced for a verbal battle.

"We should question them," Kia told Jola, trying to buy time.

"Let them go," Princess Rela said in a tone that wavered between command and plea.

"That is impossible, Princess," Jola said. "They would only attack you again."

"You can protect me," said the princess.

"That is true, but it is less than ideal," said Jola.

"The interrogators will kill them soon enough," Kia said. "We might as well learn what we can from them first."

Rela climbed off her high bed.

"Please, I do not want them to die because of me!" The princess sounded truly distraught.

"It's not about *you*," declared the girl from the floor. She spat in Rela's direction. The slimy projectile fell far short of the princess, but thankfully, it did stop her from approaching the prisoners. "If you die, he dies."

A look of horror crossed Princess Rela's face. She understood that if Lord Kezem experienced pain, she felt it and vice versa, but she hadn't actually considered dying.

"Who sent you? Is there a place we can send your bodies?" Kia asked gently. The second question was not unkind, merely practical.

The prisoners would soon be executed after unpleasant interrogations. Although sluggish in helping people, Kezem's government could be ruthlessly efficient when it wanted to be.

"Let my children go," said one of the masked figures on the floor.

At Kia's nod, Jola removed the black cloth masks. The young man who had caught the banistick across the forehead was still out cold.

The face of the older man was twisted with more than physical pain.

"I forced them to come with me to kill Lord Kezem." The man's voice trembled with fear and fatigue. "Do not hold that against them."

"No!" the girl protested. Her gray eyes flashed with passion. "Father, we have fought together to rid our planet of that monster. We will die together!"

"You do not need to die," Princess Rela said impatiently. After donning a dark blue robe with gold woven in an intricate pattern around the neck, waist, and sleeves, the princess moved forward to release the captives' bonds.

Kia moved to block her.

"Step aside!" A determined glint entered Princess Rela's blue eyes.

Kia couldn't guess where the princess had obtained the regal tone, but part of her rejoiced to see this new side of the young woman. Training took over, and Kia fell into step next to the princess. She would wait for her to release them, but as soon as they attacked, her kerlinblade would cut them down.

The father of the would-be assassins practically melted with relief as Rela reached for his daughter's bonds.

The girl looked ready to spit again.

"No, Lissa! Let her free you. Escape. Live to fight Lord Kezem another day!" His eyes begged his daughter to listen.

"I don't want her mercy or her pity!" said Lissa. A silent battle of wills raged for several long seconds. Then, her father's words finally reached her and horror replaced much of the anger. "What about you, Father? Why won't you escape?"

"My leg is broken. I won't be able to make it over the walls," said the father. His tone said accepted his fate. "Wake Brian and get out of here."

Princess Rela removed the stuncuffs, but Lissa just stared at her father.

Kia prepared to take the assassin down if she so much as twitched in the princess's direction.

"We can get you out," Princess Rela promised, turning to Kia. "You can take them down the servants' corridors and smuggle them out the waste room."

Her confidence told Kia that the princess had given escape plans much thought.

"Princess, these people tried to kill you," Kia said, letting her tone carry her disapproval.

"But they wanted to kill Lord Kezem," Princess Rela argued. "Even I have dreamed about that, Kia. Please, I am not strong enough!"

The statement about wanting to kill Kezem drained the rest of Lissa's anger and made Kia acknowledge that similar feelings had existed within her for quite some time. She had never actually considered attacking Lord Kezem, but she wasn't blind. She could see that his harsh rule was crushing the people. The thought that she, Princess Rela, and these attackers shared similar thoughts gave Kia pause. She cursed silently, knowing she was about to alter her life forever.

"Jola, you can stay here, leave, or take the boy," said Kia.

"This maneuver will be illegal," Jola commented.

"The Melian Maidens are not Lord Kezem's personal korvers. We swore an oath to trust, obey, and protect members of the Royal House. Furthermore, we swore to protect the people. I intend to fulfill my oaths tonight," Kia said, knowing the argument would appeal to Jola's sense of duty. She bent over to release the cuffs binding the older man. She paused for a final warning. "My commitment to your life ends the second you threaten the princess. Do *not* test me on this."

The man nodded solemnly, and once his hands were free, he meekly placed his left hand in her proffered right hand.

Kia grunted as she hefted the man and placed him in a comfortable position across her back.

"Lead on, Princess."

Princess Rela looked ready to protest but reconsidered.

"Hurry!" she urged.

A thrill of excitement rushed through Kia as she followed

Princess Rela down several passages. It was a long way from the princess's seventh-floor suite down to the palace gardens. Near the end of their journey, Kia's shoulders began aching. She bumped the man's leg rounding a corner and winced sympathetically. His breath rasped in her ears, but he did not cry out. Eventually, they made it to the kitchen and then the waste room. Kia wrinkled her nose at the foul smell. The others clapped hands over noses or grimaced, but Princess Rela seemed unaffected.

They burst out the disposal room door and found themselves in a dense part of the palace gardens. As Kia set her prisoner on his feet, Jola's burden woke up and managed a small cry before his sister's hand clamped over his mouth.

"Hush, Brian, we're getting out of here. Father's hurt. If you scream, the guards will hear!" Lissa explained.

"Take this and buy passage out of Rammon," Princess Rela commanded. She took a small pouch on a string from around her neck and placed it around the older man's neck. It contained most of the kefs that remained from her botched escape attempt.

Tears came to the man's eyes.

Kia couldn't tell if the tears were from gratitude or pain.

"There is no way to hide the attack from Lord Kezem," Princess Rela continued. "He probably felt it when your dagger pierced my arm, and the guards could still come any moment! Go down this first path until you reach the wall. Follow it to the right until you reach the south gate. You'll have to stun the guards, but please don't kill them. That would only make things worse."

"Thank you, Princess. It is more than we deserve," said the man humbly.

"Kia, give me your pistol."

Kia reluctantly handed the princess the kerlak gun.

Flicking the pistol's setting to stun, Princess Rela handed it to the man.

"Use this on the gate guards and take it with you. They must not discover that the weapon of a Melian Maiden aided your escape. Now, go!"

Kia was wary of the prisoners. With the princess's permission, she followed them until they were safely off the palace grounds.

***

Zeri (June) 27, 1560
Same Day

Lord Kezem's Private Chambers, Royal Palace, City of Rammon

Lord Kezem awoke to find his white sheets marred with blood near his right forearm. He frowned and concentrated, trying to think. No one could have gotten close enough to harm him, and anyone who did would never have inflicted a mere scratch. That only left one possibility.

Rela has been wounded. The thought of the princess shot anger through him, but it faded as he thought, *Why didn't she tell me?*

After a hasty morning meal, Lord Kezem summoned the princess. She entered the throne room minutes later flanked by two of the Melian Maidens he had provided her. His breath caught in his chest and he did a double take, almost swearing it was Queen Reia who strode towards him. Princess Rela wore a simple dress of royal blue shimmersilk that showed off her budding young figure. Her light brown hair was swept up away from her smooth features and woven in a manner that accentuated the few red strands.

"What happened last night?" demanded Kezem.

"There was a small incident," Rela answered, folding her hands in front of her.

"How were you wounded?" asked Kezem.

"Someone seeking your life threw a dagger at me. I failed to dodge quickly enough," she replied.

"Where were your maidens?"

"Fighting the other two aspiring assassins," said Rela.

"Why was I not given a report?" Kezem bellowed for the entire palace to hear. He leapt off the throne. "Where are these assassins? I will kill them myself!"

"They are gone."

"You let them go, didn't you?" Kezem glared at the princess. His left eye twitch with irritation.

After returning his gaze steadily for a few seconds, Princess Rela looked away and nodded.

"I did." Her answer was barely audible.

"What could possibly have possessed you to release them?" asked Kezem.

"You would have killed them," said Rela.

"Someone *will* suffer for this." Kezem's voice was low and tight.

"Why are you so angry? Why must there always be punishment? People would serve you if you served them!" The princess's face flooded with color.

Kezem flushed as well, for she had never spoken to him like that. He despised this new, independent streak.

"They will serve me because they fear me," said Kezem, stepping close to Rela.

The princess retreated a step but maintained eye contact. Only a tremor in her jaw betrayed her fear.

Still glaring at Rela, Kezem addressed his guards.

"Bind them and take them to the interrogation chamber. I have a lesson to teach the princess."

Chapter 37:
Royal Captive

Zeri (June) 27, 1560
Same Day
Princess Rela's Private Quarters, Royal Palace, City of Rammon

Twenty minutes after returning to her chambers, Princess Rela tried concentrating on a new food plan for Rammon's marked people, but her mind kept returning to Kia and Jola. She could almost feel Kezem's heavy hands on her shoulders. He had stood behind her lecturing while shocks tormented Jola and Kia.

Such a high price for defiance.

Rela blinked back tears and shuddered, remembering their pain.

Thankfully, Kezem had not been upset enough to kill them, but they would spend a week in the palace prison to appease his anger.

Linnea and Elia stood stiffly a few feet behind Rela. She didn't have to look to sense their burning anger. They blamed her for Jola and Kia's sudden absence.

I blame me too.

An empty feeling gnawed at her. She thought of the people starving for disagreeing with Lord Kezem. The subsequent anger helped her focus. She wrote a message asking Lory Pascal to send five bags of wheat to the Bann family. It was not what she had meant to do, but it would do for now.

"Elia, will you please take this letter to the Merchant Quarter?" asked Rela.

"We are here to protect you, Princess," Elia said stiffly. "We cannot do that and run errands."

"I regret what happened to Kia and Jola," Rela said softly, "but we cannot stop helping people because we might be hurt!"

"You never get hurt," Elia pointed out.

The comment stung, but Rela didn't fight the pain because she knew she deserved it. Frustrated tears slipped down her cheeks as she nodded agreement.

"I'll take the letter after dark, Princess," Linnea offered.

"Thank you." Rela wiped her eyes, reached into a drawer, rummaged around, and pulled out a ring with a small emerald in it. "Show this to Master or Lady Pascal to prove you act for me."

The Melian Maiden's green eyes widened, but she took the ring without protest.

Rela tried not to think about her mother's ring, the small link to a past she knew next to nothing about.

The door to Princess Rela's drawing room and private sanctuary burst open. Eight Royal Guards and ten Palace Security officers rushed in, the former in their dress blues and the latter in dark gray uniforms.

Experiencing a flashback to a few hours earlier, Rela leapt to her feet.

"I demand an explanation!" she cried.

Linnea and Elia dropped into defensive positions at her sides.

Lord Kezem strode in wearing his usual dark ensemble and hard expression.

"Stand down," he barked at Linnea and Elia.

Confusion and conflicting emotions crossed their faces.

Linnea's blond hair bobbed as she shook her head. Elia just frowned and rested her hand on her kerlinblade.

"I said stand down," Kezem repeated slowly.

"Do as he says," Rela ordered. A sick, anxious sensation told her what was coming. "Thank you, but you cannot help me. There is no reason for you to be hurt."

"Disarm and arrest them," Kezem instructed his men.

His soldiers moved to obey. The first man to reach Elia was laid out flat on his back, clutching his jaw. Linnea's sidekick took out a second man. The rest reached for kerlak pistols.

"No!" Rela and Kezem screamed simultaneously.

Everyone froze.

"Go with them," Rela whispered, though it broke her heart. Her chest heaved, and she breathed shallowly, trying not to faint. She looked deep into each woman's eyes, willing her maidens to save their strength for better odds. "It will only be for a time."

"It will be for as long as I wish, Princess," said Kezem.

The Palace Security guards whisked the Melian Maidens from the room. Rela could only hope Captain Tayce's contact in the palace prison would hear of the incident. She had worked with the captain and his contact several times to smuggle extra medicine in for the prisoners. She didn't know Tayce's contact well, but the man had proven reliable thus far.

He'll know what to do.

We will tell him, if you wish it, Princess of the Chosen.

Rela flinched as if burned, but she refrained from crying out.

Please, tell him!

"Arrest her, but don't hurt her," Kezem said.

Rela backed up a step but bumped into her chair.

"Relax, Princess, the cuffs won't sting you. We're taking a trip to the Frozen North. Friends of yours will meet us there."

***

Zeri (June) 27, 1560
Same Day
Captain Tayce's Office, Fort Vik
Captain Tayce.

Tayce heard the mental call but dismissed it as a trick of his overworked mind. The prisoners had nearly rioted yesterday, and he'd spent most of the night solving subsequent problems. He leaned his head in his hands, elbows propped on his desk, and let his fingers massage his throbbing temples.

Captain Tayce. Princess Rela needs you. Read the palace reports.

What?

Receiving no response, Tayce figured it couldn't hurt to obey the child-like voices haunting his head. He dug his infopad out of a drawer and set it to review palace reports. It didn't take him long to find the reports on hov crews being readied and the arrest of the Melian Maidens assigned to Princess Rela. The day-old report of a battle on the Kesler Plains resulting in prisoners also surprised him, but the prisoner list itself cleared up that mystery.

Captain Tayce wasn't sure what it all meant, but he was certain Princess Rela was in danger. He placed a secure comm call to Marksman Cory Tiridan.

"Do you know where the Melian Maidens were placed?" asked Tayce, after pleasantries.

"Yes, sir, one moment. Let me check," the marksman said. "East Detention Block number forty-five through fifty, sir."

"Thank you." Tayce pondered his next words carefully before voicing them. "Cory, you know that matter we discussed at length? I'm due for a long vacation, and I think I'll take it now. Would you like to come? And if so, would you mind bringing the Melian Maidens?"

"What's wrong, sir?" Tiridan asked.

"Something's happening. Something big. I don't know the details, but Lord Kezem's on the move, and he has the princess with him. Whatever he plans for her, it can't be good."

"Agreed, sir. How shall I proceed?" asked the marksman.

"Have you placed trackers on the palace hovs?" asked Tayce.

"Yes, sir. I did that ages ago when you suggested it," Tiridan answered.

"Good, collect the prisoners as soon as possible and meet me on the eastern shore of the Crystal Lake."

"Yes, Captain," Cory said. "But what about—"

"I'll deal with the details and contact you when everything is ready."

Tayce spent an hour filling out forms to make sure Fort Vik could function without him for a while. Next, he left word with a junior officer that he would be unavailable for the rest of the week. With a final bracing breath, Tayce used a code Princess Rela had given him to break into the palace prison system. Within minutes, he had quietly transferred several prisoners out of the East Detention Block and looped security vids so no one could witness the mass exodus. Finally, he forged orders for Marksman Tiridan, worded a brief private message to him, and sent it off.

"Ridenspeed, Cory," Tayce whispered.

***

Zeri (June) 27, 1560
Same Day
East Detention Block, Prison Level, Royal Palace, City of Rammon

Marksman Cory Tiridan moved down the dim corridors with a soldier's sure steps, but his heart raced triple time within him.

The checkpoint guards studied his orders closely but let him pass without comment. Supreme Commander Kolknir was not a man they wanted to question.

When Tiridan came to East Detention Block number forty-five, he paused and studied the occupant.

Observant hazel eyes swept up and down, measuring his threat level. The Melian Maiden was older than him by several years, yet she stood respectfully when he stopped before her cell. Her mass of brown hair was barely contained by clips. Her movements were stiff, reminding him of the unpleasant business conducted that morning.

It seems so long ago.

Cory didn't know what the maidens had done but doubted it was serious enough to merit the shock torture. He racked his brain for a name.

"Lady Kia, do you swear to protect Princess Rela of House Minstel with your whole being from now until death claims you?" he asked.

"I have sworn thus and still swear it," she answered.

"Then, you will help me rescue her," Cory announced, releasing the lock. He swallowed hard, keenly aware that she could snap his neck in a heartbeat. "Please, Captain Tayce needs your help. Lord Kezem has arrested the princess."

Without waiting for a response, Cory moved to the next cell and repeated his question.

"We have all sworn to protect the princess," Kia said. "We will follow you until she is safe."

Cory nodded and disengaged the lock. He continued down the line, releasing the Melian Maidens one by one. Introductions were exchanged, and they fell in neatly behind him as he rushed down the confusing prison passages to the hov lot.

"Half in this one, half in the other," Cory ordered, hopping into the hov's pilot chair.

Kia, Jola, and another maiden whom Cory recognized from Princess Rela's brief visits jumped in the back. He started the engine and waited for the vehicle to rise to its customary half-meter height. It seemed to take an eternity, but once that was accomplished, he tinted the windows and started at an unhurried pace through the gates. The other three maidens went to the other hov, also having the good sense to tint the windows.

"The next hov is with me," Cory called casually to the guard.

"I just received the orders. You're free to proceed, marksman." The gate guard hit a button on his control panel and the gates rose.

Cory nodded, resisting the urge to sigh with relief.

"Do you have a plan?" Kia asked.

Her tone told Cory he had better answer wisely.

"At the moment, we're getting out of Rammon," Cory replied. "Then we'll rendezvous with Captain Tayce. He'll know our next step."

"Elia and Linnea heard Lord Kezem say he will take Princess Rela to the Frozen North. We must go to Estra," said Kia.

"The meeting point is on the way to Estra," Cory said, speaking hastily lest she lose patience with him. He felt the intensity of her gaze and willed himself to concentrate on driving.

"Very well. The princess trusts your captain, so shall we … for now," said Kia.

"Lord Kezem's life is connected to Princess Rela, but I fear his emotional control over his physical self will fail when he discovers there is no treasure. He may try to harm the princess. That is unacceptable," said Jola.

Unacceptable indeed. Does she always talk that way?

They grew silent and remained so until they had safely passed through Rammon's West Gate, Glider. The name came from the legend of Kern Glider, the half-god charged with guarding Riden.

***

Zeri (June) 27, 1560
Same Day
Kevil Plains

The well-armed, heavily armored convoy carrying Lord Kezem and the unhappy princess across the Kevil Plains sped along at unhealthy speeds. Kezem scratched absently at his left wrist and watched the land slip by. A windstorm had recently flattened most of the fields. Gray clouds dominated the sky, but so far, no rain had fallen. His wrist bothered him again. Kezem glanced down at his reddening wrists and frowned. He activated the transmitter.

"Stop that!" he said.

"They bother me," Rela whined.

"Makil, remove Princess Rela's bindings," Kezem instructed, pinching the bridge of his nose. "She's about to rub my wrists off here."

"It will be done, Excellency," the faithful soldier promised.

"Does he come with any other lines besides, 'it will be done, Excellency'?" Rela mocked, doing a wonderful impression of Makil.

"Rela, stop tormenting Makil," Kezem said wearily.

"Do you honestly think this is the best way to gain my

cooperation on your silly little treasure hunt?" Rela asked, overdoing the superior princess tone.

"Who told you that?" Kezem demanded, planning executions as he spoke.

"His High Fakeness, the great Azhel Priest Benali," Rela replied, sounding bored.

Lord Kezem sat up straighter.

How does she know he's a fake?

His informants had taken over three weeks to come up with that information. She'd been in a hov with the man for less than an hour.

"She lies, Favored One," Benali protested. "I have told her nothing!"

Kezem hit a switch and a screen popped down offering him a close view of Benali's nose hairs. Grimacing, Kezem adjusted the vid to a less offensive view.

"I have known you were a fraud for months now. I keep you around because you speak some truths about Loresh."

"It's a fable," Rela said in a sing-song voice. She primly smoothed out the sleeve of the bright blue smartcloth shirt. The fibers would automatically bind closer together to protect her against cold and wind.

"I have told her nothing!" Benali repeated.

"Then how does she know?" Kezem demanded.

"His thoughts are as transparent as they are ugly," said Rela.

Kezem moved the vid camera to get a closer look at the defiant princess. Her expression was angry and very disgusted, but her clear blue eyes spoke truth. She didn't know he was watching so she would hardly bother feigning innocence. He flicked off the comm transmitter and cursed in Bornovan.

She can read minds! As disturbing as that thought was, it didn't surprise him. After all, her mother had been a Ranger witch. He turned the transmitter and receiver back on. It was time he made her options and the consequences of defiance very clear to her.

"—not believe the nasty things he's thought about me. Even now, his gaze is murderous!" Rela ranted, unaware Kezem had cut off communication for a few seconds.

"Oh, I believe you, Rela, but do not concern yourself with Benali. When his usefulness has expired, I will dispose of him." Kezem enjoyed Benali's priceless expression.

Concern flashed across Rela's face, before disgust and anger returned.

"Do you ever get tired of threatening people?"

"No," Kezem answered honestly. "Just as I'm sure you never grow tired of undermining me." He sighed, trying to collect his scattered thoughts.

This is going to be a very long trip.

"But that is not what I wished to discuss with you. Benali may be a fraud, but Loresh's treasures are real and I *will* have those treasures. You will find the entrance to the lower levels or I will slaughter your friends before your eyes!" Kezem didn't think it was possible for Rela's eyes to get any bigger, but they did.

"You are absolutely insane," Rela muttered, sinking back in the seat. "What if I cannot find the door because it does not exist?" She asked the question softly, staring out the window.

"For your sake, Princess, I hope you're wrong," Kezem hissed.

The gathering storm punctuated his statement. A lightning bolt flew from one end of the night sky to the other. Thunder crashed a second later. Rain fell so fast Kezem ordered his hovs to stop. It was unlikely they would crash into a rock or salt pillar so long as they stayed on the road, but staying on the road was difficult because rain reduced visibility to nothing. The storm delayed them for an hour, but Kezem calculated they would still reach Chara within four hours. Wearily, he rose and went to his sleep chamber for some much-needed rest.

Talking to Rela takes more effort than it should.

Chapter 38:
Crossing the Lotrian Fields

Zeri (June) 27, 1560
Same Day
Royal Guard Camp, Kesler Plains

Next morning, something kicked at Kayleen Wellum's ankles.

"Wake up. We're about to move out," Something in the man's voice told her their destination had changed.

Kayleen rolled over and realized her right arm was completely numb. An electric shock woke the arm up nicely. The jolt also provided her with enough incentive to sit up straight.

"Go where?" Kayleen asked, now fully awake.

"Wouldn't you like to know," retorted the Royal Guard.

"I asked, didn't I?" Kayleen said. She gave the soldier a knowing grin. "But you don't know, right? You're just a lowly marksman who catches the menial tasks."

"Shut up. I'm going to release the stuncuffs and the ankle restraints so you can eat and take care of necessities. If you try anything, I'll twist your friend's broken arm until she screams so loud—"

"I understand," Kayleen said, cutting him off.

He released the ankle restraints and then her arms.

Massaging feeling into her arms, Kayleen let the soldier help her up.

"Thank you," she murmured from force of habit.

He nodded curtly and released her arm.

"I'm not contagious, Marksman Reed. Promise," said Kayleen,

reading his nameplate.

He ignored her comment but backed out of the tent looking like he would rather be anywhere else.

Kayleen followed him out of the tent and was dismayed to see a whole army camp arrayed around her. A sea of blue uniforms stained the otherwise pretty countryside. Buttons winked gaily in the sunlight.

Kezem didn't have to empty the palace of Royal Guards on our account.

The soldier led her to a wash tent.

A meal bar sat on one counter along with a bottle of water. She picked up the bar and tapped it lightly against the counter. It made a solid thunking noise.

Yummy.

Kayleen set the bar aside and used the primitive sanitation facilities that came with the new troops. Next, she scrubbed her hands and face until they gleamed, rinsed out her mouth, ate the brick of a meal bar, and drank some of the water. Afterward, she fixed the braid which had come loose during the night. When she had stalled as long as she dared, Kayleen stepped from the tent and took a deep breath of cool morning air.

"That's much better," Kayleen said to absolutely no one. She glanced left and caught sight of her young guard who held the restraints. "Not again."

"You'd be done with these if you hadn't broken the hovs," Reed reminded her.

"Yes, and I'd probably be dead, too. I'll take the stuncuffs, thanks." Kayleen held her arms out like a good little prisoner.

He applied the cuffs, shrugged as if to say he didn't care, and bent down to reapply the ankle restraints.

"I could walk to where we're going and save you the trouble of carrying me," she offered.

Reed didn't look big enough to safely carry her more than a meter. Nodding agreement, he escorted her to the big tent in the center of the small camp.

A man with light brown hair, a sour expression, and a stiff posture stood, arms akimbo, watching Kayleen and her guard approach.

"Marksman Reed, why is that prisoner walking?"

Kayleen recognized the voice.

Hello, Predator One.

"I thought it would be easier than carrying her here, Captain

Holeth," said the soldier nervously.

"Well, she's here now. Bind her legs," snapped the captain. "And put her arms behind her back."

"That won't be necessary," said a man standing behind Captain Holeth. He wore the insignia of an aster captain above his heart.

"Captain Quedron, this prisoner is dangerous," Holeth protested. "She took out four of my hovs yesterday like it was nothing."

"My men will take care of her," Quedron assured Holeth.

That's ominous.

Movement to Kayleen's right drew her attention. She nodded to Marc, Anabel, and Lorian. Their clothes were rumpled, but they appeared mostly rested. Anabel even seemed comfortable in the stuncuffs.

They must have turned off the shocks.

"Shall I knock them out, sir?" inquired a soldier with a clipped Terab accent.

"No, just the one will do," said Quedron.

Kayleen felt several hands clutch her shoulders. Something small and cold was pressed against her neck. She fought against the hands holding her. A hissing sound came from the instrument and coldness spread throughout her body. Her limbs suddenly felt heavy, and she wished to sleep.

Teven, help!

***

Zeri (June) 27, 1560
Same Day
Temporary Rebel Camp, Kesler Plains

"Kayleen!" Teven McKnight awoke with her name on his lips. His breath came in gasps. Cold fear coursed through him.

The anotechs were trying to tell him something.

Teven, help!

He threw off his blanket and scrambled out of the tent.

"You're up early," Todd Wellum commented from his seat beside some glowing embers he was attempting to coax into a fire.

"It's Kayleen. She's scared," Teven said, trying to still his racing heart.

"Do you know where she is?" Todd asked, frowning.

Teven silently asked the anotechs the same question and received an answer.

"East of us … and moving south in a hov," Teven told his uncle.

"How do you know?"

"A friend of ours gave her some anotechs. I think she's using them to call me. I'll explain while we move. We've got to hurry." Teven was speaking fast, as if that would help them get to Kayleen quicker.

Captain Alexi Gordon stepped out of his tent.

"What's going on? You look worried," said the captain.

"We've got to leave now," Teven said.

Gordon opened his mouth. His expression said he was framing an apology.

Teven waved a hand.

"I know you have obligations here, Captain. Good luck finding your followers."

"We will join you as soon as possible, Prince Teven," Captain Gordon promised.

"Captain, I must ask you and your followers to keep my identity a secret until it is safe," Teven said.

"Of course, Highness. May Riden swiftly bring that day," Captain Gordon replied.

Teven and his uncle broke down their tents, grabbed their packs, and began jogging toward the Lotrian Fields. On the way, Teven explained about the anotechs, too distracted to even realize that Todd Wellum didn't seem surprised. They reached the Lotrian Fields in a little less than an hour.

"Just what I need, a lesson in patience," Teven grumbled, glaring at the foul-looking land.

The Lotrian Fields were swamps infested with nasty reptilian carnivores called goritors. Both male and female goritors could grow to over five meters in length, a size that surpassed even zaloks. Practically blind, goritors relied on movement and scent to catch their prey. Their thick hides could stop energy blasts but were surprisingly vulnerable to metal blades at several soft spots.

Todd rubbed odor neutralizing spray on his arms and legs and offered Teven some.

"The anotechs will handle that," Teven said.

"Don't rely on them so much," Todd said. "One day it's going to get you in trouble."

Teven fingered his derringer dagger and considered the advice. The narrow road stretching across the Lotrian Fields was in poor repair because no one wanted to fight the goritors to fix it. Taking a deep breath and trying not to think about the danger, he stepped onto the path.

Todd didn't follow.

"Come on," Teven urged. "There won't be any goritors for a few miles."

"I'm going to make a call first," said Todd.

Teven didn't argue but looked at Todd impatiently. The comm chimed, confirming that the transmitter was seeking another signal.

"Ranger Wellum?"

"Greetings, Captain Tayce, I need your help. My daughter has been captured by Lord Kezem's men, and they are headed south. We need to follow them fast, but it'll take weeks on foot."

"She must have been part of yesterday's skirmish on the Kesler Plains," Tayce said.

"Correct," Todd confirmed.

"Then, I have good and bad news for you," said Tayce with a sigh. "The good news is that they will take your daughter to Loresh. I am heading there now with some Melian Maidens to try and save Princess Rela from Lord Kezem's wrath. Plug the comm into your infopad, and I'll send you the coordinates. The bad news is that Kezem will use her and the others to force the princess to find Loresh's hidden chambers. Where are you?"

Loresh! Mother mentioned Loresh. Rela's there?

The effort to absorb the information left Teven dazed. He forced himself to pay attention to Todd's conversation.

"Crossing the Lotrian Fields," Todd answered. He pulled out his infopad and plugged the comm into it.

"I'll send a hov to pick you up, but you're still going to have to hurry if you want to arrive in time."

"Thank you, Captain. Ridenspeed."

Teven and Todd moved down the narrow concrete strip as fast as they dared but not nearly fast enough for Teven. Anxiety ate at the pit of his stomach, reminding him he had neglected to eat anything.

"She's getting farther away!" said Teven.

"Slow down!" Todd warned in a loud whisper, pointing left where a goritor's trio of yellow eyes stared at them.

Teven nearly screamed but held the cry inside. Winding up a goritor's morning meal would not save Kayleen, and for his own sanity, Teven had to believe that he could somehow save her. Knowing she was his cousin only enflamed his protective instincts. Each passing second seemed an eternity to Teven as he and Todd inched forward one cautious step at a time. An hour later, the end came in sight. Though a half-mile off, the goal taunted Teven until he broke into a sprint.

"Teven, no!" Todd shouted, running after him.

A blur was Teven's only warning before a goritor's teeth-laden mouth snapped at his right leg. He leapt straight up, drew his dagger, and slashed downward, burying his dagger in a soft spot in the goritor's neck.

Todd's dagger flashed four times.

The goritor hissed and screeched, thrashing about until it died.

Teven slowly pulled his dagger out and stared at the black blood oozing down the handle. He stooped and cleaned the dagger on some nearby marsh grass, still acutely aware of the danger. Every goritor in hearing range would soon be lumbering over to feast on the fallen.

We need to leave! Teven thought, even as Todd pulled at his arm. Teven stumbled, but then, a picture of Kayleen's face came to mind with sudden clarity. Regaining his feet, he took off again toward the tiny glint in the distance that should be the ride Captain Tayce had promised.

They reached the yellow hov at the same time.

"I'm driving!" Teven and Todd both claimed.

"Have you ever driven a hov before?" Todd challenged.

Teven shook his head.

"Then, like I said, I'm driving."

"When was the last time *you* drove?" Teven shot back.

"Never mind that. Get in," said Todd.

Reluctantly, Teven obeyed. Todd started the engine and had the hov racing forward before Teven had the safety restraint fastened. Teven pitched forward and caught himself with his hands, scrambling to secure himself in the seat. A rock pillar loomed ahead. Todd swerved left to shoot around it.

Teven stared in horror as the rock passed inches from his face.

"We need to get there in one piece!"

"Quiet! I'm driving here!" called Todd.

"Rock! Rock!" Teven cried.

"Pipe down!" The hov swung right, this time partially scrapping a salt pillar.

"Just give me a second to get used to the controls."

Teven shrank into the hov's passenger seat, wishing Kayleen were there and hoping he didn't die before seeing her again.

Chapter 39: Crystal Lake

Zeri (June) 27, 1560
Same Day
Northern Shore of Crystal Lake

"Great," Todd grumbled. "Just what we need."

"What's wrong?" Teven shook his head, trying to wake up from a nap.

"Low fuel." Todd pointed to an angry glowing button that grew bright orange and then faded to dull orange in an incessant cycle.

Instantly, Teven was wide awake.

"Where are we?" he asked.

"Nearing Crystal Lake, why?" asked Todd.

"Stay near the lake," Teven instructed. His expression said he had an idea he didn't really like

"If we crash, the last place on this planet I want to be is by this lake," Todd argued. "They say the water is—"

"Combustible," Teven finished with a reckless grin.

The hov sputtered, coughed one final agonized breath, and died but not before Todd Wellum wrestled it to the edge of the Crystal Lake. It settled onto the sand with a thump. The lake's water looked deceptively beautiful. The sun winked off tiny waves, but there was no sign of life in the lake. Any fish unfortunate enough to be washed from the Clear River into Crystal Lake had its flesh eaten off by the toxic chemicals.

"I hope you know what you're doing," Todd said.

"Trust me."

"Like I have a choice," Todd mumbled.

Teven searched the hov for the fuel port and found it on the side facing away from the lake.

"Help me swing this thing around."

Together, they managed to turn the hov. It was dangerously close to the water by the time they were done, but that had been Teven's intent.

"Okay, I see where your mind's at, but how are we going to get the water into the hov?"

Teven didn't answer Todd's question. Instead, he opened the fuel port, sat down, and gripped the edge with his left hand. Next, he stretched his right hand toward the water.

Todd gasped.

Teven's eyes shut against the pain as the chemicals chewed at his hand. An anotech shield prevented any damage real damage, but Todd found it painful to watch the process. Water flowed from the lake up Teven's right arm, over his neck, down his left arm, and into the hov's fuel tank.

Fifteen minutes later and only three quarters done, Teven's arms began to slump, hindering the fuel shuttle.

"Hold my arms up," he ordered. "We must save Kayleen."

Todd hesitated but knew Teven was serious, so he did as asked.

The process took twenty-three minutes, and when it was over, Teven slumped in Todd's arms in a semi-conscious state.

"You did good, kid," Todd said hoarsely.

He knew it would take just under two hours to reach Chara. They would have to stop for supplies and a water hov or wait an hour to get the land hov fitted to handle water. From there, they could make Estra in another two hours and hike to Loresh.

Todd gently picked up Teven and placed him in the back of the hov so he could sleep while they traveled. As he fixed the safety straps, Todd studied his nephew who knew his daughter better than he did. They had spoken briefly the evening before, enough so that Todd could see the boy was in love with his daughter. He assumed such deep devotion could not develop unreciprocated. His heart ached for them. It had been cruel of fate to throw them together without warning.

He will always be a royal, and Kayleen will always be a Ranger.

As he climbed into the driver's seat and started the engine, Todd shuddered at just how disastrous the last such relationship had turned out. Reia's defiance of the ancient codes against intermarrying with House Minstel had split the Rangers along ideological lines. Not wanting to think about that, Todd turned his thoughts to his daughter.

What is Kayleen like?

The last time Todd had seen Kayleen, she had been a strong-willed child with untamable fiery hair. The mental picture of her rosy cheeks and constant smile made him grin. The brief picture of her during the battle on the Kesler Plains was quite different but no less special. There she showed only grim determination to fight and live.

She's alive but a captive!

The thought brought both comfort and grief.

I must save her. Kiata would kill me if I let anything happen to our daughter.

Todd programmed the hov to pilot itself while they reached a long, straight section of open road. Then, he let his thoughts turn to his long-dead wife, Kiata Antellio Wellum, who had been very close to her younger sister, Reia. Todd had grown up with them in a Ranger camp in the Riden Mountains. Their parents had been murdered by people wanting to steal their tosh mines. For a moment, Todd wondered if Basil and Sela Antellio weren't luckier having perished long before things turned so dark for their daughters. He regretted the thought. There might be pain in the knowledge, but he'd rather know his daughter's fate than wonder forever.

Maybe Teven and Kayleen trained in the same camp.

He fondly recalled how the sisters had tormented him by speaking Kalastan backwards. He didn't even know how they managed that. Kiata had always been ready to fulfill her Ranger duties. Her heart had been wounded when the Ashatan Council cast out her sister for loving Prince Terosh. The meandering path of Todd's thoughts turned again to Reia.

She was always more serious than Kiata. Almost as beautiful as well.

His thoughts flew past the rift over Reia's choice, the secret marriage he and Kiata had attended, the death of King Teorn and Prince Tate, Prince Terosh's rise to the throne, and Reia's rise with him. The years had been both sad and happy. He and Kiata had moved to Rammon to be ambassadors to the palace. There had even been peace for several years.

He wanted to pause his thoughts in those good years, but more images flooded Todd's mind. GAPP's initial clumsy overtures to tempt Reshner to join them, Queen Reia's Safe Service Act, Rorge II's plight, more discussion over joining GAPP, King Terosh's disastrous duel with Kezem, the Colza Star explosion, Teven's birth, Rela's birth, discussions deteriorating to debates, Tavel's birth, Terosh's assassination, and finally, Kezem's attack on the palace. In one night, Todd's wife and her sister had been murdered and he had been thrown into prison where he spent many dark years. The thought of prison brought him back to his daughter.

If anyone touches her, I will end them.

Chapter 40:
Glass Coast Mercenary

Zeri (June) 27, 1560
Same Day
Ash Plains

Teven silently willed the hov to go faster. The anotechs, taking him literally, sent a detachment to enhance the hov's engine.

"Whoa!" Todd exclaimed as the machine jerked forward with a power surge. "Did you do that?"

"Sorry." Teven called the anotechs back.

"No, no. We can use all the power we can get," Todd said.

They reached Chara, a city on the Glass Coast, without serious incident, but Todd's driving bordered on reckless.

"Can I drive to Estra?" Teven asked.

Todd slipped the hov left to miss an angry pedestrian.

The blue-skinned being twirled its tentacles at them in a gesture Teven guessed was meant to be rude.

"Watch it!" Teven shouted.

Todd weaved and missed a young couple who had been gazing into each other's eyes. Now, their eyes were just wide with fright.

"Slow down. We don't want to kill somebody by accident," Teven said. As the city flew by, he gripped the seat so hard his knuckles turned white.

"Let's see how long it's going to take for them to outfit our hov to handle water," said Todd. "I'd like to keep the enhanced version."

It took Todd several minutes to maneuver the hov through the narrow streets to the marina where the necessary modifications could take place. After a vigorous bartering match with the squat owner of Teague's Water Wonders, Todd worked out a deal to have their hov modified for two thousand kefs. Another thousand kefs on top of that bought them top priority and a promise to cut the time down to forty minutes.

Teven had to use almost all the kefs he had left.

It's a small price if it'll pay the way to Kayleen.

They entered a local tavern to pass the time and get something to eat. Todd ordered a fried nefletch fish on rye bread and an ale that looked and smelled like it would be fine fuel for their hov. The anotechs couldn't decide if the sickeningly sweet, sharp smell was offensive or not, but Teven cleared up that point by instructing them to filter the ale odor. He ordered tropher cakes and lila juice.

While they waited, Teven listened to the conversations around them. He closed his eyes, released a few anotechs through his fingertips, and sent them to nearby tables. If Todd noticed anything strange he said nothing. The first dozen conversations that flooded Teven's mind were mundane, covering everything from the recent rash of storms to Glass Coast Water Tower's fight with Meritel Power Plus over rights to Crystal Lake. Teven sent the anotechs to another table. He continued in this manner until reaching a corner table where one word caught his attention.

"—ing to Loresh! I no care it pay well. I no work for that man!" said an irritated male voice.

"Keep your voice down! What difference does it make who we work for?" asked another male voice, slightly louder than the first.

"He betray king!"

Teven could almost picture the second man rolling his eyes.

"Are you ever going to get over that? It's been more than a decade. Move on. Your crazy theories are standing in the way of good money."

"I no go against conscience," declared the first man.

"I'm not missing out on that many kefs! I'll be back when the job's done." A rustling sound indicated the second man was leaving. Four seconds later, he brushed past Teven and Todd's table and exited the tavern.

"Be right back," Teven promised. He jumped from his chair like it had suddenly grown hot and charged to the back corner where the two mercenaries had been talking. Placing both hands on the table, he called the anotechs back. A bald man looked up surprised. He barely glanced at Teven. Instead, he scanned the room for danger.

His voice made him sound so much older.

The four digits on each of the being's hands kept tapping his bottled ale, but Teven's danger sense was aroused. Soon, he realized that two more hands were under the table pointing pistols at him.

"Who was offering that job you refused?" Teven asked.

"Who ask?" inquired the man, returning to his drink. Though it appeared as if the man wasn't looking at him, Teven got the distinct impression that he was under intense scrutiny.

"Does the name Ectosh Laocer mean anything to you?" asked Teven. "What makes you think he betrayed the king?"

The man's orange eyes flashed with anger.

"As Royal Guard, I see traitor talk to Kezem. I in prison many years. I shave head since king murdered!" The man had a way of cutting out inconsequential words, but Teven had understood him well enough. "I feel king die! Elish see things you not dream of."

"You were a Royal Guard?" Teven inquired, surprised.

The man's eyes narrowed.

"Once, many species Royal Guard. We fought for honor and peace, but no longer."

"Fight for peace again," Teven said.

The man, who had been staring deep into his drink, lifted his gaze to Teven and shook his head to clear the ale-induced fog.

"Voice," he said hoarsely. "You royal!"

"Shhh! It's not safe to say that here," Teven said. "I have no money to hire you, but my sister and friends are at Loresh. Help me save them, and I will do everything I can to compensate you."

"For peace, honor, and slain brother, Covin, I serve you," the Elish said, putting the pistols back in their holsters.

Does he speak the truth?

Zareb is a friend of House Minstel. Trust him.

Teven led his new friend to the table where Todd sat. By the time he returned, the food had arrived.

Todd had finished his nefletch fish and was working on a second container of ale.

"You haven't aged a day," Todd said upon seeing their guest.

"Elish age different," Zareb replied. "Look same fifty year then change. Look same second fifty then die."

"I had forgotten," Todd murmured.

Zareb and Todd continued to talk while Teven ate his tropher cakes. The forty minutes passed. They returned to Teague's Water Wonders where their modified hov sat ready to take on the South Asrien Sea. Extra steering fins, a pointed front piece, and waterproof engine covers had transformed the land hov into a sleek water hov.

To Teven's relief, Zareb drove the hov and knew exactly how to handle it in rough waves. Along the way, the Elish explained what he knew.

"Captain Laocer call many mercenary. He says camp in Loresh from day past to two day forward. I no know how he lure him, but he expect Lord Kezem soon."

"Whatever he did, it worked," Teven said, only partly listening. As usual, his thoughts dwelt on Kayleen. He could still hear her call for help. Her anotechs seemed upset about something.

We must go faster!

He again enhanced the hov's performance with anotechs.

They reached Estra in just under two hours. The ice-covered city twinkled under the sun, but Teven couldn't enjoy the beauty.

They rented a room in southern Estra.

The owner, a petite woman with flowing white hair, frowned at their arsenal.

"Great, more mercenaries," she muttered.

"We fight for honor, Lady Brina," the Elish said solemnly.

"That's what they all say, honey," the woman responded.

"One time, Zareb fight for kef. Now fight for son of king."

Brina gave Zareb a look that said he was crazy.

Teven tugged on Zareb's lower right arm and pulled him toward the room where they would stash their supplies. Teven changed into warmer clothes and strapped on a weapon belt. The weight of his banistick and kerlinblade balanced a serlak pistol taken from Todd's stash. He added a pouch of flingers.

"You're going to fall over," Todd said. "Maybe you should leave the banistick."

"I'm used to it by now," Teven replied.

They left Estra and headed south to Loresh. Teven ran, relying on the anotechs for extra traction. They had no time to waste.

Kayleen's in there. We must find her!

Chapter 41:
Escape in the Frozen North

Zeri (June) 27, 1560
Same Day
Loresh Cave System, Frozen North

The twenty-kilometer system of tunnels and caves known as Loresh best resembled a cross sectional slice of passion fruit stuck in the snow at a forty-five degree angle. The main tunnel, wide enough to squeeze a hov tank through and high enough to accommodate claustrophobic humans, sloped down into a large central cavern before angling deeper into Reshner via a twin. Two minor tunnels, flanking the main one, also emptied into the central cavern. Smaller tunnels branch off seemingly at random, leading to various side caves. Cheerful glowcrystals embedded in the walls have witnessed many explorers die seeking treasures as exotic as youth gems and as simple as gold.

The mercenaries arrived first and spent their time staying warm and preparing ambushes. Typical for their kind, the mercs didn't trust each other. Everyone's desire to kill Lord Kezem resulted in much counterproductive activity. Their master had been clear on only one other point: do not kill Princess Rela until after Loresh's secrets are unlocked. That ruled out most traps, including mines. No one would have used mines anyway for fear of collapsing the system and condemning everybody. Most specialized in brute force anyway.

Lord Kezem's soldiers escorting the Kesler Plains captives arrived second. At Captain Quedron's order, they spread out to prepare

Loresh for His Excellency. More squads of Royal Guards and RLA soldiers were slated to arrive throughout the day.

The Royal Guards deposited the prisoners in a small side cave immediately off the main tunnel. An ancient door preserved by ice converted the cave into a cold prison. The door was currently swung inward. Strategically placed portable lamps brightened the cave above the eerie light from glowcrystals.

"Kayleen, wake up!" Lorian Petole called, nudging her friend with her boot.

The guards had carried Kayleen on a hov sled, but now that they were in Loresh, they wanted the prisoners awake to meet Lord Kezem. Lorian had begged the guards to let her wake Kayleen naturally. She didn't know what chemical they intended to inject her friend with but the fewer chemicals involved the better. Kayleen shivered but remained stubbornly unconsciousness.

"Step aside," ordered a soldier. With his short military haircut, clean shaven face, and constant frown, the soldier looked like the rest of his squad.

Lorian didn't have to look to know he held the same nasty instrument that had knocked Kayleen out in the first place.

"Give me a few minutes," said Lorian. "This would go faster if my arms weren't behind me."

"Captain Quedron's orders," replied the soldier without inflection.

Lorian almost spoke the words with him, for that's all her complaints ever earned her. She carefully lowered herself to her knees.

"Kayleen, please wake up. Lord Kezem will be here soon. You wouldn't want to miss that, would you?"

Kayleen slowly opened one eye, consequently raising an eyebrow, forming a questioning expression.

Lorian chuckled.

"That got your attention." To her relief, the soldier went away.

The door crunched back into place, leaving them alone. At least, they could talk freely now.

"I have got to stop waking up like this," Kayleen muttered, opening her other eye. "Where are we? I'm freezing."

"You *are* lying like a slab of preserved tretling meat on a hov sled in the Frozen North with half a sleeve missing," Lorian said, suppressing a shiver. The derringer attire of simple beige cotton shirt and comfortable brown trousers was not keeping much of the Frozen

North out. Lorian wished she could help Kayleen climb to her feet, but the stuncuffs nixed that option.

Kayleen groaned with the effort to sit up.

It's a start, thought Lorian.

The soldier returned carrying a black stack of clothes.

"Captain Quedron says you should put these on," he said, throwing some warm shirts at them. He turned to leave.

Lorian cleared her throat. He glanced at her, and she turned sideways so he could see her bound arms.

"I'm not authorized to release you," he said, flustered. He left, presumably to seek out permission to remove the stuncuffs. The metals in the tunnel and cave walls wreaked havoc with communications.

"Are they always that inefficient?" Kayleen asked.

"Unfortunately, yes and no," Anabel answered.

"You missed the morning meal," Marc added. "That was a fiasco. They served tretling stew ration packs, and no one was authorized to give us utensils for fear we'd turn them into weapons. Then, when we did get spoons, no one was authorized to release our hands. They ended up spoon feeding us like babies!"

The soldier returned.

"I have acquired authorization to release you one by one to change," he said.

Kayleen was first. The soldier removed the stuncuffs and ankle restraints as quickly as possible, then stepped back and stared at her. She climbed to her feet and managed to slip the warm, smartcloth shirt under her derringer shirt. The soldier frowned, obviously wondering if that was authorized or not, but he said nothing as he settled the stuncuffs and ankle restraints back into position. This time though, Kayleen's hands were bound in front of her. Next, he released Lorian who followed Kayleen's example of slipping the warmer shirt under her own. After Marc and Anabel were changed as well, the soldier left. They waited for the door to completely shut.

"Are you really that cold?" Lorian asked Kayleen.

"No, but black comes fairly close to blue in the shadows, and I am not looking like a Kezem lackey when the shooting starts," Kayleen declared.

They were silent for about thirty seconds.

Kayleen appeared deep in thought.

Lorian didn't want to disturb her, so she waited.

"What do we do?" she finally asked, glancing at each of her

companions.

"I'd rather not wait around for Lord Kezem to come kill me," Kayleen said.

As Lorian watched, Kayleen's stuncuffs flew off, hit the far wall in between Marc and Anabel, and thudded to the ground at their feet.

Everyone stared at Kayleen with mouths open.

"Sorry. Guess I overdid that," Kayleen said with an apologetic grin. "The anotechs and I are still working on communication." The ankle restraints also fell off.

At Kayleen's touch, Lorian's stuncuffs promptly unfastened. She wriggled free of them and rubbed her hands up and down her arms to enhance circulation. Even with the smartcloth shirt the cold air nipped at her skin.

"Next move?" Marc asked, after Kayleen had released his cuffs. He looked to Kayleen whose Ranger skills made her the obvious leader in this strange environment.

Lorian didn't mind. Loresh was a long way from the Rammon palace, and Kayleen seemed capable. Despite having traveled with her for several weeks, Lorian realized she knew little about the Ranger turned derringer.

"First question: how are you?" Kayleen asked in a no-nonsense manner. "Second question: can you fight?"

"Fit to serve, Captain Kayleen," Marc said with a grin. "Requesting authorization to engage the enemy."

Lorian glared at him.

"I'd prefer to avoid hand-to-hand encounters, but I can still blast things," Anabel offered.

"I'm good to go," Lorian said.

"How many guards are there? Where are our weapons?"

No one had a chance to answer Kayleen's questions because their young guard opened the door. Seeing them free of restraints, he reacted like any good soldier and opened his mouth to shout a warning. Fear overcame cold, and Lorian snapped into action. She leapt toward him, flattened her right hand, and slammed it none too gently into his throat. A strangled noise escaped him, as he collapsed, drawing the other guard's attention.

Marc and Kayleen dodged Lorian and the first guard to reach the second. Marc grabbed the man by the shirt and pulled forward while Kayleen slipped behind the man and put him in a chokehold. She applied enough pressure so the man would concentrate on breathing and not screaming but not enough to knock him out. It helped that she was shorter, and thus, his back was already arched.

"Marc, get the door," Kayleen said. "I think we have the answers to our questions."

"Where's the armory?" Lorian asked. Lord Kezem's troops always kept a temporary armory or two in their camps.

"I'm not—"

"This *is* your authorization," Kayleen said, giving his throat a squeeze.

The man had a pretty thick neck. Lorian was impressed Kayleen's relatively small arms could keep such a firm grip around the neck.

"Cave!" the man gasped.

"Could you please be a little more precise? There's nothing but caves here," Lorian continued, folding her arms impatiently.

It feels good to be in control again.

"Two down to the left," their prisoner answered.

"How many soldiers will be there?" Anabel wanted to know. She fingered the kerlak gun she had acquired from the first soldier.

Lorian took over the man's kerlinblade.

Marc retrieved the weapons from the man Kayleen held.

"Don't be sad because you're second best," Marc said addressing the prisoner. "We're derringers of the Royal Guard."

"Marc, he *is* a Royal Guard," Anabel pointed out. "Besides, that kind of talk gets people killed."

"Answer the question," Kayleen ordered.

The soldier glared at Marc but said nothing.

"Wrong choice." Kayleen squeezed the pressure point on the man's neck until he passed out.

"Blade or gun?" Marc asked, once Kayleen's hands were free. He managed to make the choices sound exciting.

"I'll take the blade, thanks."

The small band of escapees cautiously entered the main tunnel. Marc slid the bar across the door, sealing the hapless guards inside. Lorian took off after Kayleen at a slow jog. They took turns searching side caves for weapons caches. It would have been ideal if they could find their own weapon belts. All derringers became sentimental when it came to their banisticks. Any quality merchant sold banisticks, but long hours on the Kireshana usually resulted in personal modifications. Also, the banisticks and kerlinblades they had acquired in Fort Riden had been recently updated.

Lorian hoped to avoid patrols, but wishful thinking was no match for fate. Barely a half-dozen meters from their prison, a patrol of four emerged from a side tunnel. Marc and Anabel shot without hesitation. Anabel's aim was a little wobbly but three of her four shots hit the front man in the left shoulder, spinning him around. Marc's blast caught the second man in the throat. Kayleen and Lorian leapt forward and cut down the third man. The fourth hastily retreated, racing down the tunnel. Marc and Anabel sent energy beams streaming after him, but he escaped around a corner.

Marc took two steps in pursuit before Kayleen halted him.

"Stop! We need to find more weapons before we take on the entire Royal Guard."

"We have to stay together," Lorian added.

"We should move the bodies," Anabel said. Everyone nodded but no one moved. "Don't look at me," she said, raising her broken arm.

Lorian, Marc, and Kayleen each grabbed a corpse and dragged it to the last side cave they had passed. Anabel got the door. When the bodies were safely stowed, Anabel closed and locked the doors. Lorian considered going back to kill the first two soldiers but dismissed the thought with a shrug.

"Shouldn't we hunt the patrols while they're vulnerable?" Anabel asked.

Kayleen and Lorian shook their heads.

"We're going to run into enough of them as it is," Kayleen explained.

"No use seeking more trouble," Lorian agreed.

Chapter 42: The Search for Turgot's Treasure

Zeri (June) 27, 1560
Same Day
Loresh Cave System, Frozen North

Lord Kezem glared at Aster Captain Quedron. The brilliance of Princess Rela's smile would have outshone all three full moons.

"We will find them, Lord Kezem," Quedron promised. "The guards they attacked were found almost an hour ago and are being treated—"

"I don't care about the guards," Kezem interrupted. "I want my prisoners back!"

"Yes, Lord Kezem, it will be done."

Rela watched with distaste as Quedron bowed to Lord Kezem and barked orders to his soldiers who retreated into the side tunnel they had appeared from only moments before.

"You underestimated them," Rela taunted. "Three derringers and a Ranger are not to be trifled with." She didn't understand why she knew the information, but something had whispered it into her mind. An artery in Kezem's forehead ticked, and Rela managed to suppress another grin.

"They will come for you, Princess," Kezem sneered, turning to face her.

"Without them, your threats mean nothing. You cannot kill me without harming yourself," Rela said. She was getting sick of this invisible link between them, and she didn't like this creepy place either. Loresh gave her chills in several different flavors. It was like a thousand soft, jumbled whispers called to her from every direction.

"It doesn't matter. They are drawn to you by misguided notions of rescue. When they come, my men will take them. In the meantime, I suggest you start searching for my treasure. For every day that passes, I will kill one of your friends as slowly and painfully as possible."

"It could take weeks to search every cave!" Rela protested.

"Find my treasure!" Kezem shouted like a petulant child.

"Turgot's treasure," Rela replied, surprising everyone.

"What?"

Lord Kezem drew uncomfortably close, breathing foul breath into her face. But just as soon as the stench hit her, it vanished.

"You seek Jaspen Turgot's treasure." Rela closed her eyes and frowned. "But I do not think you will like it." She bit her lip thoughtfully.

"I'll be the judge of that. You just find it!"

"Please stop shouting," said Rela.

"There will be shouting and pain if you don't move it," Kezem vowed.

Part of Rela wished he would hurt her just for the pain it would cause him.

"Might as well start searching," Rela said.

Kezem spun on his heel and stalked down the main tunnel.

Rela followed, desperately trying to think of a way to escape. As they walked deeper into Loresh, Rela was surprised to find herself in the lead. She stopped suddenly.

"Keep moving," Kezem ordered.

Rela swallowed a retort. Maybe if she found this secret chamber and proved that it held nothing, the nightmare would end. She let her feet take over.

The voices returned, beckoning her straight ahead.

The main tunnel dumped the party into the central cavern which spanned fifty meters in front of them and thirty meters to their left and right. The cavern itself ended prematurely. Solid rock walls rose to either side of the main tunnel's twin which began a few meters behind a small stone pillar. The ceiling was so high that it disappeared into the darkness above, a place no glowcrystal bothered growing. Like everywhere else in Loresh, the glowcrystals provided ample lighting along the walls and paths. The naturally good acoustics turned the cavern into an amphitheater. On either side of the downward sloping main path, a series of wide stairs were carved into the rock and ice.

"Beautiful," Rela murmured. She felt a familiar presence press close around her. A shove started her down the path. Soon, she approached the stone altar and read the strange symbols on it. "Etmani coress cherimon. Dantel corla asmenai."

The excited, indistinct voices inside her whispered the meaning.

"What's she saying, Lord Kezem?" asked a young soldier.

Luckily for him, Lord Kezem wondered that as well and was too shocked to punish the man.

"It means 'Here lies the gate. Enter to seek wisdom.'" Rela stretched out her hand and touched the pillar. A small cry escaped her as some anotechs left her for an instant to unlock the hidden chamber.

Having experienced the same tiny prick of pain she did, Kezem frowned and stared down at his right hand.

Large portions of the rock walls flanking the second half of the main tunnel behind the pillar swung in slowly with a loud grinding noise.

Excitement and horror battled inside Rela as she waited to see what treasures lay ahead.

***

Teven McKnight charged down a side tunnel.

Kayleen's ahead.

Lord Kezem's guards at the entrance had put up a pitiful fight. Zareb and Todd Wellum flanked Teven left and right respectively. Zareb brandished two kerlak guns and two serlak guns. As their loud nature made them poor stealth weapons, the serlak guns were only present in case the situation turned desperate.

Suddenly, a violet kerlinblade flashed toward Teven's head. He whipped out his own blade and met it. The other blade immediately turned white, and Teven found himself staring into Kayleen's gorgeous silver-blue eyes. Even with an intense expression, she was more beautiful than he remembered. Next instant, their blades were back on their belts, and they were in each other's arms.

Not caring whether or not they ought to fall in love, Teven leaned down and kissed Kayleen. Her lips were cold and soft and sweeter than anything he had ever tasted. Teven never knew how long that wonderful moment lasted. The next thing he became aware of was Todd Wellum's trembling voice whispering Kayleen's name. Teven stepped back, feeling guilty but still gripping Kayleen's hands.

"This is not a good place for a reunion," Lorian said tersely.

The group of seven ducked into a semi-private cave. Marc,

Anabel, Zareb, and Lorian settled themselves by the door and spoke softly. Todd, Teven, and Kayleen moved to the back. An awkward pause ensued. Todd stared at Kayleen like a man suddenly thrust into the presence of a goddess. His breath came shallowly, and his expression clearly said he had about a thousand things to say. Kayleen returned the steady gaze with a measured one of her own that covered Todd's face. Teven could almost feel the warm familiarity that slowly spread through his friend. He took the opportunity to openly stare at her.

"Father?" Kayleen finally asked in wonder and disbelief. Her eyes sparkled to life in a way Teven adored. Todd and Kayleen's hands clasped with desperate strength. Then, Kayleen practically tackled her father. "I don't believe it!"

"It's been near forever, Kaylee," Todd murmured into her hair. Tears flowed down his worn face. His story poured out almost faster than Teven could absorb. "I was captured when Rammon fell. Lord Kezem sent men to capture or kill every Ranger, especially those of us loyal to the queen. Your mother—" Todd's voice hitched. He took two quick, ragged breaths and continued, "Your mother was killed before I reached home, but she must have sent you away with Nils. I spent many years in the prison below the palace, but thoughts of you kept me alive! I knew I would find you if given the chance, and Captain Tayce gave me that chance."

"Nils died, Father. He was murdered," Kayleen said. Her voice was muffled because her face was buried against Todd's chest.

"Kayleen, listen to me," said Todd. "There's something more you need to know. Your—"

A shout from Lorian broke up the happy reunion. Kayleen and her father released each other and reached for weapons. Teven's kerlinblade was in his hand in an instant. Zareb, Anabel, and Marc gunned down a group of mercenaries.

"We need to leave!" Lorian called.

A strange feeling swept over Teven.

The anotechs were very excited.

"Princess Rela is near," said Teven.

"Then let's find her," Marc said impatiently.

"No, Lord Kezem wants you three as hostages. Stay here," said Kayleen.

"No way!" Marc, Anabel, and Lorian declared as one.

"You're going to need our help," Lorian explained. "Lord

Kezem will use anyone against the princess. Nobody can get caught. We all go."

Teven nodded and followed his instincts through the maze of side tunnels back to the main tunnel. The four patrols they met along the way scattered in disarray. Nothing was going to stop Teven from reaching his sister.

Chapter 43:
Fight for the Crash Site

Zeri (June) 27, 1560
Same Day
Central Chamber, Loresh Cave System, Frozen North

"Halt!" The commanding young voice bounced around the cavern in a creepy manner.

Lord Kezem had been savoring the sweet taste of victory. The treasure lay just beyond wide open doors. Nothing could stop him from claiming it. He glared resentfully at the pest who stood at the top of the path.

"Kill them!" he barked.

"I thought you wanted them alive," Captain Quedron said from Kezem's left.

"We don't need them now," Kezem insisted.

Before he could stop her, Rela touched the stone pillar again, and the stone doors began closing.

"No!" Kezem pressed the princess's hand against the pillar.

Nothing happened.

"Release the princess!" shouted the irritating boy. He began descending the path with a small group of well-armed backup.

"I was right! It does depend on her willingness!" Benali exclaimed.

Kezem ignored them all. He threw his left arm across Rela's neck and pressed her right hand harder against the pillar. He could feel an invisible hand painfully grasping his arm, but he refused to acknowledge the pain.

"Open the doors!" he ordered.

"You will never get in if you harm them," Rela promised. Her voice betrayed nothing but determination.

"Seize them!" Kezem screamed. His men scrambled to obey. Energy beams began flying, and Lord Kezem turned to use Rela as a shield. Realizing how ridiculous that was since their lives were linked, he growled and flung her at Captain Quedron. "Protect her!"

Lord Kezem snatched his kerlinblade off his belt and batted away several beams. He charged up the path at the newcomers. As he did, twenty mercenaries rushed into the main cavern and attacked both his men and the intruders. He threw himself into the fight, slashing left and right with his two-toned blade. The thin core was red, matching his anger, and the outside was bright orange. Two mercenaries fell in pieces. One of the young intruders stumbled toward him. He could have shoved his blade right through her, but he refrained for the sake of Rela's favor. Instead, he slashed the throat of the mercenary who had sent her flying.

"Kill the mercenaries! Capture the others!" Kezem commanded.

Three mercenaries blasted at him with energy guns. A four-armed intruder shot them repeatedly from behind and nodded at Lord Kezem before turning his guns on the next poor mercenary.

Kezem nearly tripped over the young intruder he had saved. She was struggling to her feet, clutching one arm protectively. Seizing her by the shirt, he tossed her down the path toward Quedron. He could not win this chaotic battle. He had too few men.

"Captain, retreat to the base! We will return with more men!" shouted Kezem.

Quedron nodded and barked orders to the men. Slowly, Kezem's soldiers forced their way through the crowd and withdrew from the battle, taking Princess Rela and one of the intruders with them.

***

Rela! No!

Lord Kezem was escaping. Teven caught a glimpse of Rela repeatedly treating her current protector to both fists, but then, he had to duck and roll away from a kerlinblade. For the next few minutes, a duel with one mercenary occupied Teven's thoughts and energies. Fear for Rela and Kayleen drove him to strike hard and fast. Once upon a time, he would have conserved his strength, worn his opponent down, danced about gracefully, and finally struck for the win, but this was different. Time he could not afford to lose slipped by while he dueled.

A kick to his left shin surprised him. He began falling toward his enemy's hungry blade. With all his might, Teven swung his blade up. The mercenary had not expected the move. When the man's weapon was neutralized, Teven whipped his blade back down and across the man's chest.

A scan revealed Kayleen dueling two mercenaries. They cautiously struck at her from opposing sides, seeking an opening for a killing blow. Kayleen fared well enough but spent her time catching strikes from one mercenary or the other. Teven went to even the odds. He maneuvered himself beside Kayleen and challenged the mercenary on the right.

"Thanks!' she called, before turning her attention to the mercenary on the left who wisely fled.

Seeing his partner flee, Teven's opponent also abandoned the fight.

A barrage of energy descended upon Kayleen and Teven. They threw themselves off opposite sides of the path, rolled, and rose swinging. One of the energy beams bent around Teven's kerlinblade and struck a mercenary in the back. The man's scream was cut short by a serlak bullet from Zareb.

Kayleen helped Lorian battle four mercenaries hand-to-hand.

Teven thought about entering the fight but feared to break their concentration. He contented himself with cracking the handle of his kerlinblade across the back of an already stunned mercenary. When he looked back again, a large soldier had his big arm wrapped around Kayleen's neck. She used her lower center of gravity to heave the man over her shoulder. He landed on his neck funny and didn't rise. Another man Kayleen had been fighting was already down, and yet another man lay in front of Lorian who grappled with the final mercenary. She almost had him in a chokehold, but he threw her arms off. The combatants glared at each other over the fallen mercenary.

"Yield," Lorian demanded, motioning around them.

Marc, Kayleen, Zareb, and Teven looked on.

"You're outnumbered," said Lorian.

"Never!" said the mercenary.

Marc shrugged, raised his energy gun, and shot the man in the ankle.

"I'd get that checked out if I were you," said Marc.

Muttering curses, the mercenary hobbled up the path to the main tunnel.

"Is everyone okay?" Teven inquired.

"Flesh wound," Marc reported. He turned his left leg so they could see the gruesome spot of charred skin and muscle framed by tattered trousers.

"A few bruises," Lorian responded.

Zareb and Kayleen merely nodded.

Kayleen tensed, and her voice reflected alarm.

"Where's my father?"

Everyone scanned the cavern.

"There!" Marc shouted, hobbling in the direction of the fallen Ranger.

Teven ran where Marc pointed, but Kayleen beat him to the Ranger by two strides. She fell to her knees next to her father at a loss for words.

"Kaylee, I love you!" Todd Wellum whispered. The simple sentence drained much of his strength.

Teven placed his hands upon Todd's chest where three energy beams had burned their way through flesh and bone.

"It's too late." The words were fainter than his first.

Teven refused to accept that. He poured anotechs into his uncle.

"Hang on!" he said.

They returned almost immediately, telling him there was nothing they could do to heal the damage.

Tears streamed down Teven's face. His hands rested uselessly on Todd's chest.

"Don't die!" Kayleen pleaded. She placed her hands next to Teven's, sending anotechs into the wound. Teven could tell by the way she jerked her hands away that hers too had returned and reported that Todd was correct.

"Kaylee, the game! Remember your mother's game!" Todd instructed. He continued looking up at Kayleen with love in his eyes before closing them and relaxing into death.

Teven opened his arms and hugged Kayleen who collapsed into his embrace, sobbing. More silent tears coursed down Teven's cheeks. It had been too good to dream that everybody would make it out of Loresh alive, and the shattering of that dream left him stunned. The others stood back with solemn expressions.

For several minutes, only the sound of Kayleen's sobs broke the silence.

***

When no more tears would come, Kayleen Wellum sucked in deep, cold breaths and waited for her heart to stop racing. Finally, she released Teven and moved to stand up. The sight of her father's body tore at her heart again, but she concentrated on her anger.

It's not fair! She had only reunited with her father, spoken a few words, and now he was gone again. *This time forever.*

During the many years of not knowing, Kayleen dreamed of the conversations they would have, pictured his face, and imagined what he was like. Briefly, she thought it might have been better had he never shown up, so she could keep her dreams. But she concluded that those few moments with him were far more precious than countless hopeful dreams. The pain would pass, but she would always carry this image of her father: the hero who had traversed the planet to find her.

His last words confused her, but she lacked the energy to think about them.

"We'll honor him later," Kayleen said, getting to her feet. "Let's deal with Kezem first."

"Right," Teven answered. He rose and took a step up the path up to the main tunnel then stopped. He turned and cast a puzzled glance at the stone pillar. "Let me just check one thing." He jogged over to the stone pillar and ran his fingers over the words inscribed on it.

The small band gathered around Teven.

"What does it say?" Marc inquired.

Kayleen glanced at it. She recognized some of the symbols, but it had been years since she'd read Kalastan.

"Etmani coress cherimon. Dantel corla asmenai," Teven read.

"Here lies the gate. Enter to seek wisdom," Kayleen translated for those who didn't understand.

Teven hesitated.

"Go on. Touch the pillar, Teven," Kayleen urged.

They had seen Princess Rela open and close the stone door. Kayleen hoped it worked for all members of House Minstel.

Teven slowly touched the pillar, and a grinding noise told them it worked.

Kayleen watched in awe as whole sections of the walls to either side of the second main tunnel swung inward.

Two doors!

The momentarily thrill burned through her grief.

"Which one do we go in?" Marc asked.

Teven approached the doorway on their right. The others followed him.

Kayleen wanted to rush through and see what lay beyond, but Lorian's hand gently rested on her arm, telling her to wait. She understood. This was a private moment for Teven.

"I'll wait here and call you back if there's trouble," Marc offered.

"I wait," Zareb announced.

"I'll be here," Lorian promised. She released Kayleen's arm. "Go with him."

Teven didn't acknowledge any of them. He simply kept walking toward the open doorway in a daze.

Chapter 44:
History Lesson in Loresh

Zeri (June) 27, 1560
Same Day
Chamber of Enlightenment, Loresh Cave System, Frozen North

Teven McKnight stepped through the doorway with reverent slowness. He wanted to run, but something pressed the importance of this place upon him. Two steps inside, he halted. The anotechs were alive with excitement, causing a disconcerting flutter in the pit of his stomach. Before him, resting peacefully on a raised mound of rock and debris sat a small ship cocked at a downward angle where it had crashed. The front end was smashed, but surprisingly, the rest of the ship seemed to be in good repair.

A small stone pillar marked the ship's side entrance. Teven walked to the pillar and rested his hand upon it. A translucent, wispy figure about the size of his forearm appeared above the stone and tipped its head forward in a bow. The man's expression was strained.

"Greetings, I was once Jaspen Turgot, chief aide to anotech creator Sebastian Seltan," the figure said.

Teven sucked in a sharp breath at the name *Seltan.*

"We had hoped to right the universe's wrongs, but the power was too much for Sebastian. He turned on us. I escaped before things got too bad, but I am afraid for my planet. I don't know how long I lay unconscious, but when I had awakened, the anotechs had carved their way through this frozen land. They initially told me we were on the top of this world, so I called it the Frozen North, but now they say the planet has been flipped. I think it more likely they were mistaken and reluctant to admit such." The figure fell silent.

"There must be more," Kayleen murmured.

Teven touched a spot on the stone pillar below where he had touched before. The figure spoke again.

"This place I have fled to is beautiful, but I fear I too will abuse the power of the anotechs. The locals already think I am a god for surviving the crash. I had to accept a royal appointment or risk horrible death. I have chosen the surname Minstel, meaning 'eternal ministry' for my old name has become bitter to me."

"I never thought about the meaning of the name," said Teven.

"It means more now than ever, Teven," Kayleen said.

"What do you mean?"

"Reshner has suffered too long. It needs your family's guidance," Kayleen explained.

Teven reached for the pillar again.

"It has been three years since my rebirth," said the figure. "The anotechs have taught me much and taken my dreams and made them reality. I now have a wife and two sons to live for, but thoughts of immortality repulse me. I will live a natural life and serve this trusting people. Anotechs will fill the blood of my children and their children forever, but when one life is spent, they shall return to this place for restoration. This site will be open to my bloodline to seek the wisdom of those before them."

"I see you have found the Chamber of Enlightenment," Jalna Seltan noted.

Kayleen and Teven spun to face her. The three sentries also whirled, astonished. Jalna looked and sounded like the young girl Teven had met in the Ranger camp all those years ago.

"Who are you?" asked Lorian.

Teven handled introductions.

"How did you get past us?" Marc demanded.

Chuckling, Jalna waved to some steps behind her.

"The Chamber of Wisdom," she answered. Noticing Teven's questioning expression, she continued, "Jenell and Karric are safely in the care of Master Niklos. The anotechs called me here. There will be time for explanations later, but for now, we must save your sister."

"Lord Kezem will bring her back here," Marc pointed out.

"We wait; he come," Zareb agreed.

Kayleen, Lorian, and Teven shook their head vigorously.

"I'm not fighting Kezem on his terms!" Kayleen said. She

gripped her kerlinblade with a white fist.

"We may not have a choice," Jalna said. "Let us seal this chamber and move the bodies to the sides of the main cavern. Another fight approaches."

About a half-hour passed while the small group handled the grim task of stacking the bodies. Teven helped Kayleen carry her father's limp form. She moved stiffly, and he could have done a more efficient job by himself, but it was a task he could not deny her. They carried Ranger Wellum a little farther than the others and laid him in a sleeping position on his back. Tears worked their way down Kayleen's face.

"What did your father mean about a game your mother played?" Teven asked, trying to take her mind off the aching loss.

"I don't know. I've been thinking about that," she replied. "I was only four when my mother died, and I think she blocked some of my memories."

The small group had gathered in front of the stone pillar that unlocked the Chamber of Wisdom and the Chamber of Enlightenment. Teven and Kayleen joined them. Everyone appeared tired and disheartened. Teven's touch sealed the chambers with a grinding noise that echoed about the main cavern.

"Come on, come on, we've got to find Anabel and the princess," said Marc.

"You are in no condition for a confrontation," Jalna said. "Sit down."

Marc obeyed, but his irritation showed up in his expression. Teven understood Marc's feelings but knew Jalna was right. Marc had been standing on his festering leg for far too long. Jalna placed her hands over Marc's wounded left leg. Soon, she had the wound cleaned and wrapped in sterile cloth taken from a dead mercenary's supply pack.

"Thanks. That feels much better," Marc announced, climbing to his feet.

Jalna poked him in the chest.

"The painkillers do not change the fact that your wound is grave. Do not overexert yourself."

"I agree. Take it easy, Marc," Lorian said.

"But Anabel—" Marc began.

"Will remain Lord Kezem's captive until we can free her," Jalna finished. "We have a much better chance of rescuing the young women when everyone is rested."

"There's no time!" Marc insisted.

"But there is," contradicted a voice Teven recognized.

Teven's head snapped up to where Captain Ectosh Laocer stood flanked by a large group of mercenaries.

"Who are you?" Marc challenged.

"Perhaps a former Captain of the Royal Guard," Lorian surmised.

"Very good, derringer," Laocer mocked. He slowly led his group to within twenty meters of Teven and his friends.

The well-armed mercenaries brandished their weapons.

"Far enough," Zareb said, resting his four hands on pistol grips. He stepped forward to protect Teven.

"Zareb. Can't say it's a pleasure to see you again," Laocer commented.

"You remember?" Surprise rang through Zareb's words.

"Of course, there weren't too many four-armed freaks under my command," Laocer said. His voice lost some of its edge when he added, "But you were Taytron's pet before I took command, and Queen Reia insisted we open the ranks to other species."

The anotechs reminded Teven of the epiphany he and Kayleen had had two days ago.

"You helped Lord Kezem take the palace!" Teven fired the accusation again with his eyes.

Laocer's answer surprised the prince.

"I did a lot of regrettable things," said Laocer. "King Terosh was a good friend, but he stood between your mother and me. My first duty was to our love."

"You lie!" Zareb yelled, clearly as incensed as Teven over Laocer's obsession with the queen. "Queen Reia always love king!"

"Step aside, Captain," Teven ordered. "Lord Kezem—"

"Will find you," Laocer finished, echoing earlier sentiments. "We will wait here until he arrives. Then, you will help me kill him, and I will take my rightful place as king."

"Rightful?" Kayleen scoffed. "What happened to restoring the throne to *Prince* Teven?"

Teven winced at her emphasis on his title.

"He's just a boy," Laocer said. "Reshner needs a strong ruler."

"Already got one. He's terrible," Marc growled.

"He will die soon," Captain Laocer promised.

Teven wondered whether Laocer heard a word of what they were saying or if an entirely separate conversation played inside the man's head. The point became moot when two serlak bullets slammed into Laocer's back just below the neck, killing him instantly.

Chapter 45: Heroes and Villains Collide

Zeri (June) 27, 1560
Same Day
Loresh Cave System, Frozen North

Kezem hated retreating, but he found fresh RLA soldiers waiting for him halfway up the main tunnel. Knowing the enemy would be prepared for his return, Lord Kezem ordered his men to get fresh weapons, eat, and rest. Benali, the coward, had slipped off, but Kezem didn't care. He would dispatch some men to kill him later, but for now, he had far more pressing matters to deal with.

The delay had been worth the wait. The traitor stood before him talking to the intruders.

Lord Kezem hardly dared to believe his luck.

"Kill him," he ordered.

Captain Quedron's response was to take out his sidearm and fire on the mercenary leader. Laocer's body fell forward and rolled down the slope twice before sliding to a stop.

Everyone raised their weapons and discharged them at once.

The mercenaries in the back whirled and fired on Lord Kezem's soldiers. The rest opened fire on the young intruders. A sideways glance revealed that Rela was safely tucked behind a wall of his finest soldiers whose only orders were to protect her.

Kezem didn't bother with energy guns. He flicked on his kerlinblade, spun the color dial, and raced forward with a yellow and green blade. Once in the center of the fray, Kezem swept the kerlinblade across two mercenaries. Then, he whipped his banistick out and thrust it into another soldier's throat with the electric shock set high enough to scramble the man's brain. Kezem returned the banistick to his belt.

A kerlinblade-wielding mercenary caught two of his strikes. Then, a kick struck the man low in the stomach, doubling him over right into Kezem's blade. He yanked the blade out and punched the man for good measure, before selecting another target. Suddenly, he found himself blocking banistick strikes from a Melian Maiden. A wave of surprised anger shot through him.

You're supposed to be in prison! Someone will die for this treachery.

"Yield! You are *my* servant!" Kezem screamed. He took out his banistick again, knowing he would need the extra edge against this enemy.

"I serve the Royal House!" Kia declared.

Kezem pounded at her flawless defenses, ignoring the bullets and kerlak beams flying around them. She backed down the slope, and he followed, battering her banistick with both of his weapons. Finally, the electric impulse from his banistick shorted the shock nullifiers protecting her weapon. She dropped it to avoid the electric charge. He lunged forward for a killing blow and met the back of her hand as she spun up the slope toward him. The blow surprised him more than hurt, but it was enough for her to scramble away.

Frustrated, Kezem smashed his banistick against a mercenary's chest and held it there for several seconds longer than necessary. The man's screams only fueled Kezem's bloodlust. He relished the feeling of power coursing through him as he roamed the battlefield seeking new opponents. The mercenaries—who had never been a coherent fighting group—scattered and ran for their lives. Kezem took great pleasure in cutting them down.

***

After having her banistick shorted by Lord Kezem, Kia split her attention between trying to stay alive and searching for Captain Tayce.

That man is infuriating.

His noble spirit and sense of duty were going to get him killed. He possessed decent fighting skills, but his administration post left little time for real combat experience. A flash of short blond hair to her left caught her eye. Kia punched out the mercenary who had a serlak pistol partially raised to shoot her. Two strides brought her up behind a soldier choking the life out of Tayce. A hard smack to the back of the neck stopped the soldier. She reached down and yanked Tayce to his feet even as she relieved the unconscious soldier of his blade, ignited it, and blocked an energy beam headed for them.

"Captain, get out of here!" Kia shouted. She didn't wait for a reply but paused long enough to see Captain Tayce shake some sense back into his head.

Three soldiers fell upon them. The first tackled her, knocking the blade away. The soldier had strength on her, but she had years of hand-to-hand combat training. They tumbled down the slope a ways before rolling off the main path and onto a flatter, more fight-friendly surface. His fist came at her face. She turned her head and took the glancing blow to the side of the head, causing her ear to throb painfully. Kia lashed out with her left foot, catching his ankle. He grunted, but she didn't give him the chance to recover. A roll brought her to her feet and a spin kick to the man's side ended the fight. She didn't bother killing him.

Tired, dirty, and far from done, Kia grabbed a kerlak pistol off the ground and shot two blue soldiers and a maroon one. The gun whined, telling her it was done for. She tossed it aside and picked up another. A bullet grazed her side. Stinging pain spread from the area. She felt herself falling. With considerable effort, she twisted around to avoid landing on the wound. The frozen ground knocked the breath from her.

I've failed the princess.

The mercenary who'd shot her smiled as he lined up his weapon for the kill shot. Her salvation came from the most unlikely of sources: an RLA soldier.

No, not a soldier, a Coridian Assassin. Interesting.

Kia recognized Tryse from training camps they'd both attended. She couldn't remember if they had ever actually met, but there was little time to dwell on that now anyway.

Tryse slammed his banistick down on the mercenary's gun arm then brought the weapon up under the man's chin. Clearly, he too had decided that Lord Kezem was a disease that needed to be cut out of Reshner. Unfortunately, Kia didn't know how to do that without harming the princess.

Before Kia could rise to help Tryse with his crusade against Kezem's forces, four energy beams struck the assassin high in the chest.

Tryse! No! Kia's mind screamed.

She had no energy to make the cry real. She could only watch as realization dawned behind his eyes. He met her gaze and nodded at her. Then, he grabbed his pistol and shot the three soldiers nearest him. With the last of his strength, he dropped the gun, drew his kamad dagger, and hurled it at the last soldier standing near Kia. Sighing, he fell forward and closed his eyes, a small smile forming on his lips.

***

Teven's arms ached from the half-dozen mini-duels he had waged and won. This current one was by far the toughest. A hard strike knocked him off balance and caused his right shoulder to throb with pain. Kayleen whirled in front of him and caught the next three blows on her shining green blade. The soldier stepped close and slammed his fist into her head. Next, the man slashed wildly and scraped his blade across Kayleen's left arm. She didn't flinch. Terror for Kayleen shocked Teven into hefting his blade and hurling it over her shoulder into the man. He followed the blade, pulled it out, and looked around for more danger.

Jalna and an opponent sailed by. The man was backpedaling as fast as he could, but her strikes were quicker than he could handle. Marc had traded his kerlak gun for a blade and was in the midst of an intense contest with a mercenary. Teven didn't see Zareb anywhere. A beam flashed toward Teven, and he dove instinctively.

When he was halfway to his feet, Teven saw a white blade out of the corner of his eye. The thought of impending death didn't disturb him so much as deeply sadden him. He knew Kayleen cared for him and did not wish to add to her pain today. To his surprise, the blade failed to strike him. Instead, it knocked down an energy beam that would have struck his head. Looking up, Teven found a tall woman with dark brown eyes and a playful grin staring at him. Her skin tone was complemented by the soft colors of her flowing light blue robes. She looked completely out of place.

"Energy beam to the head would be painful," she commented before turning and disappearing into the thrashing crowd.

Teven almost felt like the beam had struck him. Then, Kayleen was next to him, helping him stand. By this time, the mercenaries were either dead or gone.

Teven and Kayleen were about to pick another fight with an RLA soldier, when Lord Kezem's voice rang out.

"Stop fighting!"

Everyone froze.

Marc yelped.

"No!" shouted Princess Rela. She struggled to approach Lord Kezem and her friend.

Two RLA soldiers held Anabel whose arms were stun-cuffed in front of her. This time, the shock feature was definitely activated. Lord Kezem's blue and green kerlinblade blazed at her throat. The light reflected off her pained expression.

"I'll open the door!" Rela cried. Her voice was high with the intensity of her fear for Anabel. Tears slipped down her flushed cheeks. She almost broke free from the soldiers, but they caught her arms and held her fast.

"I know you will," Kezem said darkly.

"Please don't kill her!" Rela's voice, though barely a whisper, carried in the cavern.

"There is only treasure beyond for those who seek wisdom," Jalna said. "You will not find power or riches here."

Teven saw Jalna close her eyes as she spoke, but Lord Kezem was too far away to see.

"The treasure is mine!" Kezem shrieked.

Teven worried he might let the blade slip and cut Anabel. Then, he remembered Jalna's lessons on surroundings. He reached out with the anotechs. A steady stream of them flowed from Jalna to Lord Kezem. Suddenly, he understood.

When he was sure Anabel would be safe, Teven shouted and launched himself at Kezem who reacted faster than he thought possible. The blade in Kezem's hand raked across Anabel's exposed neck, but only a thin line of blood spread for the effort. Kezem howled with rage and turned his anger on Teven.

Their blades met with a crash and locked. Teven bolstered his strength by calling on the anotechs for help. They swirled through him, rejuvenating his exhausted muscles. Recognition flashed behind Kezem's cobalt eyes when they were face to face.

"A blade did not save your mother! It will not save you!"

"She defeated you that day!" Teven tossed back.

None of Kezem's men dared to interfere, and Teven's friends stood back as well. Everyone understood that this confrontation had to take place. Lord Kezem reached for his banistick. Teven had seen what that banistick could do so he disengaged. Lord Kezem swung the banistick with all of his considerable might. Teven leapt out of the way. The banistick passed close enough to raise the hairs on Teven's arm.

While Lord Kezem was slightly off balance, Teven kicked the

banistick from his hand. Kezem growled and swung his kerlinblade with both hands. Teven had no choice but to block the blade. The blow landed with enough force to knock Teven back a meter. He twisted his neck aside to keep from cutting his own throat.

"Teven!" cried Kayleen.

Teven caught a glimpse of Lorian and one of the Melian Maidens holding Kayleen back. He was grateful. He tripped over some pebbles on the slope and started falling but managed to turn the tumble into an over the shoulder roll. Somehow, he held on to his kerlinblade without impaling himself. Lord Kezem pursued. Teven expected to feel the bite of Kezem's blade any second. As Kezem heaved a devastating blow, Teven steeled his nerves and stood his ground. At the last possible moment, Teven pivoted on his right foot, letting Kezem's blade pass within two centimeters of his body. He finished the spin and planted his left foot on Kezem's back.

Lord Kezem recovered quickly, but Teven was several meters up the slope. They were back to the main group. Teven stopped running because there was nowhere to run. Lord Kezem's men completely blocked the main tunnel out of Loresh. Besides, he would never abandon his sister or friends. Teven turned to face Lord Kezem again.

Even with the anotechs' aid, Teven could barely stand. He rallied enough strength to parry the first dozen of Kezem's strikes. Then, a kick caught him in the stomach and knocked him to the ground. A triumphant smile lit Kezem's face. He threw down his kerlinblade, lifted Teven by the shirt, and slammed him hard against the ground. Two more similar assaults left the prince gasping. A series of hard punches caught Teven's face, neck, and shoulders. Then, Kezem's fingers were at his throat squeezing.

***

Princess Rela Minstel watched the young man fight Lord Kezem, knowing she should recognize him. Partway through the fight, Kezem ranted something about the boy's mother and the answer struck Rela with a near physical blow. Then, somebody shouted the boy's name, and the connection solidified. Rela's visions of her mother had spoken of the young man, her brother.

Teven!

Her mind frantically tried to conjure a means of escape. Teven kicked Lord Kezem, and Rela cheered. The soldiers gripping her shoulders did not release her, but their grasps loosened as the duel distracted them. She didn't know how Teven could fight on so long and hard, but he parried Lord Kezem's fierce strikes time and again. She silently willed him to win even if it meant her death. The air was thick with anticipation of the duel's end. To Rela's dismay, her brother's reflexes slowed ever so slightly.

Lord Kezem knocked him down and attacked with his hands. Rela's hands hurt. Kezem's hands were bloody from beating her brother. The solution came to her with such sudden clarity that she gasped.

If she thought about it too long, she would lose the nerve to do what was necessary. Dropping to her knees, Rela seized the dagger tucked into the left boot of the man to her right, scrambled away, and fell upon the blade. It pierced her right side between the bottom two ribs and sank into her up to the hilt. A sharp cry flew from her lips as she rolled onto her back, inadvertently twisting the blade deeper. Pain like she had never experienced before radiated from the wound. With monumental effort, Rela yanked at the dagger. In her haste, she pulled the blade down as well as out, further splitting her side open. Tears flowed as easily as the blood, but Rela had some small comfort in knowing Lord Kezem would feel every bit of pain.

The loud crack of a serlak gun echoed in the nearly silent chamber. A different kind of pain exploded in her stomach, and Rela passed out.

Chapter 46:
Broken Code

Zeri (June) 27, 1560
Same Day
Loresh Cave System, Frozen North

Lord Kezem felt like his insides were being ripped out. He had suffered wounds before but never like this. He stopped choking the boy and fell back in shock. Something thudded into his gut increasing the pain tenfold. The sound of the shot reached his ears ages later. Looking up, he spotted a being pointing four guns at him.

***

"No! No! You'll kill the princess!" Marc screamed, clutching at Zareb's arms.

"What mean?" asked Zareb.

"She's linked to him! If he dies, she dies!" Marc explained. His tone neared hysteria.

Kayleen observed everything with a numbness that comes from seeing too many people die. Teven lay so still that she didn't know if he still lived. That thought was too painful to follow. Kezem's men looked at each other wondering how to react. Marc was still screaming at the man who had come to Loresh with Teven and her father. Anabel watched everything in horror. Princess Rela lay on the ground with blood pouring from her side. Finally, Kayleen couldn't take it anymore. She separated herself from the pain. In that moment, the walls surrounding her memories melted.

Her mind wandered to happier times. She remembered her childhood home, the one before Nils took her to the Ranger camp.

Mother had always kept a neat house. The unit had been small but very comfortable and safe. Father had been away often, but he would always come back with trinkets and stories for Kaylee even though Mother scolded him for spoiling her. He always answered with a kiss and a promise to be stricter when Kaylee grew older. Then, the trouble in Rammon had started. News of rebel soldiers brought a sad look to Mother who summoned Nils Clavon. He was okay as a friend, but Kayleen didn't want to go with him.

Go with Nils, Neelyak, my beautiful baby.

Mother had often called her Neelyak, but only when they were alone.

Kiata.

That had been Mother's name. She had been everything Kayleen wished to be. Her long, light brown hair used to hang freely in front of her face, as she leaned over Kayleen's tiny bed. Batting the soft hair had been a favorite pastime for Kayleen.

Edolin cumani enuli asanti rimnula. Remember these words, Neelyak. They are very important.

Kayleen had cried so loudly she barely heard Mother, but the words had always stuck with her. Mother had opened her mouth to say more, but Nils took her away to escape the soldiers. He took nothing but a small pack of provisions and ran for his life, carrying Kayleen away from danger.

Remember your mother's game!

The full meaning settled upon Kayleen, snapping her out of the escapist thoughts. Mother had often spoken Kalastan backwards, especially when addressing her sister—Queen Reia. Kayleen was beyond shock at this point. She merely nodded and concentrated on the words her mother had told her to remember.

Edolin cumani enuli asanti rimnula became *alunmir itnasa ilune inamuc nilode. The time has come; break foul curse, release the royal to new birth.*

Kayleen moved before her mind officially gave the order. The soldiers had backed away from the fallen princess. Kayleen knelt over Princess Rela and took her cold, bloody hands in her own.

"Alunmir itnasa ilune inamuc nilode!"

Nothing happened.

She leaned closer and repeated the message.

Rela's shallow and ineffective breathing began to even out. She was still unconscious, but Kayleen could almost imagine color returning. She felt a hand on her shoulder and glanced up to see Jalna.

"She will live," Jalna said.

"Perhaps," Kayleen replied.

"She killed Lord Kezem," a young soldier hissed. "She dies."

Before anyone could stop him, he raised his kerlak gun and blasted Princess Rela from two meters away. Kayleen dove across the princess. Other soldiers and Marc gunned the man down instantly, but five shots had been released. One hit the ground near the princess. One struck the princess and the other three caught Kayleen across the back. By all rights, she should be dead, but the anotechs had isolated some of the energy.

Throwing out her left hand, Kayleen touched Rela and willed the anotechs to draw the excess energy away from the princess. She knew that the anotechs could either save her or Princess Rela, not both. They disagreed. Tears streamed down Kayleen's face as she willed the anotechs to ignore her wounds. She began pouring anotechs into the princess. She felt Jalna's silent protest.

"Save her!" Kayleen commanded.

Jalna nodded solemn acquiescence to Kayleen's wishes and turned her full attention to Princess Rela.

When she finished transferring her anotechs to the princess, Kayleen felt strangely alone. Every ache in her body was magnified. A deep gash on her arm, which she hadn't even noticed, began throbbing. Something soft was placed under her head.

"Kayleen, don't die. Keep fighting!" Teven's warm hand squeezed hers and anotechs rush in to heal the damage, but Kayleen knew it was too late.

"We have to finish the Kireshana!" said Teven.

Kayleen forced her eyes to fix on her friend's face.

"Teven, you'll always be Reshner's Royal Guard to me," she whispered with her dying breath.

***

Do you wish to be saved?

Of course, Kayleen answered. *Why wouldn't I want to be saved?*

You would not be the same.

Why not?

Your body is dead. We can only preserve the essence of you.

At what cost? What's the catch? Will it harm anyone?

Living beyond death can be … disconcerting. You would be more us than you, though in time we may find a suitable body

for you.

I'd be like Jalna.

Yes, you would be like the Maker's Daughter. What say you?

Do it, but only if Teven, Jalna, and the princess agree.

A war is coming. They will need every ally they can get. Sleep. Heal. Rest.

***

Teven couldn't believe it. Two minutes ago, he was dying while Kayleen watched. Now she was dead, his sister was dying, and dozens of soldiers stared down at his back ready to finish what Lord Kezem had started. He was still trying to absorb Kayleen's death when a soldier asked the key question.

"What happens now?"

"You surrender," Zareb replied.

Teven didn't have to look to know all four of Zareb's guns would be trained on the soldiers. He sensed more than saw his other friends tense for another round of chaotic battle.

"Who will rule?" the young soldier inquired, sounding lost. "Lord Kezem's dead!"

"The princess still lives," said one of the other soldiers.

"But we served Lord Kezem! We're done for if she rules," insisted the first soldier.

"The princess is not above forgiving," one of the Melian Maidens offered.

"She cannot rule!" cried the first soldier.

"Don't even think about it," warned the second man.

"You can't stop me!" Receding footsteps said the first soldier was retreating. A few others followed, but the majority stayed in the main cavern.

Teven wearily climbed to his feet.

"Put down—" Zareb began.

"Not a chance," the second soldier cut in.

"Their weapons are inconsequential," said a fair-haired Melian Maiden. "They will need them to serve the princess."

"Unhand my sister!" Marc snapped.

The soldiers reluctantly obeyed, releasing the stuncuffs and standing back looking suddenly shy. Anabel ran to Marc and hugged him. Teven envied their happiness.

Rela stirred.

The Melian Maidens gathered close to her, edging Teven away.

"He will do her no harm," Jalna informed the maidens.

"Enough harm has already been done," the head maiden replied, keeping her eyes on Teven.

"Let me take some of her pain," Teven requested.

"Do you not recognize him?" Jalna inquired.

One of the older soldiers broke ranks to move closer to the princess and gasped.

"King Terosh," he said in an awed whisper.

"Not quite," Teven answered. The right side of his face twitched up for a second, the closest he could come to a smile. "Teven."

Through the anotechs, Jalna silently urged him to go on.

Teven squared his shoulders and wiped most of the grief from his expression.

"I am Prince Teven, born of House Minstel, son of King Terosh and Queen Reia, brother to Princess Rela and Prince Tavel." His announcement left everyone stunned, even those who had previously known.

"Teven was the firstborn," the veteran soldier said. "You are king." He dropped to his knees.

"That has yet to be decided. We must save my sister first," Teven said. He approached Rela again.

This time the Melian Maidens parted respectfully.

"How can you help her?" wondered the head maiden.

Aster Captain Kia Meetcher of the Order of Melian Maidens, the anotechs said.

Teven didn't reply. Instead, he sat on the ground next to Rela, touched her neck with his left hand, and laid his right hand across her gruesome side wound. He winced as some of her pain transferred to him. Her skin was hot to the touch. He felt the anotechs working frantically to knit her torn flesh together.

Please live, Rela, I've lost so much. I can't lose you too!

When he had done everything he could for her, Teven struggled to his feet.

"You need rest," Jalna observed.

"I need answers," Teven said peevishly.

"What are your orders, Prince Teven?" asked a soldier. "With Lord Kezem dead and the princess unconscious, you are our leader."

Teven dispatched half the troops to gather supplies from the base so they could spend the night and ordered the other half to gather the bodies to be taken out of Loresh.

A chorus of "It will be done," answered him.

He eyed the departing troops warily.

"Can we move her?" Teven asked Jalna.

"I doubt it would do much good, Prince Teven," Jalna said.

Teven got the impression she was trying to get him used to the title.

"She should awaken by the morning, but sleep is good for her."

"I'd like to speak to her in private when she wakes up," Teven explained.

"In that case, we can try, but let's wait for a hov sled."

"I know where to find one," Lorian offered. "We need to collect the prisoners there anyway. Uh, that is, if they're still there."

An uneasy truce settled between the soldiers and Teven's friends. He sensed treachery, so he did not rely on them to guard him. The Melian Maidens and an RLA officer, Captain Ethan Tayce, hovered within arm's length constantly. It both pleased and irritated him.

Marc, Anabel, Kia, and Lorian had their injuries addressed. Jalna finally got a good look at Anabel's arm. A half-hour session of anotech therapy worked wonders for the broken arm. Teven was glad to see Anabel's skin tone return to a normal color.

The biggest surprise came when Teven carried Kayleen's body over to her father. He found Todd Wellum breathing.

How is he still alive? I watched him die!

Queen Reia's last gift, replied the anotechs.

What do you mean? What did she do?

She instructed us to fake his death if he ever came gravely near it. Then revive him later. He will live but recovery will be slow. His wounds would be fatal several times over.

Dizzying hope shot through Teven.

Did my mother protect Kayleen too?

Regret clung to the anotechs' words. ***Yes, but Kayleen already died the day her caretaker did. We saved her body once.***

Can't you do it again? Teven pleaded.

Her body is beyond us now, Prince of the Chosen, but if the Maker's Daughter is willing, we can save her mind.

Please ask her.

Teven wept.

Chapter 47: Anotech Deal

Zeri (June) 28, 1560
Loresh Cave System, Frozen North

When Princess Rela regained consciousness twelve hours later, she felt nothing and couldn't pick up her head.

That's odd.

She frowned, blinked, and slowly moved her jaw to see if it worked. Something stirred at her side, but she couldn't turn to see it. At least, she felt no threat from that direction.

Why am I lying on the ground, why can't I feel anything, and why am I not panicking?

"Princess Rela?" Kia called her name gently.

Rela's mouth was dry, her tongue thick, but in happier news, her jaw worked. She slowly opened and closed her mouth a few times.

"Kia," she managed to say finally. It came out barely above a whisper, but Rela could almost feel the woman's pulse quicken with joy.

"Linnea has something for you, Princess," said Kia.

Rela felt something slip onto her right ring finger. She flexed her fingers.

Well, at least feeling has returned.

"Welcome back, Princess," Linnea greeted. "I was unable to complete the mission to Master or Lady Pascal, but I'm sure the Bann family will be all right. Captain Tayce sent them some help as soon as we were safely on our way here."

"Thank you," Rela whispered.

"There's someone who wants to meet you, Princess. Are you well enough for an audience?" Linnea asked.

Rela nodded weakly.

I doubt I shall go anywhere for a while anyway.

"Prince Teven! The princess will see you now!" Kia called.

Prince Teven?

A thrill ran through Rela. In another moment one of the young men Lord Kezem had cursed knelt at her side and leaned over her. He was handsome, even sideways. His black hair appeared wind tossed, and his brilliant green eyes shone with concern. He looked exactly like her mother had described her father.

The longer he stared at her the softer and more peaceful his expression became.

"Nice to finally meet you, Rela," Teven said with a crooked grin that made him appear younger.

Rela sensed her maidens slip a respectful distance away.

"Teven!" she whispered fiercely. Saying his name made her want to throw her arms around him.

He partially picked her up in a warm embrace.

She felt his heartbeats tap a soothing cadence in her ear. Gradually, as mobility was restored to the rest of her, Rela returned his hug with desperate strength.

"You have a very healthy grip," Teven commented. "That won't last when the pain returns."

"Returns?"

Teven pulled away and looked at her with a teasing smile.

"You've probably got more anotechs in you than blood right now."

"Dare I ask what anotechs are?" asked Rela.

"It's a very long story. I'll tell it to you sometime, but I wanted to talk to you about something else right now." He paused, waiting for permission.

"I am sort of a captive audience here," Rela pointed out.

"The anotechs have a deal they wish to offer Reshner's ruler," Teven began.

"Which is you, if you're my older brother," Rela broke in calmly.

"We can deal with that mess later, but I think you should consider their offer," Teven advised. "Can you stand up? It's best if the anotechs present their case directly to you."

"Are you willing to be a crutch?"

"Sure. I'm sorry we don't have the hov sled anymore, but the soldiers are using them to carry bodies out of Loresh," Teven explained. "I needed to talk to you alone."

Rela sucked in sharply when Teven moved to help her stand.

Ouch! Pain's back.

"I see what you mean about the pain returning. What happened?"

Ceasing efforts to help her up, Teven stared at her incredulously.

"You don't remember stabbing yourself to stop Lord Kezem from killing me?"

Suddenly, Rela remembered everything: the battle, the screams, the wounded, the dying, the dead, the helpless feeling of being held by the soldiers, the pain from the dagger, and the shock of being shot. Her gaze dropped to her right side, which was dominated by a large blood-soaked bandage. A faint burning sensation spread around the spot on her side where the energy blast hit. She grimaced.

"I remember."

"This is really going to hurt," Teven warned. He must have changed his mind about wanting her to stand, for without giving her a chance to respond, he scooped her up in his arms.

The burning sensation spread, but she willed it to diminish.

"Good, you're doing fine," said Teven. "The anotechs are machines tinier than cells. They can repair and rejuvenate your tissues and rally your natural defenses. Jalna taught me how to live with them. You'll get to meet her later." He carried Rela like a child.

She rested her head against his shoulder.

"That wasn't a very long story," said Rela.

"Like I said, it's best if they explain." Teven touched the pillar then settled Rela as gently as possible on the small stack of bedrolls placed there for that purpose. "We are ready for your offer."

A translucent figure of a man appeared above the stone pillar.

"Greetings, if rulers of the Chosen not mind, we will use the figure of Jaspen Turgot who became Minstel."

Rela stared at the figured utterly lost.

"Better give her the beginning messages, too," said Teven.

Rela listened raptly to the figure's first three messages. Then, a fourth message played.

"I call this place the Chamber of Enlightenment. Here, I shall lay out the chronicles of my life. The second room shall be the Chamber of Wisdom. There, I have asked the anotechs to protect any pieces of wisdom my posterity wish to put there. It is my hope that such a collection will protect them from bringing further harm upon the universe through the power they wield. I could cut them off from all knowledge of the anotechs but that would be wrong. The anotechs are not evil, only powerful. Power can be used for great good, but only the tragedies are remembered."

"Did our parents leave messages in the Chamber of Wisdom?" Rela asked. Her blue eyes shone with excitement.

"We can check later," Teven promised. "Are you ready for the anotechs' offer?"

"Yes," Rela said, grinning as a fluttering sensation filled her stomach. "Their impatience is quite apparent."

Teven touched the pillar again and the figure of their mother appeared, complete with the voice they knew so well.

They gasped.

"Greetings, think us not cruel for taking this form. We sense you both miss her much. Perhaps seeing her and hearing her will ease that pain. We seek promises from you who are destined to lead the Chosen. Use your power well. Great factions run over Reshner, spreading animosity and corruption. You have already defeated the greatest of these threats.

"Jaspen Turgot, who built House Minstel, sought peace as did his son and his son's daughter, but several generations down the line that goal was sacrificed for greed and comfort. Restore peace. We will help you by fixing the damage we wrought in our distress. The rains will no longer eat the flesh, the wind will no longer gather so strongly, and the waters of the Crystal Lake will be clean again."

"You can do that?" Rela asked breathlessly. "Why have you not done so already?" She felt her ire rise against the anotechs.

"Destruction and hardship bind people together, we had hoped to unite Reshner, but evil persisted and so punishment persisted."

"It's cruel!" Rela protested. Her side ached and burned. "How can we judge these people?"

"You are Princess Rela of House Minstel. You must instill discipline, or more will die from the chaos. We have seen this. Our old home, Kalast, was lost to such chaos. We do not wish to lose this planet as well. Please help us," their mother's figure begged.

Rela slowly nodded.

"Life has never been fair," she reflected, "but how shall we set things right?" She felt a heavy burden descend upon her as she thought of the task ahead.

"Punish the evildoers, feed the hungry, help the lost, defend the innocent, and never compromise peace."

Teven whistled.

"Right, like that's ever going to happen. Countless generations have passed, and people still haven't figured out how to do all that."

"Never stop fighting for right!" An edge crept into the voice coming from the form of Queen Reia Minstel. "We did not ask for this task, but it is here. To not act would be wrong."

"I can only speak for me, but you have my word that my life will be spent in the service of this planet," said Rela.

"I have already sworn my service." Teven grinned crookedly again. "Welcome to the team, Princess Rela. Shall I escort you to the Chamber of Wisdom now that you have been enlightened?"

"Please." Rela barely noticed the pain this time as Teven scooped her up again. She felt comfortable in his arms. Only Sarie had ever dared to hug Rela, and Lord Kezem had driven her away many years ago. The touch of another human was both wonderful and strange.

Chapter 48: Chamber of Wisdom

Zeri (June) 28, 1560
Same Day
Chamber of Wisdom, Loresh Cave System, Frozen North

Teven McKnight felt some emotional pain fade as he carried his little sister down the stairs through the short hall and up the next set of stairs into the Chamber of Wisdom. His heart ached to have Kayleen back, but the knowledge that she had died saving Rela made his sister's presence that much more precious to him.

This chamber lacked the ship that made the Chamber of Enlightenment seem cramped. From the stairs, it was about thirty meters to the opposite wall, two meters to the left wall, and twenty-five meters to the right wall. The far wall curved gracefully after about fifteen meters, lending a comfy atmosphere to the cave. A line of meter-high stone pillars started at the far left wall and continued around the curve until it reached the wall which composed the second half of the main tunnel. A second line stood in front of it, and a third in front of that. A forth, unfinished row ended approximately halfway around the curve. Each stone pillar was about a tenth of a meter thick and stood a short distance from its neighbor.

"There must be hundreds of pillars in here," said Rela.

"Where do you want to start?" Teven asked, though he could guess her answer.

"With the end ones."

He carried her to the last stone pillar. As they drew near, the frozen dust and stone began swirling. Within minutes, two new pillars would decorate the Chamber of Wisdom.

"Impressive. I think this is a gesture of friendship," Teven guessed.

"I don't have any wise words to say now," Rela said.

"Don't worry. The first message is always an introduction."

"Always? You've only heard Jaspen Turgot's pillar," Rela reminded.

Teven stopped walking toward the pillars.

"I know many things," he said, solemnly meeting her eyes. "I am the wise, all-powerful older brother here."

"Remind me to smack you when my arms function properly."

"Of course, Princess. It will be done," Teven promised, doing his best impression of an RLA soldier.

They chuckled.

"Owww! Stop making me laugh!"

"Don't stab yourself next time," he retorted.

"I'm never going to live that down, am I?"

"Not if I can help it."

"Oh, just carry me to the pillar," she ordered.

He opened his mouth.

"Less talk more forward movement."

He smiled.

When they reached the last stone pillar besides the two new ones, Teven let Rela run her hand along the top of it. A holographic form of their mother appeared.

"Greetings, I am Reia Antellio Minstel, younger sister to Kiata, daughter of Sela and Basil Antellio, wife of Prince Terosh Minstel. Once a Ranger, now an outcast, I confess choosing love over duty and the life I was bred for." The figure fell silent and disappeared.

Rela touched the pillar again.

"Doesn't this thing have a play all button?"

"Guess not. Life's rough, Princess."

Their mother appeared again. Her expression radiated joy.

"We have a son! Terosh could not come with me this time because one of us had to stay to receive the representatives from the Galactic Alliance of Populated Planets. But I had to come. Teven is beautiful. He has his father's black hair, my green eyes, and a scream that can penetrate every corner of the palace! I know I am supposed to be recording bits of wisdom here so here is my lesson for future generations: enjoy every moment you can basking in the love of family." Her smile was steady as she slowly faded.

Teven gently pressed his right hand to the pillar then squeezed Rela's arm.

"She's speaking to us."

When their mother appeared this time, she was distraught. A haunted, far-off look lurked in her expressive eyes. She began speaking softly, but her voice got faster as her emotions raced.

"My beloved Terosh is dead. We suggested joining the Galactic Alliance of Populated Planets so we could offer further aid to neighboring planets suffering from the Colza Star explosion, but our suggestion was ill-received by the Senate and the Governors Council. Lord Kezem, Governor General Third Lord of Idonia, protested most vehemently. The debates stretched on from months into years. Terosh suspended the meetings for a time to let tempers cool but it did not help. A few days ago, Terosh received an offer of information from an unknown woman. A meeting was set up in Estra. Terosh was ambushed, and now he is gone." Queen Reia continued staring straight ahead, pausing so long Teven and Rela thought she had finished.

"So that's what happened," Rela said. "I wish I had known them."

To their surprise, their mother wiped at some tears, took a deep breath, and continued speaking. Her voice wavered with emotion.

"I fear for my children. We have three now: Teven, Rela, and Tavel. What will become of them? Lord Kezem is quickly gaining support. He will strike sooner or later, and I fear I shall not survive the confrontation. I do not fear death, but I fear not knowing what will become of my children. They are innocent. They should not pay for decisions Terosh and I have made. But they will. GAPP deceived us. They will force a joining when it suits them. I can only hope I can prepare my children for all the dangers they will soon face. The anotechs are a powerful gift. I bid future rulers to use them unselfishly. Selfish actions only cause pain, and it is better to suffer than cause suffering." Queen Reia looked like she wanted to say more, but then, she turned away and disappeared.

Rela touched the pillar again but nothing happened. After a moment, their mother's first message played again.

"Shall we hear what Father has to say?" Teven questioned, wondering if Rela had the strength to hear more. His arms were getting tired.

"Yes, I would like to see him," Rela murmured.

Teven sidestepped left so Rela was in front of their father's stone pillar. The holograph showed a boy of about twelve or thirteen who looked strikingly like Teven.

"My name's Terosh." The young man looked somewhere off to his left and rolled his eyes. His voice contained equal parts annoyance and arrogance. "Yeah, yeah. I'm getting there. Greetings, I am Prince Terosh Minstel, brother of the obnoxious I-am-great Prince Tate, second son of Kila and Teorn Minstel. I cannot sing, and I'll never be king so lots of me will you hear."

Rela laughed.

Teven chuckled as well. He'd always pictured his father as a serious man.

"Play that one again," Rela instructed.

"You like being in pain?"

"I want to see him as a child," Rela insisted.

"It'll cycle around eventually. Somehow, I don't think he has as many messages as he thought he would."

At Rela's touch, Prince Terosh returned a few years older and beaming with happiness.

"I am in love! I have come with my new wife so all future generations may learn from her as I have. She is wonderful in a hundred thousand ways which I have no time to record. Besides, I'd rather spend my time with her than this machine anyway." He winked and vanished.

Another touch to the pillar brought forth the figure of a much graver Prince Terosh.

"My father and brother are dead. They went to Mitra to help Princess Alikai avoid the Blood Harvest. Their bodies returned a few days ago, and the anotechs with them have quite a story to tell. I can barely believe them, though I know they would not lie. It now falls to Reia and me to lead this people. I never realized how much pressure Tate took upon himself, ruling the planet while our father grieved for our slain mother, the queen. It is now my task and burden. Riden help us."

"Now it is our task and our burden," said Rela. "I wonder when Lord Kezem decided to turn on our parents."

"He was ambitious, smart, and ruthless," Teven said. "I'm not supposed to rejoice over death, but I am relieved he is gone."

"Me too. Try having your life linked to him," Rela said.

"You've got me there."

Rela touched the pillar and the young Terosh appeared again and delivered his message.

Teven frowned and a sense of sadness spread through him. The three messages left so much unsaid. They fell silent, thinking of all that had transpired and silently mourning the lost years.

"Rela, I've been thinking about what our cousin said just before she died," Teven said thoughtfully.

The title—cousin—still felt strange to him.

"Who?"

"Kayleen Wellum. Her mother and our mother were sisters. She said I would always be a Royal Guard. Is that possible?"

"What are you asking?" Rela's tone mixed curiosity and fear.

"Will you take Reshner's throne?" asked Teven.

"You do not wish to be king?" She stared at him in disbelief.

"We're going to need all the help we can get to ferret out the deeper levels of corruption. I cannot do that as king. If you became queen you could put formal pressure on the Senate and the Governors Council to get their act together, and I would be free to apply my own pressure from another direction," Teven explained. When she didn't answer immediately, he hastened on. "I would always be nearby to help you as necessary. That's what Royal Guards do anyway."

"Don't make promises you don't know if you can keep," Rela said gently.

"Words of wisdom, Princess, you should record that," Teven said.

"Promise me you'll try to not die."

"I promise."

"Then I will accept the throne and serve the people for as long as I can," Rela vowed.

Teven waited, knowing she had more to say.

"But do not think you have escaped politics, Prince Teven. State dinners and formal wear await you."

She was joking but he protested anyway.

"I think it would be best if the people believed me still lost or dead." His frown deepened. "It would put you in more danger but hopefully not for long."

"That is why I have Melian Maidens," Rela said with a weary sigh.

A new idea occurred to Teven. His frown softened.

"Rela, could you make me a Royal Guard captain, so I could

stay with you?" He felt her studying his face.

"That is a high promotion for a first-class derringer," said Rela, pulling his current rank from his mind.

He didn't care. It was comforting to share thoughts with her. Now, it was her turn to think. He took the time to absorb her soft brown hair, smooth features, and passionate blue eyes.

The protective instincts stirred.

"I do not wish to be the Captain of the Royal Guard. I want to be just an ordinary captain. They can get places full commanders cannot."

"You have a devious mind, Teven. Are you sure you don't want to be king and level that deviousness against the Governors Council?"

"Positive. I can be more devious if they don't know who I am. Teven's a common enough name. No one will think twice about Teven McKnight. I could protect you and slip away to investigate our enemies as well."

"But most of the soldiers already know who you are," Rela pointed out.

"The anotechs can fix that," Teven said seriously. The thought was troublesome but necessary. "There are several others that will have to be dealt with as well. Jalna can arrange it."

Rela shuddered.

"Please do not talk like that, you sound like Lord Kezem."

"I'm sorry," replied Teven.

"What about your face?" Rela asked with a concerned expression.

"What's wrong with my face?" Teven demanded, pretending to be miffed. A twinkle in his eyes gave him away. He knew she referred to his uncanny resemblance to their father. "I think the anotechs could fix that as well."

Rela blew out a long breath.

"I do not like it, but it will suffice as a plan for now," said Rela. "Modify your face and alter their memories as needed but leave the Melian Maidens and Captain Tayce alone. They are trustworthy and someone must know the truth in case something happens to me." She sighed and tapped her fingers on Teven's shoulder. "You win, Captain McKnight, but we must forgo formalities until my legs stop rebelling."

"As you wish, Princess," Teven said. There was a tender quality to his voice. He cleared his throat. "With your permission, Highness, I'd like to put you down now. My arms hurt."

She leveled an imperious gaze at him.

"You have my permission but know that I will be relying heavily upon your advice on royal matters. You will be a hidden king. If you do not like my terms, tough."

"You would have driven our father mad," Teven commented, shaking his head.

Her expression said she took that as a compliment.

Chapter 49:
Perilous Return to the Palace

Zeri (June) 29, 1560 - Temen (July) 5, 1560
Loresh, Frozen North to Royal Palace, City of Rammon

Two days were spent in Loresh. Teven divided his attention among sitting by his sister, viewing messages from their ancestors, subtly adjusting his features, selectively modifying memories, hovering near his uncle, and helping the RLA soldiers clean up the battlefield. The anotechs cleaned the blood that had fallen on the cold ground. Most of the bodies were taken out of Loresh and burned traditionally.

Teven took care of Kayleen personally. He conducted a small Ranger ceremony with only Todd Wellum, Princess Rela, the six Melian Maidens, Rela's three friends, and Jalna present. Teven felt older and wearier than his new face could ever convey. He had the anotechs add cells to the bottom of both cheeks, making his face squarer, and then, he grew a beard to add false years to his life. His heart broke all over again when he spoke the ritual words.

"Resmundel resmunsi rel ihala ental mieltsom."

Jalna translated for the others, "Return to dust, return to spirit, rest, I hold you forever in my heart."

When only ashes remained, Teven and Todd buried them in the small cave where Kayleen had reunited with her father. With the unpleasant tasks finally done, they could return to Rammon. Teven knew Rela would face a tough battle to reach the capital, but he was determined to see her there safely.

The return journey took five days instead of one because they had to travel slowly for Rela's sake. Even with the anotechs controlling the pain, she could not be moved fast.

Princess Rela slept a lot, first on the hov sled ride to Estra, and then, in the modified hov to the coast. Teven had them camp beside the Asrien Sea for several days, reluctant to put Rela through the rough waters. At her insistence, they finally proceeded. Throughout the Frozen North, the defectors from the RLA and Royal Guard formed a perimeter. Inside, the six Melian Maidens, the recently minted Aster Captain Ethan Tayce, Jalna, and Teven formed another perimeter around Princess Rela. Marc and Lorian stuck close to Anabel, who despite protestation was also forced to rest.

Escapees from the Battle for Loresh had informed the rest of the RLA of Lord Kezem's demise. In addition, the word spread to the Senate and the Governors Council. Supreme Commander Kolknir was the most logical choice to succeed Lord Kezem, but other Royal Guard, Melian Maiden, and RLA officers vied for control. Senators and governors broke and formed alliances constantly, hoping to curry favor with Reshner's next ruler. Rumors circulated that Princess Rela might have survived, but they chose to ignore the whispers.

Three times, the Princess's entourage was attacked, once by desperate mercenaries and twice by remnants of the RLA still loyal to Lord Kezem. Teven was awed and comforted by the Melian Maidens' fighting skills. Kia whirled her banistick so fast he could barely see it. Energy beams flew away from her and the princess. Jola, Elia, and Clara seemed to be everywhere at once slashing attackers with their blazing white kerlinblades. Linnea and Nalana stood their ground, protecting themselves with banisticks and simultaneously returning fire with energy pistols. Each fight was finished in moments, but the repeated nature of the attacks annoyed Teven.

They arrived in Rammon at dawn, neutralized the guards at the southernmost gate, and headed directly to the Senate Great Hall. A scout reported that Supreme Commander Kolknir had barricaded himself and his command inside the palace. The senators were summoned because they could request an immediate audience with the ruler. If Supreme Commander Kolknir came, they would have a much easier time of dealing with him. As expected, he refused to come. His spies had reported Rela's return.

A subsection of the Senate foolishly tried to have Rela arrested. Teven and the Melian Maidens put a stop to that. A loud debate raged back and forth for a few minutes. Rela stood to the side and observed the scene serenely. Teven stood by her side, like a good Royal Guard.

Her carefully controlled expression hid the pain she must be in. Teven admired her grit.

"She is the only heir left to House Minstel," Senator Morren said reluctantly. "We have to have a ruler, and I will not serve a common soldier!"

"She's not even of age yet!" argued Senator Keel.

"We must wait for the prince to be found," Senator Rorian insisted, nodding agreement.

"If she becomes queen our positions are forfeit!" reminded Senator Keel.

The arguments continued in circles, until Rela lifted her chin and cleared her throat. They fell silent once they realized she would not bother to shout above them.

"It is not your choice. With or without your permission, I *will* take back the throne and appeal to the people. Many of you gained your positions through favoritism, not merit. That is to be expected. It is time you earned your place in this government. Many changes must be made as to how trade is conducted. There will be no more marks. Criminals will have fair trials and pay for their crimes accordingly. You will no longer be above the law. I will not tolerate graft or abuse. If you cannot abide by the laws, then leave." Rela spun away and strode out of the Great Hall. The anotechs reported great pain rolling off her.

"How are you still walking?" Teven murmured. He felt a tingling in his side just being near her.

"We need to retake the palace, right now," Rela stated, instead of answering his question.

Teven was becoming more alarmed by the second. Rela was walking awfully fast for someone with a dagger slash down her right side.

Of course, we must retake the palace, but we should infiltrate it at night not midmorning.

"We can handle that, Rela," Teven said earnestly, referring to the Melian Maidens and the soldiers they had acquired in Loresh.

Rela shook her head and talked as she walked toward the center of the city and the front palace gates.

"Reshner politics have changed very little over the years. We can still appeal to ancient customs. If I am to be accepted as queen, I need to physically take the palace *without* bloodshed. Lord Kezem never became king because his birthright was forfeited when his mother was cast out, and he took the throne by massacring half the palace staff, not to mention our mother."

"But Kezem controlled the Senate and the Governors Council. How could he not have controlled the people?" Teven asked, still following her closely.

The streets were disturbingly quiet. Having heard the news of Lord Kezem's death, most people waited inside secret chambers for the power struggle to end. They knew violence was likely.

"He *did* control the people. He controlled every aspect of their lives so rigidly that their only small revenge came in denying him the title."

"What's your plan?"

"March through the front door," Rela replied.

"Oh, they'll never expect that," Teven said.

It's going to be a very long day.

"Anabel!" Rela called.

"Yes, Princess?" said Anabel.

"Stay near the back and stick to a kerlak gun," Rela instructed. "If it comes down to a blade battle get out."

Teven guessed that was the best advice. Telling Anabel she couldn't help capture the palace would have been asking for trouble.

"Yes, Your Highness," Anabel answered, dropping back a few steps.

They came to the palace gates fifteen minutes later.

"Halt!" shouted a soldier.

"Get in line or get out of the way. Those are your options," Rela said, stopping two meters from the gates. She leveled her energy gun at the man who had spoken. A second guard slowly walked away from his post.

"Where are you going?" the first guard demanded. "Supreme Commander Kolknir will kill you for deserting."

"Exactly. The princess will not," the second guard said, pointing at Rela.

The first man struggled with that logic before lowering his weapon, opening the gate, and waving them through.

"I never liked the supreme commander anyway," the second guard mumbled.

"Set your weapons to stun if you want to come," Rela ordered. "No one is to die today."

"Yes, Highness, it will be done," answered the first soldier.

Teven sensed deception from the man. Rela gave him the

mental version of a wink via the anotechs. She felt it, too. They entered and jogged down the main path. Soldiers fanned out in front and to the sides of them, and the Melian Maidens remained in a loose circle around Rela. Their array left plenty of room for them to maneuver with their banisticks and gave Teven and Rela space to shoot. Teven checked the setting on his kerlak pistol and took out his banistick.

A pair of snipers perched in the second-floor balcony above the front doors took several shots at them. Teven traded his pistol and banistick for his kerlinblade and turned the power up to full. He batted away beams that came too close to Rela for comfort.

At a nod from Kia, Linnea lengthened her banistick farther than normal and sprinted in an unpredictable zigzag pattern toward the balcony. When she was two meters from her target, she stabbed the ground with her banistick and launched her body into the sky. She sailed over the railing and landed feet first on one of the snipers. The second sniper surrendered and was promptly chucked from the balcony. Linnea leapt down gracefully and rejoined the group. Seconds later, a squad of twenty Royal Guards charged from the ornate double doors in four lines of five.

"Halt! Surrender or be shot!" shouted the lieutenant.

Teven felt uncomfortable with twenty energy guns leveled at his sister.

Aster Captain Tayce took two steps closer to the Royal Guards.

"Stand down! I am your new commander!" shouted Tayce.

"Supreme Commander Kolknir—"

"Is a traitor and will be dealt with. Join us or be tried for treason," said Rela.

Doubt crossed the faces of two or three of the soldiers.

"My time is short. If you join me, nothing further will be said about your service to Kezem or Kolknir, but you must decide now." Rela waited two seconds for them to comply. "Very well," she said with a sigh. Turning to her companions, she said, "Deal with them."

A barrage of twenty deadly energy beams flew at them. Teven's heart climbed up into his throat. He needn't have worried for Rela's sake. Two of the front soldiers took the brunt of the attack and died instantly, but the Melian Maidens, Kia in particular, turned back the rest of the beams with swift strikes from their golden banisticks.

The rest of the hours-long, on-and-off battle for the palace passed similarly to the first few seconds. Teven and the Melian Maidens spent the bulk of their efforts keeping a hail of energy beams away from Rela. The princess and her loyal soldiers, including a few new additions, poured stun beams back at Kolknir's men.

The throne room door was code locked, and the guards in front of it were a bit more challenging than the last two hundred or so.

"Kia, Elia, I trust you can clear that door," Rela said calmly, slowing to a walk.

Kia and Elia leapt forward and engaged the guards. While they fought, Teven and Rela exchanged a glance, shared a thought, and placed both hands on the doors. The anotechs flowed from their fingertips. Within seconds, the anotechs had the doors unlocked and the bomb attached to the doors disabled. Teven and Rela retrieved their anotechs and stepped back. Linnea kicked one door in and Jola kicked in the other. The group burst into the throne room to meet the astonished crowd of soldiers beyond.

Teven didn't like the situation. A few hundred soldiers crowded into the throne room. If it came down to a fight, everyone would be hard-pressed to stay alive. The problem was magnified by Rela's insistence on not killing. The weakened energy beams would wear off soon and the soldiers spread throughout the palace would be called to the throne room to trap the intruders.

"Give me one reason—" Supreme Commander Kolknir began.

Rela's energy beam caught him in the throat. Teven saw her flinch at having to shoot him in such a vulnerable spot, but the rest of him was covered by black body armor, leaving her little choice.

Where'd she learn to shoot like that?

Rela addressed the soldiers before the shock wore off.

"Lord Kezem is dead. I am Princess Rela of House Minstel, and as such, I have the right and duty to claim Reshner's throne. Whether I become queen or not rests in your hands and the hands of every citizen. Those who lay down arms will be reintegrated into the army under new leadership. You will also have the choice of resigning and joining civilian service branches or going home and pursuing a legal trade. Either way you will help rebuild this war-torn planet. Whether you do so from a prison post or as free people is your choice. Choose carefully."

Teven held his breath. The soldiers eyed one another. A tense half-minute passed without sound. Finally, a young female soldier slowly removed her kerlinblade and placed it on the ground. Then, she reached for her energy pistol, placed it on the ground beside the blade, stood up, and bowed to Rela. Others followed the example.

"No!" shouted the first gate guard who stood to Rela's left. He lifted his energy gun to shoot Rela.

Teven's heart skipped a beat. He couldn't get through Rela in time to intercept the shot.

Kia—who was on that side—reacted with speed born of good reflexes and plenty of practice. She knocked the weapon up and twisted it from the man's grasp. In the next instant, he was on the ground kneeling before Rela with head bowed and arms twisted up behind his back. Kia hauled him to his feet and tossed him at some guards who caught him and applied stuncuffs. Her quick actions convinced the remaining soldiers to surrender peaceably.

The Rammon palace was finally secure.

Chapter 50:
Reshner Approves

Temen (July) 10, 1560
Royal Palace, City of Rammon

The next several days passed like a heartbeat. Princess Rela had never dreamed of the amount of energy it took to deal with politicians and commoners. Already their pettiness tore at her spirit.

The General Council, composed of commoners from across Reshner, had held their first meeting yesterday to discuss her bid for the throne. No one could deny that Princess Rela belonged to House Minstel and had taken the palace bloodlessly, but the Senators had rubbed off on the General Council. Part of her found it amusing to hear the same arguments, which called her competence into question, coming from a farmer with the same words used by a senator. The General Council met again this morning to make a decision.

Rela paced the throne room, waiting for an answer. She tried to convince herself she would be okay without the title.

You're lying.

She drew a deep breath and held it for a few seconds before releasing it.

"You're going to give yourself the hiccups," Teven said from behind her.

Rela turned sharply and winced as the wound stretched. She still relied heavily on the anotechs to ignore the pain from her side. Even the slightly quickened breaths caused her some discomfort.

"Do not make a habit of that," she said, annoyed. Rela checked the bandage attached to her side to make sure her blood was staying inside. This was her first day with just the bandage. She had removed the anotech barrier in favor of using them to enhance her perceptions. She needed every advantage when it came to the slippery councils.

"Your pardon, Highness, but the delegate from the General Council approaches," Teven said.

"You know something," Rela said, catching a gleam in his eyes. She hurried back to her throne to be properly seated.

"I know something," Teven confirmed in a whisper, as the throne room doors swung open.

A woman in a flowing white dress entered. She was plain in terms of beauty but held herself with impressive dignity. Her steps were swift but sure. Upon reaching the dais steps, she stopped and knelt.

"My Queen, you have the confidence of the General Council and the support of the people. May Riden give you wisdom to rule as fairly as King Jaspen of House Minstel."

Rela's heart soared with triumph.

"Thank you, Lady Zelene, I shall do my best to earn the trust placed in me, but our future is as much in the hands of the General Council, the Senate, the Governors Council, and the people as it is in mine."

"How may I serve you, Your Majesty?" asked Lady Zelene.

"My first request is a thorough report from each region," said Rela. "The governors can help you with that. I need to know what each region needs if I am to address their problems. Also, I shall require good intelligence on the movements of dissidents. Rebuilding Reshner will be hard enough without having the civilian engineers attacked. The RLA and Peacekeepers will provide some protection, but the last thing I want to do is return Reshner to the military state it has been for the last thirteen years."

Why can't I just browbeat everyone into behaving?

"I will convey your wishes to the council at tomorrow's meeting. Tonight, we eagerly await your address. Infopads will carry your message to every settlement, including Ritand, though only a few refugees have returned after the floods."

Rela had determined to address the people regardless of the council's decision. She wanted to put rumors to rest and extend her offer to help.

"Is Ritand in your region, Lady Zelene?" Rela inquired.

"Yes, Your Majesty, my home is in Resh, but I went to Ritand many years ago to help the refugees when the Ashasten nearly swallowed the island. My father was once the governor of Resh. Thus, I am one of the only people trusted by both the citizens of Resh and the Ritand people. That is why they have honored me with the council post."

"You have earned their trust, Councilor," Rela said, motioning for the lady to rise. "Guard it well."

"I shall," Lady Zelene said. She recovered her feet and waited.

An awkward silence fell before Rela realized the woman was waiting to be dismissed.

"Forgive me, Councilor, I am a little new at this. You are dismissed unless you have anything else you wish to add or ask. Please, do not hesitate to voice your requests."

"You are kind, my queen, a quality both your parents possessed in abundance. They would be proud to see their daughter on the throne. With your permission, I shall impose upon your time later." The ease with which the woman spoke of Rela's parents suggested familiarity.

Rela wondered how familiar but decided it was a conversation for another day.

Lady Akia Zelene bowed and left.

"You scared her, Highness," Teven said, clearly amused. He usually addressed her that way even when they were alone.

Kia and Jola flanked the throne and Aster Captain Tayce stood like a statue next to Kia.

Sometimes, Rela wished Teven would just call her by name, as he had done in Loresh, but she understood the necessity of the charade.

"How so?"

"She was tenser than a tretling in a korver den," said Teven.

Rela groaned.

"I don't want to scare them."

"Do not dwell on it, Your Majesty," said Kia. "Lord Kezem's reign was long, and he cultivated fear. It will take time to correct the perception of leadership."

Rela was pleased that her maiden spoke. It had taken a long time to get Kia to see that she was more than a glorified shield to Rela.

"Thank you, Kia," said Rela. "It is good to know I am not that intimidating. Just don't tell the Senators. A few of them could use a little more fear."

"Leave that to me," Teven advised.

"I have a speech to prepare, but I want an explanation for that statement later," Rela said.

I could get used to ordering Teven around.

"Of course, I shall now blend into the walls like a good Royal Guard," said Teven.

Rela suppressed the giggle at seeing Captain Tayce's confused expression. She began pacing back and forth across the small platform that held the throne, pondering what to say to her people. Every time she looked up she saw another statue of Lord Kezem's head staring at her.

That is disturbing.

"Those have got to go," she muttered.

"The ugly statues are slated for destruction three days from now, Highness," Teven said cheerfully. "The replacement heads in your likeness are already on their way."

Rela sucked in sharply, horrified for the full second she believed him. Then, she caught the gleam in his eye.

"Teven, that was very cruel." Despite herself, Rela chuckled at the mental picture of walking past her likeness every day.

"Perhaps, but I have a gift that can make you forget just about everything," Teven teased.

"What is it?"

"You'll find out later," Teven promised.

***

Two hours after the evening meal, Queen Rela stepped out onto the third-floor balcony above the palace's double doors. The huge crowd on the lawn shifted restlessly, standing shoulder to shoulder. Rela shivered under the intensity of their collective gaze.

Talk about intimidating!

The expansive palace grounds were a security disaster waiting to happen. A wall of blue Royal Guards lined the walls, giving Rela a mixture of comfort and sadness. Both Teven and Captain Tayce had insisted on the visible security, but their presence undermined what she wanted to say.

Rela slowed as she neared the balcony railing, fearing her knees would fail and pitch her into the crowd. Flattening a dozen spectators during her first speech would be a poor first impression.

Seeing the stars and the three crescent moons shining above the crowd, Rela wondered how her mother's crown fared against those night jewels. Rela's breath hitched as she imagined her mother standing on this balcony preparing to address the people. Her heart nearly broke under the strain of longing for her father to present her to the crowd as would have been his right. Rela would have gladly traded all the crown jewels for a simple farewell to her parents, but they were gone. Knowing she must carry their legacy of strength, compassion, and wisdom, Rela felt completely inadequate.

A cheer rose from the crowd as people realized she had arrived. Heart pounding, Rela stepped to the voice amplifiers set up by the railing. The deep purple gown she had commissioned for the occasion sparkled under the bright lights as she moved. She gripped the balcony railing with both hands to keep them from shaking and leaned forward. She spoke softly, relying on the voice amplifiers to carry her message.

"Greetings, I am Queen Rela Minstel. You know who my parents and brothers were. You know what happened to them," she began, already deviating from her planned speech. "You also know what it is like to suffer under a tyrant. Yet by granting me the title of queen, you have demonstrated much trust. Thank you. I have not done much with my life, but much has been destroyed and now needs rebuilding. With your cooperation, we can return Reshner to peaceful days. It may last a day. It may last several lifetimes. We can only control our own actions and hope the next generation will learn from our wisdom and our mistakes. Tyranny was a mist—"

"What about the soldiers?" a man shouted. "You have more guards than Lord Kezem ever did!"

"The soldiers you see and feel around you are there for your protection and mine," Rela explained. "For as many of us who want peace, there are those who still want war. Many feel threatened by this change in government. Threatened people act rashly. Until the broken pieces of our cities are picked up and the scars are removed from the land, soldiers will be present, but they will be you. The Peacekeepers will be a branch of the army composed of citizens. Those who do not wish to serve in this manner may choose some other—"

"So now *you're* telling us what to do?" the man challenged. He sounded triumphant.

Stop interrupting!

Rela clamped down on her temper. A display of anger would not help her cause. She tried again.

"For three years starting at the age of sixteen, everyone who wishes to be a citizen will serve in some way. That does *not* mean you have to disrupt your lives. In fact, most of you are already public servants. There will be abundant opportunities. Teachers, doctors, peacekeepers, ship builders, hov designers, scientists, artists, disaster workers, and street cleaning crews all serve. The point is not to make you miserable but to get you to do something unselfish for a time."

A low murmur buzzed through the crowd as the people quietly discussed Rela's proposition. Slowly, a cheer started from the back corner and worked its way forward growing louder every second. Rela listened carefully, a smile spreading across her face.

"Etvi vental la creshon!"

Long live the servant queen!

***

Teven McKnight watched his sister proudly.

She won.

Queen Rela had emerged victorious in the battle for the people's hearts. Teven smiled to himself and thought of the surprise he had for her once the crowds had gone and Rela had a moment to herself. His guest waited in the throne room. The surprise was Lorian Petole's idea, but it had been Teven who made the countless calls and finally tracked down the elusive woman. He only hoped he would have as much success when he tried to find his brother.

That's a task for another day.

By the time Teven finally steered Rela back to the throne room, he'd grown so impatient he practically danced circles around her. First, he was on one side of her then he was on the other.

Seizing his arm, Rela leaned close.

"What is wrong with you?"

"My surprise is near." Teven twisted out of her grasp and flung the throne room doors open with a flourish.

A large, dark-skinned woman opened her arms to receive the young queen.

Rela froze and stared.

"Sarie!" she cried, rushing forward to meet the embrace.

Despite the six silent, ever-present Melian Maidens observing the happy reunion, Teven felt his presence was an intrusion. He slowly backed out and shut the throne room doors quietly, pleased to have restored a little peace to his sister.

THE END

Appendix I: Annotated Glossary

(Expanded) Cast of Characters
Contains Spoilers

Alexi Gordon – rebel leader
Akia Zelene – representative of the General Council
Anabel Spitzer – friend of Princess Rela Minstel
Aveni – Ranger born on the planet of Wirsh
Benali – an actor hired by Laocer to manipulate Lord Kezem
Bova – Ranger from the planet of Rorge II
Carla Etan – former servant in the royal palace
Clara Arganon – a Melian Maiden assigned to Princess Rela
Clive Weldon – marksman assigned to Fort Riden
Coleth Timmer – mercenary, works for Gareth Restler
Cory Tiridan – marksman; helps Ethan Tayce
Covin – Elish male; twin of Zareb; Royal Guard; serves King Terosh
Dalonos – "dark ones"; anotechs who have a proclivity to pursue evil intent
Deanna Koffrin Minstel – deceased scientist; wife of Crown Prince Taytron Minstel; mother of Elia
Dentelich – doctor for the Royal family
Dravid Altran – Kezem's father; deceased
Ectosh Laocer – Royal Guard captain; secretly loves the queen
Elia Koffrin – daughter of Prince Taytron Minstel and Princess Deanna Koffrin Minstel; one of the maidens assigned to protect Princess Rela
Ethan Tayce – soldier in the Reshner Liberation Army; has a change of heart and helps Princess Rela and Todd Wellum
Jalna Seltan – daughter of the anotech creator; trains Kayleen and Prince Teven to use anotechs
Jenell – a derringer on the Kireshana; travels with Kayleen and Teven
Jola Westin – a Melian Maiden assigned to Princess Rela
Karric – a derringer on the Kireshana; travels with Kayleen and Teven; was trapped in the Huz Mon salt mines for a time
Kel Kiren – smuggler on Reshner to research his past, charged with raising Prince Tavel
Linnea Price – a Melian Maiden assigned to Princess Rela
Nalana Vastel – a Melian Maiden assigned to Princess Rela

Nicholas Riggs – servant in Royal Palace in Rammon, friend of Princess Rela
Gareth Restler – eldest son of Arista, Merisia's husband
Kayleen Wellum – daughter of Kiata and Todd Wellum; Ranger apprentice; Teven's friend
Kezem Altran – youngest son of Mavis and Dravid Altran; Governor General of Idonia; Third Lord of Idonia
Kia Meetcher – head of the Melian Maidens assigned to protect Princess Rela
Kiata Antellio Wellum – Nareth Talis Ranger; Reia's older sister; wife of Todd
Kila Creston Minstel – deceased queen of Reshner; assassinated by Niktrod Keldor; mother of Terosh
Kolknir – Kezem's agent; mercenary; former Ranger master; serves the Lady as well; trains Lucas Telon
Liam Deliad – Ranger Master of Arms, Ashatan Council member
Lorian Petole – servant in Kezem's palace, friend of Princess Rela Minstel
Marc Spitzer – friend of Princess Rela Minstel
Mavis Altran – mother of Eldon, Mitrek, and Kezem; former princess; disowned by her father when she married Dravid Altran to escape an arranged marriage to a Gardanian prince; Teorn's elder sister; also known as the Lady
Merek – Lord Kezem's adviser, tries to understand the anotechs by studying Princess Rela
Merisia Restler – daughter of Vera and Tyko; Gareth's wife; ran away from the RT Alliance to protect her unborn child
Mitrek Altran – middle son of Mavis and Dravid Altran; Governor Judge and Second Lord of Idonia; brother of Kezem; husband of Delia; father of Silvia, Arabeth, and Sullivan
Nala Wellum – wife of Terik Wellum
Nathan McKnight, Jr. – called Nate, raised as the brother of Prince Teven, son of Pria and Nathan McKnight
Niklos McGreven – Ranger Healer master; substitute father for Reia and Kiata
Niktrod Keldor – man who assassinated Queen Kila, father of Ariman; grandfather of Talyon
Nils Clavon – servant and friend of Kiata and Todd Wellum
Pria McKnight – palace servant who smuggled Prince Teven out before the coup

Quasim – derringer on the Kireshana
Quedron – Aster Captain in Kezem's army
Reia Antellio Minstel – Ranger's new queen; Kiata's younger sister; adopted by Antellio family
Sarie Verituse – Melian Maiden; caretaker of Princess Rela
Talyon Keldor – RT agent; Ariman's son; Merisia's friend; Niktrod's grandson; also Peter Estan, the man who trains Princess Rela how to fight
Taytron Minstel – deceased elder son of Kila and Teorn Minstel; Terosh's brother
Teorn Minstel – deceased father of Taytron and Terosh; Mavis's younger brother
Terik Wellum – brother of Todd Wellum
Terosh Minstel – Reshner's king, son of Kila and Teorn Minstel
Todd Wellum – Nareth Talis Ranger, often works with his wife, Kiata
Trina Kiren – wife of Kel, agrees to raise Prince Tavel when they escape Reshner
Tryse – Coridian assassin in training
Zareb – Elish male; twin of Covin; messenger for Prince Taytron

Creatures

Cannafitch – Thin-boned mammals with semi-hollow chest cavities that have leathery wings and can glide across vast distances. Although color can vary slightly, the majority are brown. They feed on small woodland creatures, though on rare occasions they will attempt to take on a korver or a tretling.
korvers – Until scientists began purposefully enhancing korvers, the average animal was about a meter tall and a meter and a half from nose to tail. Genetic alterations have resulted in several specimens that are about twice as big as normal korvers. Scrappy pack animals that live and hunt together, normal korvers do not usually pose a threat to human travelers. The new breed of korver can command much larger packs, which definitely poses a threat to travelers.
Shiners – Small insects that prefer dark caves or tree hollows where their inner light can make a difference. They feed primarily upon marin moss. They in turn are a food source for many species of birds.
Tretlings – Prized for their abundant wool, tretlings are hearty, yet simple creatures.

Voracerflies – a species of carnivorous flies native to Reshner and several other Edge planets

Wallays – These small, thin creatures happily burrow by the hundreds under nice, flat farmland. They harden the walls of their tunnels with a mucous-like substance called cradul. Farmers spend a lot of time and effort combatting wallays. When a wallay colony moves to a new location, the tunnel walls eventually weaken. This can lead to graveground.

Zalok – Majestic creatures that can grow several meters tall. Before the discovery that their scales could have hallucinogenic properties when treated with crela dust and heated, zalok packs dominated the many cave systems in the Riden Mountains. Scale color can vary slightly, but the most coveted color is purple.

Notable Places on Reshner
(Each city has formed its own personality over time.)

Azhel – The unofficial spiritual capital of Reshner, Azhel features temples and holy places for nearly every religion practiced on the planet. The citizens who call Azhel home tend to be calm and deeply committed to exploring spiritual matters.

Calsola – All manner of racing provides the backbone of Calsolan commerce. Although hovs, hov bikes, and even footraces have a place in Calsola, the residents have always had a special fondness for horse racing. The citizens on a whole tend to be wildly free-spirited. Fittingly, this is the first city encountered by derringers on the Kireshana.

Chara – A refined southern city located southwest of Rammon and right along the Glass Coast, Chara has the perfect climate for growing things. As such, it has cultivated quite a reputation for its famous wines and performing arts.

Estra – This sparsely populated city is located south of Chara on the poorly named southern continent called the Frozen North. The citizens here are no strangers to harsh conditions, but they are also proud of their patch of frozen paradise.

Huz Mon – Probably as noteworthy for its infamous salt mines as it is for being the second major city encountered by Kireshana derringers, Huz Mon is located just north of the Riden Flats.

Idonia – Home to the Altran family, Idonia generates most of its income by processing ore from the Nedis Crystal Mines. Idonian glass swords are prized as collectibles by those rich enough to purchase them.

Kalmata – Located near but not quite on the western coast of Reshner's habitable continent, Kalmata is known for processing salt from the West Remon Sea as well as tosh from the Imberg Tosh Mines.

Kerimia – Although not technically a city, this large village has a thriving black market, especially for firfe spice.

Korch – Nestled along the top edge of the Talmeth Mountains on the southwest corner of Reshner's habitable continent, Korch had built a reputation for being hearty. This probably springs from the difficulties of pulling a living out of the inhospitable, volcanic mountains and the dangerous Talmeth Forest. Every few years, Korch hosts the Colored Crossblades Tournament.

Meritab and Meritel – Often called the Twin Cities, Meritab and Meritel, are located southeast of the Riden Mountains and northwest of the Clear Mountains. Naturally, the nearness has produced a healthy atmosphere of friendly competition in everything from dance performances to colored-crossblades tournaments to shooting contests and even cooking competitions.

Osem – This port city mainly draws its living out of the North Asrien Sea, but Osem is also notable for its large contingent of Rangers.

Rammon – The Capital city of Reshner boasts a bustling Merchant Quarter and an elegant Palace District. Nearly every important noble house maintains a residence in the North Quarter or the West Quarter of Rammon. The East Quarter and Merchant Quarter houses most of the middle-class families. Poor folks tend to stay in the South Quarter where they can easily get jobs working for farmers on the Kevil Plains.

Resh – The city that marks roughly the half-way point of the Kireshana lives up to its name, which means "rest" in Kalastan.

Ritand – The name is shared both by a city and a fiercely independent island province northwest of the main continent. The long history of hostility between Ritand and Rammon has its roots in a family feud between two brothers from House Minstel.

Ritten – Known mainly for its many factories, Ritten takes raw materials from the Riden Mountains and the Imberg Tosh Mines and produces many of the technological wonders enjoyed in the cities. Everything from the latest model of klipper fighter to the newest comm can be found in Ritten.
Terab – Separated from the rest of the habitable continent by the Felmon Desert, Terab has developed largely apart from the rest of Reshner. Its citizens tolerate the rule of House Minstel in name and submit to royal or Ranger rulings in most legal matters, but they also keep culturally isolated from the rest of the planet.

Planets, Moons, Regions of Space

Corid – One of Reshner's three moons.
Edge Planets – a thin ring of planets that form the perimeter of known space. GAPP strongholds near the galaxy's core would love to conquer the Edge planets and use them as outposts for taming and exploring the Wilds.
Gardan – This close neighboring planet to Reshner is ruled exclusively by the Creston family. Recent history has seen some progress but mostly setbacks in efforts to align Gardan and Reshner.
Gemuln – One of Reshner's three moons.
Kalast – The long-dead planet that both Jalna Seltan and the anotechs once called home. Few know much more than that Kalast has had a strong influence upon Reshner's culture and language.
Marishaz – Reshner's largest and most majestic moon. It is named after the goddess of secrecy.
Mitra – This neighboring planet is probably most known for the Blood Harvest which sweeps away the Royal House every thousand years so none can claim a longer reign.
Porit – An edge planet close to both Reshner and Gardan, known mainly for its famous crystals and deadly vipers.
Reshner – A small, Edge planet rich in wildlife and a wide variety of plants. Reshner is ruled jointly by House Minstel, the Senate, and the Governors Council.
Wilds – A region of space that is largely unexplored. As the Core planets experience overcrowding and depletion of resources, many minds think the Wilds may hold the solutions. Unfortunately for them, Edge planets hold the key to accessing the Wilds.

Plants

Alipo – The sap found inside the delicate stems of alipo plants has mild paralytic properties that can be strengthened in combination with cormea and radon.
Amtea – The leaves of this plant can be made into a reviving tea that will counter most mildly paralytic agents and sedatives.
Astera – Both the pointed leaves and velvety petals of this delicate plant have healing applications. Blue astera petals can be boiled down to make a bitter broth which is known to cure Kemloth Fever. Adding a few wuzle roots to the broth can neutralize much of the broth's bitterness.
Bovas – A plant species that first thrived in the toxic runoff from a klipper manufacturing factory. It can absorb and utilize almost any liquid.
Cal – A strong, durable tree that grows in abundance in the Calsol Forest but can also be found elsewhere on Reshner.
Clava – A species of hearty grass that can grow nearly everywhere on Reshner.
Colbies – Small, green flowers thrive in cool, high altitude environments such as the Talmeth Mountains.
Copalas – Orange and yellow wildflowers native to the Riden Flats but spread everywhere by windstorms.
Corlia – A common plant used to relieve pain.
Cormea – This plant's leaves can deaden pain quite effectively, but too much cormea can paralyze the patient. Cormea has long been combined with radon to make stun weapons more potent.
Crela – Although used sparingly in healing substances designed to treat physical wounds, dust made from powdered crela leaves should not be ingested. Combining crela dust with powdered zalok scales and heating to just the right temperature can create a strong hallucinogen. This fact was discovered by Channer Mazai.
Dandi – The sap of this tree can be used to stick toom leaves together as bandages.
Danesque – A type of deciduous tree with strong, hearty wood sought for furniture and wooden weapons.
Dayde – Native to dark forest locations such as the Felmon Forest, dayde flowers come in a variety of fluorescent colors.
Deklov – A bitter-tasting herb that promotes faster healing.

Fireblooms – These beautiful but dangerous plants can be found everywhere on Reshner, but the most brilliant displays are located on the Ash Plains. Fireblooms come in a variety of yellows and reds, so fields of fireblooms appear to be on fire.
Fossa – A plains tree that can survive without much water.
Ira – Dried ira petals can provide a convenient, lightweight food source for Rangers traveling long distances. If treated with bastrel, ira petals will also turn flames purple, which can be handy if one needs to signal distress. Ira petals are also used to treat fever. They have a sweet, tangy scent.
Kintral – A type of evergreen tree with soft wood good for carving. The root systems of these trees have evolved to be nearly twice the length of their height because of Reshner's infamous windstorms.
Krinton – A fast-growing grain.
Marin Moss – The major food source for shiners.
Mesta – Shoots of this plant are part of the basic requirements for curing Cornada.
Mintas – A very common plant that can be found across Reshner's habitable continent. Some people believe it only has uses as a flavoring agent for teas or candy, but just as many people believe the leaves contain a relaxing agent that can cure foul moods.
Neralas – Green or gold wildflowers found in most flat areas.
Porlas – Red wildflowers found on the Balor Plains and Riden Flats. They have a very strong scent if crushed.
Quemin – Small, scrappy bushes that grow in dense patches.
Radon – Nareth Talis Rangers will combine radon, alipo sap, and cormea to give their kamad daggers the ability to safely knockout foes. Shootav pellets typically contain both cormea and radon in various amounts, depending on the intended use.
Rineth – An evergreen tree found all over the Riden Mountains.
Ristal – The wedge-shaped leaves of this mountain weed can be used to answer for several known poisons, but only skilled healers should be sent to collect it as ristal leaves resemble several other leaf-types, including a few that are poisonous.
Sanda – A staple crop for most farmers who make their living on the Riden Flats.
Sannin – Used to treat both acute and long-term aches.
Sholcas – Brilliantly white wildflowers that grow well after acid storms.
Toom – Common plants with wide, thick leaves ideal for binding wounds or creating makeshift bowls for mixing healing pastes.

Wuzle – The roots of this scrappy little grasslands plant can be used to make strong teas and broths. Ironically, although capable of turning a substance bitter, wuzle roots can also effectively cancel out other bitter substances.

Weapons and Objects

Banisticks – These weapons can be as simple or complex as the maker desires. Starting in their third year, or sooner on rare occasions, Ranger apprentices spend as much time as needed designing his or her weapon. Although it is possible to make them of soft metals, most banisticks are fashioned of kintral or danesque wood. Reia chose to use the latter wood because its softer nature takes better to carving. The tiny, curved leaves linked together are shaped like mintas leaves. Through careful arrangement, Reia also placed the likeness of astera, ristal, corlia, and ira because each represents a different aspect of the healing profession.

Criessa Darts – Darts are the most common way to inject somebody with criessa, a powerful sedative that has an unpleasant side effect of intense cold.

Flingers – These pronged throwing weapons are popular both with Kireshana derringers and Coridian Assassins.

Kamad Dagger – Beautiful and deadly, kamad daggers are highly favored by the Coridian Assassins. The graceful, gently curving edges hide sharpened teeth along the full length of the blade. These invisible teeth provide a swift way to inflict deep wounds upon an enemy. Individual blade length may vary slightly, as they are designed for a specific assassin. However, in keeping with royal tradition, each kamad dagger must bear a zalok's likeness somewhere on its handle.

Kerlak Pistol/Rifle – Kerlak weapons are based on energy. Typically, they can fire either blue or red beams. Blue beams are for stunning opponents while red beams seek to destroy. Occasionally, kerlak weapons will be created with only a blue setting, but most of these are for competitions like the annual mock-war waged between Meritab and Meritel.

Kerlinblade (fire-light blade) – In the hands of a skilled fighter, a kerlinblade offers many options for both offense and defense. Quality and functionality differ as certain kerlinblades are crafted for military purposes while others see only action in dueling arenas. Weapons created for colored-crossblades combatants tend to have a limited range for width but, a wider range of colors. The handle decorations usually have more to do with personal preference, but those wielded during team events during tournaments are much more standardized. Prince Terosh's kerlinblade was commissioned by his father, King Teorn, as a Kireshana gift.

Klipper Fighter – a single person aircraft used mainly for defense of small installations. Occasionally, klipper fighters are also used in racing and practice battles waged among the few reckless, bored, and very rich young nobles.

Serlak Pistol/Rifle – Serlak weapons fire pieces of metal. They have fallen out of favor with the nobility, but still see plenty of use as they are generally cheaper to make than kerlak firearms.

Shootav – These are relatively small, cylindrical weapons that fire pellets capable of stunning most medium sized creatures that could threaten a traveling Ranger.

Appendix II: Kalastan Language Guide

Months (all months = 30 days)

Idela - January
Lanolin – February
Jira – March
Enis – April
Retsi – May
Zeri – June
Temen – July
Allei – August
Pirua – September
Kest – October
Lalri – November
Ferrim – December

Words and Phrases

Alunmir itnasa ilune inamuc nilode. – The time has come; break foul curse, release the royal to new birth.
Ensueltsom icretton, mef sela. – In your heart, I will dwell, my daughter.
Etmani coress cherimon. Dantel corla asmenai. – Here lies the gate. Enter to seek wisdom.
Resmundel resmunsi rel ihala ental mieltsom. – Return to dust, return to spirit, rest, I hold you forever in my heart.
Sela – dear one, daughter

Thank You for Reading:

I hope you enjoyed this third entry in the epic science fiction Anotech Chronicles saga. The trilogy constitutes my most ambitious project to date. One day, I hope to return to Reshner and continue chronicling the adventures of the Royal House.

Although there are no more Reshner tales, you may wish to try a different brand of science fiction (Devya's Children) or switch over to some fantasy. There are 7 stories set on a different planet, Aeris.

If you want to keep up with any of my series or get some bonus content, sign up for my **newsletter (https://www.subscribepage.com/n7e818)**.

Sincerely,

Julie C. Gilbert

Made in the USA
Middletown, DE
14 September 2023